Also by

Jennifer Armintrout

AMERICAN VAMPIRE

Jennifer Armintrout

MIRA

All the characters in this book have no existence outside the imagination of the author, and have no relation whatsoever to anyone bearing the same name or names. They are not even distantly inspired by any individual known or unknown to the author, and all the incidents are pure invention.

First published in Great Britain 2011
MIRA Books, Eton House, 18-24 Paradise Road,
Richmond, Surrey, TW9 1SR

© Jennifer Armintrout 2011

ISBN 978 0 7783 0439 5

54-0511

MIRA's policy is to use papers that are natural, renewable and recyclable products and made from wood grown in sustainable forests. The logging and manufacturing processes conform to the legal environmental regulations of the country of origin.

Printed in Great Britain
by Clays Ltd, St Ives plc

Jennifer Armintrout was born in 1980. She has been obsessed with vampires ever since the age of four and her first crush was on Vincent Price. Raised in an enormous Roman Catholic family, Jennifer attributes her interest in the macabre to viewing too many funerals at a formative age. Jennifer lives in Michigan with her husband and children.

Visit her at
www.jenniferarmintrout.com
jenniferarmintrout.blogspot.com

Follow her on Twitter:
JArmintrout

This book is dedicated to Rob Riddle,
my former roommate whose wok I destroyed,
and Oliver, his Cabbage Patch doll
who had a licence to drive a submarine.

One

If there was one power a vampire could really use, Graf McDonald figured it would have to be internal GPS. Steering his car—a black 1974 De Tomaso Pantera L, a total snatch magnet—with one hand, he jabbed at the tiny screen of his TomTom GPS thingie and said words his mother would have made him eat soap for speaking.

His BlackBerry vibrated against the leather of the passenger seat, seconds before Lady Gaga blared from its tiny speaker. He ripped the GPS from its suction cup base and took it in his left hand, steering with his knees while he answered the phone with his right. That was another thing vampires could use. Extra limbs, to be utilized whenever they willed it.

"Sophia," he said into the phone as he pounded on the TomTom screen. "What do you want?"

"Darling!" Sophia called everyone darling. It was her thing. "You're on your way, yes?"

Of all the traits that got Graf all hot and bothered about his sire, the way she would end questions with the answer she wanted to hear was in the top five, at least. He couldn't help but smile to himself at that. "Slight delay. This stupid GPS thing isn't working."

"Oh, no, no!" Sophia clucked her tongue, and even that sound had an Italian accent. "Darling, you're not going to miss my party, no?"

Graf flicked his gaze to the windshield, to the straight road that hadn't changed since the last time he'd bothered to look at it. "Not if I can help it."

"Well, where are you?" she asked earnestly.

"I'll be honest with you, Soph. I have no fucking clue where I am." He braced himself for the reprimand that was sure to come.

"Graf, your language! You sound like a peasant." She sighed. "You have my address, yes?"

"Yes, I have your address. I programmed it into the thing."

Fucking technology. Usually, he loved it. The internet, thank God for that. High-definition television, yes, yes, yes. Little weaselly devices that pretend like they're going to help you and then stab you in the back? Those could suck his big, fat—

"Honestly, I do not know how you have such difficulty with directions. Get on the highway and go toward Washington, D.C. It is not difficult!" Sophia pouted over the line. "Do that!"

"Well, I would, pumpkin butt, but I dropped the damned TomTom in the parking lot at Denny's, and now it's all in Spanish and I can't get back to the map screen." He took a deep breath and propped the phone against his shoulder as he fished for the cigarettes in his jacket on the seat beside him.

"I do not understand you, you men," Sophia said, sure to lean on the word enough to let him know she meant it as an insult. "You know, I only turn women now, yes? Because they are not as...vulgar and stupid. I do not wish to hurt your feelings, sweet Graf, but it is true, it is just my opinion. Now, why do you not find a place to pull over and ask for directions, and then you hurry here. Okay, good boy. Bye-bye!"

As always, she hung up without a chance for rebuttal. He tossed the phone back onto the seat, threw the TomTom on the passenger side floor, and lit a cigarette. When he looked up at the road, the biggest deer he'd ever seen stared back at him.

With a shout, he jerked the wheel and veered onto the shoulder, narrowly missing the animal. Tall grass and a ditch loomed just past the shoulder, aching to chew up his paint job and destroy his aftermarket ground lighting. Unacceptable. He fought to get the car under control on the gravel shoulder, and brought it to a stop in the center of the road.

Very few things got Graf's adrenaline pumping

the way a threat to his car did, and he leaned over the steering wheel, his heart—which usually didn't beat—pounding in his chest.

"Christ," he muttered, easing the gearshift back to First. Okay, maybe Sophia was right. It was time to swallow his pride, ask for help, and keep his eyes on the road.

The trouble was, he reflected as he slowly rolled down the road, scanning the fields on either side for more white-tailed devil creatures, there didn't seem to be anyplace to stop; he'd passed plenty of farms, lots of little ranch houses with decks, aboveground pools, and absolutely no shade trees in the lawns, but nothing that would indicate a town was nearby. He'd passed a grain elevator, but it had been abandoned. When he tried to remember the last time he'd seen anything that promised civilization lay ahead, he had to reach at least an hour back. And he was cutting his trip close… If he wandered around all night, he'd have to find a hotel to stay in. And if he didn't find one before sunup…

He swallowed the lump in his throat and forced himself to take things one step at a time, without panicking. He'd been stranded at sunup before. The memory of prickling pain flaring into full-blown, fiery agony spread over his arms in a heated warning. A cold sweat of blood broke out over his forehead, and he wiped it away with a curse, ordering himself to get his fear under control. Yes, being burned by the sun had been excruciatingly painful. Yes, it had taken a long time to heal. But he'd been younger then, with less healing ability. The entire situation could be avoided, if he kept a cool head.

To distract himself, he thought of all the fun he'd have at his intended destination. Sophia's July Fourth parties were legendary. All those years ago, she'd been in England when news of a potential uprising in King George's colonies had caught her attention and Sophia, never wanting to miss out on anything exciting, had hopped a boat and relocated. Thus, she'd been at the very first July Fourth, and the revolution that followed it.

"Darling," she had told him once, "it was either going to be a historic moment, or it was going to be chaos. How could I miss either? All of those bodies lying around, the countryside unprotected as the men went off to war. Delicious."

Graf smiled at the memory. His sire was…well, she was spectacular. The only thing he didn't like about her was that he had to share her with her other fledglings. She turned about three a year and sent them on their way, like she was a friggin' vampire factory, but, somehow, she made them all feel special and loved. Just receiving her blood was an act of love in itself—what more precious gift could you give someone than the gift of eternal life?

From the corner of his eye, he spotted light. Not enough that a human could have seen it; vampire eyesight was beyond excellent. A beam of light swung wildly through the darkness. A flashlight. Inside a structure of some kind. He hit the brakes and pulled over, examining the source of the light. The building was a gas station, all closed up snug for the night, because nothing in these Midwestern middle grounds stayed open later than ten.

A gas station would have a map. And if someone was robbing the place, he could get one for free. And pick up a snack.

He pulled closer, then killed the engine and let the car drift into the gravel lot, not closing the door when he got out. The element of surprise somehow made people taste better, and if they had a gun, he didn't want to get shot. It wouldn't kill him, but it would hurt like hell.

As he approached the building, it became apparent that the place wasn't just closed, it was abandoned. Several of the windows were broken, but no one had bothered to board them up. The price of cigarettes displayed on the faded sign in the one nonshattered window would have made Graf weep with joy had it been current. He pushed open the unlocked door and a bell jingled. So much for surprise.

The shelves were bare, so the place had clearly been looted. Why would someone even bother to break in?

"Hello!" he called cheerfully. "Anybody home?"

Something scurried in the farthest corner of the store, near the empty, glass-fronted coolers.

"Look, I know you're in here. I saw your flashlight." This was, Graf reflected, the kind of thing that would happen at the beginning of a horror movie. Cocky, confident guy walks into a creepy place, thinking he's the toughest thing in there, something horrible jumps out of the shadows...

But he knew he was the most horrible thing there at the moment, so the horror-movie comparison made him grin. "Okay. You want to do this the hard way? We can do it the hard way."

Whoever it was scurried across the floor. But they didn't move away from him. They approached on hands and knees. A hand grasped his ankle, and he kicked to dislodge it.

"Stop! It will hear us!" A feminine voice, consumed with panic. "Get down! It's coming!"

"What's coming?" He crouched, but not out of fear of whatever this woman thought was heading their way. He needed to get a better look at her, to decide if she was crazy or just plain terrified.

Maybe both, if he had to judge by the eyes staring back at him. The whites shone like the moon in the darkness, with huge pupils obscuring nearly all the green around them. Her lips, the same pale of her skin, pursed against the agonizing wait. Fear radiated from her, from the scent of her sweat to the unrelenting grip on his wrist she'd secured when he'd knelt. Suddenly, she released him, turned her face up to the windows just above their heads. She pressed one finger against her lips and moved backward in a slow crouch. Graf followed, though he still had no idea what the hell was going on. A meal was a meal, and this one looked pretty tasty, despite the bone-chilling terror that gripped her.

She pushed open the door to the back room of the store, and they crept inside. She motioned, still silent, to the desk in the corner, a clunky metal contraption that no one had seen fit to take with them when they'd closed down. Climbing beneath it, she motioned for him to follow.

Here was a predicament. She was a hot little piece, and under normal circumstances, he wouldn't have minded squeezing into a tight spot with her. But if there actually was some ominous thing coming for them, being trapped when it got there didn't seem like the best idea. On the other hand, hiding out in the back room would be fine once the sun came up, because it was mercifully windowless.

An inhuman roar shook the walls, and that made Graf's decision for him. He dove beneath the desk, and the girl tried to avoid him with a squeak. "It's here!" she screamed, covering her ears with her hands and squeezing her eyes shut tight. The sound of her rapid breathing and wild heartbeat filled his ears, and his fangs slid down in anticipation.

Then, the groan of rending metal sent daggers

of instant "Oh, that can't be good" shooting to his brain. As ridiculously quick as vampire reflexes were, he didn't have time to react before a gas pump shot through the wall like a knife through hot butter, and asbestos tiles rained from the ceiling like snowflakes in hell.

"We should probably get out of here," he said, but it really wasn't up to the human to decide if she wanted to leave or not. He grabbed her by the wrist and pulled. If she wanted to keep her hand, she would follow. She did, but screamed, "Don't go out there!" even as he pulled her through the door.

"There's my car!" he shouted over the sound of the gas station's roof tearing off. Something moved in the darkness, but getting away from it was more important to Graf than getting a good look at it.

The girl hesitated, and he shoved her through the driver's side door and climbed in after her as she scrambled into the passenger seat. "Drive!" she screamed as a chunk of roof fell on the hood of the car.

She didn't have to tell him twice. The engine roared and the transmission protested as he pushed all three hundred and fifty of the horses under the hood to haul ass and get them out of there.

"What was that?" He checked the rearview mirror. The gas station, a crumbled ruin, stood alone at the side of the road, but nothing around it had been disturbed. The power lines stood, the cornfield waved placidly. "Was that a tornado?"

"How did you get here?" The human trembled, gripping the dash with one hand as she sat sideways to face him. Her voice held some of the same panic she'd had in the darkened station, as though whatever the hell had just happened to them hadn't ended yet and that his relief was premature.

Very few things rattled him anymore, but the strangeness of her question did. Not a good feeling. "How else do people get here? I drove."

"No, that's impossible." She sat back, stared blankly out the windshield. "This can't be happening."

Shell-shocked human. Fantastic. He should just pull over and eat her, dump her body in the ditch and keep going, but some instinct that was smarter than him warned that it wouldn't be a good idea. "Well, I hate to tell you, but it is happening, and I'm about two seconds away from kicking you out of this car if you don't stop acting so damn crazy. If you're lucky, I might even hit the brakes first."

"Oh my God, you're really here. From the outside." Her eyes got even wider, if that were possible.

"The outside of what? Ohio? What, are you Amish or something?" He pulled the car to the side of the road. Something about the whole situation was fishy, and he had a personal rule about getting caught up in human problems. And he definitely didn't eat crazy. "Look, I don't know what's out there, or why that place got ripped to shreds, but you need to get out of my car now."

"No!" She grabbed his arm, her fingers digging in through the sleeve of his shirt. "No, you have to go back!"

"My dear, I don't have to do anything. Get out, or I'm going to throw you out." If there was one thing he didn't have time for tonight, besides being lost, it was being lost with a human who was deranged past the point of making any sense. She continued to babble as he opened his door and grabbed her by the arms, dragging her out over the gearshift. Even when she was out of the car, she kept pleading, as if she didn't realize she was already on the ground. He pushed her back to get her desperate, clawing hands off him, and got back in the car and slammed the door before she could grab him again.

He rolled the window down just a crack. "Where's the nearest town?"

"You're in it," she snapped at him, wiping her eyes. "I hope you enjoy your stay, asshole."

Right…so, she wasn't going to be any help. Sure, he was leaving her on the side of the road, but he had just saved her life. Humans could be so ungrateful.

He pulled away. She'd called him an outsider. What the hell had that been about? As much as he didn't want to head back toward…whatever it was that had destroyed the gas station, he really didn't want to drive straight to the heart of some religious commune, either. He blew past a THANKS FOR VISITING PENANCE sign with peeling paint and a faded metal Rotary Club seal on it and pressed the accelerator to the floor. He didn't want to see the gas station when he passed it—at least, not as anything more than a blur. It had been about three miles since he'd passed the last county road. He'd backtrack to that and take it wherever it ended up leading. If he had to sleep in the trunk to stay out of the sun, well, he would. It wouldn't be pleasant, but it would be a hell of a lot more pleasant than being held hostage by religious freaks.

After a few long, silent moments, he turned on his iPod. Weird stuff happened all the time. It didn't bear thinking about. He found Lily Allen's latest album and turned it up, singing along absentmindedly as he struggled with the TomTom once more.

Three songs later, he noticed he hadn't made it back to the road yet. No, that couldn't be right. He probably was just too distracted trying to change the settings back to English to notice that he'd passed it. He pulled a U-turn and headed back. He'd only gone about a quarter mile before the ruined gas station loomed to his left, and he passed a WELCOME TO PENANCE sign on his right.

"What the…" Up ahead, a figure walked at the shoulder of the road, her head hanging, arms wrapped around her middle. He slowed beside her, double-checking the odometer. He'd driven fifteen miles. It was right there, in black and white on the little dials that worked just as well as the rest of the car.

The girl shot him an angry look over her shoulder, then faced forward again, tossing her long, brown hair.

He drove past her and waited, watching in the mirror as she tried to look anywhere but at the car she approached. He couldn't help but notice her long, suntanned legs sticking out of a nice, short pair of denim cutoffs. Country girls. Yum. He rolled down the window as she walked by. "Something strange just happened."

She didn't answer, but kept walking. He gave her a little room, then rolled after her. When he pulled up even again, he continued, "I just tried to drive back to county-road-number-whatever-that-number-was, but I don't seem to be getting anywhere. Got any idea what that's about?"

Still no answer.

He let her get ahead again, then drove up beside her once more. "You can either get into this car, or stay out here with whatever that was that just wrecked a building."

She laughed humorlessly and kept walking. "You didn't seem to care about leaving me out here when you thought you were going to be able to drive away and never see me again."

"Well, yeah," he said, creeping slowly alongside her. "But that's only because I thought I was going to drive away and never see you again… Why didn't that work out?"

"You're a real gentleman." She shook her head, still walking. "You can't leave because It keeps us here."

"It?" She'd said the word like it was a name, like it should be obvious what she was talking about, but Graf had no clue. "What do you mean, 'It'?"

There was something hard about the way she wrinkled her nose, as though she had been defeated a long time ago and didn't like talking about the fight. Whatever bad memories were associated with the subject, they made her voice a little less strident. "I don't know. No one does."

"Well, what do you mean I'm—" His foot slipped on the accelerator, and the car lurched forward. He hit the clutch and downshifted into Neutral. "Damn it, get in! This is ridiculous."

To his surprise, she walked around the front of the car and opened the passenger door. "Are you going to drive me home, or just abandon me on the side of the road a little farther down?"

He ignored her. "You told me to enjoy my stay. So, I take it other people have had this same trouble?"

"No. You're the first." She wasn't being sarcastic. She dropped into the seat and pulled in her long legs as she closed the door. "The rest of us have been trapped here, but outsiders never stop."

Trapped. Well, that sounded great. "'Never' meaning...how long exactly?"

"Five years." She pointed to a dirt road ahead.
"Turn there."

He complied, too confused to do much other than
ask questions and take orders. That wasn't like him
at all, and it made him uncomfortable. "Five years,
no one has been able to..."

"To leave Penance, or get in. No visits to or from.
No one with car trouble on the side of the road." She
closed her eyes. "No ambulances."

"So, I'm the first person to come to Penance for the
past five years?" There was a fallow field to one side
of the road, a swamp to the other. "What is this?"

"A town." She looked at him like he was crazy.
"A small one, but a town. And everything within the
city limits has been trapped for the past five years.
No one gets in, no one gets out."

That explained the lack of cars on the road, the
closed-down gas station. "So, what's this 'It' that
you're so worried about? The 'It' that tried to bring
a building down on us. What's with that?"

"I don't know." She got a faraway look, as if she
didn't want to talk about it. "I've seen It before. A
lot of people have. It kills. Not every night, not on
a schedule. Some people have had It come right up
to them and not do anything at all. Other people get
slaughtered."

"Okay." He pinched the bridge of his nose. "But what is it?"

She looked dead-on at him like he was stupid. "It's a monster."

Two

Realistically, Graf couldn't doubt the existence of monsters. It just wouldn't make sense. Obviously, vampires existed. And werewolves. He'd met one of those. Zombies, he'd never heard of those existing, but he wouldn't have been surprised. Witches? Wouldn't want to tangle with one. But unclassifiable bogeyman-type creatures that could bring down a gas station roof right over his head? It wasn't that they couldn't exist, they probably did, but such information was hard to believe when it was coming from a human.

"A monster?"

The woman nodded, still eyeing him like he might be a little bit "special." "Yes. You don't really think a tornado did that? And left the power lines up? And us able to run? And your car sitting right there, not getting a scratch on it?"

"I thought they were notorious for that kind of thing," he muttered, but he didn't admit that everything he knew about tornadoes came from the movie *Twister.* "So, what kind of a monster are we talking about?"

"I've never exactly asked It to classify itself while it was chasing me." She blew out a breath and raised her hand to push her hair back. She still shook, giving Graf the visual interpretation of the old "like a leaf on a tree" expression. She didn't stink of fear anymore, so she must have just been burning off adrenaline. "It's just a monster. That's the only way to describe it. Some people thought It was some mutant kind of giant possum when it first started attacking people, but..."

He frowned. "When did it start attacking people?"

"About five years ago," she replied in a "Gee, what do you think?" tone. "Right after we all got stuck here."

For a few minutes, Graf didn't say anything, just kept his eyes on the painfully straight road and let everything she said tumble around in his mind. For five years, an entire town had been held captive by some kind of monster, and no one on the outside had noticed? There was clearly more at work here than just plain old monstering. That was the kind of thing only a spell could accomplish, not that he'd tell her that. He never liked to reveal the existence of the supernatural to a human, even if they had already experienced it in some form. There was always a ton of explaining to be done, and the same tiresome questions. Questions a lot like the ones he'd had for her.

"My place is right up there." The girl indicated, pointing to where a mercury light cast the side of a white farmhouse in a sickly green glow.

Graf pulled into the driveway, lined on both sides with milk cans rusting under their coats of white paint. "Nice decor." He sneered.

"Yeah, well, I've been really worried about my curb appeal during the last five years that I've been unable to leave town and lived in constant fear of a monster, so go fuck yourself," she snapped, pushing the passenger door open.

She was feisty. Now, he didn't know if he wanted to fuck her or eat her. Or, he could do both, but only if she let him into her house.

"Wait," he called after her, turning off the engine.

He got out of the car, and she stopped, hands on her slim hips as she turned to face him. "I hope you don't think you're coming into my house."

"Look, I know that we got off on the wrong foot—"

"The wrong foot?" She laughed, tilted her head back, and gave the trees above her an imploring look, like they could save her from his stupidity. "I'm going to have to disagree with your assessment of the situation. You see, getting nearly killed by It and then being left for dead by the person you think is trying to save you, that's not getting off on the wrong foot. That's called getting screwed, and I'll be damned if you're going to do that to me again."

"I'm not trying to…screw you." He forced away an immature giggle. That would not help his cause in the slightest. "If I'm trapped here, I'm going to need a place to stay. Can't you at least give me directions to a motel?"

"Yeah. I can." She smiled sweetly. "It's about twenty miles away, just over the state line in West Virginia."

He cursed and turned away, then turned back. "Is there anyone in town who would put me up?"

"As charming as you are, I'm sure you'll find someone delighted to have you as a guest in their home. But not here. There is no room in this inn." She walked up the lawn, toward the wide front porch.

"Just, wait…" He wasn't asking this time. The sun would be up soon. The sky was already turning that weird grayish-blue color that it did toward dawn. She was going to let him inside, or she was going to die trying to keep him out. "I need a place to stay, and you owe me."

She stopped with a noise of disbelief. "I owe you? For what? Stranding me on the side of the road?"

"For saving you from your monster. And for the

ride home." He could have left it at that, but he didn't, striding up the lawn to loom over her. "You stranded yourself. You ran out there. You were going to be walking home, anyway, so I was good enough to give you a temporary reprieve, not really stranding you at all."

Her jaw dropped, but thankfully no words came out of her pretty little mouth.

"I won't be here for long. Just give me a place to stay until I figure out a way to get out of here." It still sounded like he was asking permission. What he needed to do was rip out her throat and go right on inside.

"We've been trapped here for five years, and you think you're going to waltz right on in and out in a few days?" She shook her head. "Oh, yes, please do come into my house and continue to insult me."

"Look, I know I've been a huge asshole. But listen, I have this…medical condition." He fished in the pocket of his pants. It was time to play the card that most people saw right through, the one that practically screamed, "I'm a vampire, put a coffee table leg through my heart." His fingers closed on the slender piece of metal and chain. "See this? It's a medic alert bracelet."

"Good for you, you're allergic to penicillin." She turned away and took the steps up to the porch two at a time. When he followed, she whirled and shouted, "Get away from me!"

"Would you listen to me for a minute? I have photosensitivity. Polymorphous light eruption. I won't go into details, because it's disgusting. Pus is involved. I can't be in the sunlight. I need to be indoors." He had one more trick to pull out of his sleeve before he decided to bite her and be done with it, an option that was looking less and less appetizing the more she opened her mouth. It was drastic, and he hated to say it, but he braced himself and added, "Please."

She considered a moment. A sick part of his mind wondered if she would look so serious and doubtful if she knew the only option left was getting her blood sprayed across the faded white siding. Finally, with an annoyed sigh, she said, "Look. I don't know you. You could be a psychopath. There is no way that, under normal circumstances, I should let you into my house. But normal circumstances went out the window about, oh, five years ago. You can't stay here permanently, and I think it's only fair for you to know that I have my dad's double-barrel shotgun inside and it'll be the last thing you see if you try to lay one finger on me."

He held up his hands and tried not to smile at the absurdity of her statement. He was too strong and way too fast. He could do anything he wanted to her; she wouldn't even have time to load. At this point, though, he didn't want to do anything but get her to shut up. "Understood."

She hesitated a moment, then turned to open the door. "You're going to stay in the basement."

"That's fine." He'd slept in worse places. And most basements he'd been in had couches and pool tables.

Inside, she flipped on a light switch, and the full Midwestern horror of the house became instantly apparent. Everywhere Graf looked, doilies covered end tables and decorative plates hung on the walls. Beyond the living room—and the hideous floral couch—the archway leading to what Graf assumed was the kitchen had a pair of antlers mounted over it.

"This is…" He closed his eyes for a moment, trying to mentally erase the figurines of chubby German children on the fireplace mantel. "You decorate this yourself?"

The girl stopped, her mouth again in the increasingly familiar half-open position, like she'd never heard someone say that her place was hideous before, which Graf couldn't believe. "Don't worry. The basement isn't anywhere near this nice."

She marched into the kitchen and turned on the lights there and a ceiling fan began to whirl gently. Graf watched it for a moment, something nagging at his brain. "No one can leave, and no one can really arrive, right?"

"Yup." The woman went to the refrigerator and took out a pitcher of plain water. "Thirsty?"

Yes, but not for anything you're going to give up willingly. He shook his head and took a seat at the small island. A pot rack hung overhead, with oven mitts shaped like chickens' heads dangling from a hook. "If no one can get in and no one can leave, then there isn't any way that mail is getting out."

She poured herself a glass of water, keeping her eyes on him as much as possible. "You just found out you're trapped in a town where no one has been able to leave for five years, and you're worried about the mail?"

He shrugged. "Not worried. Curious. You've got electricity. Who's paying the bill?"

"I don't know. It just never turns off. Water neither. Some people think we're frozen in time, but I don't buy it. The physics teacher over at the high school held a town meeting to explain it once, but he's gone now." She took a swallow from her glass, her slender throat moving as she did so.

Usually, that would have been a temptation, especially on a woman as good-looking as she was. But while the package was sexy, what was inside was annoying as hell, and he wanted no part of it. "I thought you said no one had left in five years."

"Not 'gone' gone. Gone. He put a gun in his mouth over on Pleasant Creek Road." She looked down sadly. "He didn't live here. Just worked here. His family was over in Bucksville County. He hadn't seen them in a year when he finally gave up hope and did it."

Graf couldn't bring himself to actually care. "That would suck."

He looked at the refrigerator, where a magnetic chore list adhered to the door. Someone had written on it in dry-erase marker: MOM, DAD, JONATHAN, and another name half swiped off and unreadable. "So, I know you're not 'Dad' or 'Jonathan,' so should I call you 'Mom'?"

"What?" She looked in the direction he pointed, and she stiffened. "Oh. That's just...old."

He studied the stilted way she moved as she went to the refrigerator and pulled down the chart, scattering little round magnets with pictures of dishes and brooms all over the floor. She opened a drawer and shoved the whole thing in, then slammed it closed.

"So, I'm going to guess that Jonathan, not being a feminine name, belongs to someone else. Maybe someone who used to live in this house, but doesn't anymore." He drummed his fingers on the island. "Is this really your house?"

"Yes, it's my house." She didn't turn to face him. Her shoulders were tense and she gripped the edge of the counter as though it supported her. "Jonathan was...Jonathan is my brother."

"'Is' or 'was'?" Graf asked absentmindedly, examining the carved wooden chickens in wacky poses on the windowsill. A family had lived here. A family with very bad taste in interior decorating. "That's kind of crucial to the story, I'm guessing."

"Is. He's dead, but he's still my brother." Her voice trembled. She was crying.

Oh, this is just precious. He rolled his eyes and managed a semi-interested-sounding "I'm sorry."

She turned, a fake smile on her face. She didn't need to pretend anything. Graf didn't care. And smiling was the exact opposite of what she'd been doing to him all night. She killed the lying expression and pushed away from the counter. "You're probably tired. Let me show you where the basement is."

To his left was the outside door, the window covered in a red-and-white-checked shade. Perpendicular to that, a door covered with too many coats of thick, white paint, with an antique porcelain knob. About a foot above the knob there was a chain lock, attached by two measly screws. That wasn't going to keep him out, no way, no how. But he wouldn't tell her that. "I have some stuff I need to get out of the car, before it's too late. I'll meet you down there."

Nocturnal though he might be, he wasn't prepared to descend into his tomb yet. He already felt trapped. In the basement he would feel completely claustrophobic.

As he unloaded his bags, he caught sight of his BlackBerry lying on the passenger side floor, and he dove for it. Miraculously, four bars glowed reassuringly on the screen. He redialed the most recent call—if anyone would know how to get out of this mess, Sophia would—and held his breath.

It never connected. It rang—once, twice, four times, five—and the voice mail never picked up. Seven, eight rings, ten and still nothing. He waited out twenty rings, then cursed and hurled the phone to the ground.

"I know the feeling."

Graf whirled to face the girl. She stood behind him, an expression of true pity on her face. He didn't need her pity. He needed a way out.

"When we first all started to realize that we were stuck here…we didn't know how long it had gone on. We thought there was something wrong with the phone lines." She looked down at her hands. "You'll get used to it. We don't really rely on each other here, but you'll learn to rely on yourself."

Oh, for Christ's sake, I had to get trapped in a Lifetime original movie, didn't I? He couldn't take any more homespun wisdom from the woman who appeared to be the queen of all mood swings. "Well, that basement is sounding awfully comfy right now. You can lead the way."

He carried his overnight bag and cursed his light packing. Not only would a pair of jeans and change of shirt not last him for eternity, if he was really trapped here that long, but he hadn't brought an eternity's worth of blood with him. He'd fed off a waitress when he'd stopped earlier in the evening, but he'd been planning to gorge himself like a tick at the Independence Day party, so he'd only brought emergency rations. Like her or not, he'd be tearing into this woman before too long.

He followed her down the basement stairs. It was not the kind of basement that the word *basement* described in his mind. A "basement" was a place where somebody puts the aforementioned pool table and maybe a miniature refrigerator. They put up drywall and maybe some wood paneling and called it a den or a family room. This place, with its bare rock walls and dirt floor, was more like what someone would call a cellar. Or a hole. "You're seriously going to keep me down here?" He wiped a finger through the cobwebs clinging to visible floorboards of the house over his head.

"I'm not going to serve you breakfast in bed, if that's what you were hoping," she called over her shoulder as she tugged futilely at a mound of various, unrelated objects stuffed in a corner.

That's what you think. He watched her struggle for a while with whatever it was that she was doing, then reached past her, shouldering her out of the way.

"Very gentlemanly of you," she griped, wiping her hands on her jeans.

"I never claimed to be a gentleman." The metal frame and musty canvas of an army cot pulled free from the rubble of tent parts and Christmas decorations. He untangled a string of colored lights from the cot and set it on the ground at his feet. "Is this what I'm sleeping on?"

"That or the floor." Beneath the moldering wooden stairs was a stack of plastic totes. She pulled one out, examined the label, and popped open the lid. "Blankets in here. They're old, but they'll do."

"Your hospitality amazes me," Graf quipped, snapping open the cot's folded frame.

"I'm sorry, I must have missed the Holiday Inn sign at the end of my driveway." She put her hands on her hips, where she might as well just keep them permanently, they ended up there often enough. "I could always rescind my invitation, you know."

I'd like to see you try.

"Sorry." The word left his mouth almost less frequently than *please,* and it had to make its way past his clenched back teeth this time. "You have to understand, you've had five years to get used to this whole 'being trapped' thing. I've had five minutes."

"You've had an hour. Suck it up." She went up the stairs. They creaked, and a fine rain of sand fell from each step. "This isn't permanent. At sundown, you start looking for a new place to live."

The door closing at the top of the stairs was a judge's gavel falling, and the scrape of something heavy being dragged in front of the door was the sound of a jail cell locking up tight. He'd been sentenced to living in a basement and putting up with a warden so insufferable, he didn't even want to eat her.

If she had known that a flimsy lock wouldn't keep him in, would she have still taken that precaution? Probably. Humans did silly things to reassure themselves when they were frightened, which she most definitely was, with a strange man in her basement.

Still, if she had wanted to make him feel like a prisoner, she couldn't have been more effective. Graf decided he could bide his time; the thing about caged animals was, they only stayed caged for so long.

Three

Jessa stood, hands still braced on the heavy wooden bench, and wondered if it would be enough to hold a grown man inside. She wasn't worried about him running away. Actually, she would prefer it. Contrary to the rumors around town that she was a man-hungry spinster, she did have some established criteria when it came to weeding out the bad ones.

This guy was one of the bad ones. That was why she was so worried about him getting out. He wasn't bad in the hot-guy-who-was-nothing-but-trouble kind of way, though she had plenty of experience with that type. He was bad in the he-was-always-so-quiet-serial-killer kind of way. It was something about his eyes. There was a void there, an absence that had chilled her the moment she'd seen him. She'd almost been willing to take her chances with It, rather than hide in the gas station with him. But she had stayed, and gotten into his car on a desolate stretch of road in the middle of the night, and even let him sleep in her house. History had proven she wasn't a very good judge of character before, but this example was like a neon sign that flashed You Dummy.

Keeping him close wasn't necessarily a bad thing, though. It wasn't by chance that he was the first person to be able to stop in Penance. Nothing happened by chance anymore. Maybe she was a hard, cynical bitch—no, she was sure she was—but she wasn't going to trust that he was just a stranded traveler. Having him on her side could be an advantage, or it could be a huge mistake.

She kept one eye on the basement door as she filled the kettle and set it on the stove. The sun would be up soon, and it would be too late to go to bed. Not that she could sleep, anyway, with a stranger in her basement who might or might not be trustworthy.

Then why did you let him stay? She scrubbed her hands over her face, blocking out the kitchen, blocking out the world. Blocking out the knife drawer, the scene of so many failed attempts to escape life, escape Penance, escape everything. Was it that same self-destructive urge that had convinced her to let him in?

It didn't matter why she had offered up her basement, and it didn't matter why he was here. What mattered was she had chickens to feed and chores to do.

She had to survive, because, so far, not surviving hadn't been an option she'd been able to follow through on.

She left the kettle to boil, vaguely aware that it could be used as a weapon if he did sneak out of the basement. That line of thinking was counterproductive. All thinking was counterproductive. Once she thought about one aspect of her situation, she would have to think about all of it. The guy in the basement. The reason he was here. The thing that might have sent him. The town, the past, the future, all of it. The only way she got through the days and nights was by blocking all of it firmly out and pretending something else was happening.

She drifted up the stairs, imagining it was a Friday night, and she tiptoed to avoid waking her parents, who, once upon a time, would have been sleeping behind the closed door to their room. If they found out she'd been running around at all hours, they would tan her hide. There was no way she was going to get grounded this close to the homecoming dance. She went into the bathroom and closed the door, holding her breath when the light clicked on. It was the little sounds that would wake her parents, like the light switch flicking or the creak of the floorboards in front of the sink. She shed her dirty clothes and dropped them into the hamper. Mom did wash on Fridays, so that was why it was nearly empty. Not because Jessa was the only one left.

Downstairs, the teakettle whistled, and she closed her eyes, squeezed them shut tight against the intrusion of reality. She turned off the light and went to her bedroom, not bothering to sneak or avoid the squeaky spot in the hall. Her parents were gone. Jonathan was gone. The only things lying behind those closed doors were empty rooms, shrines to the dead she could hardly bear to look at. Everything she knew and loved had vanished, replaced by a nightmare world that mocked her with its familiarity.

She padded across the white area rug in her room, over the stain where she and Becky had spilled the wine cooler snuck from the fridge in seventh grade. The sky outside the window, what she could see of it through the branches of the tree—the very one that Derek used to climb to get into her room at night— had lightened to the white that preceded the arrival of the sun in the sky. Another fifteen minutes, maybe, and the rooster would start crowing.

She dressed in clean clothes, a tank top and denim shorts, and went downstairs. In the kitchen, she checked the basement door again, then put some dried raspberry leaves in a cup, pouring the steaming water from the kettle over them. Coffee, like everything else that couldn't be grown or handmade in Penance, had gone from common item to luxury to extinction in the last five years. She had learned to substitute homemade soap for shampoo and live with the results. Coffee…she would kill a stranger with her hands to get a cup of coffee.

The thought of strangers brought her mind right back to the man in the basement. If he hadn't been such a jerk, he might have actually been attractive. If she went for that slick, well-groomed type, which she didn't. But she'd always been a sucker for blonds, and his gorgeous blue eyes were the kind a girl could get lost in, if she didn't know they covered up a whole batch of lies, which they probably did.

He had to go, as soon as possible. If he had been polite—if he'd just been a little less rude—she might have more sympathy toward him. But he hadn't been, so she didn't, and she wouldn't feel bad about kicking him out. She took a sip of the tea, wincing as she scalded her tongue. She was always doing that, always being too impatient, and hurting herself in the process. She finished her tea and headed out to the barn, trying hard to shake the feelings of guilt and responsibility that plagued her. It wasn't her fault that the guy had stopped at that gas station. It wasn't as though he'd stopped to help her. He shouldn't have been able to stop at all.

A light sheen of dew glistened on the lawn, chilling Jessa's bare feet as she made her away across the grass. There was something satisfying about being up with the sun, or at least there would have been had she actually gone to bed the night before. Lack of sleep aside, the morning seemed as close to normal as it got in Penance. The chickens chased each other through the hard-packed dirt of the farmyard in aggressive anticipation of feeding time. They didn't know they were locked in a never-ending nightmare, and their ignorance comforted Jessa. She pushed the barn door open, ignoring as best she could the long slashes across the wood. It had come here before, and It liked to leave reminders.

Inside the barn, she checked her feed stores. Damn. She would have to go into town soon. She'd have to go, anyway, to unload her freeloader. But she didn't have anything to trade, and supplies were running out. She leaned her head against the door, fighting the feelings of hopelessness that washed over her. She usually traded peaches from the orchard, but this year's crop hadn't yielded what it had the year before, and she'd lost a batch of preserves when the cans didn't seal. She'd already traded away the tractor to Jim Wyandot, and he'd melted down the metal to make bullets for black-powder rifles. Without gasoline the farm equipment in town had been pretty much worthless, anyhow.

Gas. She barely thought of the word anymore, after nearly five years without any. They'd tried to ration it, but with It coming so close to the harvest, the majority of it had been sucked down by combines. There hadn't been a drop of gasoline in Penance in a long, long time…. But there was, now.

Between the time she grabbed the garden hose

and a red plastic gas can from the wall, and the time she made it down to the car, she didn't think about anything but the amount someone, anyone, would pay for a gallon of gas. Once she stood beside the car, though, she thought about the guy in the basement. He'd gotten here. He might be able to leave. He couldn't do that with an empty gas tank.

Did it matter, though?

She doubted he would send help back, if he could get out. Even if he did, help might not be able to make it back to their town. No one else had been able to so far. They'd figured at first that people just didn't need to stop, then later feared what would happen if someone did. They'd feared the town would quickly become overrun with lost tourists, and resources would be obliterated. After a few months, they'd stopped worrying about unexpected arrivals and concentrated on getting out themselves. As the buildings started looking pretty rough and the store and gas station were reclaimed by nature, surely someone outside had to have noticed that Penance had become a ghost town—a missing town!—but still, no one had stopped or sent any help. And everyone left behind had stopped wondering long ago what it was that kept people out or in. They were too busy just trying to survive.

She frowned at the car. The night before, she'd thought it was a Corvette. In the light of day, she realized how wrong that first impression was. Maybe it was a Mustang, but it would have to be a custom job. More likely, it was a fancy foreign import, and she wrinkled her nose in distaste. That just proved what kind of a guy he was, driving around in a ridiculously expensive car.

She tossed the gas can and hose on the grass, figuring she probably wouldn't even know where the gas tank was, anyway. The windows were open, and she leaned inside. The dew had settled over his leather interior. That wasn't great. His phone wouldn't be worth much, but he had to have CDs in there somewhere, and maybe even some convenience-store food. She opened the door as quietly as possible and climbed in. A leather jacket lay crumpled on the floor of the passenger side. Who wore leather in the middle of the summer? There was a pack of cigarettes in the pocket; those would fetch a good price. She rummaged beneath the seats and in the glove box, and found the car depressingly devoid of food. No chips, no popcorn, no beef jerky. Not even an empty soda can. The guy was probably a health nut. "Vanity," she said to no one, clucking her tongue. Sure enough, he was some slick city guy who thought hard work happened in the gym. She climbed out of the car and closed the door, again as quietly as she could, to avoid alerting him to her snoop search.

Jessa finished her chores quickly, though her muscles still ached from her late-night flight from It. When the chickens had been tended and the garden watered, all the tomato plants inspected, when she checked up on the beehives, when she tacked the siding back up from where It had brushed its huge, scaly back against it and knocked it down, she put on her boots and approached the fallow field that surrounded the yard and headed to the woods beyond.

Though It rarely struck the same place twice in a row, a chill left over from the night before crawled up her spine. The woods didn't seem frightening now, just a bunch of trees and May apples swaying on the shaded ground between them. "Elf Umbrellas," Mom used to call them. Jessa squeezed her eyes shut tight as she stepped over the tall-grass border and into the trees. There was nothing in the woods. Nothing but her gun, and she needed that. It was the whole point of coming out here, where it wasn't safe, where she shouldn't be. What had brought her out here the night before, though…

She opened her eyes and saw the shotgun, gleaming black and simulated wood grain at the base of a tree. The tree itself was wounded, from where her first shot had missed. She never missed twice. She'd struck the creature, but that had only infuriated it.

She ran to the gun and snatched it up, her hands shaking, heart hammering, and looked for the blood trail. Closing her eyes, she remembered the scene the night before. It had been charging her, and she'd fired the first barrel, hitting the tree and exploding wooden shrapnel into the air, leaving behind an angry wheal of white tree flesh. It had kept coming, and she'd fired again, the second shot hitting its center mass, filling the air with a fine, red mist and the stink of burned flesh amid a disgusting sulfur-and-mold smell. It had roared and swatted at its chest, where the scatter shot had peppered its skin with bloody holes. It hadn't stopped coming for her, but the wound had given her time to run.

No one had ever stopped It. They knew that evasion was the best they could settle for.

When she opened her eyes, she faced the direction she'd fled the night before. A path of ruined trees and uprooted plants showed where It had chased her, and she followed the trail. Blood stained the forest debris on the ground, volumes of it, but It had barely slowed. Its impossible strength hadn't faded in the least, leaving it capable of destroying an entire building with its bare hands. No, not hands. Claws.

"Jessa? Jessa, where the hell are you?"

She startled at the voice, and nearly dropped the gun. She sprinted toward the field, resisting the ridiculous urge to look behind her as she charged toward the house. The monster wasn't behind her, wasn't chasing her to the safety of her own yard. The impetus to run had just called her name. Derek, the one dependable part of her life for the past five years—if she could really call him dependable—wouldn't have missed the strange sight of a car sitting in her driveway. If he went inside and found the basement door barricaded, he would go down there. And if he found the guy...

No, on second thought, it might not be so bad for the smug prick in the basement to get beat up by her smug, hillbilly prick ex-boyfriend.

Once past the tree line, she slowed, tried to appear unhurried as she caught her breath. The last thing she needed was for Derek to think she would literally run every time he called for her.

"Stop making so much racket. You'll upset the chickens, and they won't lay." She raised her hand to shade her eyes from the sun and dropped the gun onto the grass as she stepped onto the lawn.

"Jesus, Jessa. You scared the hell out of me." Derek nodded toward the woods. "What were you doing out there?"

Before she could answer, Derek turned, pushing his Ohio State baseball cap up on his forehead. He hadn't gone to Ohio State, but still he wore the Buckeye leaf proudly. "Where did that car come from?"

"That all kind of ties into the story of me being in the woods with a gun." She laughed nervously, hating that she cared if he would be mad at her or not. She rubbed her face and took a deep breath.

Derek turned, his confusion increasing by degrees, as evidenced by the frown that drew his eyebrows down. "You don't look so good, Jessa."

"Thanks. I've been up all night." She swallowed. Saying it out loud made her more tired, just like the part that followed made her more scared. "Running from It."

His expression frozen in shock, Derek looked to the house, then back at her. "Again?"

She nodded, and felt her face crumpling before she realized she was about to cry. It didn't even matter that she was crying in front of Derek, the one thing in the entire world she hated the most.

"No, no, no, come here," Derek said, pulling her into his arms before she had a chance to object. Not that she was entirely sure that she wanted to resist him. The instant she was there, in the comforting familiarity of his embrace, she knew it was a mistake. It was too easy to pretend again, to fall back into the fantasy that always hurt her more than it salved her wounds. More than once she'd given in to temptation with him, and it always felt wonderful until reality crashed down on her once more. She pulled away. "How's Becky?"

Derek couldn't stand feeling guilty. It was his biggest weakness, and Jessa wasn't afraid to exploit it. He knew that, and he looked away, scrubbing a hand over the back of his neck. "Damn it, Jessa…" His voice trailed away, and he glanced again at the car parked in the driveway. "Are you going to tell me where the hell that car came from?"

She followed him as he stalked across the lawn, relieved for the change of subject. She'd brought up his wife as a stalling tactic. She hadn't really cared to hear about her, or his kids, at all. Before he could change his mind and start telling her all about them, she started explaining. "You're not going to believe this, but someone actually stopped at Dale Elkhart's service station last night."

"Really?" Derek stood beside the car, hands on his hips. He tore his fascinated gaze away from the sleek black machine to look at her. "Why were you all the way out by Dale's?"

That, she didn't want to get into. "It chased me, and that was the way I ran. I got a shot off, though. Hit it right in the chest. It just kept coming."

"Hell of a car," he said, as though it didn't matter that she'd been chased down by a monster and barely escaped with her life. That was Derek, in a nutshell. Easily distracted by shiny objects.

She was grateful for the change of subject, though, and gestured to the open driver's side window. "Take a look. The guy was on his way to some party or something and got lost, I guess. I don't know why he would have stopped at the service station, though. It doesn't exactly look like it's in business."

"I'm wondering how the hell he managed to stop at all." Derek leaned in the window and gave a whistle of appreciation. "All-leather interior. This is a hell of a car, whatever it is."

"Well, it's a good thing he did stop. Otherwise, I would have been It's dinner." She wondered if those terrifying words would come back to haunt her in the night. And she tried not to dwell on the fact that she'd brought It up again. A hot flush flamed in her cheeks, embarrassment at herself for wanting him to acknowledge the danger she'd been in. She didn't want to be scolded, but a sick, jealous part of her wanted him to care.

"Hell of a car." Derek looked around the yard, an increasingly agitated expression on his face. "So where's this guy, now? You didn't let him stay here?"

"I did." She drew herself up to her full height, which was pretty impressive for a woman, or so she'd been told. She was still shorter than Derek, but he would damn well listen to her. "I'm a grown woman. I can have anybody stay the night that I want to."

Derek gave her a sideways look that said, *Over my dead body.* "Nobody ever said you couldn't, but how did you know this guy wasn't dangerous or something? I mean, he could stop here…how do you know he wasn't sent here?"

"Sent?" She hadn't thought of that. Maybe she should have. The creature had never sent anyone into their midst before, and it didn't make a whole lot of sense that it would now. Such a complicated strategy for a basically ragtag monster, but then, It didn't make a whole lot of sense, period. Nothing in Penance did anymore. "You think so?"

"Could be. Don't know until we talk to this guy." Derek started for the house, and Jessa followed.

"We can't. Not now. He's sleeping."

"Well, I guess we're gonna just have to go and wake him up," Derek said, his worn-out boots striking a determined rhythm on the porch.

Jessa hesitated. It wasn't that she wanted to protect the guy in the basement from Derek, but she didn't want the two to meet, either. Something about the guy reminded her of the reality of her—and the whole town's—situation. If she stood in the same room with the both of them, the safety and familiarity of another aspect of her pretend world would be fractured. If she kept losing pieces of her fantasy refuge, where would she go to escape the here and now?

She didn't have much of a choice. Derek was already headed toward the stairs to the upper level of the house.

"Wait," she called out to him, not sure if she meant to stop him entirely or just stop him from going up. "He's in the basement."

"Why would you keep him in the basement?" Derek moved with equal determination toward the kitchen.

First he didn't want the guy in her house at all, then he wanted her to be putting him in plush accommodations? She rolled her eyes, glad Derek could see her. She didn't have the energy for a fight about her "tone." "It was the only place I felt safe keeping him."

"Don't you worry about safe," Derek reassured

her. "I'm about to make sure this creep doesn't lay a finger on you."

Yeah, from one creep to another, she thought, but she still had to squash a spark of triumphant feminine pride as she followed him down the basement steps.

Four

Waking to the disturbing sensation of not knowing where he was or why he was there, Graf sat up on the rickety cot. Someone was coming toward him, but his vision hadn't cleared enough for him to make out who. He did know that he was naked, and he didn't want that kind of vulnerability. He put a hand out to reach for his jeans and started to stand.

Someone yelled, "Whoa!" and someone else yelled, "Don't get up!"

He rubbed his eyes. His skin was on fire, and he felt like he hadn't slept at all. He was thirsty, parched, in fact. He needed to eat somebody. "What time is it?"

"Who the hell are you and what are you doing in Jessa's basement?"

Graf cracked one eye, but the brightness of the basement made it difficult to focus. "Could you cover that window over there?" He hadn't seen sunlight in thirty years—at least, not willingly.

"Hungover?" the male voice asked, kicking the leg of the cot, and Graf put his arms out to keep from tipping over.

"Jesus, Derek, we're not interrogating a suspect! He's allergic to the sun. Put that gun away!" The woman from last night—Jessa, apparently—scrabbled through the boxes and camp gear in the corner and eventually found something to block the light from the dirty, ground-level window. A deflated pool raft stuffed into the hole covered the glass, filtering the light through thick blue vinyl.

The male voice spoke again. "Allergic to the sun? That sounds like something a *vampire* would say in a *vampire movie.*"

Very astute. His vision clearing, Graf examined the guy, who certainly did not look like the astute type. Derek, Jessa had called him. A lot of new, human names to remember that he didn't care to remember. Derek had a college emblem on the hat he wore and a T-shirt with a varsity football logo on it that screamed, *I didn't willingly leave my high school days behind.* He looked strong. Small-town strong. Farm-chores strong. Not strong enough to take Graf in a fight. He might not win, but he'd sure put up one, and the last thing Graf wanted was any kind of hard work. Derek slipped a handgun into the back of his jeans. That was another thing Graf didn't want to deal with.

Jessa stood beside him, not close enough to tell Graf that they were lovers, but close enough that it was apparent they once had been.

"What's his name?" Derek asked, and Graf let the woman falter for a little bit before he looked up.

"His name is Graf. He was trying to sleep after he was attacked by a monster last night." Graf rubbed his eyes again. "What is it, 8:00 a.m.?"

"It's one in the afternoon," Jessa snapped. "And you weren't the only one running from a monster last night."

"I was the only one saving you. I guess I thought that would be good enough reason to let me sleep in!" He thought about standing up and choking her, but then he would be the only naked person in the room, and he tried to avoid that whenever possible.

"Okay, both of you, shut up." Derek gave Graf what was supposed to be a threatening look, but really just made him look like an angry gorilla.

"Now, listen, Graf." He leaned on the name like it was an accusation. "I don't know where you came from—"

"Detroit." Graf pushed his fingers through his hair. "You can stop your tough-guy act. I'm not going to cause any trouble." *That you'll be able to do anything about.*

"You're in my girl's house. You scared the shit out

of her, and you pissed me off. You've already 'caused any trouble.'" Derek gave the distinct impression that if Graf had been wearing a shirt, he would be yanking him up by the front of it. It was a good thing he'd turned down Sophia's offer to pierce his nipples.

Graf filed the "my girl" remark in the back of his mind, for later use. If Sophia had taught him anything, it was that the most effective injury to inflict was to an opponent's pride. Maybe he would sleep with Jessa, after all.

He leaned his elbows on his knees and let his hands hang between his bare legs. "This isn't just an inconvenience for you guys. I don't want to be stuck in some podunk town forever. If I could redo last night, I wouldn't have gotten all turned around in Cleveland. I damn sure wouldn't have stopped here."

"Well, you're not here forever. You're just here until you die." Derek cracked his knuckles, probably imitating some mobster he'd seen in a movie. "You get my draft?"

"It's drift, you moron." Graf lay back down on the cot. At sundown, if Corn-fed was still hanging around with his stupid tough-guy act, Graf was going to drain him dry. At the very least, he would be doing Jessa a favor. If this was the kind of guy she really went for, it would probably be doing her a favor to kill her, too.

"What did you just call me?" Derek demanded, his voice dripping with unspent testosterone.

Graf didn't bother to open his eyes. "I'm too tired to repeat it. Come back later."

From the sound of Jessa's feet shuffling on the dirt floor and the rapid-fire, "No, no, no!" she uttered, Graf knew Derek had lunged for him, and that most likely Jessa had held him back. Though it took considerable effort not to sit up and rip out the guy's windpipe right then and there, Graf restrained himself. It would be better if he waited, until the sun went down and he had a place to hide the bodies.

"That son of a bitch has a big problem on his hands now, a big problem." Derek swore, his voice accompanied by the creaking of the stairs.

When the door slammed, Graf sat up and pulled on his jeans. He cocked his head to listen to the muffled conversation upstairs.

"You can't just go around punching people!" Jessa had a different angry voice with Derek than she'd had with Graf the night before. There was more frustration invested in it. That was interesting.

"There's something weird about that guy, and I don't like it!"

"It doesn't matter if you like it! It's not like he can leave!" There was a strained silence, and Graf imagined the two humans staring at each other, daring each other to try for the last word.

"And...go," Graf prompted quietly.

On the heels of his words, Jessa spoke. "Look, I'll take him over to June's Place tonight, see if I can't get someone else to put him up."

Derek huffed in reply. "Yeah, well, you better take him over to Tom Stoke's place, too. He's going to want to know what's happening, and you don't want to get Tom pissed off. I might go over there, too, and let him know I'm not real keen on the notion of some guy staying out here with you, alone."

"Oh, yeah, and what's Tom going to do? Make me wear a big, red letter *A* on my chest?" She lowered her voice. "Besides, this guy isn't dangerous. He's just a prick."

Graf couldn't help but smile at that. They were so trusting sometimes. His smile died when she followed up her statement with, "He seems kind of like the whiny type. Not real intimidating."

"Don't make me worry about you," Derek warned, and the implication went beyond fearing for her safety. And…confirmation. Graf had figured there was something going on between the two of them. So, he was a jealous boyfriend? Where the hell had he been when his girl was running from—and being rescued by—monsters?

When Jessa spoke again, her tone was hard and cold. "You should be getting back on home to your wife, shouldn't you?"

That was interesting. Very interesting. Better than

the soap operas Sophia had forced him to watch with her.

Derek swore, and the floorboards overhead creaked as he stomped across them. The outside door slammed.

Graf expected to hear Jessa crying—the spurned lover, the other woman, reduced to tears by the man she couldn't give up. Instead, all he heard was an exasperated sigh, then footsteps through the kitchen.

If it hadn't been so damned sunny out, he would have gone upstairs and shown her exactly how nonintimidating he was. Knowing the way the place was decorated, there were probably yellowing lace curtains on the windows and he'd be incinerated instantly. And a sick part of him still wondered if he'd kill her or have sex with her. If she was getting it from that Derek guy, it probably wasn't that good. He could do things to her that would make her forget she ever gave a shit about Country Boy.

Thoughts like that made his fangs ache, and other things, too. Hunger, even the sexual variety, was too exhausting to deal with at the moment, so he lay down and went back to sleep.

"Wake up. Allergic to the sun does not mean 'lazy as hell.' I saw those girls on 20/20."

Graf peeled open one eye. Jessa stood over him, scowling. *Be patient,* he urged himself. *You can't eat her yet. You don't know how to find anyone else to eat without her help.*

The way he figured it, he could follow her to this Tom guy's house, and then to June's Place, whatever that was. He could get acquainted with the town tonight and then finish off Jessa and her backwoods Casanova before polishing off the rest of the hillbillies as necessary.

He stood up and reached for his shirt. When he pulled it on, she turned away quickly, a guilty expression on her face. She'd been sneaking a peek, and the hungry look in her eyes told him her opinion of what she'd seen. Very interesting, considering Everybody's All-American hadn't been all that bad-looking.

"So, what, do you spend, like, forty hours a week at the gym?" she snorted, starting for the stairs.

"No, I don't work out all that much." It was true. There was really no point in a vampire working out. For the most part, he looked exactly the same as he had the day he'd been turned. Sure, his muscles had become more toned from the boost in strength, and his wardrobe was a lot different, and he didn't have a lame haircut anymore, but physically, not much could be changed about the way a vampire looked. A lesson Sophia had learned when she'd stupidly tried to get collagen injections in her lips. At least the plastic surgeon had been delicious.

Jessa made a noise that told him she didn't believe

him. "Meet me in the kitchen. We've got eggs and apples for dinner."

"I'm not really all that hungry," he called after her as she jogged up the stairs. He followed, his stomach jerking in response to the smell of the food. Another physical thing that couldn't be changed. "Eggs and apples?"

"All I can afford." She shrugged as she scraped scrambled eggs from a large, cast-iron skillet. "We have to make do with what we've got."

He rolled his eyes. "I appreciate that fact. You can stop acting like a dust-bowl farmer."

The skillet clattered to the stove top, and she braced her hands against the counter. "You have got some nerve, buddy."

"I have some nerve? You get me trapped here, you let your boyfriend come down to beat my ass—"

"Derek is not my boyfriend!" she shouted as she whirled toward him, the spatula in her hand whipping flecks of egg through the air. Her shocked gaze followed their trajectory.

Graf ducked the flying food and gave a low whistle. "You don't say?"

"I don't even know why I'm explaining it to you. It's none of your business." She took a deep breath. "What were you doing at the service station? You shouldn't have been able to stop there in the first place. But couldn't you tell it wasn't open, from the fact that it was all dark inside?"

Before he could stop himself, his gaze flicked guiltily to the countertop in front of him, and he knew he was caught. Usually, he could lie convincingly enough to fool a polygraph machine, but for some reason that skill had failed him now, and in front of a woman who was, he had to admit, a pretty smart cookie.

"Oh my God!" She put her hands on her hips. "You were going to rob it!"

"I was not!" The quick denial sealed his fate. He should have laughed it off, like it was the most ridiculous suggestion in the world. "Well, I was going to steal a map—"

"Ha! I knew it!" She pointed at him, like an actor in a courtroom drama who was really enjoying her role. "You were going to rob the place. What are you, some kind of criminal? I should have known you couldn't afford that car."

"That car was a gift," he sputtered, then, realizing that he was defending himself to a woman he planned on making a meal of, stopped himself. "Look, what does it matter? I was there, and I saved your life."

"And you're probably going to steal my silverware when my back is turned." She shook her head, glaring off at seemingly nothing, as though accusing the air of ruining her evening. "This is just great."

"Yeah, I'm having a hell of a time, myself."

Her eyes narrowed as she glared back to him.

"You're out of here tonight. We'll go down to June's Place and foist you off on someone else."

"Foist?" He chuckled. "That's a pretty big word for a farm girl."

Ignoring the barb, she dropped a plate in front of him. As she sauntered out of the kitchen, she snapped, "Eat up."

"Oh, believe me, I will," he said under his breath, and reluctantly lifted his fork.

They set out right after sunset. Jessa's understanding of sunlight was that when the sun went down, there was no sunlight. It was a simplistic belief, but he couldn't really expect much else from someone who was basically a Hee Haw personality. The residual light prickled his skin, but didn't burn him. It did bring back the unpleasant memories of being nearly roasted alive in the trunk of his car, which he didn't appreciate.

Before he killed her, he'd have to ask her where he could find a map to get back to the highway, so he wouldn't get stuck in a similar situation once he got out of here. Who knew how many void towns there were in Ohio?

"You need to behave yourself," Jessa scolded. He hadn't even done anything yet. "Tom Stoke is the sheriff here. He doesn't take lip from anybody, not even guys with fancy cars. And he has a way of dealing with people who don't fall in line."

"Tar and feathers?" Graf guessed, but Jessa didn't smile. She pressed her lips together into an unattractive line and kept walking, head down.

Maybe this Tom person thought he was a tough guy, but most tough guys crumbled like dust when a vampire started sticking their teeth in them. Not dust…more like rag dolls.

"People in town don't like different," she warned ominously. "Bad things can happen."

He would worry about bad things later. Right now, he needed to figure out a way to get out of town. He would think about bad things and this place when he was driving far, far away from it.

Tom Stoke's house wasn't a house so much as it was a single-wide trailer parked on a depressing lot surrounded by tall grass. Just after the grass a rotting wooden bridge spanned the gap over a ditch that ran through his driveway, giving the place the appearance of having a moat. It was like the worst castle in the history of all castles.

"Sheriff?" Jessa called, picking her way across the collapsing bridge. "It's Jessa Gallagher. I'm coming to your door."

Graf noticed the hand-painted, misspelled TRESPASERS WILL BE SHOT ON SITE sign as he crossed the bridge behind her. The front door of the trailer swung open, and a dumpy man—who looked to be about sixty in Graf's estimation—came out to stand on the cinder-block steps. He held a rifle at his side. Totally normal way to answer a door.

"Who's that with you? Derek?"

"No. This is what I came here to talk to you about," Jessa shouted back, indicating Graf with a jerk of her thumb. "Sorry to come out so late, but I can explain."

They crossed the yard, mostly hard dirt with a few pathetic yellow clumps of grass, and Graf ducked into the shade beside the trailer. In the twilight, nearly everything was shade, but this was a cool patch that had been sunless for hours, far more comfortable than the residual heat that lingered everywhere else.

The sheriff looked Graf up and down, stroking his beard with two fingers. "I'll be damned," he said, beady gray eyes squinting even further in his wrinkled face. He looked like Santa Claus's brother who'd done some time in jail for DUI. Multiple DUIs.

Jessa pushed some stray, sweat-dampened hair from her face. "I found him on the road last night, out by the service station. He said he stopped for gas, but I'm pretty sure he stopped to rob the place."

Narc, Graf thought. Maybe she was hoping the sheriff would arrest him right then and there, and take her problem guest off her hands. "It was a good thing I stopped, though, or you would have been dead."

"That's true," Jessa agreed, surprisingly. "I was out there running from It, and if he hadn't been there…I don't want to think about what would have happened." She said the last part the way bad actors deliver lines in Westerns. Not convincing, and you knew that they were mimicking the performance of someone better. Which gave Graf the distinct impression that she would have rather been caught by the monster. Either she was suicidal, or she hated him enough that she would rather be dead than know him. Either way, he had the solution to her problem.

"Doesn't really matter why he was out there, does it? Not when there ain't nothing out there to rob." The sheriff put out his hand. "Tom Stoke. Sheriff. Let's not worry about what you were doing out there. Let's talk about how you got into this here town at all."

He welcomed them inside the trailer. The interior was in a lot better shape than the exterior, though on a purely functional level only. On an aesthetic level, it was the seventh circle of hell. The walls were covered in wood paneling, save the small, open kitchen wallpapered in a print of huge mauve roses with metallic gold leaves. Not that much of the wall coverings were visible between the commemorative Elvis plates and shelves of Precious Moments figurines.

This decorating schema was as close to wholesome as Graf figured he'd ever get, and just standing in the midst of all of it made his skin itch.

"Marjorie, you wanna go to the kitchen? I got official business here," the sheriff said to a woman about his age dressed in a sweat suit with a picture of two kittens snuggling on the front. She set aside the tattered crossword puzzle book she had been working on and nodded, not in a friendly way, to Jessa as she walked past.

"Sit down, young man," Tom said, taking up residence in what was probably his regular chair, a wooden rocker with padded seat and arms. "Tell me how you got here."

Graf took a seat in the armchair Marjorie had vacated, leaving Jessa standing awkwardly by the door. "Well, I got off an exit on 75 hoping to bypass a traffic jam, then I got all turned around. I was running out of gas and needed to get somewhere to sleep, so I pulled over at the gas station. I figured it was closed, but I thought I could sleep there and get gas when it opened in the morning. It was a win-win situation."

"And that's where you saw Jessa?" The sheriff glanced suspiciously at her. Maybe she had a record. Stealing street signs or something smalltownish like that.

Either way, the sheriff seemed to believe him more than he would likely believe Jessa. Her antagonistic glare cut right into him, practically carving *liar* on his forehead.

"Yeah. I saw the beam of a flashlight in the windows, so I went in to investigate. That's when It attacked us. Mighty nice monster you got out here, Sheriff." Graf tipped his imaginary cowboy hat, but Stoke didn't crack a smile.

"I don't know how much Jessa has told you about this town, but we ain't had any strangers here in five years." The sheriff rocked in his chair like a shark circling a wounded seal. "You'll have to pardon me if I get a little suspicious when I hear your story."

"That's fine." Graf held up his hands. "I'm suspicious, myself. I'm supposed to be meeting friends down in D.C., and they're going to be worried if I don't show up soon."

"D.C.?" Stoke's eyebrows shot up at that. "You FBI?"

Graf hesitated. "No…I was on my way to a party."

"He's not FBI," Jessa said with certainty. "He's too dumb to be FBI."

I'm smart enough to F. U. Up. He didn't give her the satisfaction of acknowledging her remark. "The FBI has probably tried to get in here a million times, you've just never noticed. Think about it—all you people suddenly missing, not contacting your loved ones, not paying your bills. Heck, someone in this town has to have a car loan they defaulted on. You're so far lost, even a skip tracer can't find you."

Stoke stopped rocking and leaned forward in his chair. "We know all about that, boy. If you ain't FBI, and you ain't the IRS or some other government agent, just a normal guy, how'd you get here?"

"That's something I am dying to find out." The sooner he found out how he'd gotten in, the sooner he could use that information to get out.

"Ain't we all?" Stoke glanced up at Jessa. "I don't know what you think I'm gonna do about him."

"I couldn't just keep this kind of news from you. You're the head of the town council. You're the sheriff. They'll all want to know about him, won't they? Besides, he needs a place to stay," Jessa piped up, her arms folded tight across her chest. Everything about her body language said that she wasn't intimidated by this man, from the way she leaned casually against his door to the expression of boredom on her face. She feared him, though. Graf's sense of smell was too good to miss that.

Stoke's mouth canted sideways in the depths of his beard as he considered. Finally, he said, "You got that big house all to yourself out there, don't you?"

She shook her head adamantly. "No, he can't stay."

"Put a crimp in your love life, does he?" Mrs. Stoke said blandly from the kitchen.

"Marjorie, you stay out of it, now," the sheriff warned. Then, in the same warning tone, "Jessa, there are too many people in town and not enough room. What am I supposed to do with him?"

"Put him in over at the school," she said with an exasperated sigh. The fear smell intensified, but so did her stubborn insistence that Graf wouldn't stay with her. "Nobody's using it!"

"Why, you know I'm using it for the jail. And school is neutral property, for the community. It ain't a hotel." Sheriff Stoke looked Graf up and down, like he was considering buying a cow. "Why don't you take him on down to June's Place and see if anyone there will take him? If you don't want an extra hand around your place, there's plenty who might."

"I'm sure you'll find something to do with him," Marjorie put in dryly.

Apparently, Jessa had a reputation. Was that why she wanted him out of the house? So she wouldn't sleep with him? Jessa, so uptight and moody, yet so unable to resist a roll in the hay with any guy who stumbled across her path. It was actually kind of hot. The reality was probably not that interesting. She probably just didn't trust him, and didn't want him to get in the way of her romance with a married man.

Jessa made a disgusted noise, but she didn't do anything else to express her disapproval. "We better get heading over there, then."

"I'm not quite done with your friend here," Sheriff Stoke said, leaning back and putting his big, square hands on his knees. "I don't believe in coincidences. Him just showing up looks a little fishy."

"In my own defense, Sheriff, this whole town looks a little fishy," Graf replied, annoyed. "It wasn't my idea to get stuck here. And I will gladly leave at the first opportunity."

"Wouldn't we all?" Stoke agreed, but his expression was still hard, accusing. "I'm gonna have my eye on you, boy. Just keep your nose clean, and we won't have any problems."

"Squeaky, I assure you." Graf stood, eager to be out of Elvis hell and away from these people who probably made a habit of needlessly mistrusting others.

"You have a good night, now," Stoke said with a nod as Graf and Jessa stepped through the door and down the cinder-block steps. "And, Graf, keep your eye out. You got hit by It once, but until it draws blood, it'll keep coming after you."

"Well, that was a waste," Graf muttered as they crossed the broken-down bridge.

"Not a waste, believe me." Jessa sounded more worried than she had on the way over, definitely more frightened than she had in the trailer. "If we hadn't come by, we would have heard about it."

"What did he mean, about It drawing blood?" Was It some kind of mutant super-vampire? Graf didn't know if he liked the idea of something else above him on the food chain.

Jessa's mouth opened and her brow scrunched up. "Uh, well, that depends on who you ask. Some people in town have a theory about its movements and patterns."

"You don't agree with it?" How unlike her, to be contrary.

She shrugged. "I just have experience that runs counter to it."

He waited a moment as they walked to see if she would continue explaining. When she didn't, he snapped, "You wanna let me in on it?"

With a heavy sigh, she explained, "Except for the people It has killed, once it injures somebody it never goes back for them."

"Could be a coincidence." Graf kicked a rock and watched it bounce across the asphalt in the twilight. He frowned when he realized how entertaining that was to him.

"That's what I'm leaning toward, myself. It does seem a little weird, though…" Her voice trailed off and she shook her head.

"No, tell me." This was the kind of stuff he needed to learn so he could get out of town as fast as possible.

"Well." She hesitated. "According to Mitch Moody, when It cornered him in his barn, it slashed his arm, then immediately backed off. Like it didn't like the way he reacted or got bored with him."

"Maybe he didn't smell tasty," Graf wondered aloud. "I mean, maybe there was something about the guy's blood. Animals won't eat prey that smells sick."

"It doesn't eat people," Jessa snapped with disgust. "You don't have to be so gruesome-minded."

He changed the subject quickly. "What was up with the sheriff's wife? Did you piss on her birthday cake or something?"

Jessa didn't answer. She kept her head down as they walked, still hugging her arms around her chest.

"Well, let me feel free to form my own conclusions, then," he went on. "You have a reputation."

"What are you, from the sixties or something?" she snapped. "A 'reputation'? Who am I, Rizzo?"

"I see I have struck a nerve." He followed behind her, kicking stones down the road. "And, while dated, *reputation* is a perfectly good word. You have one. Either that, or you stole Marjorie's boyfriend when the two of you were in high school."

Jessa stopped walking and dropped her hands to her hips. Without facing him, she ground out, "Yes, everybody in town thinks I'm a whore. Are you happy?"

"I don't care either way. But if I'm going to be shacking up with a woman, I would prefer her to be a loose woman."

The minute she turned around, Graf knew his joke had not been interpreted in the spirit with which he had intended it. Jessa's hand slashed out, her palm connecting with his cheek with a crack. It stung a little, but he made sure to grimace and rub his jaw. Little tricks like that made a vampire seem more human.

"Sorry," he said, and he meant it this time. Being an asshole on purpose was one thing; being an asshole by accident was worse, somehow.

Jessa shook her head and turned back to the road, marching away from him with purpose.

"Look, that was uncalled-for, I admit." He jogged to catch up with her, then slid smoothly in front, cutting off her forward progress. "We should at least try to get along until this whole mess is straightened out."

"It's never going to be straightened out, pal. You're here for a while." But she stuck her hand out, anyway, and shook the one Graf offered. "Just so you know, we'll get along a lot better if you can refrain from calling me a whore."

"I will file that away," he promised.

"…and then it became a kind of co-op for everyone in town. A central meeting place."

Graf nodded, though he hadn't been listening for some time. As they walked through the dark, he'd asked one innocent question about their destination—June's Place—and had received a history lesson that had lasted at least a mile. His feet ached, his throat was dry, and his ears were his worst enemy.

"So, there's going to be someone there willing to take me in, then?" He slapped a mosquito off his neck.

Jessa shrugged. "Maybe. Despite what Sheriff Stoke said, you might be able to get one of the rooms at the old high school, if enough people argue on my side. There aren't classes anymore, because of It."

Scanning the road behind them, then ahead of them, Graf took some comfort in the shotgun tucked under Jessa's arm. He didn't have a clue what "It" was, but he didn't feel the burning need to run into the thing again to try to figure it out. "So, people are afraid of It, enough that they won't send their kids to school anymore, but they'll come out to this June's Place in the middle of the night?"

She shook her head. "It's different, when it's kids you're talking about. People know they're taking a chance coming out, but they're more comfortable taking that chance when it's just them and not their babies likely to get killed. Anyway, the people who've already been attacked don't have anything to worry about, in their minds."

"How many people has this thing killed, then?" he asked. "Like, has it ever killed a kid, for these fears to be warranted?"

"It has. One." Jessa's face got the same bitter, far-off look she'd had in the kitchen when he'd mentioned the stupid chore chart on the fridge the night before. It was the kind of expression that was visible even in the dark.

"Ah," he said in understanding. "So, I take it that's what happened to your family?"

"No. Someone else…" she said, and then a brightness in her voice signaled that their conversation would not be heading down that particular road. "Really, it hasn't killed that many people. And the ones who've died either got in It's way, or they picked a fight with It. Protecting livestock or their kids, you know?"

Well, It probably had nothing on Graf. And he'd be adding to his body count by the end of the night, if he played his cards right. As she launched into a forced-cheerful description of the local waitress who'd been killed by the monster and exactly what extracurricular activities she'd been involved in back when they'd been in high school, Graf gave Jessa a good once-over. She looked a lot better when she hadn't just been running for her life. Her thin cotton tank top clung to her body from the humidity, and the light sheen of sweat that made her bare arms sparkle in the low light wafted her scent to him. He breathed it in, and his mouth watered. Her nipples stood out against the ribbed cotton of her shirt, and her hair, pulled back in a ponytail, swished against her neck. He imagined gripping her by that hair, winding the length of it around his fist as he jerked her head back.

That was where the fantasy ran into a snag. He didn't know if he wanted to pull on that ponytail while he was eating her, or fucking her.

They came to the junction of the gravel road and blacktop and took a right. It wasn't the road he'd come in on, Graf realized, and added it to his mental map. Not that it would be accurate in any way. If he was good with directions, he wouldn't be in this mess to begin with.

A few more minutes of walking in tense silence brought them within view of a long, low building with a flickering neon OPEN in the window. A weathered wooden sign in the empty parking lot proclaimed it JUNE'S PLACE.

"Is anybody here?" Graf asked, frowning at the lack of cars. Then, he recalled Jessa's reluctance when he'd suggested driving there. "Oh, I get it. No gas…"

Jessa nodded. "No cars. Right. And I thought you should keep your fuel for when you needed to barter for something. If you brought that car here, you'd come out to find all the useful parts stripped off it."

"Like, someone might try to siphon the gas out of it while I was inside?" He enjoyed her guilty expression for a moment before he said, "I saw the hose and the gas tank on the lawn."

"Right. Well, I do what I have to." The proud set of her chin didn't match the still-remorseful look in her eyes.

They entered June's Place through a small mud-room, its walls little more than the clapboard siding that covered the rest of the building. Jessa pushed open the door to the interior, and the thick, heavy smell of alcohol and something else—sweet and smoky and skunky—assaulted Graf in a cloud.

"Is that…pot?" he asked, covering his mouth with his sleeve.

"We can't grow tobacco here," she answered with a shrug. "People need something to smoke."

Graf made a face. He liked a cigarette, and even a joint, every now and then, but he preferred his humans keep the oxygen in their blood free from pollutants. He looked around the room, trying to find one acceptable meal to replace Jessa when he finished her off, but everyone in June's Place looked rough and leathery, and they all puffed on pipes or joints, big jars of clear alcohol in front of them. If he ate one of them, he'd be buzzed for a whole night.

He noticed the hungry way he was surveying all of the people in the bar. And they were all looking back at him, he realized with a shock.

"Who's your friend, Jessa?" someone asked, and Graf turned toward the bar, where a slender woman with hair in a long, sandy-brown braid stood wiping a glass with a rag.

Jessa nudged him forward, and they walked to the bar, Jessa's back stiff under the stares of the rest of the patrons.

"June," she said with a smile as she hopped onto one of the bar stools. "This is Graf. He's looking for a place to stay."

"He picked a hell of a place," June said, her ruddy face breaking into a smile. She reached across the bar to shake Graf's hand with surprising firmness. Her smile faded as she looked back to Jessa. "Where'd he come from?"

"I ran into him out on the road last night." She lowered her voice. "Out at the service station."

"What were you doing there?" June had a way of talking without moving her mouth, and the words came out as though they were tied together with string. Graf liked that. It made everything she said seem tense and important.

Jessa shrugged casually, but leaned in so as not to be overheard. "I was running from It. Chased me all the way out there."

June looked up from the bar with a plastered-on smile and nodded to the rest of her patrons. Then, she leaned back down. "Jesus Christ, are you okay?"

"She's fine," Graf said, slapping Jessa on the back. "Aren't you? I got there just in time."

The door opened, and a group of five guys stumbled in. Their entrance was loud and rowdy, but they didn't draw the rapt attention of the patrons away from Graf and Jessa. They all held mason jars, half-full of clear liquid, and they could barely stand up straight. One of the guys was Derek.

"Oh, here we go," June said with a sigh.

"What are they drinking?" Graf asked, his eyes watering from the drunken stink that nearly overpowered the smell of the marijuana smoke in the bar.

"Shine." June jerked her thumb at the wall behind her. "It's all we got. For a while, we tried prohibition, but with our situation…well, people deserve to numb the pain whatever way they can."

"I couldn't agree with you more, June," Graf said, slapping his hand down on the bar.

"They're drunker than skunks," Jessa said, making a face. "What the hell do they think they're doing? Derek knows what happened last night. Why would he go out?"

"Probably celebrating," June said, then, with a cautious glance at Jessa, went back to wiping down glasses. "You knew him and Becky were pregnant again, right?"

Graf stole a look at Jessa's face. Apparently, she had not known, and the information wasn't sitting well with her. She slid from her bar stool with a quiet "Excuse me."

"So, what's with that?" Graf asked, watching Jessa make her way to the corner booth the men had crowded into.

"How do you know Jessa?" June asked, her icy blue eyes fixing him like a straight pin through a specimen bug.

"I don't," he admitted. "I met her last night, when my car...ran out of gas by her house."

June nodded, the wry smile on her lips letting him know that she didn't believe his story, but she wasn't about to argue with him. "No one's been able to stop in Penance for years. Why you?"

He shrugged. "I guess I'm just lucky? I honestly didn't have any trouble at all, until I got out at the gas station and nearly got killed by Godzilla."

"Godzilla is a guy in a rubber suit," June said, turning to take down a bottle. She poured him a shot, saying, "Our monster is very real. Here, this is for you."

"I don't have any money," he said, shaking his head as she set the glass in front of him.

She pushed it toward him with the tips of her fingers. "What would I do with money?"

He took it and threw it back, knowing that refusing wouldn't exactly ingratiate him to her. Human food, human intoxicants, what next? Would they demand that he use the toilet?

Raised voices from the corner caught his attention, though it seemed everyone else in the place was trying to ignore the fight going on between Derek and Jessa.

"A lot of people aren't happy with Derek and Becky, having more kids when there already isn't enough to go around in Penance as it is," June offered by way of explanation.

A noble try, but Graf wasn't buying it. "Yeah…I think she's probably angry about being the other woman."

"I thought you said you didn't know her," June teased. Then, with a sad sigh, she continued. "She wasn't always the other woman, though. Becky was, until she swooped in and got the ring."

Graf made a noise. He wasn't as interested in the tragic romantic history between Jessa and Jethro

Clampett as he was in the fight between them right now. The four guys with Derek all exchanged amused looks and open laughter as their buddy fought with his jealous ex-girlfriend. Graf experienced a pang of secondhand embarrassment for Jessa.

"Does this happen a lot?" he asked June.

The woman shrugged. "Not so much anymore. It used to happen a lot before Becky had the first baby. Now, she stays home with the kids, so things stay pretty civil between Jessa and Derek."

After a long silence, June continued. "It's a shame, though. He wasn't good to her. Her whole family died, and he expected her to just get over it and go back to normal. But I don't think there is a normal after something like that happens."

Graf nodded, guilt pricking him. He still had living family, siblings and nieces and nephews. He hadn't seen any of them since it had become too hard to cover up the fact that he wasn't aging. Jessa probably wanted her family, and they'd been killed. Maybe he'd been a little harsh to her.

"Oh, shit," June said suddenly, and Graf looked up in time to see Derek stand and grab Jessa's arm, wrenching it toward him.

"Stop it!" Jessa shouted, pulling back, but Derek was stronger.

Before he could realize what exactly he meant to do, Graf was on his feet, pushing through the maze of tables in the center of the floor. He willed himself to slow down, to look less like a supernatural creature and more like a human, but it was damned difficult to do when Derek was raising his hand to smack her.

Sure, he was planning on eating her, but that didn't mean Graf liked to see a woman get knocked around. And he didn't treat the ladies bad, either. They never saw it coming. Hitting a woman was a low, vulgar thing to do, and he'd be damned if he sat back and watched a punk like Derek do it.

"I suggest you put your arm down, before I break it," he said, and though he kept his voice low, he knew everyone in the bar had heard. Not that they needed any inducement to eavesdrop; they'd all been watching him, waiting to see what the new guy was up to.

This was a sticky spot. If he hit Derek, would the cast of *Deliverance* decide they didn't like some mysterious stranger wandering in and beating up the locals? Or would it establish a kind of grudging respect, like all those prison movies claimed?

There was only one way to find out, and Derek wasn't going to give him much of a choice. "Don't tell me how to treat my woman!" he shouted drunkenly, pushing Jessa back. She stumbled backward into a table, but at least she was out of striking range of Derek's fist.

"Far as I can tell, Pilgrim, that's not your woman. Your woman is at home, probably waiting for you. Why don't you run along back there." Pilgrim? Graf cursed his love of John Wayne movies, and prayed he still knew how to throw a decent punch. He was more of a lover than a fighter. More pertinently, he hoped that if he did land a decent hit, it wouldn't shatter Derek's head like a pumpkin thrown into a mailbox. That would be embarrassingly difficult to explain to all these people, and he didn't have the energy to kill this many witnesses.

"You son of a bitch," Derek shouted as he lunged. He grabbed the front of Graf's shirt and hauled him off his feet, literally wiping a nearby table with him.

So much for worrying about not appearing weak and human enough. The inbred yokels at the tables around them scooted the chairs back and howled with laughter.

"Don't you ever talk about my Becky that way!" Derek warned, and while Graf tried to remember if he'd said anything derogatory about Derek's wife, Derek got a swing in. His fist connected with Graf's jaw, and, vampire or not, a hard punch from a strong man was not a pleasant experience.

Graf swore and held up his hands. "I don't want to have to hurt you," he mumbled. That made the yokels laugh again, and Graf couldn't blame them. He was getting his ass handed to him.

He waited for Derek's next swing, and ducked it, taking advantage of the human's momentum to grab him and hurl him to the floor. When he flipped onto his back, confused at his suddenly changed perspective, Graf took a handful of Derek's T-shirt and pulled him up as his fist shot down. Derek's head snapped back, blood gushing from his nose.

"Now, are you going to keep your hands off Jessa?" Graf growled, pulling his arm back again. When Derek didn't answer, Graf punched him again.

"Stop it!" Jessa shouted, running to pull Graf back. She shot him a dirty glare as she knelt on the floor beside Derek. "What are you trying to do, kill him?"

"I'm trying to stick up for you!" Graf got the distinct impression that his valor was unappreciated. "Unless you want to be his punching bag?"

"I don't want you to make him your punching bag!" She helped Derek to his feet and pushed him toward his friends. "Get him out of here, you guys."

"And you best get your friend out of here, too," June called from behind the bar. "He can come back when he cools off."

"That's bullshit, June!" Derek shouted, his eyelids fluttering closed as he wiped blood off his chin. "You should ban him!"

"You should mind your own business, Derek, before I throw you out of here with my own two hands. I don't want to see you beating on any women, I don't care who they are." June didn't sound angry. She didn't have to. Her word was obviously meant to be obeyed as law, like she had no reason to expect otherwise.

"June, I've gotta find a place for him to stay," Jessa protested, and that was all she needed to say to get every hillbilly in the place to look away from Graf and into their drinks.

The kindly barkeep would not be swayed, it seemed. She pointed to the door wordlessly.

"Let's get out of here," Jessa grumbled, grabbing Graf by the elbow.

The fact that she was put out by this turn of events touched him on a profoundly personal level. The joy that radiated through his whole being was only slightly displaced by the fact that her misery came at his expense, too, because now he was stuck with her.

"Hey, I don't have a place to stay yet," he reminded her as he followed her into the deserted parking lot, wanting to prolong the magic.

"You think anyone back there is going to take you in, after what you just did?" She shook her head and kept walking. "You'll be lucky if they don't come over with a noose and run you out of town the only way possible."

Five

The tall grass whipped against Jessa's legs as she cut across the ditch and up the lawn. Graf followed, still silent. It was good that he knew when to keep his mouth shut, because one more wrong word would have set her off in a big way, and it seemed like none of the right words came out when he opened his trap.

It wasn't that she had wanted Derek to hit her. In fact, the thought that he was perfectly willing to stung her to her core. He'd never raised a hand to her before. He'd been angry and stormed off, and he'd punched a wall once or twice—once in her kitchen, and her father had repaired it while lecturing her on what was and was not appropriate behavior from a boyfriend. She wondered if there had been times before when Derek had wanted to hit her, and if he'd hit Becky. Was it a normal thing at their house?

No, he'd been drunk. Drunk people did things they wouldn't normally do when they were sober. She knew that from experience.

Still, it wasn't right of Graf to step in the way he had. It would have been one thing if one of Derek's friends had, or someone else at the bar. But not Graf. Not when he was staying with her, and everyone knew it. They would start to think things about her, things they already probably thought, but it would give them a sort of confirmation. By the time the people who'd seen it happen had sobered up enough in the morning, the guys wouldn't be fighting about one of them hitting Jessa, they would be fighting over Jessa. Then rumors would spread all over town that Jessa the slut was screwing around on her married boyfriend. People would love that bit of gossip.

Not that ridiculous, maybe. She'd slept with Derek before, more recently than she would like to remember, and there was something attractive about Graf, even though he acted like a complete jackass.

That must have been the common element in them that had sprung her gears.

She charged up the steps to the porch, then stopped, catching sight of the car from the corner of her eye. "You wanna move that thing before you attract too much more attention? Anyone who walks by here is going to see it!"

"Do a lot of people walk by?" he asked. For a guy who'd just gotten punched in the jaw, he spoke remarkably clearly. He should have at least a tooth knocked loose, or a puffy lip.

She shook her head in annoyance. "If I'm stuck with you, you're going to do what I say, when I say it. You got it?"

"Yes, ma'am," he responded, accompanied by a mock salute.

Jessa ground her teeth. "And you're going to have to pay me rent." She waited until he reached for his back pocket, then folded her arms across her chest. "Not what I'm looking for."

Hesitantly, he put his wallet back. "Is this…is this a sexual thing?"

Ugh! She stomped into the house and headed straight for the kitchen, where she pulled a mason jar of clear liquid from the refrigerator.

Graf followed her, and watched as she lifted the jar to her mouth. "Look, I know you're pissed off because I beat up your boyfriend, but I'm not going to just sit back and watch a guy hit a girl. It's not my nature."

Wincing at the burn of the moonshine as it tore a path down her throat, she set the jar down. When she spoke, her voice was rough. "I told you, he's not my boyfriend. And to be honest, he's been needing a good ass whipping for some time now."

"Okay…" Graf sat at the island and braced his elbows against the counter. "If you're not mad about that, what are you mad about?"

"You've never lived in a small town, have you?" When he shook his head, she continued. "Imagine if every time you walked down the street, every person you saw knew your business. They know about all the bad things you've ever done, and they know about all the bad things anyone in your family has ever done, and they're all rooting for you to fail, because if you do, they've got more gossip to spread around. That's what it's like living here. You said yourself that I have a reputation. I'm not proud of it, but I earned it.

"I showed up with you tonight, and that drew attention to me. They were already wondering who you are and how you got here, and what it has to do with me. That's dangerous enough. People here are suspicious of everyone for the littlest things, and I don't want knowing you to become a liability!"

"A liability?" He snorted. "What are they going to do? Burn you at the stake?"

"They've done it before!" she shouted, then clamped a hand over her mouth.

"Okay, I can sense by your hyperbole that you're afraid of people here." Graf nodded, actually looking sorry for something for the first time since she'd met him. "I didn't think about how showing up with me might affect you."

"You didn't think about it, because you have no idea what it's like to live here. Since It came around and we all got trapped here, all of the malice and bad feelings have just grown and grown." She took another swallow of the alcohol. "You'll see. The first time you do something wrong, you'll see."

He reached for the jar, and she passed it to him. He took a big swallow and grimaced. "Let me guess…the 'something wrong' that you did involved Derek?"

She worked hard to keep her expression neutral. Eventually, Graf would know all about her and Derek, every sordid detail. That didn't mean she wanted to spill it all right now. Still, if he was going to be living there, he'd have to deal with Derek in the future. "People…don't like the way I behaved after Derek married Becky. And before Derek married Becky."

Graf nodded. "You beat her up? Key her car?"

"No." She took another swig of moonshine. "No, I kept sleeping with her husband."

"Ah." There was a hint of judgment in Graf's tone that Jessa didn't care for. "Well, from what I understand, he was your boyfriend to begin with."

"June tell you that?" She shouldn't have bothered to ask. June wasn't a gossip, but she wouldn't withhold information from someone she thought needed to know something. If she'd suspected there was something between Jessa and Graf, she couldn't have been more wrong, but she would have thought it only fair to warn him what he was getting into.

Graf nodded. "She didn't give me the full history, but she said that Derek wasn't exactly supportive after your family died. Which I'm sorry to hear about, by the way."

Clearing her throat, Jessa screwed the top back on the moonshine and shoved it to the back of the refrigerator. She leaned down, hiding her face behind the door long enough to force back the tears that never failed to flood her eyes at the memory. "Well, it's better off this way. Becky can have him, for all I care."

"That's not how it looked this afternoon. And it's not how it looked at the bar tonight." His voice startled her, as it was closer than it had been before. When she turned, he stood behind her, gazing down at her with pity.

Yeah, like she needed his pity. She stood and pushed past him. "I don't have any idea what you're talking about. Derek comes sniffing around here like a hound dog most days, but I haven't encouraged him." It was a bald-faced lie, and she had a feeling Graf knew it. She wanted nothing more than to lure Derek away from Becky, knew she could have him in her bed with a snap of her fingers. But she didn't want to be that person anymore. She didn't want the guilt when she saw the kids playing in their grandma's yard, or when she ran into Becky at June's Place. She didn't want to be the town tramp. She just wanted her old life back.

"Well, guys like that, they don't need a lot of en-couraging," Graf said, and there was a sneer in his voice.

"You don't know him. You don't know me. You

don't know any of us, so where's it your place to judge?" She put her hands on her hips and wobbled slightly. She hadn't eaten much, and she'd cut way back on her drinking in the past year. Now, the moonshine hit her like a truck. That was probably why she found herself defending Derek right alongside herself.

The booze was making her tired, and she rubbed her eyes with one hand. "You think you have everything figured out."

"I think you're in a bad situation with a bad guy who doesn't treat you right." Graf fell silent a moment. "But you're right, it isn't my place to say anything."

She opened her mouth to let him know just how much of his place it was not, when the sound of something scraping against the siding stopped her.

"What was that?" Graf turned wide eyes to Jessa. "Seriously, is that—"

"Get down!" she whispered, dropping to the floor. In an instant, the murky drunk feeling fled, replaced with an all-too-familiar fear. She inched cautiously toward Graf, motioning for him to meet her halfway. "Sometimes, It comes sniffing around houses. But if you stay on the floor, and It doesn't see you, it usually leaves."

"Usually? How often does this happen?" He put an arm over her back, and she shrugged it off. Though it felt good beyond belief to have that little bit of comfort, she didn't need him getting used to rescuing her. She definitely didn't need him getting used to casually touching her.

"I don't know. Every now and then. It's not a nightly occurrence, if that's what you're asking." She nodded toward the living room. "I'm going to crawl out there and get my gun."

"You didn't bring your gun back from the bar!" Graf whispered, his voice going almost comically high in fear. It would have been a lot funnier if she wasn't terrified, herself.

He was right. She ran through her memories of the night. She'd had the gun with her when she'd gone inside June's Place. She'd leaned it against the bar, like she always did. She'd broken up the fight. She'd been admonished. And then they'd left. In her memory she could see the shotgun, from the corner of her eye, sitting right where she'd left it. It mocked her, because it would have been so easy to pick it up and carry it away with her, but there wasn't a damned thing she could do about it now. She leaned her head against the cool linoleum. All that was left to do now was pray that It moved on, but she'd been doing about as much praying as she had been drinking lately, which was not a lot.

It scraped against the siding again, the screech of bony spikes against metal vibrating through the kitchen.

"What should we do?" Graf demanded. "Should we go into the basement?"

"It isn't a tornado!" she whispered back. "Just shut up, I need to think!"

There wasn't a lot of time for thinking. He grabbed her and pulled her to her feet. She shrieked in protest, and the sound was swallowed up by the roar of It, the rending of metal, and the splintering of wood. One wall of the kitchen was gone, and suddenly they were plunged into darkness, the only light coming from the moon outside and the broken wires whipping sparks out of the hole in the house.

Before she could blink, they stood on the lawn, her head swimming. Graf shook her by the shoulders. "You hit your head and blacked out—" a strange thing to tell someone in the midst of an emergency "—run and hide! Do it!"

She wanted to argue that she had definitely not hit her head, but she couldn't account for the missing time between being in the kitchen and being in the yard. It burst from the wound in the side of the house and charged across the lawn, and she ran, too, every breath that pushed out of her raw throat a cry of terror. She made it to the barn, turned to slide the big door closed, and saw It run past Graf, who stood directly in the thing's path, toward the barn. Toward her. She pushed the door closed with all her might and sank to the ground, leaning against the weathered wood, expecting It to thrust its massive claws through the wood and grab her at any second.

"Hey! Hey!" Graf shouted. Jessa, certain that It

would shred Graf to pieces, pressed her eye against the crack between the boards and looked out.

It stopped, turned from the barn, and seemed to sniff the air. Its long, curled horns grazed the ground as it lowered its head. One clawed, humanlike hand ripped grass and soil up in a clump, and its forked tongue snaked out for a taste. No, a smell. That was what snakes did with their tongues. It was scenting the trail of its prey.

"Forget about her!" Graf shouted, waving his arms. "Forget her, she's nothing. Come here! Come and get me!" He pulled his shirt over his head, his muscles rippling, tense for a fight. Like an animal.

Jessa gasped and pushed back from the door, then, unable to stand the suspense, pressed her face against it again.

Graf hunched over, like a football player bracing for a tackle, and cracked his neck. "Let's go," he growled at the creature, his voice lower, rougher, than normal.

It tossed the clump of dirt aside, bent into a similar posture, and rushed at Graf. Jessa squeezed her eyes shut and waited for the screams.

They never came. Instead, there were feral growls, more animal than man, and when she opened her eyes, Graf was on It's back, biting and clawing. It had an impossibly long reach, though, and swiped him down with razor-sharp claws. A spray of blood showed black in the green mercury light, and Graf howled with rage. But he didn't fall. He didn't seem to be concerned with the long strips of torn flesh hanging from his chest. In fact, he pounded his fist against them and roared, "Is that all you got?" before he leaped at the monster again.

Jessa had seen many unexplainable things in the past five years. This definitely had to be one of the stranger ones.

It grabbed Graf by the neck and slammed him into the ground, then hurtled its fist toward the back of his head. Graf rolled, but he wasn't quick enough, and there was a crunch as It fractured the back of his skull.

"Oh!" Jessa cried before she caught herself, and It turned as if having heard her. But Graf, impossibly, got up. He swayed on his feet, and his scalp hung from the back of his head like a torn dishcloth, but he jumped on the monster's back again and bit its neck, tearing a huge chunk of the scaly flesh away. It roared and shook him free, then made a ground-shaking retreat through the cornfield.

Trembling, Jessa watched as Graf touched the back of his head, swore, and started for the barn. Her first instinct was to go to him and help him, but the extent of his injuries, the way he'd taken on It…none of it seemed right. She stood, not really feeling the ground beneath her feet, and pushed the door open.

"Jessa," he said, almost guiltily as he walked

toward her. The bones of his ribs showed through the slashes on his chest.

"Stay away from me!" she screamed, and ran. It was possible that he would catch her, if he tried. No, more than possible. He'd gotten her out of the house so fast. She hadn't even felt him move. But he didn't come after her. Maybe he'd fallen down and died. She didn't care. All she cared about was that she made it into the house, up the stairs, and into the bathroom before she vomited up the little dinner she'd eaten.

Doubled over the sink, the moonshine burning her throat again with every retch, she remembered the hole in the house. He could get in. There was no way of keeping him out.

"Jessa?" He was right outside the door. She hadn't even heard him come up the stairs.

Wiping her mouth, she straightened. She could lock the bathroom door. If she dove for it right now, she might be able to lock it before he came in. Her stomach disagreed, and she gripped the edges of the porcelain sink and groaned.

Graf, whatever he was, opened the door. He'd put his T-shirt back on, covering the wounds in his chest, but blood still flowed down his face and neck from the back of his head. "Oh, God," he said quietly. "You're bleeding."

She shook her head, and it felt like the inside of it had been put together too tightly. "No, you are."

Still, she pushed her hair back from her face, and her hand came away wet with blood.

In that horrible moment, she knew that Graf was dangerous, not to be trusted. And that she was about to lose consciousness.

Six

Idiot. You're a fucking idiot. Always have been. Graf whipped a towel off the edge of the claw-footed tub and wound it around his head, turban style, to try to hold his scalp in place, or keep his brain from falling out, or something. Then he knelt beside Jessa and examined the bloody patch at her temple. It wasn't a serious head injury, or at least, it didn't look like it. The vomiting and passing out weren't great, but she had drunk a lot of moonshine and had a pretty big scare. He was no doctor, but he guessed she'd probably passed out from shock.

He lifted his fingers to his lips, but didn't taste her blood. If he did, he wouldn't be able to stop. She smelled so sweet, and her body was so warm. He'd probably sink his fangs right into her skull. And that would be very bad.

While he had intended to eat Jessa, that had been

before he'd called such massive attention to himself at the bar. Now that everyone in town knew that he was staying with her, it would be the dumbest idea in the history of dumb to kill her. If he were staying somewhere else, or had some other alibi, a little nibble would be no problem. Of course, the giant hole in the kitchen, that could be a good alibi. A couple of whacks to the head. Whoops, the creature, whatever It was, got her.

That was a dangerous line of reasoning. It would look too suspicious, a death right after he'd arrived in town. And if Jessa had been serious about the burning-at-the-stake thing, he didn't want to anger locals. He wiped her blood on her tank top and lifted her in his arms. In the hallway, he examined his choices. The door with the cheerfully painted wooden sign proclaiming JONATHAN'S ROOM probably wasn't the right one. He kicked another door open to find a queen-size bed with an ugly, upholstered headboard and a thick layer of dust on everything. The next room he checked out was soft and white, with an iron bedstead painted to match the walls and fluffy white pillows piled on top of it.

"So much for the fallen woman's boudoir," he said to the unconscious woman in his arms. He dropped her in the center of the bed and slid to the floor, head throbbing. Whatever that thing was that he'd fought, it wasn't anything he'd want to see again. Easily fifteen feet tall, its chest and arms made him think that a human and a dinosaur made a baby together, and then that baby grew up to be Dinosaur Mike Tyson. Huge muscles and slimy scales, not a good combination. Then, there had been the long tail, and the bony spikes down the spine. The head could have belonged to a particularly ugly bull, or maybe a dog with a smashed-in face that had grown horns like a handlebar mustache out of its head. It was like a monster built out of entirely spare parts. But the worst thing about it had been the stink.

Once, Sophia had called in a favor with Graf. One of her other "babies" had gone off the deep end and holed up in a house with some ghouls, humans who survived off vampire blood, and, as a result, had became dangerously insane. She'd wanted Graf to go in and kill the ghouls, retrieve the vampire, and return him to her, so she could make sure that it didn't happen again. When Graf had gotten to the place, though, the vampire had been one up on him. The ghouls had been dead. Long dead. Tarry black stuff seeping out of them and into the carpet dead. The house had been completely shut up, in June, in Utah, with six dead bodies in it for God alone knew how long. The smell had been unbelievable, a combination of rotting meat and the sweet scent of almonds and the stink of human excrement.

This hillbilly creature had smelled ten times worse.

Cursing, Graf unwound the towel from around

his head and gingerly felt the edges of his torn skin. The bleeding had stopped, and things had started to fuse together. He needed a shower to get the stink of blood—It's and hers—off him.

He didn't know how long Jessa would be out, but he could guess that it would be a while. As far as he was aware, she hadn't slept all day, or all the night before. And there was no chance of her waking up and hightailing it back to town, if he judged her right. She would be too afraid of It to leave the house.

Really, the only danger was in her staking him while he showered, he thought as he turned on the taps in the ancient tub. First, she would have to figure out that he was a vampire, and then remember, in her state of shock, how to kill one. He would hear her if she tried. The house was so full of squeaky boards and loose joists that it was a miracle the whole thing didn't come crashing down around them. With a missing wall now, it just might. He would have to try to do something to shore that up, he realized. The house, and the girl, would be no good to him if either fell apart.

Not that the girl was much good to him in the first place. He stepped into the tub and pulled the shower curtain closed along its oval track. He had to duck under the arched shower head to sluice water over his hair, and he wiggled his toes in the bloody pink stream that cascaded toward the drain. Jessa really was a waste, now that he couldn't eat her.

Well, not entirely useless. She was hot, in a girl-next-door way that drove Graf crazy. The rush of blood that headed straight for his groin argued valiantly for her usefulness. But Jessa was damaged goods. Dead family? Ex-boyfriend? Definitely not something he was interested in dealing with. He grimaced. Jessa: not good for sex or food. All he really needed was her house, but now, unfortunately, she was there to stay. And he had a lot of explaining to do.

When he'd scrubbed the blood from his scalp, which was still tender but healing into place nicely, and soaped the smell of the creature from his body with horrible homemade soap, he dried, dressed, and headed downstairs to survey the damage. He felt as weak as a human, with the amount of blood he'd lost.

The creature had been big, but it had created damage ten times its size. Nearly an entire wall was missing. The kitchen door was gone. Cabinets were strewn across the yard, broken dishes in their wake. Electrical wires hung, deceptively calm, from the ragged edges of the hole.

Graf was no independent contractor. The biggest building project he'd ever done was a birdhouse he'd made in sixth grade. And the roof of that had fallen off in a stiff breeze. Still, he knew that the splintered wooden beam in the center was some kind of framework, and its absence would probably be missed by the rest of the house. With a sigh, he hopped through the hole and walked toward the barn.

The stink of It still hung in the air, thick like the smell off an open manhole on a hot day. Graf had never been a fan of barnyard smell, but it would be a welcome change.

Chickens scattered and clucked nervously at his intrusion. He hadn't really seen one up close before. Now that he had, he was glad that he wasn't human anymore and didn't have to eat them. Graf had no idea what the inside of a barn was supposed to look like, but he had expected more hay, maybe a tractor. All he saw were ugly chickens, some rope, some yard tools, and, pushed against the wall, a workbench and a tall, red cabinet that would most certainly hold tools.

The job took less time than he thought it would. Once he came up with a plan, he went back to the kitchen, tapped the bowed, splintered ends of the support beam back together with a rubber mallet, then braced it on either side with smaller pieces of wood that he screwed together. Like metal plates on a broken leg, he thought, feeling pretty good about himself.

Another look around the barn yielded a big canvas car cover and some blue waterproof tarp, which he used to cover the hole where the kitchen used to be, fixing it in place with a staple gun. It took more time collecting up the crap from the yard than it took fixing the house. By the time the sun rose, he'd done all he could do, and he pulled the curtains in the living room and sank onto the couch, tired, but too wired to sleep.

He made a list of all the problems facing him, and it looked something like this in his head.

Trapped in Deliverance.
Missing Sophia's party/possible sex with Sophia.
It.
Need blood.
Obnoxious baggage.

None of these problems could be solved on his own steam. He was going to have to enlist help. Which meant convincing Jessa not to rat him out to the townies. They seemed like the pitchforks-and-torches types.

When Jessa stumbled down the stairs, holding her head, he sprang to his feet to help her. "Hey, you okay?" he asked, in his best sensitive-guy voice. "I was worried about you."

She pulled back, bleary eyes uncertain. "Stay back!"

"What?" He injected a little laugh into his statement. "Jessa, what's the matter?"

"What do you mean, 'what's the matter?' You should be dead! I saw It attack you last night. I saw what happened to you." She retreated up a couple of steps. "What are you?"

He reached out a hand to soothe her, but she jerked violently away. Okay, so she wasn't buying the concerned, nice-guy act. "You're confused. You hit your head last night. I tried to get you help, but I couldn't remember how to get back to that bar. And I was worried It would return."

"No—you're some kind of freak. I remember." She glared at him, her anger overcoming her fear. "What are you?" she repeated.

He conjured up an image in his head of Sophia, what she would do when caught in a lie. The result was an imperious declaration of "You're being ridiculous."

"What are you?" Jessa shrieked, flying at him with fingers bent like talons. "What are you?"

He could either get his face scratched off by a demented hellcat, or do something that could potentially hurt her. He chose hurting her. He gripped her by her arms and tossed her from the landing to the floor at the bottom of the stairs. She writhed where she fell, gasping for the air that had been knocked out of her lungs. "Okay," he said, dusting his hands off on each other as he leaned over her. "You want to know what I am? I'm a vampire. And I'm not in a very good mood."

Her eyes widened and she struggled to her feet. He lunged for her, but she was surprisingly fast, and he came up with empty arms as she threw open the front door and flooded the living room with sunlight.

The brightness and heat hit him like a special-effects explosion. He recoiled with a shout. Jessa crossed the porch, her tennis shoes the last thing he could see as she jumped from the top step and fled into the burning white.

He had to stop her. The sun—his most feared enemy—stood between him and her escape. If she told anyone, he would be in deep shit. If he went out there…

It was best not to think about it. He plunged head-first through the door, trying to shield his burning eyes and still keep a bead on her as she raced across the lawn. She went for his car, not bothering to open the door—smart girl—but he got her as the top half of her body disappeared through the window. He grabbed her by one ankle and pulled her, fighting and screaming, onto the lawn. His skin blistered and charred, stiffening his movements, and he screamed as his exposed parts burst into flame. With as much strength as he could muster, he pulled her up the porch steps and into the house, slamming the door behind them.

He sank down, pain arcing like a 120-volt charge through every square inch of his body. His head lolled to the side. His eyelids, baked to his eyeballs, tried to close, but stuck open. Jessa scrambled forward on her hands and knees, and started to climb to her feet.

"If you take one more step I will not hesitate to kill you," Graf wheezed, and she stopped, trembling, to face him.

"Vampires can't go out in sunlight," she whispered.

His natural inclination was to respond with "No shit, Sherlock," but he restrained himself. She was in shock, and at this point, sarcasm would be lost on her. "No. We can't."

"Are you going to die?" There was something hard and hopeful in her voice that would have killed him if he were one of those sparkly movie vampires who gave a shit about what humans thought of him.

He tried to shake his head, but it hurt too much. It would be hard for her to believe, faced with someone who looked like a campfire-roasted hot dog, but he would be fine in a half hour. "No. Sorry to disappoint."

Tension started at her feet and worked its way up. The muscles of her calves tensed; her fists clenched. The dumbfounded expression on her face tightened to cold fury. "You're a part of It, aren't you? You're here because of It."

"I'm here because I couldn't get my fucking GPS to work." The healing had started, deep in his muscles, working toward the burned surfaces like pieces of barbed shrapnel from an old war wound. "Whatever It is, I've never seen anything like it. And I've never heard of a town being trapped for all eternity, either."

"We're not trapped for all eternity," she snapped. "We're going to get through this and get out of here. But I thought vampires knew about stuff like this. Aren't you linked up with the rest of the oogie-boogie stuff in the world?"

He lifted a shoulder in a shrug, the pull of his burned skin making the movement harder. "Not that I'm aware of. I know other vampires. I've never met anything like your It out there."

"You're lying." She folded her arms over her chest and took a deep breath. "So, what do you eat, blood?"

"Yes." No getting around that. If she knew about the sunlight, she'd know that vampires drank blood.

"Were you going to eat me?" She tapped her fingers on her arm, waiting.

"Yes," he answered honestly. "But I can't, now. Everyone has seen us together."

Her eyes flared in anger, and she turned, as if she'd leave.

"Don't do that," he called after her. "I can still chase you. And I'm giving you this one chance."

She turned again, stomped up to him, but didn't touch him. Instead, she glared down at him, and he had no doubt that if he had cared, the hatred in her eyes would have burned him far worse than the sun had. "You think I'm afraid of you? After you saw what I've been running from night after night? You think I'm afraid to die? I live in a tomb. If you think you're going to intimidate me by threatening to kill me, go ahead. Kill me."

"Point taken." He was able to close his eyes again, so he did, to appear defeated and tired. She walked to the kitchen, and he gave her just enough time to reach the spot where the back door had been before calling after her. "After I kill you, though, who's to stop me from killing someone else? Someone like Derek?"

She came back. He knew she would.

"So, here's the plan." He got to his feet, painfully, the skin sliding off his toes inside his shoes. "You and me, we're going to have a little chat. We're going to figure out how you can help me, and how I can help you, and how we're going to get out of this mess."

"Why would I want to talk to you? You're a disgusting…thing." She spat the word out as though it were the most bitter insult she'd ever tasted.

"You haven't even thanked me for fixing your kitchen." He put a hand on the back of the couch to steady himself as he walked toward her. "Or saving you from the monster."

"Which you probably summoned," she insisted.

"Summoned?" What the hell was this, *Dungeons and Dragons?* "No, I don't know how to 'summon' anything. If I did, I could have gotten him to leave a

lot easier. You don't seem to remember that I got torn up real bad distracting that thing from killing you."

"Yeah, but you could have been doing that to make yourself look good." She didn't sound as certain now of his involvement with the beast. "It could have been part of your plan, if you knew you weren't going to get hurt or anything."

"I did get hurt," he pointed out again. "What you're saying is that I somehow captured this town, which has absolutely nothing interesting in it, full of people I don't know and probably won't like, five years ago. During that five-year span, I was never once seen, but I decided to show up spontaneously just the other night for some reason. I control the creature, but I let it kick my ass, and I send it out to kill townspeople, who would be my food source if they weren't ripped apart by a monster. That make a lot of sense to you?"

"Everyone says that once it draws blood, it gives up. It kept fighting you," she accused.

He sighed, feeling more and more tired of the argument. "I guess I'm just likeable."

Her eyes narrowed. "So, what, you're here because of a coincidence?"

"That's all I can figure." A thought occurred to him, one that made him a little sick. "Maybe it's because I'm a vampire. Maybe that's why I was able to stop here."

"Then why can't you leave?" She probably didn't

believe his innocence yet, but at least she was done with her line of absurd accusations. "If being a vampire got you in, how come it hasn't got you out?"

"It just might!" If he hadn't just had a painful reminder of what the sun could do to him, he would have bolted out the door right away to check.

Jessa scoffed at him. "You think you can leave."

He nodded. "I think so. I'm going to try again as soon as the sun goes down."

"Well." She looked him over, burns and all, and her face screwed up like she couldn't tell if she hoped he would succeed or hoped he would fail. "If you're right, I look forward to never seeing you again."

"You and me both," he snarled.

Seven

Nightfall could not come fast enough. Jessa gave Graf a wide berth. She was still afraid of him. Probably because when she'd all but ordered him to let her lock him in the basement again, he'd threatened to kill her, again. Now, he really had to get out of there.

"Getting dark," she called from the kitchen, where she cleaned the dishes. "You can go at any time."

He pushed aside the curtain over the front window and leaned back cautiously. His burns might have healed, but he got a new respect for the light every time he disrespected it. "You're not going to miss me?"

She turned and tossed her dishrag into the sink. "No. Because I assume you'll be coming back."

"What, you don't think I can make it?" He made a face at her and peered out the window again. The sun just had to sink behind the tree line, and he would make a run for the car.

"You didn't make it before. On some miracle chance that you do get out, you'll come back to help us all get out. And bring supplies." Her hands were on her hips. She was dead serious.

Graf forced down a laugh. "Yeah, that's going to happen."

"I'm not joking." She stalked into the living room, her jaw clenched. She hissed through her teeth, "If you do get out, you will help us."

"I'm going to do exactly shit for you. I'm going to get in that car, put my foot to the floor, and roll into D.C. before sunup. Then, I'm going to party like the world is ending tomorrow and forget all about this hellhole." Maybe it was the fact that he kept taunting Jessa with his surety that he would be leaving, but he was actually starting to believe it himself.

"No, you won't." She shook her head. "No one could be that heartless."

"I could. I'm a vampire." He flicked the curtain aside. "What do you know? Time for my exit."

She followed him onto the porch and stopped at the top step as he opened the trunk. He pulled a bag of blood from the cooler there—not cold, but pleasantly warm now—and bit off the corner with his back teeth. "I guess I should say it's been a pleasure, but, you know. It hasn't."

"I hope you die in a car wreck," she spat.

Graf chuckled to himself as he slipped behind the wheel and started the engine, gulping down the blood like it was the last he would ever taste. He was never so happy to see something in his rearview mirror as Jessa and her stupid house.

He remembered the turns he'd taken to get there like something out of a nightmare, and soon he was on the same damned highway that had trapped him, passing the same damned gas station. This time, he kept his eye on the odometer, and punched the accelerator. If a DeLorean could travel through time going eighty-eight miles an hour, a Pantera could break out of this prison town at one-twenty. He shot past a figure on the side of the road and pumped his fist. He was actually going to make it! Ten miles, fifteen.

A deer—the same goddamned deer!—lunged from the cornfield, and he hit his breaks, swerving to avoid it. The car fishtailed, then did a one-eighty in the center of the road. And there, in the edge of the glow of his headlights where it shouldn't be, was the ruined shape of the busted-down gas station.

Graf launched himself from the car and took off after the deer, whose hind end bobbed merrily over the stalks of corn as it ran. Deer were fast, but vampires were faster, and he was on the creature in five seconds. He pinned it by the neck and tore its throat with his teeth, spilling the animal's blood all over the broken stalks around them. When it stopped struggling, its eyes frozen open in death, he let it go and punched it in the head.

"Fuck you, deer." He nudged the body aside with his toe and pushed his hair back with both his hands. Then, he stood, straightened his clothes, and came up with a new list.

Still trapped.
Still need blood.
Homeless.

There was no way Jessa would let him back into her house. He hadn't just burned that bridge. He'd gone full *River Kwai* on it. And he wasn't going to feed off the deer he'd just killed. He spat to clear his mouth of the taste. It would be like drinking piss out of a jug of spoiled milk.

He trudged up the bank of the ditch and back to the road. His car waited patiently, like a horse in a cowboy movie. He patted the hood and got back inside. He should have just leaned out the door and punched the accelerator, running over his own head. He would rather do that than go back to that harpy and her house of decorating horrors.

"Hey!" someone called, and he looked up to see a rail-thin woman in a pair of denim cutoffs and a too-tight shirt that read CLASSY in pink cursive across the chest.

Does it rain white trash in this town? He motioned

to her, and she strolled boldly to the passenger side and got in. She took one look at his bloodied shirt and paled. "What happened to you?"

"I hit a deer." It was kind of true.

"Your car doesn't look like you hit a deer," she said doubtfully. "There's not a scratch on it."

"Well, there's a lot of lead on this car. Real durable," he lied.

She bought it, but didn't bother to ask if the blood was his or not. "You're the new guy, huh?"

"Word travels fast." He frowned as she pulled a joint from her pocket and lit it. "You mind not smoking in here? Pot, I mean?"

"I don't have anything else to smoke," she said, slipping her lighter into the V-neck of her shirt. If she'd had much cleavage there, it might have been a sexy move. "Do you?"

He nodded toward his jacket. "In the pocket."

She kept her eyes on him as she pulled the garment up from the floor. "Leather. Nice."

"Well, that's why I bought it." God, could she be any more obvious? If he weren't trapped in this town, and if she wouldn't be missed, he would have opened her up two minutes ago.

On second thought, maybe she wouldn't be missed. "What's your name?"

"Becky." She closed her eyes as she sniffed the open cigarette box.

"Becky?" He chuckled. This was his lucky night.

If he got any luckier, he'd trip down some stairs and break his neck. "Derek's Becky?"

She nodded. "Oh, yeah, I bet you've heard all about me. Staying out there with the wicked witch."

"No love lost there, huh?" No wonder. Not many women would be thrilled if their husbands were still sniffing around old girlfriends. But something about Becky didn't exactly inspire his sympathy. Maybe it was the fact that she was sending out "I'm easy" signals like Morse code. Jessa couldn't be the only one with a bad reputation in town.

"What, she didn't tell you all the stuff she's said about me over the years?" She slowly pulled one cigarette from the pack. "You know what? I don't even want to talk about it. I haven't had a real cigarette in five years, and I'm going to enjoy this one."

As much as he would have loved to sit in his car all night while this gem of a woman talked shit about her enemies and smoked all of his cigarettes, Graf cleared his throat and asked, "So, is there somewhere I can drop you off, Becky?"

She moaned as she exhaled, a look of pure rapture on her face as the smoke drifted in perfect rings from her mouth. "Yeah," she answered, coming to her senses. "You can drop me at June's Place."

"June's Place is in the opposite direction," he pointed out. "What were you doing way over here?"

She shrugged, taking another long draw off the cigarette. "I wanted to see the service station."

"At the risk of getting killed by It?" He pulled cautiously away, a sick feeling in his stomach. He'd thought he'd been so close. He'd thought he'd been free. Now, he headed straight back into the very hell he'd sought to escape.

"I had to see if she was lying," Becky said with a snort. "She says all kinds of crazy shit for Derek's attention. She's the only person in town who's been attacked by It more than once. It leaves everyone else alone, if they survive getting attacked."

He nodded, pretending to be sympathetic. As annoying as Jessa was, he'd take three of her to one Becky any day. "So, she's lied before about the thing attacking her?"

"She claimed it got some chickens not too far back, but for all I know she could have killed those chickens herself. And everyone just fawned all over her for it. But folks are starting to come to their senses now." She tipped the ash off the end of her cigarette out the window. "People in town don't have patience for drama anymore. She needs to keep her head down."

"You've been attacked by It, then?" He tried to catch her expression when he asked, but the threat of demonic deer rushing in front of the car kept him facing forward.

She blew out a long stream of smoke. "Nah."

"So, you risked your life coming out here, then? Just to prove Jessa wrong? If no one believes her, anyway, what's the point?" He had his own idea about why she was out there, on the edge of town. He had a feeling she wasn't the only one to do it.

"I was testing," she admitted, almost daring him to call her out on her earlier lie. "Every now and then, I test."

He'd been there a day, and he'd already tested the barrier keeping him there. "Has anyone ever gotten out before?"

She took another draw off the cigarette. "There's some controversy there." Now that she had him hooked, she took her time, exhaling loud and long. "There's one guy who got out. At least, I think he did. About a month after we all got stuck here, he got in his car and just drove off with the last of his gas. Some people think he escaped, but others think he drove into a field and killed himself." She took another midstory smoke break, then added gravely, "But if he did, wouldn't we have found the car by now?"

She carefully stubbed the cigarette out, leaving half unburned. "I'm going to save this for later."

"Don't tell anyone where you got them," he warned. He didn't need to get jumped by a bunch of hillbilly muggers who thought he had pockets full of goodies.

"Suit yourself." She tucked the stub of the cigarette behind her ear. "But you could get a lot in trade for those. Everybody is kinda wondering when you're going to come back to town and start trading."

He pulled into the parking lot of June's Place. Several faces, drawn by the sound of the engine and the crunch of tires on gravel, crowded at the window. His eyes flicked from them, back to Becky. "You better get in there, before they come shake this thing down for parts."

She laughed. It was a phlegmy laugh that turned into a cough. "Thanks for the ride. Hope I'll be seeing you."

He leaned across her to open the door. What the hell, give the married lady a thrill. She got out and crossed through the headlight beams in front of the car, a smirk on her face. She thought she'd seduced him. She thought she'd stolen something from her enemy. What sick, vicious creatures women were.

"Hey," he called to her through the car window. "You say people want to trade? You think somebody would trade me for lodging?"

"I don't know who has room," she replied, clearly disappointed that he hadn't called her back for something more intimate. "And they don't like getting beat up."

"Yeah, sorry about that." He wasn't, really, but it was good manners to apologize for trouncing someone's husband.

She smiled. "The way Derek tells it, he should

be apologizing to you. But he's an asshole when he's drunk."

And pretty much every other time, too, Graf thought. "Well, I'll try to keep my fists off him."

"Good," she said with a pout. "He's my baby's daddy. I need him to stay around for a long time." She patted her stomach, and flounced through the door of the bar.

Graf shook his head and pulled out of the parking lot.

The house was oddly quiet once Graf had left. That didn't stop Jessa from jumping at every slight noise. She sat on a stool at the kitchen island, glass of water in her hands, staring at the steady drip from the faucet. The knowledge of what her houseguest had been, what he had planned on doing... She forced a shiver away. It had been hard to accept the existence of the monster that kept Penance captive. Now that it was part of reality, it wasn't as difficult to accept that another monster might be here. But there was a difference between a monster being out there, and a monster being in her house.

This week, there had been two.

She shot a nervous glance to the plastic-covered hole in the kitchen wall. Before, her house had been a fortress. She'd never had any actual illusions that its walls could keep her physically safe. But it had kept her from cracking up. Now, the wound to the house was a wound to her security. The presence of a vampire within her sanctuary made it unclean, and, worse, uncertain.

The reminders were all over the house. The closed curtains in the living room, which bore stripes of fading and dust from hanging too long in one position because her mother had never closed them, and Jessa had never thought to, either. The ruined towel on her bedroom floor. The blood and dirt in the bathroom. She'd gone to shower and, standing under the spray, had seen the gouges his broad fingers had made in the jar of soap. Everything had been tainted by the presence of a monster, and now that he had left, he seemed more present than before.

The problem was not knowing what he was doing. Had he actually managed to leave Penance? Good riddance. But what if he returned? What if he rounded up his vampire pals and came back to finish off the whole town? What if he was already busy decimating the whole town, by himself?

What if he came back and got her? No one would ever know what had happened. Even fewer would care. But they deserved to know, didn't they? So they could protect themselves?

She could go down to June's Place and tell them all about what had happened, but only a handful would believe her. June might, but she wouldn't press the issue with those that didn't. She had a business to run, a town to run, really. The town council wouldn't believe her, and they thought they ran everything. Thanks to Becky's rumor-mongering and Derek's insistence that she was crazy, it would just look like Jessa crying wolf again. Jessa: trying to get attention again.

She should have given Graf a list of people to eat before he left. She snorted at the thought, but her amusement was cut short by the sound of a car pulling into the driveway. It was a strange sound after five years without it, and she knew it could only be one person. One vampire.

She jumped off the stool and contemplated diving out the hole in the wall and running to Jack Tilly's across the field. Strangely, her fear of Graf the vampire was overcome by her annoyance at Graf the obnoxious man, and she decided instead to march out to the front porch and face him. She waited until he sheepishly emerged from the car to say, "You're back."

"Happy to see me?" He put his hands in his front pockets as he walked up the lawn. "You were right. I'm not heartless enough to leave all you people trapped here. I came back to make it right."

"You came back because you couldn't leave," she responded flatly. "I suppose you think you're just going to come back in here and make yourself at home in my basement?"

"I was hoping you'd let me stay in a bedroom,

actually, but yeah." He stopped at the bottom of the porch steps.

She shook her head slowly. "Not a chance in hell."

He looked seriously surprised at that. "Why not?"

It was so absurd that she had to laugh. "Because you're a vampire!"

"So? You saw what'll happen to me if I go out in the sun! I need a place to stay." This was a side to him that she'd seen before. The calculating, wheedling, look-how-pathetic-and-in-need-I-am side that disappeared the second he got what he wanted.

It had been hard to deny him the first time. This time, it was easier. "You were going to eat me."

"I'm a vampire!" He threw up his hands. "It's what we do!"

"I'm not going to let a mass murderer into my house just because it's what you do!" She looked up at the sky. "You've got the whole night ahead of you. Go out and find some other dumb sucker to take you in."

"Fine, then some other dumb sucker can have my stuff," he said, backing up.

She didn't want to, but she had to ask. It was almost a sick curiosity. The unbelievable gall of him, to come back here, after everything he'd said to her, after he'd admitted to wanting to kill her. She had to know what stupid thing would pop out of his mouth next. "What are you talking about?"

"Well, I met Becky out on the road tonight, and she said that my stuff, like my cigarettes and my jacket, were things people wanted to get their hands on." He turned away slowly. "But I guess if you don't want it…"

She did want it, damn it. "Becky is a moron. No one is going to want your flimsy jacket."

He turned back. "When have you seen my most excellent jacket?"

She didn't meet his eyes. "When you picked me up the other night. I saw it in your car."

"You were snooping. When you were planning on siphoning my gas, you snooped," he accused. "Did you take anything out of my car?"

She lifted her chin and looked down at him, like he was a really gross bug she wouldn't stoop to viewing. "No! I'm not a thief like you."

"I'm not a thief. I'm a vampire." He held out his hand. "Do we have a deal?"

"No." She gestured to the door. "Come inside and we'll talk. Lock up your car, though. If Becky knows where you're staying and what you have, you won't have it for long."

He followed her into the house, not heeding her warning. "She didn't have much nice to say about you, either."

"I'll bet she didn't." Jessa went to the kitchen junk

drawer and pushed aside screwdrivers, rubber bands, one of Dad's old watches, to retrieve a pen and a small legal pad. "Sit down. We're going to make a contract."

"A contract?" He looked at her doubtfully.

"A lease agreement, then." She dragged one of the stools to the opposite side of the island. "Sit. Get comfy. I have a feeling this is going to take a long time."

"Fine." He leaned on the counter on his elbows.

"First condition," she said, drawing a number one on the paper and circling it. "There is going to be absolutely no eating me."

"I couldn't now, anyway," he grumbled. "Too many people know I'm here. If you disappeared, it would look suspicious."

"That's very comforting." She rolled her eyes as she wrote it down. "But I've seen you fight. Maybe you could take them all down if need be. So, second, you have to give me all your stuff of value, so that I can trade it as needed."

"And what do I get?" he asked, putting out his hand to stop her from scribbling down rule number two.

When his hand touched hers, it was ice-cold. She jerked her fingers away. "You get to not roast alive, and I keep your secret so that the town doesn't do to you what they wish they could do to It."

"Fair enough," he said after a moment. "But you

know, I'm going to need to eat something. So I think condition number three should be that I'll obey your first two conditions as long as you find a way to feed me."

She scrawled his demand down with a shaking hand. "I hope you like chicken blood."

"No, none for me, thanks. I want the real stuff. And I know there are some people in town you don't care for." He raised an eyebrow. "Derek? Becky? The jerks down at June's Place?"

She slammed the pencil down on the counter. "No. I won't help you murder innocent people, even if they are jerks."

"I'm not talking about murder. I'm saying, you know, maybe get a guy back here, get him drunk, and I'll have a little while he's passed out." He sounded almost ashamed of the idea. "Look, I'm more than happy to feed off a willing donor, but I don't think I'm going to find one of those around here. Unless you want to do it?"

"Uh, God, no!" Not that it looked all that bad in the movies. Against every rational thought in her head, she imagined Graf holding her to his chest, bending his mouth to her throat as she moaned in ecstasy like a soft-core porn actress. She closed her eyes and slapped her hands on the counter to bring herself back to reality. "Fine. We'll see what we can do. I know at least one guy in town who can't hold his liquor, but that doesn't stop him from drinking it."

"Condition number four," Graf continued. "I want a bedroom. A real bedroom, one of the ones upstairs. And I don't want to be locked in."

Her heart pounded in her chest. Of course, she'd seen how strong he was when he was battling the monster. And fast. Even if she locked him in the basement, that was no guarantee that he wouldn't get out and hurt her. Letting him sleep on the same floor seemed like she was inviting disaster with open arms, though.

Not to mention, the only two rooms besides hers were Mom and Dad's...and Jonathan's. "You couldn't sleep up there. There are windows."

"I can cover them. Let's be honest, I'm going to be stuck here for a while, right?"

She began to write it down, then paused. "What are we talking about, exactly? I mean, in terms of the stuff you have?"

"Do we have a deal, or not?" He stood, as if to go. "If not, I've got to go see a man about a horse."

Wouldn't everyone just love that? The new guy in town, and Jessa turned him out, turned down a fair trade. It would be plenty of ammunition to make her seem even crazier.

Jessa quickly filled in line number four, and stuck her hand out, meeting Graf's cold one. "We have a deal. You can have the first room on the left upstairs."

"Your parents' old room, right?" Why did he say it like that, like he knew she was avoiding talking about it? Didn't he know things would be so much easier if she just ignored the past?

"I won't mess anything up, or throw anything out," he continued. "I'll just cover the windows and rumple the sheets."

She stood speechless. He had admitted to wanting to kill her, had asked her to help him steal blood from people, and he'd been incredibly rude to her since they'd met. Now, he was worried about her sentimental attachment to her parents' bedroom? "Get your shit together, and we'll walk down to June's Place."

"Why not just take the car?" he asked. "They've all seen it, when I drove Becky down there."

"You drove Becky to June's Place?" Why did that make her strangely unsettled?

"Yeah. I don't know what she's doing down there, in her condition, but that's where she wanted to go." He paused. "I really didn't like her."

"Welcome to the club." She sighed and rubbed her suddenly pounding temples.

Eight

The walk to June's Place was more pleasant than the one they'd taken before. Jessa wondered if she had subconsciously realized something was wrong with Graf before, and if that had made her nervous. But she was probably giving her intuition too much credit.

The night might have been more pleasant because Graf was in a better mood. It wouldn't be hard to top any of the moods he'd been in, but at least he wasn't giving snotty answers to her questions. And she had a lot of them.

"So, sunlight is a no, garlic isn't a big deal, you can't turn into a bat, but you're really strong and fast?" She ticked the points off on her fingers and struggled to keep the satchel under her arm.

Graf took the bag of his stuff from her and slung

it over his shoulder. "You got it. Also, shockingly few of us are from Transylvania."

He was teasing her. That was a nice change from sarcasm. It was as if their knock-down, drag-out fight had been cathartic, and now they could be at least civil to each other. Like one usually was with new roommates. "Well, pardon me. All I have to go on here are the movies."

"That's how it is for most people. Not that I tell a lot of humans." He smiled, and she could see his teeth in the dark. No fangs.

"So, 'human.' Do you consider yourself not a human?" Wrapping her mind around the vampire experience was weird, but not as uncomfortable as she had anticipated when she'd first begun interrogating him.

"I was human, once." He said it like the thought made him uneasy. Like admitting that he'd been a drug user, or an alcoholic. "And then I met Sophia."

"And Sophia is, what, your girlfriend?" Jessa imagined the vampire brides in Bram Stoker's *Dracula,* all exposed breasts and writhing body parts, and got strangely jealous. It wasn't like he was going to get out of this town and see her again, right?

No, that wasn't the point. She tried again. It wasn't like she cared if he had some exotic bride of the damned waiting at home for him, right? Much better.

He laughed. "No, no. Sophia is the vampire who made me."

"So, she's like, what, a mom to you?" God, she hoped all that incestuous vampire stuff from Anne Rice's books wasn't true. Because it would be gross, not because he was cute.

"No, not exactly." He paused, the only sound their feet falling on the broken asphalt. "It's more like she's my mentor. I definitely do not have mother-son feelings for her. But I can't imagine ever being good enough or hip enough to be anything to her. So, I just sit back in awe and worship from afar."

"From afar, but you were going to a party at her house?" Jessa raised one skeptical eyebrow. "That sounds like more, or less, than 'afar' to me."

"Well, metaphorically speaking. It's not like we've never gotten physical or anything—"

Vampire sex was probably all hot and dangerous and wild and animalistic and… "Don't need to hear about that!"

"But," he continued, "I would never dream that we could be emotionally close. She's been alive since the Italian Renaissance. She was a model for Titian, for Christ's sake."

"I don't know what that is," Jessa said quietly.

Graf didn't seem to care that she didn't know, because he didn't bother to explain it. "There's no way that I could ever possess the depth of experience she has. So, I study her, spend time around her, and learn how to be a better vampire."

"A better vampire." Was there such a thing? "She teaches you how to kill more people?"

He shrugged guiltily, which was more of an answer to her question than he knew. "She blends in really well. She appears human, and it's little tricks, like accidentally knocking over a glass or faking a headache—things you learn by watching, not just hearing about them. When I was new, that kind of knowledge saved my ass more than once."

"And when were you new, exactly?" She almost didn't want to know how old he was. "Like, are you two hundred years old, or did you become a vampire last week?"

"I was turned in 1967." He switched the gun to his other shoulder. "It was funny, actually. One minute I'm living in Detroit, working in research and development at Uniroyal Tire, and the next I'm a vampire, traveling all over the world with this beautiful, sexy vampire who has people—I mean, vampires and humans both—fawning over her. Buying her presents, a villa in Spain, cars—anything she wanted, she could get by crooking her little finger."

"She sounds amazing." Jessa's voice held a note of wistfulness that she couldn't hide. Growing up in a small town, she'd had typical dreams of leaving and having the glamorous life he described. Minus the vampire part. Though her mother had done her best to impart feminist wisdom to her daughter, Jessa still had guilty daydreams about being able to get anything she wanted from a man just by being beautiful and sexy.

They walked in silence a few minutes, Graf no doubt reminiscing about his flashy vampire friends and their fleets of private jets they had sex all over. "So, what about you? Have any big plans that this whole 'trapped like rats' thing squashed?"

He couldn't have put it more bluntly if he'd tried. This was the guy she had to get used to. Insensitive, rude, snobbish. And no wonder, if he thought the only value a person could have was what they could get other people to give to them. She'd be damned if she would share her private thoughts with him, now. "No."

"Oh, come on. You had to have some desire to rise above the simple lives of all of these peasants." He chuckled at his own joke. "There's one of you in every town."

"Well, we can't all be Sophia," she snapped.

He stopped walking. "Hey, don't be like that. It's a compliment. It means that I don't think you're on the same level as all these yahoos."

She stopped, too, and turned. "These yahoos are the people I've been living through hell with for the past five years. What makes you think I think I'm any better than them?"

"You aren't. But you're more interesting." He

didn't sound apologetic, or even like he'd realized he'd insulted her. "Something about their eyes. I didn't notice it until I met Becky, but there's this kind of dead-fish stare looking back at you with these people."

"That's fine," she said, stomping forward. But she couldn't help but feel validated by his assessment. She'd always secretly dreamed that, one day, she'd be more than anyone in this town could dream of being. But it was one thing to hear someone else disparage the people around her, and another thing entirely if she did it herself. Graf hadn't earned the right to hate any of them. "Keep up. You're the one with the superpowers."

"And you're turning your back to me. That means you must trust me," he said cheerfully, suddenly at her side, though she hadn't heard him move.

It unnerved her, this reminder of what he was, and what he was capable of. "You're a vampire. If you wanted to kill me, even my gun wouldn't be able to stop you, but remind me to pick it up at June's tonight."

"True. I could just drag you into the tall grass over there and tear your throat out with my teeth."

It didn't seem like he was trying to rattle her on purpose. The fact that he was saying this stuff accidentally made it worse. "Yup, I reckon you could."

"But I won't. Because I'm a man of my word." He

sounded awfully proud of himself. Like he deserved some kind of trophy for not killing her.

They walked in silence the rest of the way to June's Place, but in the parking lot, she stopped him. "When we get inside, we've got to get permission from June to hold an auction tonight. Then, we announce it. Anyone who's interested has two hours to round up what they want to trade, and to spread the word to their neighbors. Then they all convene back here, and hopefully we make some good trades."

"So, what, we just wait around here all night?" He didn't sound so cocky now. "Are we going to get back before sunup?"

Now it was her turn to shrug and act like his death was no big deal. "I don't know. We might."

"Well, I'm cutting out of here with enough time to get to shelter, whether you're done bartering or not." He nodded to the little red wagon she pulled. "And you can bring home as much as you can carry in that."

"We won't be able to bring everything home tonight." She hoped. "Some people will drop stuff off tomorrow."

He scoffed. "God, eBay is so much faster."

June's Place was busy tonight. Good, they needed it to be busy. Or, rather, she did. Jessa had no idea how she was going to feed her boarder, but she knew she had to get supplies for herself. She'd worry about him later. Maybe he'd shrivel up like a mummy she could just prop up in the corner, then chicken blood wouldn't sound so bad to him.

"Uh-oh, here comes trouble," June called, a wide smile on her face.

Jessa waded through the cluster of tables to the bar, where she stepped up on the tarnished brass rail and leaned over to speak with June more privately. "You up for an auction tonight?"

"Probably a good night for it." There was a weary note to her voice as she continued. "Yeah, we can do that."

Jessa turned to Graf. "Give me a boost."

He complied, putting his hands around her waist and lifting her up to sit on the bar. She climbed to her feet, wobbled a little, and he caught her hand in his.

"Don't fall," he warned, naturally, as if he hadn't just talked calmly about murdering her on the walk over. She snatched her hand back.

"Listen up, everybody," June called, though most of the patrons had turned to see what crazy Jessa was doing standing on the bar in the first place.

Jessa took a deep breath. "This is my friend, Graf. He's new in town."

A murmur went around the room, the confirmation of the rumors most people had already heard and repeated to their neighbors.

June whistled to get their attention, and the bar

fell silent. Jessa continued. "He's brought some stuff with him, and he's looking to trade."

"How'd he get here?" someone shouted.

June hollered over the sudden surge of raised voices. "He don't know. If he don't know, how would she?"

"Get out of here!" another patron yelled.

This was not going the way she had planned. People were suspicious. Why shouldn't they be? But their fear and anger were making this an unstable situation, and there were no established rules for dealing with it.

To Jessa's surprise, Graf hopped up on the bar next to her and called, "Hey!"

The crowd silenced, though they still looked like they'd rather kill him than listen to him. Graf looked around the room, body tense as though he realized this was a mistake, but when he spoke, he sounded confident. "I'm not here to cause any trouble. In fact, I'd rather not be here at all. For some reason, whatever keeps you guys trapped here chose to trap me, too. I would appreciate it if you would all just give me the benefit of the doubt. If I got in, there must be some way to get out, right?"

There was another uproar from the bar patrons, and Jessa held her breath. Getting out was something they never talked about. It was a sort of unwritten rule; no one had ever discussed it, but everyone knew to hold their peace where leaving Penance was concerned. Maybe it was the last thread that kept them all from unraveling, but they had to cling to whatever would keep them sane.

"Hey, hey!" June called over the noise, her usually good-natured tone giving way to something harsher and less patient. "Now, they come down here to trade with you. Either you want to, or you don't, but I'm not keeping this bar open all damned night while you make up your minds."

The people fell silent.

"That's what I thought." June nodded toward Jessa and Graf. "Now get off my bar. Everyone's got two hours to get their shit together. We ain't waiting for any of you, so get back quick as you can."

"And spread the word," Jessa called, over the sound of scraping chairs and scooting tables. "Let everybody know."

"If I were them, I wouldn't," Graf said, hopping down and offering Jessa his hand. "I would want as few people to show up as possible, so I could get a better deal."

"That's the difference between you and us, then," June said, wiping the place where Graf's sneakers had been. "We don't just look out for number one."

Yes, we do, Jessa replied to herself, not that she would tell him that. She let Graf help her down and got away from him as fast as possible.

They took a table that had been abandoned. Only a few bodies remained, people who either didn't have anything to trade or didn't care to go to the trouble of participating, anyway.

Jessa groaned inwardly when she realized that one of those bodies was Becky. It helped a little to see Graf having the same reaction, a look of mingled horror and disgust that deepened as he realized Becky had gotten up from her table and was presently staggering in their direction.

Becky had never been a subtle person. She was clear as a pane of window glass when she was drunk, which she definitely was. She gripped the hem of her denim skirt at crotch level and yanked it down, her ankles crossing as she stumbled forward. "There's my friend," she called, laughing up a puff of smoke.

Graf looked distinctly uncomfortable. Good. For all the hell he'd put Jessa through for the past couple of days, he could have this little slice of hell for himself. "Uh-oh, looks like you're friends now."

He puffed out a breath and said, long and pinched, "Yeah."

Becky pulled out a chair next to Graf and fixed on Jessa with narrowed eyes. "I went out to the service station. It doesn't look like anything happened out there."

"It's completely torn down," Graf said, calm and even.

"It probably just fell down," Becky said with a roll of her eyes. She leaned closer to Graf. "What are you doing later?"

"Not getting shot by your redneck husband." Graf pushed his chair back and leaned away from her. "You might want to ease up on the shine, if you don't want your baby born with cirrhosis."

Better to let white trash nature take its course, Jessa thought, and instantly heard her mother's voice admonishing her for wishing Becky ill.

Becky, translating Graf's statement into a joke the way drunks were prone to do, slapped his arm. "You're not being very nice!"

He shrugged. "I'm not very nice."

She was starting to catch on. Jessa could see it. She also knew what Becky was like when she felt insulted or rejected. Her self-confidence was mostly fake, and once she couldn't fake it anymore her lack of self-esteem and her nasty temper became a volatile mix.

Becky laughed, a halting, disbelieving sound, and said, "The way you act, I'd think you don't like me much."

"Because I don't," Graf said with a weary sigh. "Just because I didn't want you to get eaten by a monster doesn't mean that I want to be BFFs, okay?"

Almost faster than Jessa could see, Becky grabbed one of the mason jars from the table, and threw the contents of it in Graf's face. He blinked, then clapped his hands over his eyes, swearing.

"You don't get to talk to me like that!" Becky shouted, listing on her feet as she stood.

"Chad, get your buddy's wife out of here," June called calmly over the laughter of the remaining patrons.

"That's bullllschlit!" Becky slurred.

June flicked her long, brown braid over her shoulder and put up her hands in a gesture of helplessness. "Them's the rules, and you know it. Break a rule, get thrown out."

Chad Brown stood up from his seat and, with a weary groan, said, "Come on, Becks, let's get you home."

Jessa didn't see whether Becky put up a fight or not. She ran behind the bar, grabbed one of June's bar towels, and wet it under the faucet. She didn't know whether Graf was faking being in pain to keep from blowing his cover, but moonshine in the eyes couldn't be a good feeling.

"Here." She tried to move his hands, but he batted hers away. "Oh, stop it, you big baby."

He dropped his hands. His eyes were puffy and red, which he probably couldn't fake. She dabbed at his face with the towel and made a sympathetic hiss along with him as she pried the lid of one eye open.

"Why didn't you duck or something?" she asked quietly, casting a quick glance to the other tables. They still laughed and jostled one another, retelling the tale of the most recent time Becky embarrassed herself. They weren't interested in the cleanup.

Graf eyed them, too. "Because she was too quick."

That was bull. She'd seen how fast he moved. He was certainly committed to appearing human. "Well, if you're lucky, you won't go blind."

"Oh, good." He watched her through bloodshot eyes as she wiped the rest of the alcohol off his face. "Are you being nice to me? Dare I ask, nurturing?"

She made a face. "I guess I am. Probably because we're in a bar full of assholes, and you seem less obnoxious by comparison."

"Except for June," he said with a nod toward the bar.

"Well, yeah. Except for June."

They spent the rest of their wait mostly in silence. Jessa wasn't a big fan of small talk, and Graf seemed incapable of making any effort toward it. It wasn't a fully comfortable silence, but it was at least a mutually agreed upon one.

Folks started trickling in about an hour later, with their items for trade. The rules of the auction were simple, and everyone knew them, so when it kicked off, it went quick and neat. Jessa was pretty happy with most of the trades she got.

"Hey, I can make pasta out of that," she'd said excitedly when Graf's leather jacket went for a sack of flour. "God, I haven't had pasta in so long."

"Doesn't it get cold here in the winter?" he'd

grumbled, but he'd been easy enough to ignore. In fact, he'd been remarkably easygoing.

"Bar needs fresh music," she'd said, admiring her newly acquired MP3 player, and Jessa was glad. The same old CDs on the jukebox were wearing on her nerves.

After the auction was finished and Jessa's sense of prolonged death by starvation had eased, she relaxed. Even had a second drink. All while Graf sat, quiet for one blessed moment, watching her.

"What?" she finally asked, too aware of his scrutiny.

He leaned on the table, elbow propped up, chin on his hand. "You're like a different person."

"I'm a little drunk." She took another swallow from her cup. "You'd better get a drink, or they'll get suspicious."

"Not if you stop saying things like 'they'll get suspicious.' Now they probably wonder what they should be suspicious of." He pried the glass from her fingers. "You won't fit in that wagon, so we better leave while you can still walk."

"Yes, I can still walk," she insisted, before remembering that he hadn't asked her a question.

As he led her toward the door, his hand at the small of her back—people would talk about that— the other pulling the wagon loaded down with supplies, Chad staggered in. His hat was missing, and his shirt was torn.

"It almost got me!" he shouted, his lips trembling. "It almost got me!"

Nine

The scent of blood was all over the guy who'd burst through the door.

Graf's first instinct was, of course, to eat him. His second instinct was to cower and cover his eyes. Like the smell would disappear if he couldn't see it? Didn't make any sense. The coppery tang would invade his nostrils no matter what he did, forcing the part of him that was more monster than man into hunger overdrive. Oh, who was he kidding? He was always more monster than man.

"Sick at the sight of blood?" June's arms were folded across her chest, and she was smiling at Graf during her good-natured teasing. But her eyes weren't smiling. They were accusing.

There was no way she could possibly know. Humans weren't that smart. They believed what they were taught to believe, that there was no such thing as monsters, that vampires were bogeymen for nightmares and Halloween.

Occasionally, though, he ran into a human who did know. Someone who probably didn't guess "vampire!" right away, but knew something was up. They could tell that something wasn't right about the way he moved, or the way he looked. June was one of those people.

"Come on, we should get you home," he said, putting his hand on Jessa's arm without turning away from June. Finally, he broke her suspicious gaze. He swallowed, unnerved. He wasn't used to being intimidated. He was used to being the one doing the intimidating.

"Are you crazy? Chad is hurt." Jessa pulled away to join the people crowded around the injured human.

"I sh-shot It," Chad stammered, his pale face turning from one pair of concerned eyes to another. "It came after me."

"How'd you get away, son?"

Graf couldn't tell who'd asked the question. It was the grizzled, honest country voice that could have come out of any of these farmer types.

Someone helped Chad pull his shirt over his head, revealing a long, jagged slash down his ribs. The scent of his blood grew inescapable, and Graf took a deep breath, hoping he looked like he was trying to keep from tossing his cookies all over the floor, rather than savoring the smell. The smell of blood affected him the way the smell of apple pie had when he'd been human.

At the sight of the wound, a couple of the women gasped. It looked worse than it was, Graf could tell from his vantage point. Long, but not deep. Nothing like what the monster had done to him. If the thing had wanted to kill Chad, it would have been able to, easily. What kind of a monster picked and chose who to kill amid its rampages?

"It's just a scratch," Chad said quickly when someone recommended stitches. "I caught myself when I crawled under the barbed wire around Stapp's old pigpen."

"You ran that thing onto my property?" someone, Stapp, most likely, shouted.

Chad shook his head. "It wasn't chasing me. I was taking a shortcut."

"Best you all get home while It's still hurting," June called to silence the chaos. "Chad, you be able to make it?"

He nodded, still white as a sheet. "Yeah, I'll be fine. Lost my gun, though. Dropped it running."

"Take mine," Jessa volunteered. "I've got—"

Graf held his breath. It would be fitting for her to let his secret out in some stupid way, like this. It never came out all big and dramatic. It would be one slip of the tongue and then it was all torches and pitchforks.

Luckily, she wasn't too drunk to remember herself. "Because I've got a shorter walk."

Graf let out the breath he'd been holding. "Yeah, and there's two of us. I could just throw her to It and keep running, so I'll be fine."

His joke fell on unappreciative ears. Fifty pairs of hillbilly eyes glared at him with disbelieving hostility. Like he'd taken a piss on Elvis's grave.

"Shut up, Graf," June commanded from behind the bar, in the same way a friend would kindly advise another friend to shut up. He wasn't sure if he should be touched at her simple, country-folk acceptance or if it was a cover for the fact she'd figured out he wasn't exactly what he was supposed to be. "Jessa, best you leave your loot here, so you don't have to abandon it to a quick getaway."

"Yeah, now that she knows It's out and about, Jessa'll run into it for sure," a woman's voice snapped, and there were a few unkind chuckles.

"Thanks, June," Jessa said quietly, tugging the little red wagon behind the bar.

Graf picked up the shotgun and handed it over to Chad, who took it gratefully and promised, "I'll return it tomorrow."

"See you then," Graf said, trying and sensing that he had failed to sound hometown and welcomey. Fuck it, he tried; that was all they could really expect from him. He could lure normally intelligent people to their deaths just by flashing a smile, but hillbillies seemed to be immune to his charm.

The crowd cleared quickly. Graf and Jessa were the last to leave the bar, partly because Jessa wanted to make sure June was okay.

"What are we going to do if she's not?" Graf had grumbled, juggling the sack of flour Jessa had insisted had to be carried home right now rather than in the morning.

Graf had a feeling her reluctance to leave had more to do with the food packed into the little red wagon than concern for the bartender. Not that he could blame her. If that wagon had been full of blood, they would have had to pry his fingers off it to get him to leave it behind.

After they'd walked down the road and were surrounded by nothing but crickets and darkness, he asked her about it.

"Look," she said with a heavy sigh. "When you're so used to doing with nothing, it's hard to let go of what little you have. Even if you know for sure it's going to still be there in the morning."

"And you're sure it will be there?" He wouldn't have left his last bag of blood in that place, if the townspeople were vampires. Lucky for him, it wasn't his dilemma.

She nodded. "Yeah. I mean, I know some of the people down there aren't totally honest. There have been some feuds, some disputes in town. But no one would dare mess with June. If people lost their one avenue of sociality and commerce, well, I reckon they'd go crazy."

"You reckon, huh?" He laughed. "I'm sorry. I just feel like I've fallen into a Tennessee Williams play. Not that you'd even know who that was."

"I know who Tennessee Williams is," she said, her brow furrowing. "*Cat on a Hot Tin Roof.* It was a movie with Elizabeth Taylor and Paul Newman."

"Very good." He didn't bother to cover up his surprise.

"I'm not some inbred yokel. We did have TV here, you know. Some of us even had sa-TEE-lite." She adopted an exaggerated country accent. "Yes, sir-ree, we got us one of them thar talking picture boxes, hyuck hyuck."

"Point taken," he muttered.

"No, I don't think it was. Did you know I went to college?" She waited for him to respond and let him stammer helplessly for a few seconds before she cut him off. "No, you don't know that, because you just assumed I'm uneducated because I live in farm country."

"Okay, fair enough, I made a stupid assumption." Though he couldn't picture Jessa at college, he had to ask. "What was your major?"

She shrugged. "Mathematics. I wanted to be a high school teacher."

"I wouldn't have pegged you for the type who'd

want to teach. I thought you'd have planned on being a veterinarian." He'd prided himself on being a good judge of people, but every now and then he found someone who surprised him.

"There you go, making assumptions again." She sniffed and cocked her head to the side, like she was indicating the bar they'd just left, though it was far out of sight. "So, pretty good haul."

"Yeah, I'll remember that in the winter, when all the food is gone and I'm freezing to death because you sold off my jacket." As if summoned by his words, a wintry chill crept up his spine.

"You'll be fine," she said, sounding pretty darn unconcerned, in Graf's opinion. "I have some of my dad's old Carhartts in the basement."

"Oh, good. I'll look like an ice road trucker." By this time next year, he'd probably be chewing on hay stalks and saying "reckon," just like Jessa.

A year. He would stake himself if he was stuck in this town for a year.

"Do vampires even get cold?" she challenged, still not seeming at all guilty about giving away all of his personal effects. "You're dead, right?"

"That's not the point—" he began, and his words abruptly cut off when she grabbed the hand swinging casually at his side and lifted it up to examine it. Drunkenly, she leaned over their clasped fingers, bringing his hand perilously close to her neck.

"See, you're cold right now. So how does the cold

bother you?" She dropped his hand and started walking again.

It took Graf a second to recover. Something was definitely wrong with him. After Chad had wandered into the bar, bleeding like the main course, that one little touch from Jessa should have pushed him over the edge. And Lord, how he wanted to go over that edge and drink her dry, but he couldn't.

He was starting to trust his captor. He had Stockholm syndrome.

"Yeah," he said quickly, hoping his stunned silence hadn't lasted too long. "I'm room temperature. But I can still get cold. I've still got blood moving around in here. If I go into a walk-in freezer, I'm not going to drop to that temperature."

"Huh." She walked the walk of a happy drunk, sprawling steps slapping the pavement with her whole foot at one time as she looked up at the stars. Then she stopped, her face creased in concern. "Wait, then wouldn't you get really hot in normal temperatures?"

"Yeah, but you get used to it. Like living in the desert," he answered. "Keep walking."

She obeyed his order, but her frown remained as they crossed the paved road to the dirt one that would lead to her house. "So, why did you have a leather jacket with you? In July?"

He smirked. "Because leather is sexy."

"Ugh," she groaned in disgust. "Can you still get a hard-on? I mean, if you're dead."

"Whoa—'ugh' to leather, but you're worried about my *dick?*" He smirked, she blushed, and they both fell silent.

They approached the house, the sickly green glow of the mercury light like a toxic candle in a dark window. Graf had to admit, he liked the isolation of the place. Usually, he preferred someplace busy, lots of people, lots of cars. Since the people in Penance weren't that great it didn't bother him to have some distance. Same thing with the cars, since there apparently weren't any.

He stopped at the end of Jessa's driveway, jolted by the realization that there weren't any cars there, either.

"What the fuck?" He pushed the sack of flour into her arms and charged up the lawn. Futile, obviously. The car wouldn't be hiding. If it wasn't where he'd parked it, it was gone.

"Your car," Jessa said slowly and drunkenly. "It's, like, not here."

"Really? Thanks for pointing that out!" He punctuated his sentence by kicking a cloud of gravel across the driveway. There wasn't even anything good to kick in this town.

Jessa stumbled up to stand beside him. "Where did it go?"

"That's a great question." He sniffed the air, as

though telltale exhaust would linger there. If it did, what good would that do him? Confirm that someone had driven the car away, rather than pushed it?

"Well, it couldn't have gone far." Jessa trudged toward the porch. "We can find it in the morning."

He opened his mouth to argue, then realized that she was right. Whoever took the car could drive it all night, but they weren't going to leave Penance.

"It stings, though, just leaving her out there on the road, all by herself," he said as he followed Jessa through the door.

She startled at his sudden presence. "Jesus, don't do that!" She set the sack of flour on the coffee table and folded her arms over her chest. "Why do you guys do that?"

He shrugged. "I guess because we forget we freak humans out if we move too fast? Or we just don't care?"

"Not that." She rolled her eyes, like he should have been able to follow her shifting conversation topics as well as she did. "Call their cars 'she.' Cars aren't feminine."

"First of all, it's not just a car. It's a 1974 De Tomaso Pantera L. And I don't know why men call cars 'she.' It's not like I've ever done a sociological study of the phenomenon." He peeked out the window, half hoping he'd had some kind of hallucination and the Pantera would be sitting in the driveway. Lonely and undriven, but still there.

"That's a stupid answer. You have to have some kind of idea." She flopped on the couch and clicked on one of the end table lamps.

Graf couldn't decide if Jessa was more annoying drunk, or less. She said anything she felt like saying now, but she hadn't really been restrained and polite before, either. She was less hostile. Maybe that didn't have anything to do with the alcohol. Maybe she was just too tired to be a bitch.

"Do you think it's because you don't have a woman in your life, so you make your car into your girlfriend?" she mused, leaning her head back and closing her eyes. "That's pathetic."

"Hey, I pull my share of tail, okay?" Not that he could remember recently. He'd been an eat-and-run kind of guy as of late.

"Ugh. You're disgusting." She let out a long sigh and reached up to play with her ponytail. Her brown hair lay against her neck, dotted with a thin sheen of sweat like dew on grass. Her pulse beat beneath her skin, nice and slow and relaxed, flexing a visible point on her throat.

Graf's gums ached, and his fangs lengthened. She seemed drunk enough. Maybe she wouldn't notice a quick bite. Hell, maybe she would be into it. Some of them were.

Her eyes snapped open. "Did you hear that?"

Over the sound of her blood teasing him into a feeding frenzy? No. But he waited for a moment more, and the sound came again, a thunk, then a scrape, and the tarp wall in the kitchen rustled. "Stay here," he ordered.

The kitchen was still dark, though the mercury light glowed through the blue plastic. A shadow moved behind the sheet, where the kitchen door used to be. A human shadow. At least it wasn't the monster again.

"What's going on?" Jessa asked from the kitchen doorway.

Graf cursed. "Didn't I tell you to stay in the living room?"

There was another scrape and thunk, and the intruder spilled into the kitchen. Graf caught him by the back of his T-shirt and the belt around his waist and hurled him back through the hole, partially ripping down the tarp barrier. He jumped out after him while Jessa shouted things like "Stop," and "It's just Derek!"

The moment the words penetrated the fog of violence in his brain, Graf wanted nothing more than to crush Derek's head between his palms until it popped like a water balloon. A water balloon full of skull and brain matter. But that would probably upset Jessa, what with her obsession with the guy.

He stepped back. "What the hell are you doing?" he asked, wiping his palms on his jeans. "I could have killed you."

"Yeah, I bet," Derek muttered, swaying as he got

to his feet. Another drunk. The whole damned town needed AA. "You can't do shit to me. This is between me and Jessa."

Jessa leaned against the edge of the hole, a scowl on her face. "You couldn't just use the front door?"

"I didn't want to disturb your guest," he said with a sarcastic sneer.

Graf shook his head. "That doesn't make any sense."

"What do you want, Derek?" Maybe Jessa was sobering up, because the bitch was back in her voice. Graf figured it was nice to not have it directed at him, for once.

"Where's my wife?" He reached into his back pocket and pulled out a crumpled piece of notebook paper.

Jessa hopped down through the hole, and Graf restrained himself from going over to help her. He didn't want her to get the wrong idea and start thinking he was a gentleman. She snatched the paper from Derek and frowned. "I don't know where the hell she is."

While Jessa read the note, Derek turned his anger to Graf. "Chad brought her home from June's Place all torn up and crying, saying she got kicked out after she got into a fight with Jessa. What the hell did you say to her?"

"I didn't say anything to her." Jessa thrust the note

back at Derek. "She was drunk and coming on to Graf."

"Bullshit," Derek spat. "Chad said it was something to do with you."

"Chad wasn't there!" Jessa shouted. "He was all the way across the damn bar!"

"Okay, okay." Graf pinched the bridge of his nose and closed his eyes. "There's been some misunderstanding. Derek, we haven't seen Becky since she got thrown out of June's. She was coming on to me and didn't like it when I turned her down."

Derek squinted at Graf like he'd just spoken Greek and he needed time to translate. Then he stepped back, his head cocked to one side. "You turned her down?"

"I can't believe this." Jessa spun around as if to go to the front door.

Graf caught her arm. "No, this is your mess, you're staying."

"This ain't nothing to do with her, now." Derek still had the expression of a man who'd just been hit, but had frozen midfall. Offended, astounded, pissed as hell, and flat-out stupid. "Becky was coming on to you and you turned her down?"

"What was I supposed to do, fuck your wife?" The argument was so ridiculous Graf didn't have any idea what side he was supposed to be fighting on. "You're drunk. Go home and look for your wife. Take care of your kids."

"The kids are gone! She took 'em!" Derek slumped to the ground, suddenly weeping. "She took 'em. I looked everywhere. Her mom said she saw her—she stopped by with the kids in a car and told her to come with her. Saying all sorts of crazy things. Now she's gone."

"What kind of crazy things?" Dread gnawed Graf's stomach.

"It's in the note," Jessa said. "She's leaving town, she's never coming back, blah, blah, blah… I'd like to see her try."

"Is anyone looking for her right now? Besides Drunkey McGee here?" If she'd left town, and left in Graf's car…if he'd had a chance to make it out and that skinny bitch had left instead of him… No. No, no, no, no, no.

"They'll find her in the morning at some friend's house," Jessa said, not sounding the least bit worried. "Go home. Get off my lawn."

"Jessa, baby." Derek looked up at her with pleading eyes. "I'm in pain here."

"So?" She pulled free of Graf's grip. He hadn't realized he was still holding on to her.

"You're just going to leave me? Alone?" Derek looked like a kid who'd been told his trip to Disney World had been canceled.

"You'll survive." She walked away, around the front of the house, leaving Graf and Derek in the side yard. Awkwardly.

"I guess you got your answer," Graf said, offering Derek a hand up.

He didn't take it and stumbled when he got on his feet. "You turned down Becky?" He snorted. "Your tough luck, pal. Because you ain't never going to get any from that stuck-up bitch! You hear me, Jess? You're a stuck-up bitch!"

Graf let his fist fly before he could truly examine his motives. It was better that way. His punch landed on Derek's jaw with a loud crack, and laid him out in the grass. Graf didn't bother to check if Derek was still breathing. He gave him a light kick in the side. "Get the hell out of here."

He didn't look back. It would have been too tempting to chow down on the guy while he was knocked out. The world wouldn't miss him—that was for sure.

"Did you hit him?" Jessa asked when he came through the door. Her eyes were rimmed with red, and the tracks of tears stained her face.

Graf nodded.

She smiled a little, but it faded as a fresh wave of tears erupted.

Of all the things in the world Graf felt physically able and willing to confront, female tears were not on that list. He stood in place for a second. Realized that the decent thing to do would be to comfort her. Warred with himself over whether or not he was a decent guy who did decent things. Then, unable to stand it anymore, went and put his arms around her.

To his surprise, she didn't resist him. She tucked her drunken head under his chin and pressed her hands against his chest, letting him hold her up. "Why are guys like that?"

Fantastic. He'd gone from houseguest to one of the girls in the time it took for her eyes to form tears. "Guys aren't like that. Some guys are like that. Not all of them."

All of them in this town probably were.

"Is he okay?" she sniffed against his chest.

Does it matter? Compared to the rest of the people in town—the bartender excluded—Jessa had seemed pretty smart. Women were stupid when it came to their feelings. "He'll be okay. Unless he wakes up and decides to come back in here. Then, he won't be okay."

She pushed away with a noise of disgust.

His arms felt oddly empty, and he didn't know what to do with his hands, so he put them in his pockets. "What now?"

"What now?" She laughed, disbelieving. "You basically just said you're going to kill him if he comes back! Why wouldn't that upset me?"

Something had gone really wrong, if she was mad at him and not the asshole lying on the lawn. "Why would it? The guy is a jerk."

"That jerk is the only person in this town that

cares about me!" She shook her head and marched toward and up the stairs. "Never mind. You wouldn't get it."

"Yeah, he really cares about you. So much that he married the town skank instead of you!" He dropped onto the couch. Great. She'd gotten his shirt wet. He hoped it was tears and not snot. His stomach growled, and his fangs ached. He was going to have to eat somebody, and soon.

With a groan, he got back on his feet and went into the kitchen, where the paper outlining their lease agreement still lay on the island. That was a dumb move. If Derek had come inside and found it, it would have either exposed Graf or made Jessa seem more crazy than everyone thought she was.

He felt a pang of guilt at that. Jessa wasn't crazy. She'd been trapped in a town with no allies—Derek did not count—for the past five years. She'd withstood the isolation much better than Graf would have. He was ready to stake himself with a broken two-by-four and he'd only been in town a couple days.

Feeling sorry for Jessa wasn't going to change her situation, and it would just make him weak. Next thing he knew, he'd be out killing rabbits for food and crying about it. He grabbed the list and headed upstairs. He opened Jessa's door without knocking and thrust the paper through the gap.

She sat up on her bed, her eyes red and swollen.

"What?" She looked at him expectantly, as though she awaited an apology.

"Number three. I'm getting hungry. You better figure something out by tomorrow night, or I'm going to pick someone, and you won't have any say over who."

She nodded, looking for all the world like she wanted to incinerate him with her hate. "Fine."

He didn't say anything else. He didn't think he needed to.

Ten

The sun across Jessa's face woke her. She opened her eyes reluctantly and squinted past the white eyelet curtains to the illuminated green of the tree outside.

An insistent knock on the door startled her. It had been that, then, and not the sun, that had woken her. She sat up, rubbed her eyes, and called, "Be right there."

She took the steps two at a time, alternately pleased, then dismayed, to see the shape of a man outside the door. If Derek had come crawling back to apologize, she would probably let him in, accept his apology, and go right back to being his doormat.

If it annoyed Graf, it would be worth it.

"Hey," she said, not making eye contact as she opened the door.

Chad, not Derek, stood on the porch, his lips

compressed over a tight breath. "Did I do something wrong?"

That was Chad, always trying to be nice and not step on anyone's toes. She laughed and shook her head. "No, sorry. I saw you through the curtain and I thought you were someone else. Come on in."

He ducked his head as he came through the door, though there was no danger of him not making clearance. "I stopped by June's and brought you your stuff. I hope that was all right."

Jessa looked past him, to the little red wagon sitting on the lawn. Her father's gun leaned against the uprights of the porch. "That's real nice of you, Chad. You didn't have to do that."

"No, I did." He made a pained face. "I heard Derek came by and caused trouble for you last night."

"Did you?" Had Graf gone back into town? She'd thought she'd heard him moving around in the bedroom before she'd fallen asleep. Had he left, maybe for good? The thought should have relieved her, but it troubled her to think she might be alone again.

"Yeah," Chad continued. "Derek came by June's early this morning, still drunk as a skunk and raving about Becky going missing. He said your boarder hit him."

"He did. Is Derek okay?" She remembered the damage Graf had managed to do to It. Of course, if the damage had been too serious, Chad would have probably said, "I heard your boarder killed Derek," so she stopped worrying. "Did they find Becky?"

"He's fine. There's another search party going out this afternoon." Chad looked toward the stairs, a kind of homesick-puppy look suddenly coming over him. "You think your friend would want to help out?"

"I don't think that's a good idea, do you? After what Becky did down at June's, and what he did to Derek?" At least Graf had given her an easier way to explain why he couldn't come out. "Allergic to sunlight" seemed too obvious, now that she knew what he was.

Chad gave her a sad half smile. "Yeah, you're probably right. Look, I gotta get back. Is it okay if I check up on you later?"

"Why?" Ever since she was a teenager, she'd maintained careful boundaries when it came to Chad's worship from afar. Maybe it was cruel of her, but she didn't want to lead him on or raise his hopes. She didn't want to take advantage of him. That had become an even bigger danger now that they were trapped in Penance. It would be so tempting to ask him to come back and check on her, to help patch up the wall, to get in her bed with her when she'd just be thinking of his best friend. He would have done all of that willingly, and she didn't want the opportunity to see if she could resist temptation.

"Yeah, that's stupid. I know you've got your... friend. He can look out for you." He turned and headed out onto the porch, then stopped. "I hope we find his car in one piece. You remember what kind of a driver Becky was."

Jessa smiled. "Yeah, I remember." She watched him as he descended the few steps to the lawn. Perfect. Now that she and Derek had had a fight, Chad would be over here checking on her more and more often, until Derek got pissed off and put him in his place. With Becky missing, he wouldn't notice or care what Jessa was doing for a while. And Jessa had her own problems to deal with, and a hungry boarder to feed.

"Chad?" she called, her heart pounding in her throat. There was no way she was doing this. Was there? "You know, on second thought, I wouldn't mind it if you'd stop by later. I don't really know this guy living here. I just had the extra room. If you would stop in and maybe just make sure that I'm okay…"

"Why? Did he try something?" Chad asked, the sudden transformation from eager puppy to guard dog setting Jessa back a few steps.

"No!" she said quickly. "Nothing like that. I'm just getting used to having a strange face around here. It would help to see somebody familiar."

He nodded. "Okay. Yeah, I'll come by later tonight. Maybe I'll bring some weed? We can smoke and talk about old times?"

"See you later, then." The words tasted awful on

her tongue. She watched him walk down the driveway, smiled and waved when he looked back occasionally. It was almost too easy. She felt like a serial killer.

She fed the chickens and went back upstairs. She passed the door to her parents' room and wondered if Graf was in there. She half hoped that he wasn't, but the other half of her had gotten a little used to having him around.

Maybe it was that he was so terrible, she thought as she turned on the taps in the tub. He was so terrible, probably the worst thing in town next to It, so she'd been knocked down a notch. She was a liar, a loser, a whore. She was fucking a married man, when the opportunity presented itself, and it often did. She was a terrible person, but she wasn't a killer.

Not until tonight.

She stripped off her clothes and sank under the water, listening to the dull thumps of her limbs against the porcelain and the slow leak of water slipping down the drain. If Graf ate Chad, and she lured him there, that was the same as killing him, wasn't it? She might as well have shot him in the face while he stood there on the porch. She opened her eyes under the water and watched the ceiling distort with the movement of the water. What kind of a monster did it make her that she really didn't care if Chad died? That she could rationalize it away as one less person straining the town's resources?

That she cared more about Graf surviving than Chad?

No. She couldn't think like that. Graf being here with her wasn't a good thing. He was as much of a monster as It was. He had violated her sanctuary, shaken the tightrope she walked every day to maintain her sanity.

She scrubbed her skin raw, delaying the moment she knew was coming. She had to decide. Was she going to be a monster? A killer? Was she going to let the presence of a monster rule her life, outside of her house and inside?

Before she could waver in her decision, she stood and shook the water out of her hair. Wrapping herself in a towel, she tiptoed across the hall. If he wasn't in the room, it would be that much easier. If he was, well, it wouldn't be too difficult to rip down the blinds and watch him burn.

She felt a little sick to her stomach at the memory of what he'd looked like from just a short exposure to the sun. How painful it had been. But if that was all it took, it would be over quickly. She pushed the door open, her breath frozen in her chest.

Graf was there, sprawled naked across the bed. He lay on his stomach, face turned away from the door. If she'd had to see his face, maybe she wouldn't have been able to do it. Clutching the towel closed at her chest, she slowly walked into the room, the way she had done so many times as a child woken by a nightmare, afraid to be sent back to her own bed.

He had covered the windows with quilts from the cedar chest at the foot of the bed. She gripped the fabric, took a breath, imagined the sunlight streaming in, the dust motes dancing in the wholesome light. The burning. The dying. Her fingers flexed, her arm jerked.

Something struck her, knocking the breath from her lungs. It was the floor, on the opposite side of the bed. Graf was on her, his face twisted in fury. She screamed and clawed at his shoulders, but he was strong, so strong. She reached over her head for the tail of the quilt covering the second window, but her fingers came up empty, then caught in his crushing hand that pinned her to the floor. His eyes flashed with hunger, his mouth opened, deadly fangs poised to sink into her neck.

The space of two heartbeats became an eternity. His mouth lowered to her neck. She arched her back, moaning as his teeth pierced her skin. She opened her legs, let him sink into her, writhing against his hips and gasping in desperation. He drank deep, and she threw her head back, screaming.

In an instant, she broke free of the fantasy. She sat up in the bathtub, water sloshing over the sides, her chest heaving from lack of air. Shame crushed her. She drained the tub and dried off, then dashed down the hall to her room to dress and comb her hair. Killing Graf was not an option. Getting near Graf was not an option. Something was desperately wrong with her.

She didn't dare look at the door to her parents' room when she passed it. She went downstairs and got a glass of water. Usually, she would figure there was no harm in fantasizing a little bit about a good-looking guy, but when the guy was a vampire, and when the fantasy involved death and violence, that was where a line had to be drawn. Besides, she had work to do. Things just didn't stop because someone throws a wrench into the works.

When she went to the front door to unload the wagon, she stopped with a shock. June stood on her porch, her back to the door, looking out over the front lawn.

"Hey," Jessa said, stepping outside and closing the door quietly behind her. "I didn't hear you knock."

"Well, I didn't yet." June wore a brown ball cap over her hair, her long braid trailing out of the hole in the back. "I was just enjoying the view."

"I thought you'd be out with the search party," Jessa said cautiously. June didn't just show up places for no reason.

"Nah." She put her hands in her pockets and looked out at the road. "Becky's long gone."

Jessa took a breath. People didn't talk about leaving Penance. And here June was, showing up out of nowhere to talk about it.

"I think you figured the same thing?" June probed. "I'm not trying to upset you, but—"

"No, no. I didn't think that you were." Jessa motioned to the house. "Come on in. You want something to drink?"

"Glass of water would be nice. Let me help you carry some of this stuff inside." June followed Jessa down the steps to the wagon and picked up a plastic ice cream bucket full of cherry tomatoes.

Jessa collected a box of shotgun shells and six ears of sweet corn tied together with a rubber band. "Thanks. And thanks for holding this stuff for me. I think I was too drunk to get it all home."

"Your friend wouldn't have helped you?" June asked casually as they walked through the living room.

Jessa's cheeks flamed suddenly. June was a good judge of people. Sometimes, she figured out things about them before they did. Had something she had done or said tipped June off to an attraction toward Graf? God, she hoped not. It certainly wasn't something conscious, and certainly nothing she would act on. "I think he had his hands full getting me home safely."

"That's true." June chuckled, a deep smoker's chuckle that hadn't quite lost its rattle after five years without nicotine. "So, Becky took his car, and he punched out Derek."

Jessa shrugged. "Derek had it coming."

She filled two glasses with water and nodded toward the living room. June sat in the overstuffed floral armchair and fixed Jessa with an ambiguous stare, before flicking her gaze downward. "You said you shot It just before this Graf got into town?"

"I did." Jessa sat her glass on the coffee table and pulled her legs up to sit cross-legged on the sofa. "Why, are people talking about that?"

"No. I was just thinking." June fell quiet for a second. "If you shot It, and Graf got in, and Chad shot It, and Becky got out—"

"Assuming she is out." Not that it wouldn't give Jessa some sick pleasure to know that Becky wouldn't be bothering her anymore. "They might still find her."

"I don't think they will. And I think the reason is because Chad hurt It." She shook her head. "It's crazy to talk about, but I just… You know when Steve Siler disappeared? It was right after."

June didn't have to tell Jessa what she meant by "right after." He'd disappeared a couple weeks after Jessa's parents had been killed, the night after some of the guys in town had hunted down the creature and shot it about fifty times. They'd thought then that It would be gone forever.

"I think," June said slowly, as though afraid to say it, "that whatever is keeping us from leaving is gone when It gets hurt."

Jessa didn't say anything. She couldn't form a coherent thought.

"Once might have been a coincidence. I could even be talked into believing that lightning struck twice. But this time, I think it would be stupid to ignore it." She waited a moment before continuing. "I thought maybe we could consult your friend about it."

"W-why would he know anything?" Jessa stuttered. "I mean, he just got here."

June sighed. "Come on, Jessa. I'm not as thick as some of the people around here. I could tell there was something up about him the minute I saw him."

Well, I didn't, Jessa thought irritably. *I guess I'm just thick.* "I don't know what you're talking about."

"Look, I don't know exactly what it is, but there's something different about him. I won't tell anybody. You know how they can be."

Jessa did know. Prickles ran up her back. "You're worried I'm going to end up like Sarah."

Something painful flickered in June's eyes. "I don't want anyone to end up like that, so I'm going to keep it a secret. But I don't think it would hurt for you to ask him. See what he thinks."

"I can do that," she said, as though she were psyching herself up to face him. God, maybe she was. What was happening inside her head?

June stood and finished off her glass of water. She wiped her mouth on the back of her hand and said,

"Well, I've got work to do. When that search comes back empty-handed, they'll be wanting to get good and drunk."

When June was gone, Jessa put away the rest of the supplies. She washed the glasses in the sink and set them in the dish drainer to dry. She dusted and vacuumed the living room. She checked on the peach trees and watered the vegetable garden. All the while, she kept checking on the position of the sun in the sky, wanting it to be sundown, dreading it at the same time.

At five o'clock, she faced reality. She went back in the house and ran some water in the tub and shaved her legs with her dad's old straight razor. She brushed her hair and let it hang loose around her shoulders. She found the floral print dress she'd worn under her graduation gown. It didn't fit as well anymore; she had to tie the sashes at the back a little tighter, which pulled the fabric. She pawed through her old cosmetics case and found some crumbling powder. She sprayed some ancient Love's Baby Soft on her neck and wrists, then faced the long oval mirror in her bedroom. All she could see was a murderer.

"I hope you didn't get all dolled up for me," Graf said from her doorway, and she jumped. Outside, the sun was still up, but it had dipped behind the trees, bathing everything in a warm golden light.

Graf stayed in the doorway, far from the fading light. "Hot date with Derek?"

She bristled at that, and whirled to face him. "No. With Chad. You're welcome."

He didn't seem to get it at first, but when he did, his face lit up like a kid on Christmas morning. "*Wow.* I didn't think you'd have it in you. So, what's the plan? Am I going to get him on his way out in the morning, or what?"

"Ugh, no!" The thought of sleeping with Chad wasn't entirely repugnant, but the idea of doing it knowing that he was just going to die was…no. "He said he was going to bring some weed, so I thought we'd smoke, and get drunk, and hopefully he'll be good and passed out, so he doesn't feel it when you… kill him."

"If you get him drunk, I won't have to kill him," Graf said with a shrug. "If he's drunk enough to black out, he won't even remember. And if he does, who'll believe him?"

June would. But she decided not to mention that.

"You were okay with me killing him, though?" Graf asked, sounding impressed.

"Not okay with it. But I'm going to do what I have to do to keep you from killing me." It had been too easy, though, and that concerned her. "Let's just not talk about it. Before I change my mind."

"Fine," Graf agreed. "Cover up that window, would you?"

She rolled her eyes, then snatched her bedspread and hung it over the curtain rod. She was aware that he watched her. She could feel his eyes on her legs as her skirt hitched up when she raised her arms.

"So, did they find my car?" he asked, coming in to sit on her bed.

"No. And I'm supposed to talk to you about that." She turned and folded her arms over her chest, uncomfortable being in such a small space with him. Walking right next to him outside was one thing, sitting across the kitchen island from him, that was something different, too. Now, she felt trapped, and her earlier imaginings came back to haunt her. She could practically feel him on top of her, and she shivered. "June knows there's something wrong about you."

"Hey, there's nothing wrong with me," he insisted.

"Well, that's debatable. But she knows you're not human." Jessa shook her head. "Maybe. She was sure driving at something when she came by today. She has a theory, and she wanted me to run it by you, in case you know something."

He lay back on her bed, his arms behind his head. "I'm all ears, cupcake."

She gritted her teeth. "Someone did get out of Penance before. At least, some people think he did."

Graf nodded. "Yeah, Becky mentioned that, in the car. She said it caused some controversy at the time."

"It still causes controversy. That's why no one

mentions the name Steve Siler in town if they want to keep their friends." That, and the town had a way of forgetting the unpleasantness of the past. Especially if they had caused it. "But the night before Steve disappeared, a bunch of guys had gone out and hurt It. The night that you came into town, I had shot It—"

"And last night, Chad shot It. And the night before, I fought with It and hurt it." Graf sat up. "Holy shit."

"It's just a theory June has," Jessa said quickly.

"But she's right. Holy shit, we could get out of here tonight—"

"No!" Jessa's heart pounded in her chest. "Look, we can't say anything about it right now."

"Why not? People are going to want to know!" Graf shot to his feet, as though he would run downstairs and outside and through the streets screaming it at the top of his lungs.

"No, no, no!" Jessa rushed forward and grabbed his arm. The coldness of his skin registered with her briefly, and the hard muscle of his arm. What the hell was wrong with her? "You have to listen to me about this, and just trust me, okay? If this is true, and it works, that's great. But something happened before. We have to tread carefully."

"You tread as carefully as you want, but I'm getting out of here." He took a few steps, then stopped. "Not right now. After I eat."

"Yeah, and what are you going to do? Walk to the next town? I hope you make it before sunup," she snapped.

"I'll get a motel room or something. Hitch a ride with someone and steal their car." He paused. "Fuck me, my wallet was in the car, and my phone. Shit, I can't even call for help once I get out."

"Besides, we'd have to find It, first. I don't know how long the gap lasts." She ran her fingers through her hair. "Please, just don't say anything to anyone."

"What are you so damn afraid of?" Graf asked, sitting down on the edge of her bed and dropping his head into his hands.

She closed her eyes and repeated, "Something happened."

The sound of crackling fire filled her mind, the heart-pounding fear of that night. "It was right after the first of us got out. There was a girl in town—she was about seventeen years old. Sarah. She was a goth kid, dressed all in black. Everyone thought she was a devil worshipper. When Steve got out, she started saying some crazy things around town, about It being a demon, and we should all band together and make a circle and do a spell to banish it. She wasn't going to hurt anyone, she was just a kid. But she talked about It too much, made too big a deal about knowing how we could all get out. Some people around town started getting suspicious about all of her talk of spells and magic and witchcraft. And in the end..."

"They did something to her?" Graf finished for her.

Jessa nodded. "They burned her."

"Jesus H. Christ, what is wrong with you people?" Graf scrubbed at his face with his hands. "So, we're damned if we do, damned if we don't."

"No. We just wait until June finds the right way to tell everyone," Jessa assured him. "They'll listen to her."

He sighed, loud and long. "Okay. I think you've got something on that score. She's a bright one, I could tell that last night. She saw right through me."

"It doesn't take much," Jessa snapped. Then, softer, she said, "You're a nice guy, for a vampire. And it's not too bad, having a vampire on my side. Don't do anything stupid."

He opened his mouth to reply, and was cut off by a knock at the door.

"Delivery guy is here," Graf said, clapping his hands together with a grin. "Where do you want me?"

Eleven

Graf followed Jessa to the top of the stairs, then appreciated the view as she went down the rest of the way. He had to admit, she looked good in her cliché little flowered dress, like Alicia Silverstone in that Aerosmith video. There was something inherently wrong about liking something that looked so straight-outta-the-trailer-park, but damn it, he couldn't help it.

The living room was dark, and Jessa turned on just one table lamp before opening the door. The guy from last night, with the delicious-smelling blood, stood on the porch. He wore a button-down blue denim shirt, and he didn't know what to do with his hands. He should have brought a bouquet of wildflowers; it would have made the whole situation that much more funny.

Jessa welcomed Chad inside and flicked cautious

eyes toward the stairs. From his hiding place, Graf shook his head, though she wouldn't be able to make out the movement in the dark. He didn't need her acting cagey and tipping Chad off.

"You look real nice," Chad said with a wide grin. "Is that for me?"

"Maybe it is and maybe it isn't." There was something sweet about her voice that was utterly foreign to Graf's ears. She was never that nice to him.

"Sorry," Chad said, scuffing his toes on the carpet. "I thought maybe…"

"Oh, don't be silly." Jessa moved out of view then said, "Have a seat, get comfortable."

Chad did as she instructed, and Graf crept farther down the stairs. Jessa sat on the couch, her bare feet pulled up beneath her, causing her to lean far too close to Chad to just be expecting a friendly evening.

"Did you guys find Becky?" she asked, as if she couldn't see the poor guy's shaking hands.

"N-no," he stuttered. "Nobody did. Derek is just beside himself."

"I'll bet he is." Though her words sounded sincere, Graf knew she really meant "I'll bet he isn't."

So did Chad. "Aw, don't be hard on him. I know he's done some stuff in the past that wasn't too great—oh, and he smoked the weed I was going to bring over…"

"Let's not talk about him. Derek is not here

tonight." She twirled her hair around her finger, then tossed the curl over her shoulder.

"Yeah, probably better not to." He sat silent for a moment.

"Yeah." Jessa jumped up and disappeared into the kitchen. Graf wondered if she knew that Chad never stopped looking at her the whole time.

Graf wished he could see her. He imagined her moving around in the kitchen, confident and at ease, as though she weren't in on the elaborate trick she was playing. She would have made a fantastic con man. Or vampire.

"You want something to drink? I got some of the cinnamon-stick shine Bill DeGraff made last fall," she called.

Chad nodded nervously. Still didn't realize that this was a sure thing. Or, would have been, if the intent wasn't to anesthetize and leech him, not seduce him.

Jessa returned with two generous portions of the drink, but when she raised her glass to her lips, she barely swallowed. Good girl. She knew she needed her wits tonight.

"Jessa, we're friends, right?" Chad said suddenly.

This took Jessa off her guard a minute, but she recovered quickly. "Of course we are, Chad. You know that. What's all this nonsense about?"

Chad shook his head quickly. "Oh, no, Jessa, I

didn't mean it like that. I just meant… Look, can I tell you something in secret? It's been bothering me all day, and I don't know who to talk to."

"You know you can always talk to me," Jessa said, quickly swallowing a gulp of her liquor.

Don't lose him now, Graf urged silently.

But Chad was too focused on whatever it was he wanted to tell her to notice anything else. "I know we're not supposed to talk about it, but…I just have this feeling that Becky is gone for good. Not dead. I mean, that would be horrible, if her and the kids—I mean, I don't want to even think about that." He dropped his head. "I don't mean to upset you saying this, but do you think it's possible for people to leave? Like Sarah was saying?"

For a split second, Graf thought Jessa was going to blow it all. She stared at Chad, like she was torn between two outcomes to this night, and when she opened her mouth she didn't look sure that she had made the right choice. Then, very slowly, she said, "Chad, you have to be careful saying something like that. You know how people are."

"I know, I know." He exhaled loudly, then picked up his drink, rolling the glass between his palms. "I just don't think we're going to find her. And Derek, he was crazy. He was ranting and saying all sorts of crazy things."

"What kind of crazy things?" Jessa's eyes were

wide, and her body tense. She wanted to look up at Graf. Badly. Bless her, she resisted.

Chad shook his head. "I've been fine here for the past five years. I mean, sure, times have been hard all around, but I never had any illusions about leaving Penance anyway. I like it here, it's where I grew up. But Derek, he was saying… It was strange. It was like he was saying he caused this to happen, all of us getting stuck here."

"That's stupid." Jessa dismissed Chad's concerns with a wave of her hand. "And awful. Ain't that just like Derek to take credit for something he didn't do?"

That loosened up the mood a little, and made Chad laugh, but she hadn't shaken him completely free of his fears. "Don't tell anybody I said that, all right? You remember what happened to Sarah, and I don't want that to happen to Derek."

"Yeah, but everyone thought Sarah was a witch. She even thought she was."

"I know. But if you had heard what he was saying, Jessa." Chad stopped. "Ah, hell, let's forget all this nonsense. I came over here tonight to check up on you, show you a good time."

"That's right, you did!" Jessa laughed, a little too loud and a little too strong, but she took another drink and smiled and the poor yokel boy was just as lost as ever.

"Hey, are we, uh, are we alone tonight?" Chad

asked quietly. "Not that I'm trying to make a move on you. I'm just wondering."

She smiled slowly. "Now, why wouldn't you want to make a move on me?" While he was still stunned, she flipped her hair over her shoulder and laughed. "No, we're alone. The poor guy is out looking for his car. Was all last night, too, after Derek came by. Didn't get back until sunup."

"Fat lot of good it will do him, in this town." After a long slug of shine, Chad grimaced. "Out of everything, that's the one thing I really miss."

"Cars?" Jessa asked, reaching for her own glass. This time, she did drink. Good Lord, what was she doing, getting drunk? Graf scowled. She was supposed to be getting him fed, not having a good time.

"Yeah, cars." Chad settled against the back of the couch and looped his arm comfortably around Jessa's shoulders. "Cars. And girls."

He leaned just slightly toward her, and she let him, inviting him by sliding just an inch or two closer. She smoothly set her glass down on the coffee table as his mouth finally met hers, and her breasts rose beneath her flowered dress as his arm fell to her waist.

Graf didn't know how to judge a kiss on sight alone, but it seemed pretty clear Jessa was enjoying this one. Maybe she was a good faker, but the little whimpers that came out of her, the way her head fell back as Chad moved his mouth down her jaw and onto her neck, made it seem like he was doing something right.

It was doing something for Graf, too, and it wasn't the usual excitement that came with the anticipation of feeding. That was always crazy arousing, no matter who he was going to bite. This was turning him on in a much different way. Watching Jessa moan and grip Chad's shoulders as his mouth moved over every inch of exposed skin above the neckline of her dress… Graf felt like he was watching her star in his own private porno.

Even weirder, Jessa knew he was watching her. She couldn't have just forgotten he was there, but she pulled Chad with her as she lay down, and lifted one leg to hook around his waist. Was she getting off on this? Was that her kink, being watched? It would be so unfair to find out now that she was hot, when he could have been banging her this whole time.

Chad ran his palm down her tanned leg, following the line of it around his hip, then reached into his back pocket. Instead of pulling out a condom, like Graf expected, Chad pulled out a pocket hunting knife.

Graf moved to the bottom of the steps.

Underneath Chad, Jessa stiffened. He had the knife at her throat, then. That answered that question.

"I'm sorry, Jessa." Tears obscured Chad's voice. "Derek said this is how it has to be."

It took precisely the space between "has to" and

"be" for Graf to reach Chad and pull him off Jessa. He pinned the human's arms behind his back and dragged him, kicking and cursing, away from the couch. Farm-boy strong, Chad put up a good fight. But not good enough.

Jessa didn't scream. A sudden sweat of fear stood out on Graf's forehead, and he called out, "Jessa, you okay?"

"Yeah, I'm fine," she said, surprisingly calm. She fumbled for the other light and ran to collect the knife that had tumbled to the floor.

"What the hell did you mean by that?" Graf snarled into Chad's ear.

The blood was pumping furious through the human's veins. Anger, not fear. It was a different kind of struggle, a different kind of perspiration. "He didn't know, okay? He didn't know what would happen. That bitch lied to him!"

"Me?" Jessa shrieked, standing frozen in place by the couch, as though the words had just passed the blood-brain barrier and made it into her consciousness.

"Who the hell are you talking about?" Graf demanded, tightening his grip on the human. "And what does it have to do with Jessa?"

"Blood," Chad gasped, and Graf realized then that he held the human too tightly. The skin of his face had begun to purple with the need for oxygen. "Her blood. Sarah lied about the spell."

The words sent Graf over the edge. He had been too long without blood. He was too desperate. And the idea of this jack-off killing Jessa on the orders of another jack-off...he couldn't handle it. He gripped Chad's hair, wrenched his head to the side until it crackled like bubble wrap, and sank his fangs into his neck.

Jessa screamed, but Graf shot her a warning glare over Chad's neck, and she silenced.

The blood ran hot and fast over Graf's tongue. His eyes locked on Jessa's as he sucked down gulp after gulp, the torrent too much for him, leaking out the corners of his mouth to stain Chad's T-shirt.

To her credit, Jessa didn't look away. She stood there, her dress crumpled, dingy cotton bra showing above the skewed neckline, and met his gaze while he gorged himself on Chad's blood. She clutched the open knife in her hands, the blade cutting into her skin. Droplets of crimson fell to the carpet at her feet, but she didn't react.

Graf drank until he couldn't anymore, then dropped Chad's heavy, dead body to the floor. "You got a saw?" he asked, wiping his mouth on his arm.

Finally, Jessa noticed her bloodied hand, and dropped the knife with a scream. Of course, she would lose it now, when it was time to clean up the mess.

"Do you have a saw?" he repeated patiently.

She trembled and stared at the body on the floor. "What for?"

There was no use sugarcoating it. "Because he won't fit into several garbage bags in one piece."

She ran to the kitchen and vomited into the sink.

Dropping the corpse, Graf followed her, keeping a respectful and safe distance from the puke. "I know this is probably the first time you've seen something like this—"

"No, it isn't!" She whirled, fists clenched at her sides so violently that her arms trembled. "I have seen worse!"

"Okay." He took a step toward her, cautiously, not wanting to set off any more explosions of anger or vomit. "Look, I know you're rocking this whole traumatized shtick and I get it. I really do. But you have a dead body on your floor, and a drunk pseudo-boyfriend who likes to drop by unannounced and who apparently wants you dead. What do you think our next step should be? Freaking out and barfing, or getting rid of the body? It's up to you, but I'm just saying you need to think about which choice is more productive."

He figured she would either slap him or see reason, or both. Luckily, she chose door number two, nodding meekly. "Fine. What do we need?"

"A saw," he repeated. "And trash bags. Four of them if they're regular ones, three if they're the stretchy kind."

"I don't have any trash bags, you moron," she snapped. "We haven't had anything like that for years. What are you going to do, saw him up for fun?"

It would be more fun than standing here arguing with you, he thought, but he knew when to hold his tongue. "All right, good point. We move on to plan B. Shovels."

"There's one out in the barn," she said, more subdued. "But where are you going to bury him? People will notice a patch of torn-up grass that big."

"Good point. Now you're thinking, and not just barfing." He rubbed his chin, staring out the window at the backyard. "What about the woods?"

She shook her head. "You'd never find the space. The roots would be too close together."

"But we could leave him out there, maybe hack him up a little bit and let a search party find him." Graf made a mental note to never rely on Jessa for covering up a murder ever again. "People would believe he got attacked by It and died."

"But he was supposed to be coming here," Jessa argued. "People are going to wonder why he came out here and never returned."

"He never got here. You waited for him to show up, even put on a pretty dress. When he didn't arrive, you figured he changed his mind and went to bed rejected." People would believe that. Graf hated to rely on the town's bad opinion of Jessa to make their lie work, but at least they had a few cards in their hand.

He could tell from the expression on her face that she didn't like the idea. But he could also tell that she knew there weren't many better options.

"Do you want to go with me?" he offered lamely. "Maybe you wanted to say some words or—"

"Leave my footprints all around the body?" She glared at him. "You really think we're all ignorant country bumpkins, don't you? The men who'd be out combing the woods looking for him are the same men who hunt in the winter and can track a deer better than most wolves could."

He gritted his teeth. "I was just trying to be considerate."

"And get me hanged for murder, that's real considerate." She turned to the sink and ran the water, splashing it around the basin with her hands.

"Fine. You do puke cleanup and I'll do body cleanup. That's fair." He went to the living room and checked out the window before opening the door. The last thing he needed was to walk out with a corpse slung over his shoulder just to run into some smiling townsperson.

Oh, who was he kidding? There was nothing to smile about in this town.

He gave Jessa one last look before he left. She still

stood at the kitchen sink, with the water running. Didn't surprise him. There was a lot to process after an attempted murder.

Disposing of the body took longer than Graf had anticipated. Finding the spot to dump the guy wasn't difficult, but Jessa had spooked him with her talk of CSI: Walton Mountain, so he did a little extra work. He bashed up the trees, and shredded Chad's clothes a little. After crushing Chad's torso to a pulp and obscuring the bite wound on this throat by decapitating him entirely, Graf felt pretty confident with his work and returned to the house.

Jessa wasn't downstairs. Her bedroom door was closed. Graf went into his room and stripped off his bloody clothes, leaving them in a pile on the hardwood floor. In the morning, he would take them out and burn them. In the meantime, though he'd promised Jessa he wouldn't mess with her parents' stuff, he needed something to wear. He rifled through the drawers in the bureau and prayed her father had been approximately the same size as him. He'd just found a pair of pajama bottoms and a T-shirt that looked like they would fit when he heard a quiet, persistent noise like the sound of a television on in another part of the house. The springs of Jessa's bed squeaked, momentarily covering the sound, and he realized what it was. She was crying, alone in her room.

He sat at the foot of the bed and listened. He

should go in and ask her if she was okay. No, that didn't seem right. Since when "should" he do anything? He was a vampire. Did a human ask a bowl of soup if it was okay before he ate it?

With a shock, he realized that he didn't intend to eat Jessa. He didn't know exactly when he'd crossed her off the menu, but she'd somehow moved into the strictly "do not kill" section of his brain. The thought of eating her was ridiculous; the thought of listening to her cry herself to sleep nauseated him.

He pulled on the clothes and walked to her room, tapping on the closed door softly. She didn't answer. Was she intentionally ignoring him, waiting for him to go away, or did she just not hear? He knocked again, then pushed the door open.

Jessa lay on her bed, curled into a ball with her arms crushing a pillow to her face as she sobbed. She hadn't wanted him to hear, still didn't know he was in the room. He could back out and leave her there, and claim that the strain of the evening and the pot Chad had smoked before he'd consumed him were to blame for the momentary lapse in sanity that had caused him to think of her as something other than a possible victim.

But he'd already moved toward the bed, and any further argument would be futile. He sat beside Jessa and put one hand on her shoulder.

She startled and pulled the pillow away from her face. "What are you doing?"

The genuine fear in her face shot straight to Graf's heart like a wooden stake. He couldn't find the words to explain himself. "I'm…sorry?"

"What are you doing in here?" she repeated, sitting up and drawing her knees to her chest.

"I wanted to check on you." Why did caring about someone have to sound so lame out loud? "I heard you crying. Are you okay?"

"My ex-boyfriend sent his buddy over to kill me," she reminded him.

"I know." He leaned away from her, but his hands seemed determined to touch her, as though he could reassure her. "Do you know why?"

"Now that his wife is gone? No. Unless he's gone completely crazy and managed to take Chad with him, I don't know why he would ask Chad to do something like that. Or why Chad would agree." Her face crumpled, fresh tears spilling down her cheeks.

"Hey, hey," Graf said softly, the words painful as they left his throat. "I'm not going to let anybody hurt you."

Confusion momentarily broke through her grief. "You threatened to kill me before."

"Yeah," he said helplessly. "That was before. It seems like there's competition for the job now, and I'm not one to follow a trend."

She laughed through her tears, then fell quiet, playing with the hem of her skirt. "So, are we friends now?"

Friends. He couldn't remember a time when he described anyone that way. Not even when he was human and therefore supposedly normal. "Are you going to stop being mean to me?"

"I have to, don't I? You saved my life. You could have let him kill me."

He didn't point out the obvious, that which they had already discussed—that he couldn't have her showing up dead if he wanted to evade suspicion. He wished they had never had that conversation. He motioned to the head of the bed. "Do you mind?"

"Go ahead," she said uncertainly, and he swung his legs onto the bed, lying beside her. He pulled her down, and she lay easily at his side, her head propped on his shoulder.

"Are you wearing my father's jammies?" she asked with a hitch of quiet laughter in her voice.

"Sorry. My clothes are destroyed. We'll have to burn them tomorrow." He looped his arm around her and stroked her hair. "Think of a good excuse to have a fire."

She yawned and lay silent. He thought she was sleeping, until she said, "Why would Derek want to kill me? He doesn't hate me. Becky does, but Derek… no matter what he says, he doesn't hate me."

Graf believed her. Derek had married Becky, but he had history with Jessa. A fucked-up history, from what he understood, but there was something between them that wouldn't break. It made Graf strangely sorry for her, and sorry for himself. He'd never had that kind of connection with anyone. He'd thought it made him free. Maybe it just made him kind of pathetic.

Twelve

Jessa didn't know what time Graf had left her room, but since she hadn't woken to a pile of ashes in her bed, she'd figured he'd made it out before sunup. She had woken with a lot of unanswered questions in her head, though, and those needed taking care of before she could do anything else.

She wiped the sweat from her forehead with her forearm, but she didn't stop walking. The day was beyond hot; it was downright hellish. Damn Becky for taking Graf's car. There would have at least been air-conditioning in it. This was a mission Graf couldn't be involved in, though, so she had to do it during the daylight hours.

Derek lived in a small house at the back of his in-laws' farm. Once upon a time, it had housed Becky's elderly grandfather, but when he passed, Derek and Becky moved their brood into it. A lot of families had done that in the last few years. Pulled together geographically to form their own little compounds. It made them feel safer, she guessed.

Jessa had never been inside Derek and Becky's house. It had been easier for Derek to come to her, and there had been less risk of getting caught, in those early days when they'd still thought no one was onto them. From the outside, the house looked bleak. Derek was too busy running around with his buddies to keep the place up probably. The siding was dented and splashed with a long streak of roofing tar beneath where a sloppy patch job covered a hole in the roof. The screen over the storm door hung in a limp curl, and Jessa didn't bother with the rust-stained door-bell. She opened the storm door and hissed as it first stuck, then released violently, bashing her shins with the sharp bottom edge. She hoped that thing about tetanus shots lasting sixty-five years was true.

"Derek?" she called, knocking on the rusted inside door. "Derek, you home?"

At her house, Derek always just barged in, and expected her to be okay with it, but she wasn't sure if she should do the same at his place. For one, Becky lived there. She was missing now, but there was some-thing just plain not right about "the other woman" walking into the family home. Another knock and a couple minutes of waiting made up her mind, and she tried the knob.

No one in Penance used to lock their doors.

Nowadays, with the monster and the isolation and the mistrust that had grown between neighbors, people didn't just lock up their houses, they fortified them. When the knob turned and the door swung inward, Jessa thanked God that Derek had never lost his teen-ager's sense of immortality.

The inside of the house was dark. Sheets pressed into service as curtains kept most of the light out, a smart choice on such a hot day. Still, the dark and heat of the interior suffocated Jessa, and the stench of unwashed dishes and untended trash made her gag. This wasn't a mess Derek had made before Becky had left. It was evidence that she'd checked out a long time before leaving.

Picking a path through strewn toys and unwashed cloth diapers, Jessa checked the living room and the bathroom. The children's bedroom, with its dirty walls and dingy, bare mattresses on the floor, was likewise empty. The door to the master bedroom was closed, and Jessa knocked on it before she opened it to find it empty.

She'd told herself that she had come to interrogate Derek, to find out if he truly had sent Chad to kill her. But that would have been a bad plan, revealing that she had seen Chad, that there had been violence. When they found him, all fingers would have pointed her way, and who would have believed her?

Staring down at the rumpled sheets of the bed he'd shared with his wife, she realized she'd come here to prove to herself that he still cared for her, and that he would never have wanted to hurt her. But if that had been true, why would he have chosen this life, with Becky, and not her?

She brushed tears from her eyes and cursed her stupidity. Derek had so casually hurt her in the past, when she'd needed him to stay true to all the promises they had made each other. While she'd tried to put back together the pieces of her broken life, he'd grown tired of waiting. When she'd welcomed him back, he'd been unwilling to come to her—at least, not fully. He'd wanted her, but he'd wanted Becky more, and Jessa had let herself believe a lie.

From the corner of her eye, she caught a flash of black lying on the bed. A book. Did Derek keep a journal? It seemed unlikely, but she crawled over the mattress, pulling a black plastic three-ring binder from the tangled sheets. She flipped it over, a lump of dread in her throat at the thought it might be their wedding album. Then, she saw what had to be a devil symbol drawn in silver ink on the front—the circle around an inverted star—just like she'd seen warnings about all through her youth group years. Silly superstition yanked her hand back, but she forced herself to open the book. The heavy-metal loser kids in high school had carved the same lines into the desks and the devil had never materialized in English class, even if it had felt like hell. She flipped open the cover and the fleeting feeling of relief fell into the sinkhole of her stomach. There, with heart-dotted *i* and all, was Sarah Boniface's name. It was on the bottom of every page.

It had been a mistake to come here. She turned away from the bedroom and started back down the hallway, the sound of footsteps in the living room jolting her into panic. She'd never been afraid of Derek before, but now as she stood clutching stolen property, she didn't know how he would react. The footsteps came closer to the hallway. Those familiar footsteps, the sound of his breathing. She knew him so well, and not at all. Her heart hammered against her ribs. He didn't know she was there. She could hide in the bathroom, and sneak out when he left. But if he found her there, how would she explain herself?

It was too late. He rounded the corner and looked at her with wide-eyed shock, and his gaze dropped to the book in her hands. Then she knew. And he knew, as well.

With all of her might, Jessa rushed him and threw her shoulder into his midsection, keeping low and exploding up the way he had taught her when he'd been on the football team. Only now he wasn't wearing pads and bracing for the force in a practice drill, and he stumbled back with a loud grunt, leaving her free to run for the door. A row of plastic ducks on a cord wrapped around her ankle, and she fell painfully to one knee as a chorus of quacks went up around her.

The binder sprang from her hands and she grabbed for it, tucking it close to her chest with one arm. Derek grabbed at her shirt, and she twisted free, kicking the ducks away and lunging for the door. She opened it and slammed it hard into his face before sprinting through and into the overgrown lawn.

The hot air burned her lungs, and pain shot through her knee with every step, but Derek was strong, and she knew he would follow her, so she had to keep going. Heads of blackjacks thumped against her legs as she ran for the road. She crossed it, then cleared the ditch on the other side and plunged into the cornfield.

"Jessa," Derek called behind her, his calm tone a put-on if she ever heard one. "Jessa, come on back, baby. I'm not gonna hurt you!"

Yes, you will, she pounded into her brain, to keep running. And strangely, she thought of Graf's promise the night before: *I'm not going to let anybody hurt you.* She trusted him more than she trusted the man chasing her, and she forced her aching body to keep moving forward. Trapped between two tightly planted rows, she had no other choice but to move forward, pushing glossy green leaves aside so they wouldn't slap her in the face.

At the end of the rows the ground rose up, and she stumbled, clutching at the tall grass to grope her way up the bank with one hand as she struggled to hold the binder with the other. Her shoes slipped on the soft dirt, and the plants she used as handholds lost their footing in the soil, so she clawed at the dirt, shoulders aching, until she reached the top. Just another few hundred feet, and she would be home safe. She raced across the blacktop for the dirt road—she wouldn't go through the stand of trees and risk seeing Chad's mutilated body, even if it was the difference between life and death. Her every instinct screamed to look over her shoulder, to see if Derek still followed, but that would be a mistake; she knew it in her heart. She would turn her head and see him, and that would be when she stumbled and he overtook her. She wouldn't let that happen, not when she was this close to safety.

The lawn had never looked so welcoming as when her feet finally landed on the grass, and her whole body ached to drop down and rest now that she was beneath the sheltering arms of the oak in the front yard. But she pressed on, her breath wheezing from her lungs, the steps to the porch almost her undoing. She reached the door and pushed it open, summoning as much air as she could to scream, "Graf!" as Derek finally overtook her and carried her to the ground.

Derek's hand twisted in her ponytail and he wrenched her head back, slamming her face forward into the floor. Then, he lifted off her, and in the mind-blowing pain that paralyzed her, all Jessa knew was that Graf had saved her, and now everything would be okay.

She rolled to her back in time to see Graf open his mouth and rip the skin just beneath Derek's ear. Smoke rose off Graf's shoulders from the light streaming through the windows, but it didn't deter him from sucking down Derek's blood. Before Jessa could cry out a warning, Derek ripped the HOME, SWEET HOME placard off the wall beside the door and bashed Graf in the face with it. Stunned, Graf let go, just for an instant, and Derek elbowed him in the chest and took off through the door, leaping over the porch railing as Graf ran after him.

Jessa shot to her feet and caught Graf by the arm before he could reach the top of the porch steps. She tugged, hard, bringing both of them crashing to the floor just inside, and covered him with her body as she tried to kick it closed.

"What were you doing?" she screamed as he struggled from under her. She climbed to her feet almost as fast as he did and blocked the door with her body. "You're going to get killed!"

"He knows what I am now! I've got to go after him!" Graf argued, but he didn't make another attempt to leave.

"You'll never catch him now, not before you burn up." She knew he already had given up for that reason, but it felt like it needed to be said out loud. They weren't giving up. Their hands were tied.

"Look at you," Graf said, reaching for her face. She

flinched, and the motion made the contact between his fingers and her flesh more painful.

"He's going to tell everyone," she said, ignoring Graf's hand gently cupping her jaw. "We have to get out of here."

"Where are we going to go? It's full daylight out—I can't leave. And we can't get out of town." He said this as though she were a child being told she couldn't have a birthday party. Gentle, understanding, but firm. "Let's get some ice on your nose."

She marveled at Graf's calmness as he got ice from the freezer and towels from the kitchen drawer.

"You got a first-aid kit?" he asked.

She nodded. "In the bathroom."

"Let's go up there, then," he said, almost cheerfully reassuring. She'd expected him to say, "I told you so," and possibly even do a jackass end-zone dance when he said it. His kindness really threw her for a loop.

Jessa showed him where the kit was, and watched with fascination as he removed alcohol swabs and bandages. She covered the single window with a towel, then looked in the mirror and saw a long scrape across her forehead, and blood clotting at both of her nostrils, two long tracks of blood across her lips and down her chin.

"Sit," he ordered, lowering the toilet lid. She obeyed, and he tore open a swab and began to gently dab at her forehead.

"We should be boarding up the windows and preparing for siege," she said, drawing in a breath at the stinging cold.

"Why do you say that?" He frowned as he wiped the blood and dirt from her wound.

Jessa thought of the binder downstairs, lying forgotten on the floor. If anyone walked in and saw that, she'd be in a world of hurt. She'd be right where Sarah was now. "I found something in Derek's house. A notebook. He's going to want it back, and he can definitely use the fact that I've got it in my possession against us."

"Like what kind of a notebook?" Graf leaned close and blew a stream of cold breath over the liquid on her forehead. "That help?"

"My mom used to do that with peroxide," she said lamely.

"I'm a nurturer. Wait, did you say, 'in Derek's house'?"

Jessa sucked in a breath, and waited until he looked up, into her guilty eyes.

"Oh, come on. You didn't go over there." His frown deepened into one of disappointment.

"I had to know. I don't expect you to understand." She looked down at her hands. They were torn up from fighting.

"Damn it, Jessa!" Graf threw something at the bathtub, and it ricocheted loudly around the porcelain interior.

"You don't have to yell," she said meekly. It was a ploy to keep him from being too mean, too loud. If he was, she wouldn't be able to stay calm. She would respond in kind, and she didn't know if she had enough energy for more fighting.

Thankfully, his anger seemed to diminish. "That was stupid," he admonished, dropping to one knee and taking her foot in his hands. "And now your ankle is all fucked up."

She winced and pulled her leg back. He was right, it did look bad: swollen and purple with bruises. He pulled her shoe off carefully, though it couldn't have been done completely painlessly, and tossed it aside. His hand was cold against her calf.

She closed her eyes, but she couldn't stop the tears from coming.

"Don't, don't," Graf murmured, his arms closing around her. She leaned her head on his shoulder. Though his body was cold and his shirt was soaked with blood, he felt safe to her. Safer than she'd felt in years.

"There's only so much of this a guy can take," he whispered. "We're not going to do this holding-and-crying thing every day, are we?"

Despite the sadness swelling under her ribs, she laughed through her tears. "This is ridiculous."

His breath was strangely warm as it stirred her hair. "Yeah, well, don't tell any of my friends. If this gets out, I'll lose a lot of vampire street cred."

She laughed again, and he continued. "I'm serious. It would be like someone finding out you console ice cream cones."

"I'm an ice cream cone?" she asked, sniffling. "That's not very flattering."

"I could have said 'side of beef,' but I'm a gentleman." He leaned back and hooked a finger under her chin, tilting her face up to his. "Fine. A strawberry sundae."

"That's not much better," she began. "What about a coo—"

His lips gently brushed hers, and the rest of her sentence was lost to a sharp, startled breath. As suddenly as the kiss had happened, it was over.

"Sorry." He wouldn't meet her eyes. "Your ankle, right."

She sat, silent, as he fumbled with the first-aid kit. He pulled out an Ace bandage and began unwinding it. With surprising quickness, he bound up her sprained ankle and immobilized it, then got a washcloth and wiped the blood from her face with efficiency that lacked the tender concern he'd shown before.

It wasn't a difficult change to adapt to. Derek had been a master of expressing, then immediately withdrawing, affection.

The fact that she'd compared Graf to Derek bothered her more than it should have.

"We need to think about what's going to happen

when Derek tells everybody in town that you're a vampire," she said, taking up Graf's cues to stay detached.

"It's all going to depend on whether or not they believe it." Graf tossed the washcloth over the side of the pedestal sink. "Or whether Derek is stupid enough to tell them how he found out."

"He won't be. He'll make up some story." But Graf had a point about them not believing. "Maybe they'll think he's drunk. Or stupid. But we still have that binder."

"They already know he's stupid… But you're right. We might have a fight on our hands, eventually. What's in that binder that he's going to be so hot on keeping under wraps?"

"I'm not sure, but it's Sarah's." She cleared her throat. "Sarah Boniface's, that girl I told you about. Everyone thought she was a witch, and with the way things in town are…"

"Right, angry mob. Hue and cry. Gotcha." He rubbed a hand over his chin. "Okay, so what do you think we should do? Hide someplace else?"

The thought of leaving her house sent flutters of panic careering through her body. "No! No, we're safer if we stay here."

"Why?"

That was a good question, one Jessa wasn't prepared to answer. If she wasn't safe here, where would she be safe? "We have the gun. And supplies."

"Yeah, and we could take that stuff with us," he countered. "There has to be a bomb shelter or a cave or someplace we can hide where no one would look for us."

"Until when? Until they just give up? Anyplace we go, they'll find us. We have limited options, and they have unlimited time to search us out." She hadn't realized the sense to that before she said it. She just wanted to stay here, where she felt safe, where it seemed nothing bad could get to her.

Graf considered a moment, then agreed. "Yeah, I suppose you're right. I'm not use to thinking with the 'trapped rat' mind-set you all have. I don't think I like it."

"None of us do. All we can really do is wait and see what happens." She hated waiting. She hated the entire situation. "If we start barricading ourselves in here, or we run, we're going to look like we have a reason to be guilty. It's going to be a hell of a lot easier to deny that you're a vampire if we don't do anything out of the ordinary."

"I can't say I've convinced tougher audiences." Graf paced the length of the bathroom, his index finger tapping his lips. "Usually, people don't realize I'm a vampire until I'm eating them."

Her stomach went sour at that. "I might never eat ice cream again."

He looked up and said, "Sorry about that."

"Don't be." She struggled to stand, unable to stay in one place any longer.

She expected him to put out an arm to steady her, but instead he scooped her up in his arms again. "Let's get you somewhere you can elevate your ankle. If we do have a fight coming to us, it'll be easier if we have four working legs between us."

He carried her to the door of her bedroom, then, seeing the sunlight streaming in, turned around and headed for her parents' room. She opened her mouth to protest, but he cut her off before he could even begin. "I know, you have issues. That's terrible, and I feel really bad for you. But not bad enough that I'm going to get burned twice in one day. You can stay in here while I sleep, so if you need anything, or anything happens, I'll be able to get to you."

"If the angry villagers storm in with pitchforks and torches?" She bit back a noise of pain as he lowered her to the mattress.

A smile quirked the corner of his mouth. "Don't joke about that. It actually happens."

Their eyes met, just for a second, and she raised her head, tried to make their mouths connect, but he turned away.

"I want to kiss you," he said, before his rejection could sting her any deeper. "I want to do a lot more than kiss you. But I don't want it to be because Derek hurt you."

"It's not—" she began, but he shook his head, cutting her off.

"It's a big thing for me to admit, about a human. Don't make it harder to turn you down." He kissed her forehead, then grabbed a pillow and propped her foot up on it. Then he pulled the bedspread off the bed and headed for the door.

"Where are you going?" she asked, a little desperately.

"I'll be out in the hall, if you need anything."

The door closed behind him, and Jessa flopped back on the pillow, staring up at the popcorn ceiling, and listened to him settle down just on the other side of the door.

Thirteen

Graf couldn't sleep, and it wasn't just because every seam and join in the hardwood floor had some personal vendetta against his spine.

What the hell had happened? He pored over every second of the last few days, scrutinizing every one. Jessa sure hadn't gone out of her way to welcome him when he'd first gotten into town. And she hadn't been pleasant…ever. Maybe he didn't like pleasant. He sure liked Jessa.

Maybe it was some kind of cabin fever. Maybe it was inevitable, if you were stuck with someone for long enough, you'd start to like them. You'd have to, or go crazy.

All he knew was that when he'd seen Derek putting his hands on her, he'd wanted to kill. And the night before, with Chad.

That was it. He was feeling bad for her because two people had tried to kill her since he'd arrived.

No, he couldn't convince himself of that, either. Normally, he hated helplessness. If he hadn't depended on her so much, he would have killed her the first night he'd been here. And she wasn't right in the head. She was too attached to this damned house, and to the past. And she was human.

So, why did he want to go into that bedroom and hold her and tell her everything was going to be all right? Nothing else—he'd meant it when he'd said he didn't want to be consolation for Derek. That was just more to worry about. Why not go in for the kill, figuratively? She was rejected and hurting and willing. Totally easy lay. But he couldn't do it.

He dozed off for a while, and woke to a dark hallway. His internal clock told him it wasn't sundown yet. A soft roll of thunder prompted him to get to his feet, and stretching the kinks out of his back, he went to the window in Jessa's room. Outside, fat drops of rain pelted the house, and an electric gray coated the underside of the clouds. On top of the vanity with too many coats of rubbery white paint sat framed photos. Jessa and Derek, in their caps and gowns, and Becky at Jessa's side, beaming. Jessa and Derek at prom. Jessa and her parents. He picked up the graduation picture and tapped the frame against his palm.

He carried it with him to the next room, where Jessa lay asleep, a tattered paperback open over her face. An unwilling smile twitched Graf's mouth, and he lifted the book off her, wondering how she hadn't suffocated. The motion was enough to stir her, and her eyelids fluttered open. "I fell asleep."

"I noticed." He set the book on the bedside table, facedown to keep her place.

"What time is it?" She sat up, yawning.

He checked the alarm clock. "If that's right, it's five o'clock."

"It's right." She frowned at the picture he still held. "Snooping in my room?"

"I was checking the weather, accidentally snooping." He sat beside her. "Nice picture."

He'd expected Jessa to look sad, maybe shed a few more tears for Derek the dickhead. But she actually smiled as she studied the picture. "Ah, the good old days."

"So, what happened between then and now?" He took the frame from her hands and placed it on the nightstand.

"The usual stuff," she said with a shrug.

"I don't think it's very usual for a best friend to steal someone's boyfriend." Then again, he wasn't familiar with the female concept of friendship. It seemed like a lot of backstabbing and bitching, from what he'd seen of Sophia's relationships with other women.

"She didn't steal him. I threw him away." The sadness in her voice was different now when she talked about him. Like someone talking about a person who'd done them wrong a long time ago, not just this morning. "After my parents died, he tried. He wanted to be there for me, but we were so young. And we were stuck here… It was a lot for anyone to take."

"You lost your parents," Graf said, surprised to find himself arguing on her side. "He couldn't have expected you to—"

"No, I know. That's what everyone said. But if I couldn't be a good girlfriend for him, how could I have expected him to be a good boyfriend? I isolated myself for months. I didn't want to leave the house or have anyone come into it." She paused. "That hasn't changed much. If we had stayed together, I would probably have kept shutting him out. And the college thing—I came back here when the accident happened." An audible wobble hit her voice when she mentioned it. "And the morning I was supposed to go back, we got trapped."

"Bad timing."

"You're telling me." She laughed bitterly. "But even going to college was the real beginning of the end for Derek and me. He thought he was going to get some big football scholarship, but it never materialized. So, he started working on Becky's parents' farm. And from there…"

"He started working on Becky."

She nodded and grimaced. "It's amazing how

clear it all is when you look back on it. At the time, I thought it was the ideal situation. He was going to be making enough money that he could move to Columbus to be with me, eventually. But I guess he'd always had a little crush on Becky, and vice versa."

A louder crack of thunder preceded a knock on the door downstairs, and they both jumped.

"I'll get it." He got to his feet. "Stay here, unless I tell you otherwise." He would be damned if whoever it was would hurt her. Not after he'd kept her alive through two attempted murders. Three, if monsters can be said to "murder" people.

He realized halfway down that he still wore the stained T-shirt, so he whipped it over his head and tossed it behind him, hoping it landed bloody-side down.

The visitor knocked again while he made his way down the stairs, and again as he paused to kick the black binder under the couch. One more knock brought him impatiently to the door. He opened it in the middle of the next knock. "What do you want?" he snarled, before realizing who stood before him.

June's features were lost in the recesses of a hooded sweatshirt and a rain poncho. "Good to see you again, too." She gestured to the three figures behind her. "Mind if we come in? They need to talk to Jessa."

"Jessa's in bed," he said, knowing what they would

think from his shirtless appearance. "Can you come back later?"

"Well, we don't mean to interrupt you," June said with a grin.

"This is serious business, son." Tom Stoke, the sheriff, stepped through the door, crowding June out of the way. It chafed Graf's nerves to be called "son," even though the man couldn't have known that Graf was older than him.

Graf blocked the rest of them with his body. "What's going on?"

"We're really more interested in talking to Jessa," one of the other men said, and June shrugged.

"I'll go on up and get her," Graf said eventually, opening the door and ushering the rest of them inside, where Sheriff Stoke wandered the living room, examining it as though it were a crime scene. "Make yourselves at home for a minute. She's gonna need help. She had a bad fall."

He hoped she'd heard him up there. He had no doubt she'd been listening. When he got to the top of the stairs, she stood in the doorway already. "Who's down there?" she asked, a little louder than normal. To show she wasn't hiding anything, he assumed.

He picked up the shirt he definitely needed to hide and pushed it under the bed before returning to her side to help her limp downstairs. "Some dudes, and June." He noticed her shudder as he lifted her and cradled her against his bare chest. He hoped it was a shiver of restrained sexual desire and not fear at the mention of the council, but he figured it was, sadly, the latter.

When they reached the living room, June, who'd remained standing by the door, gasped. "Honey, what happened to you?"

"Bad fall," Jessa said with an unconcerned laugh. "I was going after an egg up in the hayloft and lost my balance."

"Fell straight down," Graf supplied. "I thought I was gonna get to her and she would be dead."

The same man who had spoken before cleared his throat. "Well, I'm sorry to hear about that, but we really need to get down to business. None of us want to be out past nightfall, not with what's been happening lately."

"Why, what happened?" Jessa asked as Graf set her in the armchair. Lies rolled off her tongue smooth and convincing. It amazed him and scared him, just a little. He'd never met a better liar than Sophia, and Jessa wasn't far off.

Before the man could answer, Jessa laughed, startling everyone in the room. "I'm sorry, I just realized that my friend here doesn't know most of y'all. This is Graf."

"We've met," Stoke said, smoothing a hand over his yellowed beard. "This here's Dan Beech and Wade Cook."

"Nice to meet you. I hope it's under good

circumstances," Graf added quickly. "But I'm guessing not."

"No, son. We're here because there's been another disappearance." Tom fixed his beady gaze on Jessa. "Chad Shelby."

Jessa didn't miss a beat. "*What? Oh my God!* Well, where did he go?"

"We don't think he went anywhere," the one named Wade said, scratching at the short stubble that covered his head. "We think something happened to him."

"Well, how long has he been gone? Did anybody tell his mom?" Jessa asked, looking each man straight in the eye.

"She knows," Tom said. When he spoke, only his mustache moved.

"Well, how's she doing?" Jessa continued, as if blithely unaware that they had come here to interrogate her about the murder.

The second he thought it, Graf realized he must have looked guilty from the start. And damn it, June had seen. She shifted her weight from one foot to the other and pushed her hood down.

"Not so good, Jessa. That's why we're here." Tom looked to the other two men as if seeking support. "We know he was headed out to see you last night, after the search party came in. And we know that he never came back."

"Is he here now, Jessa?" June asked quietly.

"No, he's not here," she said, still giving those honest, bewildered glances. "He didn't come by last night, either. I waited up for a while, but he never showed. The last time I saw him was yesterday morning, when he brought over the stuff from the auction."

The men exchanged glances. There was something they weren't telling her. They were trying to let her hang herself. Graf would have been worried, if he didn't have total faith in Jessa's deceptive little mind.

Tom clicked his tongue and rested his hands on his knees. "The thing is, Derek says he walked over with Chad. Says he saw him come into your house."

"Well, if Derek said, it must be true," Jessa said, dropping all pretensions of friendliness.

Dan broke in. "We're not saying we believe his word over yours, Jessa. Hell, I'm wondering what he was doing skylarking around while his wife and babies have gone missing. But we had to check it out."

"I know you did. And I know you gentlemen like to keep a real tight ship around here. But I gotta say, it's pretty insulting to have you come in here and insinuate that I did something to Chad." She paused. "That's what you came to check out, isn't it? Or were you hoping you'd find him here, so you could run back to town and spread the gossip around?"

"Now, you know we ain't that type of people—" Tom began.

Jessa interrupted him. "Yeah, well, you're the type of people who would believe Derek when he hasn't told anything more than a half-truth in the past five years. I didn't see either Derek or Chad last night. I guess that was a good thing, because my new friend here is pretty possessive. We hit it off right away, and he doesn't really care for other guys coming around."

Graf wondered where she was going with this lie—okay, maybe it wasn't a lie, because he hadn't liked the two guys who had come around so far—when it all became clear.

She smirked. "If you all saw Derek today, you saw what Graf here did to him for sniffing around me this morning."

"He said It did that to him," Wade said with a grin. "I guess he didn't want to admit he got his ass kicked."

Tom didn't look like he was enjoying the exchange as much as the councilman was. "If you don't want trouble, you'll all stay away from each other from now on, you hear?"

"It's a small town, sheriff," Jessa said, meeting his cold glare. "Believe me, I haven't been trying to run into him."

Tom stood and held out his hand to Graf. "I told

you to keep your nose clean, and we wouldn't have any problems."

"Clean as a whistle, sheriff," Graf said, but he couldn't manage to make it sound sarcastic. It came out mostly nervous.

The council filed out after Tom, but June hung back. "You just made yourself some enemies," she warned Graf. "And there's blood on your carpet."

Then she closed the door and left.

"We're so fucked," Jessa whispered, staring in horror at the door. "We're so fucked."

Graf held a finger to his lips and went to the window to make sure they were all out of earshot. All four figures were walking across the lawn, Tom gesturing broadly with his short arms, the rest nodding in agreement. June had pulled up her hood and rain poncho, and walked with her hands in her pockets.

Graf turned back to Jessa. "You did so good. I almost believed you when you said you hadn't seen Chad."

"They could tell," she said, trembling. "I lie all the time. They know better than to believe me. And June saw the blood on the carpet."

"Yeah, but she didn't say anything in front of the other guys." Why she hadn't was anybody's guess, but Graf wasn't going to complain. "She knows something isn't right about me, that's for sure. I can tell by the way she looks at me. But she's not ready to tell them about it. Which makes me think she's not too keen on her town council buddies."

"They're not too keen on her, either," Jessa agreed. "Tom thinks she pokes her nose where it doesn't belong."

"She does, and that's why she's valuable to have on our side." *If she is on our side,* Graf thought, but he didn't need to say anything like that to Jessa and get her all paranoid.

"And Derek didn't say anything about you biting him." Jessa paled. "Oh, God, he had that bite. And he said It did it, which would have covered for us. But I told them."

"It's okay, they seemed pretty satisfied to believe Derek got smacked down." If anyone asked, Graf would be happy to admit to taking a chunk out of Derek. It wouldn't make him seem like the sanest person in town, but it would at least keep people from messing with them.

"They're going to find Chad's body here, close by the house, and they're gonna know we did it." She dropped her head to her hands. "I wish we could run, just get out of here and never look back."

"Says the woman who didn't want to leave her house just a few hours ago." Graf took her by the shoulders. "It's going to be okay. Just keep doing what you did tonight. I don't think I've ever seen a better liar."

"Thanks?" she said tentatively.

"Believe me, that means a lot coming from me." He stepped back. "Do you think we need to talk to June? Handle things with her?"

"I don't know. I guess it wouldn't be a bad idea. But what are we going to tell her? 'Hey, he's a vampire, don't say anything'?" Jessa chewed her lip. "Maybe we could ask her what the town council wanted with me, and if there's anything I should be worried about… We can go after I get my chores done."

"How are you going to do chores with a sprained ankle?" He didn't like the idea of her just walking around on it. If they were in as much trouble as she thought they were, it wouldn't help if she didn't at least try to heal.

"I'll get by. This isn't the first sprained ankle I've ever had. And chickens get hungry regardless of how you're feeling." Farm-girl logic.

Graf wondered if she knew how stupid she sounded. "Look, this storm doesn't seem to be letting up. It'd probably be safe for me to help you out."

"But it's daytime."

"The cloud cover will protect me. If it breaks up, you'd be free of at least one problem, right?" He laughed a little, but it sounded lame when she didn't laugh with him.

She sighed and said, "If you think you'll be okay," but it was obvious that she didn't want his help, and didn't even think she needed it.

He took a T-shirt out of the bureau upstairs, then helped her limp out to the barn. They were barely halfway across the backyard when Jessa said softly, "Oh, no."

Graf caught the tang of blood above the electricity in the air. The warm rain battered down on the white and brown feathers scattered in front of the barn door.

When they reached the animals, Jessa bent down and lifted one limp body. "Oh, no," she repeated, tears that she didn't shed coming out in her voice.

"I don't think It was here," Graf said, scanning the yard. "I don't see any tracks, or smell it."

"You could smell It?" she asked, dropping to one knee to inspect another dead chicken.

"It has a very distinct scent." He knelt beside her and gingerly lifted one torn wing. Ugh, chicken blood. "This is all crawling with salmonella, you know."

She sat back on her heels, making a pained face as she jostled her wrapped ankle. "No, It has taken chickens from me before. All that's left are feet and feathers. It eats the rest. Someone else did this."

"The council guys?" It didn't seem like a good way to get reelected, but they had also put someone to death for witchcraft and scored votes.

She shook her head. "No, we saw them go, and they wouldn't have had time to double back. This was a warning."

"Oh, that was nice of Derek." He paused. "That is who you're thinking of, isn't it?"

She nodded. "Let's take these into the barn and start butchering them. No sense wasting the meat."

Graf helped her, unenthusiastically, to bring the chickens into the barn. Fifteen of the poor bastards, hacked to pieces by the chicken-murdering son of a bitch.

"Go in the house and get the big silver pot out from under the sink," Jessa ordered. "Fill it up and put it on to boil, so we can scald 'em. I'll wring the heads off the ones who still have them."

There was really no place he would rather be than away from something that involved twisting the heads off anything. Unless it was him doing the twisting, and the head being Derek's. He stepped out of the barn, back into the rain, and immediately the smell of It hit him in the face like a dead chicken. "Jessa, we have to get back in the house right now!" he hissed over his shoulder.

And as soon as he spoke, It came around the corner of the house. He got back in the barn and had his hand over Jessa's mouth before she could say a word.

"Listen very carefully," he whispered. "It is out there right this second. Where is the best place to hide?"

She raised one finger and pointed up. He tossed her trembling body over his shoulder and scaled the ladder into the hayloft. When they reached the top, he dumped her down onto a pile of folded burlap sacks and whispered, "King Kong made that look a lot easier."

"Quick, get behind the engine." She stabbed her finger toward the rusting shape of a tractor engine sitting on a platform of cinder blocks. A rope sling looped around the hunk of metal from when it was first lifted up to be forgotten in the hayloft.

Graf let her crawl into the space behind the engine, right up against the wall. If It somehow made it up to them, It would have to go through him to get to Jessa. It would probably still get her, at that point, but at least he would put up a fight.

She pressed her face to the light seeping in between the boards and said, "Oh my God. Derek's out there."

Good, was the first thing Graf thought. Then he thought of what it would look like if Derek turned up dead on Jessa's property, and Chad not far from it. "I'm going out there."

"No—" Jessa whispered harshly. "Don't. It…"

"It doesn't see him?"

"No—no. It's…" She covered her mouth. "He's leading…It!"

Graf joined her at the wall. Outside, Derek walked five steps in front of the creature, taking a slow path around the house. They circled it two or three times, then headed toward the barn.

Graf held his finger to his lips in warning, but he was pretty sure Jessa couldn't have spoken if she'd wanted to. Shock and confusion were plain on her face, but anger was there, too, as though she had some idea what was going on.

Which was good, because Graf sure as hell didn't.

Derek stepped inside the barn, and Graf and Jessa ducked. "Jessa?" he called cheerfully. "Jessa, baby, are you in here?"

Jessa's fingers curled into a fist as she crouched beside Graf.

"Honey, we need to talk about what happened this morning," he continued, his boots falling heavily on the floorboards below. "We both lost our tempers, is all. I thought you were a burglar at first, you know? We were both just freaked out and reacted badly. Why don't you come out, sugar?"

Just when Graf thought the jackass would wander around and talk to himself all day, Derek swore and stomped out of the barn. They waited until they saw him walk toward the house again, the monster tagging behind him like a pet dog, before they spoke again.

"What is going on?" Jessa asked, her voice low. "What was Derek doing with It?"

"Well, I think it's pretty clear how It got here." Graf shut up when he saw the creature whip its massive head around to stare in their direction.

Mercifully, Derek called out, "Come on, you stupid demon," without looking over his shoulder. The creature sniffed the air, big puffs of steam issuing from its nostrils, then turned and followed its master.

"Derek can't even do his own laundry, how'd he manage to get that thing here?" Jessa hissed, pushing away from the wall. "And why would he want it?"

"I don't know." Graf stood to get a better view of the two leaving the yard. "The important thing is that now we know who's behind It. If he did it, he can undo it."

Jessa rubbed her temples. "He has to have something to do with it, but I don't know that he's smart enough to actually do it."

They waited in the barn until sundown, to be sure It was gone and Graf was safe to be outside. Then they climbed down from the hayloft and retrieved the gun from the house. Immediately, Jessa turned right back out the front door and Graf followed after.

"Who do we go to with this info?" he asked over the crunch of their shoes on the driveway.

"June." Jessa had the gun over her shoulder, and, even with her ankle banged up, she marched like a toy soldier on some kind of revenge mission. Graf kept up with her, and hoped her anger would last until they reached the bar.

June's Place was even more crowded than usual; Graf could tell from the shapes moving in the window. Bicycles stood in parking spaces that cars used to occupy. Jessa slowed as they entered the lot. "Something isn't right."

"I was just thinking that." The nagging feeling that they should run prickled in the back of his mind. "I guess the only way we find out what is by going in there."

Jessa went in first, her fingers clenched tight on the butt of the gun. The second they stepped through the door, the loud conversation ceased, and all eyes turned to them.

Derek stood on the bar, and at the sight of them, he grinned an evil-looking grin.

Fourteen

Hands closed around Jessa's arms, and she saw Dave Stuckey going for Graf. *Please, don't do any vampire superstrength thing,* she prayed silently. Graf wasn't dumb, though. He shrugged Dave's hand off his arm, but when he grabbed him again, he let him.

"What the hell's going on?" Graf demanded angrily.

June wasn't behind the bar. For once, she sat on the other side of it, watching the commotion with an expression of sadness.

It was Sarah Boniface all over again. Jessa's knees went weak, but she forced herself to stand. They weren't going to get any sign of guilt, real or imagined, out of her.

Sheriff Stoke rose from his seat behind June and hitched his pants up by his huge oval belt buckle. "You two are under arrest on suspicion of witchcraft."

"You have got to be kidding me," Graf growled. "Witchcraft? Do I look like a witch to you?"

"You look like a vampire to me," Derek shouted, and everyone else in the bar began shouting. It was clear that some didn't believe him. But worse, it was clear that some did.

"Quiet!" Sheriff Stoke yelled over the noise. "I said quiet, goddamn it!"

Jessa looked to June and, once the crowd had quieted, said, "Are you really going to sit there and listen to that? In your bar? Tell them how ridiculous he's being!"

She shook her head, true regret written on every feature of her face. "I'm sorry, Jessa. I can't do that."

The hush that fell over the bar was eerie, and strangely convincing that Jessa and June were the only two standing in it. Jessa shook her head slowly. "You don't really believe—"

"I've thought for a long time now that there was something not right about him. And Derek shows up with a scar that looks like somebody bit him, saying Graf's a vampire.… There was blood on your rug when I was there today."

A chill ran down Jessa's spine. "This is crazy."

"If you want a witch," Graf said, nodding toward Derek, "look at him. He's the one who brought that demon here."

"How'd you know It is a demon?" Sheriff Stoke

asked, like a detective in a TV show. "Seems to me the woman who's hanging around with a vampire might have more call to consort with a pet demon than a man who lost his wife recently."

"That doesn't make any sense!" Graf shouted, incredulous. "In the first place, I'm not a vampire. That's ridiculous. Everyone knows vampires don't exist. And you can't say that Derek wouldn't summon a demon because his wife just left—the demon's been around for years and his wife just left yesterday."

"Summoning sounds like some witch talk, if you ask me," Sheriff Stoke said with satisfaction, and several people cheered.

"You're out of your minds!" Graf shouted, but it was pretty clear no one was listening.

"I know why she did it," Derek called over everyone's voices. "She thought if she trapped me here, I'd have to marry her. Or I'd leave Becky for her. She came over to my house and told me all about it this morning."

Jessa opened her mouth, but closed it when she realized that anything else she said would be even more damning. The entire town believed she was some kind of crazy, desperate mantrap. And a liar. It wasn't too big a leap to witchcraft, she guessed. They'd taken Sarah for less.

"Are we even going to get a trial?" Graf asked Sheriff Stoke, his jaw clenched.

"We aren't barbarians. You'll get your trial." It

was clear he was proud of his efficiency. "We'll need about a day to gather evidence. In the meantime, you'll be held at the jail."

"Just let us go home," Jessa pleaded. "Where are we gonna run?"

"There are procedures that have to be followed," the sheriff said, his chest puffed up with the posturing of his office. "Come on, boys, let's move 'em."

Jessa fought against whoever it was that held her—she couldn't get a good look—and glared at Derek as she got dragged toward the door. He looked back guiltily, like a dog that's done wrong and knows he can't hide it. She hoped the sight of her being dragged away to die haunted him to his final days.

She held out hope that once they were outside, Graf would fight their way free, but he didn't resist as they marched them out. His hand found hers for just a second as they were jostled by the throng that followed, and it gave her some comfort.

The "jail" wasn't far up the road. The combination police and fire and ambulance station had housed a single, lonely jail cell that had rarely been occupied for more than a few hours before the state police would come and pick up the detainees to take them to the county jail. That building was long gone, destroyed by It in the first, early days of their confinement. They hadn't had much call for a proper jail, so since then, if someone caused trouble they spent a few days in the teachers' lounge at the old high school.

"Are you kidding me?" Graf said with a laugh as they walked up the long drive. "We can break out of here in no time."

Sheriff Stoke panted a little as he tried to keep up pace. "Don't be foolish, boy. We're going to watch you like a hawk. You step one foot out of your cell, and we'll put a bullet in your heart."

"My heart? Not my head?" he asked. "That sounds cruel and unusual to me."

"Not for your kind," the sheriff said, and he elbowed him in the chest. The blow wasn't as hard as it was meant to be, because the sheriff was having a tough enough time talking and walking.

When they reached one of the three entrances to the school, Sheriff Stoke found a key on his key ring and unlocked the double doors.

Jessa hadn't been inside the building since she'd graduated five years ago. Despite being abandoned and shut up for so long, the halls smelled exactly the same as when she'd left on that last day of high school. When the sheriff flipped on the lights, every illuminating bulb took her back to strolling the halls with Becky, slipping notes into Derek's locker. As Sheriff Stoke marched them down the hall, Jessa took note of her old homeroom, the stairs down to the gym.

They reached the teachers' lounge, and Sheriff

Stoke opened the door and motioned them inside. "I'm locking you in, but if you get any bright ideas about escaping, know that there will be some real angry folks waiting on the lawn all night to see you put up to trial. They'll rip you apart, if I don't shoot you first."

"Thanks for the hospitality, Sheriff," Graf said dryly as he followed Jessa inside. The sheriff didn't bother with a retort, just closed the door, leaving them in total darkness.

"There isn't a window in here," Jessa said, trying to sound positive about it. "At least there's that, right?"

The sound of a light switch flipping back and forth filled the darkness. "They could have at least turned the lights on."

As her eyes adjusted to the darkness, Jessa could make out the general shape of the furniture in the room. A couch and two armchairs surrounded a low oval table, and an area rug covered the space. Where the carpet ended and the default school tile resumed there was a taller lunch table and heavy plastic chairs, beyond that a kitchenette. Jessa inspected the sink, where a slippery stalactite hung from the faucet, proving that it was still connected to a water source. A small bathroom stood to the left, and nearly a whole roll of toilet paper was still on the dispenser. She made a note to come back and steal it somehow, if they weren't sentenced to death.

"Did you see how ready they were to believe him?" Graf asked, flopping down on the couch. "It's like they were just waiting for some excuse to come after you."

"That's how it works in a small town," she said, pushing on the pump top of the soap dispenser on the sink. Jackpot. "Why didn't anyone think to loot here?"

"I've never been to a small town that tried people for witchcraft. I mean, I went to Salem as a tourist, but centuries after the fact." He got up and paced from the refrigerator to the couch and back again. "Is this how it's going to end? Death by hillbilly? I'm not even a hundred years old yet."

"Don't open that refrigerator," Jessa warned. "Nobody's been here for five years, it looks like. It won't smell pretty."

Graf stopped his pacing, and though it was dark, she could tell he stared at her. "Are you completely suicidal or something? Aren't you the least bit worried about what's going to happen to you?"

"Not really. You'll figure something out." She truly believed that. "You said you weren't going to let anybody hurt me, and you haven't gone back on any of your promises yet."

"Oh, no pressure or anything, Graf." He went back to the couch and sank down. "I don't know how we're getting out of this one. If I do anything that shows them I really am a vampire, we might be able to escape somehow, but they're still going to come back. Even when I'm gone, they won't leave you alone."

His words struck her as painfully obvious, but painful nonetheless. "What do you mean, when you're gone?"

He sounded a little embarrassed when he said, "Well, it's not like I can stay around here forever, is it? I've got a life outside of Penance."

"Right, your life. Your vampire parties and your slutty friends," she said, recoiling inside at the naked hurt in her voice.

"What the hell?" Graf said angrily. "You want me to rescue you from these redneck witch hunters, but you're going to insult my friends?"

No, she wanted to say. *No, but you're the only good thing I've had happen to me in five years, and I don't want you to go.* But she was wounded, so she just shrugged, deliberately exaggerating the movement so he could see it in the dark.

"That's really nice of you. Really nice."

"I never pretended to be nice," she shot back, though she had to struggle past a lump in her throat to speak.

Silence pressed down on her, filled with his anger, as she went through the drawers and cabinets. There wasn't anything to eat, the people who'd been incarcerated before her had taken care of that, but behind a box of trash bags under the sink she found a six-pack of Coke. She smiled at the thought of her old teachers hiding their food from one another in a futile effort to keep their coworkers from consuming their lunch. She didn't figure Coke would go bad, not even in five years, so she pulled one out and popped it open.

As she stood, she became suddenly aware of Graf standing behind her. She turned to face him, steeling herself to feign anger again, when he gripped her shoulders and pulled her against his chest, smashing their mouths together painfully. She dropped the can in surprise, and before it could hit the floor, Graf caught it and slid it across the counter.

"You're mad at me," he said, breathing fast. "You're mad because you don't want me to leave."

"Don't be stupid." She shoved at his chest, but it was a halfhearted effort. "I've been trying to get rid of you since you showed up in town."

He didn't bother with an answer, but kissed her again, and though she thought it might be wise to resist, she couldn't help herself. She put her arms around his neck, opened her mouth to the cold slide of his tongue. It was all she could do to keep from wrapping her legs around him and climbing him like a tree.

"Don't leave," she begged against his mouth. "Don't leave me."

"I'm not going anywhere," he promised, smearing a kiss across her jaw.

"I know you're not," she said with a laugh that dissolved into a moan. "But don't."

He lifted her up to sit on the edge of the counter, kissing a wet path across her neck as his arms slid under the back of her T-shirt to unhook her bra.

It had been so long since she'd felt this good. So long since she didn't have to shut down the voices in her head telling her that she was a whore, filthy, just reaffirming everyone's suspicions of her. And it felt good to be wanted, not because she was comfortable and familiar and stupidly willing. Well, she was stupidly willing to let a vampire put his mouth on her neck, but she trusted him. Maybe that was stupid, too.

"I swear to God, if some inbred redneck busts in on us, I'm going to rip their goddamned throats out." And as if to prove his point, he yanked her shirt up, and she had no choice but to raise her arms to let him pull it over her head. He turned fast, taking her with him, and she locked her legs around his hips. The cold Formica tabletop shocked her as he laid her on the table. He stood between her legs and pulled his shirt over his head, exposing the ridges of muscle she had covertly admired earlier in the day. God, it had been hard to concentrate on keeping her lies straight in front of June and the town council while he stood not two feet from her, all shirtless and looking like a naughty firemen calendar. Just the sight of him before had made her wet and achy, and now anticipation tightened muscles she rarely acknowledged.

He smoothed his hands over the cups of her plain

cotton bra, and the look in his eyes as his gaze drifted over her breasts made her feel sexier than if she were wearing black lace. He slid the straps down her arms, then tossed it aside with a helpless groan as he leaned down to suck one tight nipple into his mouth.

She threaded her fingers through his hair and stroked his neck, then over the wide planes of his shoulders. His tongue swirled over her skin, taking a wandering path over her other breast, then down her stomach. He reached the waistband of her jeans and she sat up, pushed him back. The look of shock on his face was almost funny as she hopped down from the table and pushed him again, backing him into the cupboards. When she dropped to her knees, her meaning became clear, and he swallowed audibly as she reached for his zipper.

When she unzipped it and slid her hand inside, he brushed her hands away and pulled his jeans down over his hips. Not trying to be cool or in control, like Derek would have done. She pushed that thought right out of her head. Derek wasn't going to be in this room right now.

"Oh, wow," she said on a sigh as she gripped him, and on a throaty exhale he laughed, "Well, thank you."

She slid her hand down the considerable length of him, then trailed her tongue up, around the wide head, before closing her lips over him. She'd forgotten how much of a turn-on it was to give a guy head, how hot it was to hear him make nonsensical sounds and repeat the same words over and over, like a prayer, only profane instead of sacred. She certainly wasn't an expert, but from what she could tell, Graf was enjoying himself.

She cupped her hands around him, stroking up and down in time with the movements of her mouth, and he laid his hands on her head, then pulled them away as if he didn't trust himself.

It had always amazed Jessa how something so simple as sex could make a person forget everything else. She knew they were in danger. She knew there were a million other things they could be doing to try to save themselves. When Graf stopped her with a gentle hand on her shoulders, she didn't care about any of those other things. When he carried her to the couch and pulled her jeans off, then her panties, she didn't care about anything but the way his hands felt on her body, the way his fingers felt stroking the slick, hot flesh between her legs.

"I want to make this good for you," he rasped against her ear as he pumped his fingers in and out of her. "Just tell me what to do."

She couldn't articulate what she needed, not beyond "now" and "please," but he understood the gist of it. And she was so grateful he had, as he pushed into her, stretched her almost painfully. Then he moved inside her, each thrust forcing the breath from her lungs, each withdrawal dragging new breath down. She arched underneath him, twisted her legs around his hips, and she almost lost him, but he gripped one of her legs by the calf and hooked it over his shoulder, bent her almost in two as he drove into her. She clung to him, her hands greedy to touch more, to feel the muscles flexing under his tight, cold skin, to know every piece of him before it was all over.

She panted into his ear, moaned her appreciation over and over, until, almost too soon, she found herself back at the familiar and completely alien edge of the pleasure battering through her. In an instant, everything seemed too cold, too hot, too big, too much to feel, and then she burst, screaming, holding tight to his shoulders as he groaned and drove harder into her. As she quaked beneath him, he collapsed over her, his limbs trembling from exhaustion.

Could vampires be exhausted? She laughed at the absurd thought, at the absurd idea of where they were and what they had done. Her back stung from the rough upholstery, her legs ached like she'd run a mile. It had all been so erotic in the heat of passion. Now, it just seemed silly.

"Oh, that's very encouraging, thank you," he said, pushing himself off her.

She could only laugh harder, and she sat up, hugging her knees to her chest. "I'm sorry. I was just thinking…you're supposed to be this supernatural creature, all strong and tough, and here you are, looking like you're going to pass out or have an asthma attack from sex."

"I don't have asthma," he corrected. "And that's hard work. Always has been. You women don't think it is, because you don't have to do it."

"I'm pretty sure I had sex, too." She scraped her hair back from her face.

"Oh, yes, you did. And you're welcome, by the way." He grinned, and it sent all sorts of hot shivers through her.

She wished they could lie there longer, but she knew what was coming.

"So, when do you think they'll come get us?" he asked, reaching to the floor for his jeans. "I don't want to get caught with my pants down, literally."

"I don't know. They want to 'gather evidence,' so I guess however long they need to find proof that I'm guilty." She pressed her hands against her head. "Oh, God, they'll find Sarah's book, and we'll be doomed."

"We are not going to be doomed," Graf said with so much certainty that it was hard not to believe him. "I'm going to figure something heroic out, and you'll be fine. You said so yourself. You wouldn't lie to me, would you?"

An unexpected wave of remorse tugged her down from the giddy swell she'd been riding on. "How would you know? I'm a great liar."

"That you are." He leaned forward and gave her a

quick peck on the cheek, then stood and pulled on his jeans before strolling to the kitchenette. "You forgot your Coke."

"What are you doing?" she asked as she limped after him, feeling strangely modest. She reached for the T-shirt he'd discarded on the floor and pulled it over her head. It was one of her father's old T-shirts, but it didn't smell like him anymore. It smelled like the cedar drawers of the bureau, and the bizarre absence of scent that clung to Graf's body.

"I'm thirsty." Graf knocked the calcified crust from the faucet and ran the water until it turned from sputtering brown to clear. He left it running as he went through the cupboards.

"You can drink just plain water?" She leaned on the counter beside him, watching with fascination as he filled up a mug that proclaimed TEACHERS DO IT BY THE BOOK, as though she'd never seen anyone get a drink of water before.

He took a long swallow and wiped his mouth with his hand. "Yeah. I drank the moonshine, didn't I?"

"Yeah, I reckon you did." She knew her smile was big and goofy, but she couldn't help it. "I just had sex with a vampire."

"You did." He took another drink, and above the rim of the mug, his eyes glittered with amusement.

She bit her lip. "It was hot, too."

"That it was."

They went back to the couch, and she curled in the

corner, using the armrest as an uncomfortable pillow. Graf reached for her, saying softly, "No, come over here," and pulled her into his arms. She curled at his side, his arm around her shoulders, her head against his chest.

"Are you going to sleep sitting up?" she asked, the pull of slumber tugging at the space between her nose and mouth, the place where yawns always started.

"I'm not going to sleep. But you should." He kissed her forehead and leaned his face against her for a moment. "You can lean on me." Tenderly, as if he truly had meant every word he'd said to her before.

She burned with the need to know whether he'd just said those things, promised he wouldn't leave her, because he was looking to get laid. At the same time, she couldn't ask, because she knew he would tell her the truth, and the truth might not be what she wanted to hear. She faked a nonchalant laugh and said, "Thanks for not biting me, by the way. On *Buffy* they always want to bite when they're having sex."

"I had more important things to do than bite you," he said with a chuckle that she felt under her cheek. "Go to sleep."

Love me, she wanted to order back, and the ferocity of that desire shocked her.

It might be better not to know.

Fifteen

Graf had played it off like he hadn't wanted to drink her blood. And Jessa thought she was a good liar.

He paced the room, trying not to look at Jessa sprawled on the couch, but still glancing at her nervously every few seconds. God, the sex had been incredible. If he killed her, he wouldn't be having incredible sex with her again. Not that he would want to kill her, anyway. He was pretty sure.

Hunger was driving him crazy, and boredom, and the smell of stale nicotine that stained the walls and asbestos tile above his head. He needed a cigarette, and some blood, and even just a *People* magazine would be good after nearly a whole night of silence and worrying.

On top of that, Jessa was expecting him to come up with something brilliant to save them both. He should have told her that he wasn't brilliant. He was a good talker, but what good would talking do with a group of hill folk who probably had a combined IQ of a hundred?

But he'd promised Jessa. He had no idea what it was he felt for her, but he didn't like it. Or maybe he liked it too much. She was bossy and cranky and she lied and had tons of fucked-up emotional problems. But damn it, he was pretty sure that he…

Nah.

He scrubbed his hands over his face and went to the sink. He was so goddamned thirsty. The cup took too long to fill up, so he bent his head and swallowed straight from the tap.

"Graf?" Jessa's voice was sexy and sleepy. She sat up, scanning the darkness. "Are you okay?"

"Fine," he said, and the forced cheerfulness made him sound deranged. "Just thirsty."

"Yeah, I see that. You've got your whole head in the sink."

Lifting his mouth away from the water was like walking away from a pile of money and naked women, but he managed it and stuck the cup under the stream.

"You're thirsty for something other than water, aren't you?" she asked, and there was fear in her voice. Not on the surface, but hiding under the layers of fake sympathy. He didn't blame her. Being the only human locked in a room with a hungry vampire, he wouldn't have had sympathy for the vampire, either.

"I haven't been eating like normal since I came to town," he admitted. "I'll probably adjust, but it's like the first week on a diet, I guess. I'm miserable."

Wow, that was humbling. Telling a human that he had a weakness.

"Do you need..." Her words trailed off, and she swallowed. "I mean, you could drink some of my b-blood. If you need to."

He didn't think he'd ever needed anything as much as he needed blood at this very moment, but he couldn't do that to her. Could he?

No. For one thing, he'd gotten out of control when feeding before. He chalked up those people he'd accidentally dispatched to learning experience, and it didn't bother him. Vampires ate people. But he didn't want to risk it with Jessa.

"If you don't eat—drink, sorry—are you going to be able to stand trial and get us free?" She had a good point, but Graf still wanted to snap at her that it wasn't his fucking job to save her from the pitchforks-and-torches crowd.

He took a long, slow breath to clear his head. He wasn't angry with her. He was just cranky and hungry. "I'll be a little weak, but I'm pretty sure it will be okay."

She was a good enough liar that she could recognize his. "You don't sound okay. And you're acting like someone trying to quit smoking."

"Well, I haven't had a cigarette in a while!" he snapped. "You're not helping with all this pushing."

"I'm not helping because you're not cooperating. I'm trying to help." Her tone was surprisingly gentle and understanding. It was irritating as hell. "Why won't you let me help you?"

"Because I might kill you!" He closed his eyes and pinched the bridge of his nose. He hadn't just blurted that out, had he? It sounded weak and stupid, like he couldn't control himself. And worse, she might not trust him anymore. Worse than that, he was more worried about the trust thing than his pride.

"Well...I might die tomorrow, anyway," she said, the trace of fear gone from her voice. Maybe that was just wishful thinking.

And he felt himself getting sucked into her strange logic, wanting to believe that it would be okay to open up a vein on her and damn the consequences. "I don't like to drink from people I know. It's nothing personal. I wouldn't feel great if I killed you by accident."

"You'd feel great if you killed somebody else by accident?" she countered.

"Probably not great, but I wouldn't really care." It wasn't the answer she wanted to hear, that much was apparent from the long moment of speechlessness that kept her silent.

Finally, she cleared her throat and said, "That's not the point. You need something. We just had sex, for God's sake. The most intimate thing two people can do with each other, and I can't do something simple like this for you?"

Intimate. That was a scary word to hear out loud. "It's not about…intimacy. I don't want to hurt you."

"You won't," she insisted.

"Have you ever been bitten by a dog?" he asked, determined not to win in this battle she was trying so hard to lose.

She shrugged. "No, but it can't be that bad."

"Maybe not, but my bite would be." He came as close as he dared to her and opened his mouth, letting his fangs slide down. "Believe me, you'll feel it when these get into you. They're not precision instruments."

Her eyes widened in shock as she stared at his teeth. Then she recovered quickly and lifted up her leg to show him a scar. "They can't be worse than accidentally sticking a pitchfork tine through your foot. I don't want you to suffer."

"I don't want *you* to suffer. My answer is no." He finished off the rest of his water and tried to coax his fangs back into their resting positions. Fang blue balls were the worst.

He went back to the sink and filled up the cup again, too aware of the hurt in her silence. Comforting her wasn't an option, not when she was so willing.

"You're the first person in a long time who didn't want me to suffer," she said with a sad laugh.

He wanted her so badly. He wanted her body and her blood. He just wasn't sure which one he wanted more.

She got up from the couch and walked toward him, her feet making soft padding noises on the tile floor. Panic rose in his chest, worse than when he'd faced It, worse than the first time he'd been caught in the sun. Panic that she might touch him and send him flying off the edge, and he would hurt her.

She moved carefully, as though she felt the tension that snapped like a live wire in all of his muscles. She opened the kitchen drawers, one after another, until she withdrew something gleaming and metal. A pair of scissors.

The thought that she would cut herself to tempt him made cold sweat pop out on his forehead. He half wanted her to do it, half dreaded that it was exactly what she intended. Walking slowly toward him, she raised the scissors, and just when he thought she would make a cut, she pushed the point gently against his neck.

"If I stabbed you, what would you do?"

The weird turn of the moment took him by enough surprise that he didn't want to grab her. He kind of wanted to run from her. "I would...probably cry? Stabbing hurts."

She arched a brow. "If you were drinking my blood, and I stabbed you, would you stop?"

The answer was yes, but he couldn't tell her that. Then, there would be no reason to refuse her. Her trust overwhelmed him, crawled inside his skin and forced him to consider things he didn't want any part of.

She pushed her hair away from the left side of her neck. "Go ahead. I want you to. I'll make sure you don't hurt me."

Little did she know, if she got to the point where she was in danger, she wouldn't have the strength to stab him. He should tell her that, argue harder against her suicidal wish, even opened his mouth to do so, but what he said was, "No," and reached out to tilt her head the other way. "Not the jugular. The blood isn't oxygenated. It's not as good."

She uttered a sharp noise of surprise to find herself beneath him on the couch, too fast for her human mind to sort out the movements it had taken to get her there. Her arm fell slack at her side, hand still clutching the scissors, and he gripped her wrist, pulling the point of the blades to the side of his neck as he bent his mouth to her skin. The beat of her heart taunted him, and he seated his fangs against her throat.

"Always here," Sophia had told him on the night she'd made him. She'd held down a twisting, raving homeless man and encouraged him to kill—"A mercy killing," she'd said to encourage him—instructing him to tear not into the main artery, but into the smaller pathways that fed it. "Less mess that way."

The same heady rush of his first feeding flooded him, gave new strength to his already powerful muscles, new hunger to his already starving body.

She'd said she could handle the pain, but as he bit down, harder, harder, unrelenting until he felt the crisp pop of her skin breaking under his fangs, her body tensed beneath him, an ascending chorus of "ow's" escaped her, then finally dissolved into helpless screaming. But she didn't use the makeshift weapon in her hands.

He wanted to tell her that the worst was over, but he couldn't lift his mouth from the blood that pumped into his mouth, faster and faster as she wailed beneath him. Her blood was thick and sweet; it tasted better if you knew the person and liked them, inasmuch as a vampire could like his food. He'd stopped thinking of Jessa as food, and somehow that made her even more delicious. Her blood calmed the raging thirst in him, a tidal wave over the drought in his mouth, a wash of warm, wet comfort to his shrinking, cracking tissues.

"Stop!" she begged finally. "Please, stop!"

The point of the scissors dug farther into his throat, but he didn't need that kind of inducement. The pleading in her voice turned the taste of her blood in his mouth to something spoiled and horrible, too sweet and sour at the same time, like rotten milk. He lifted his head, and she pushed him off her, panting, tears streaming from her eyes as blood trickled from her neck.

The sight turned Graf's stomach. He got up and went to kitchenette and grabbed the roll of paper towels off their plastic spindle. He wadded some in his fist and returned to Jessa's side to press it against the two small puncture marks in her skin. Next to them, the dark outline where he'd bruised her with his bottom teeth marred her smooth neck.

He felt like he was going to barf.

"I'm sorry," she said, sniffing and wiping her eyes with the back of her hand. "Wow, you were right. That really, really hurt."

"I tried to warn you." He sounded more defensive than he would have liked to. "I'm sorry I hurt you."

"I asked you to." Her watery eyes gleamed in the darkness, and he hated himself even more.

He'd promised her that he wouldn't let anybody hurt her, and then he'd gone and done it. He was just as bad as Derek.

He let her replace his hand on the paper towel, after he checked to make sure her blood was slowing. To focus on something other than how he'd hurt her, he looked at her foot. "How's your ankle?"

"Umm," she began shakily, "I think it's okay. It only hurts when I bend it."

"I shouldn't have let you walk on it." He dropped to the floor and took her foot in his hand, gently unwinding the tan bandage. "I'm going to rewrap this and then you're going to put it up again."

He worked in silence, not wanting to look at her face or her trembling hands or her bloody neck. The whole experience had cured him of wanting her blood, that was for sure. It wasn't any fun to feed off someone you cared about, no matter how good they tasted.

"Thank you," she said quietly as he hooked the metal closures through the bandage.

He shook his head. "Think nothing of it. I remember being human. The healing time on little shit like this is ridiculous."

"Not that. I mean, thank you for that, too, but thank you for drinking my blood." It was such an odd statement, it had to be genuine.

"Don't thank me." He didn't mean it in the way John Wayne said it to the women he rescued in the movies. "I mean, really, you shouldn't thank me for doing that to you."

"I learned something from it." She carefully settled her ankle on the arm of the couch and lay back.

He snorted. "What, that being bitten by a vampire hurts?"

"That you care about me." Her eyes drifted closed, and he pressed the back of his hand to her cheek, relieved to find it warm. If she had been clammy and cold, he would have known he'd taken too much. There was only one cure for that.

Luckily, she was just experiencing the natural exhaustion after a painful experience. Her fingers captured his and held them by her face. "Thank you," she whispered again, before her grip relaxed into sleep.

He pressed his lips against her forehead and held them there, breathing in the scent of her. Not the smell of her blood, but the perspiration and the homemade soap and the skunky smell of the marijuana smoke from June's bar. They might as well have been flowers and homemade cookies and baby powder; because they clung to her, they smelled that much sweeter.

"Thank you," he whispered against her forehead. "Thank you."

From what Graf could tell, based on his own need for sleep, it was sometime around four o'clock the next afternoon that someone came to their cell. It was June, bearing two paper bags. One held cooling ears of cooked sweet corn, the other, a pan of hard bread and Tupperware containers of strawberries and blackberries.

Jessa, dressed in her own clothes, her hair down to hide the marks on her neck, took the bags and slid them onto the counter with a terse "Thank you very much."

"Why don't you eat? You must be hungry," June

urged, guilt written on her face in letters big enough for a billboard.

Jessa turned, sliding her hands into her back pockets. "Well, since I don't know how long we're going to be stuck in here, I figure we need to ration it. Isn't that the smart thing to do?"

"It won't be much longer." The way June said it, Graf knew what she meant. It wouldn't be much longer, not until the trial, but until they wouldn't have to worry about stuff like food and water and living in general.

Jessa held her head high and replied, "No, I don't expect it will. They aren't going to find anything they can use against me. Just Derek's testimony, and yours. Derek's a drunk and liar, and you…well, the town council doesn't like you always trying to run things behind their backs."

"That's true," June said, accepting the criticism without complaint or defense. "But they did find something."

"Bullshit." Jessa's glare never wavered. "Whatever they found, you all put there."

"I didn't put anything anywhere," June said, bristling at the accusation. "I was on your side, Jessa. Even when you let this vampire come to your house—"

"*Not* a vampire," Graf interrupted.

June continued, as though he hadn't spoken. "—even when everybody else thought you were telling tales. But I can't defend you against the whole town, not when they found the stuff they did at your place."

"What did they find?" Graf asked, dreading the answer. Of course, they would have uncovered something. Derek would have made sure of that.

"They found what you two were up to in the barn," June said, without elaboration.

"They found out I was cleaning up chickens that someone killed when they snuck onto my property?" Jessa asked, moving her hands to her hips in a defiant pose. "The chickens that have now gone to waste?"

"If you were just cleaning them, why did you make that circle on the floor? Why did you have a knife and a cup out there with blood in it?" June wanted to understand, Graf could see that much, but she had reached the limits of belief.

"There was no circle!" Jessa insisted. "There was no circle. No cup. There were just some dead chickens. Derek put all that stuff out there! Derek was leading It around. It might as well have been on a leash!"

Graf's heart ached for her. She didn't realize that it was too late; there wasn't anyone on her side anymore.

"Jessa, how can I believe a word you say, with the evidence they found?" June sighed. "I didn't come here to argue. I just wanted you to have something to eat before they came and got you tonight."

"It's going to be tonight?" That took a load off Graf's mind. He'd been terrified that they'd drag them outside in the daylight and he'd get his execution quicker than they'd planned.

"Well, thanks for thinking so kindly of me," Jessa spat, then turned away, refusing to face June like an insulted cat.

June waited a few moments, compassion and doubt warring with themselves on her face, until finally her jaw set and her eyes hardened. She left, locking up the door behind her, and Jessa and Graf were alone again.

The silence stretched between them. "Do we get a lawyer, or…"

Jessa laughed, a loud burst of disbelief. "Do you think we get a lawyer?"

"Okay, we'll have to represent ourselves, then." Graf scratched his head. "At least they didn't find that fucking binder. Why is Derek going to such crazy lengths to frame you? What's he think is going to happen when you're dead and the monster is still around?"

"I'd like to be there to tell everyone 'I told you so,'" she said with a weary smile. "Maybe I will be."

Probably not, he thought miserably. The way out of this thing was looking pretty bleak.

After a few hours of sulking with a rumbling stomach, Jessa ate, and Graf watched silently, seated across the lunch table from her. It seemed highly unfair that he'd found a woman who looked sexy eating corn on the cob and now they were both going to die. As demented as it seemed to him, he wanted to see her eat all kinds of things. He wanted to know her more than he knew her, outside of the context of a tragedy. He wanted to spend time with her out of choice, and not because they were trapped somewhere.

"What are you looking at?" she asked, raising a suspicious eyebrow.

He shrugged. "I don't get a lot of chances to watch a human eat."

"I'm not a zoo animal. Quit staring at me, it's creepy," she ordered, dropping the stripped cob to the table.

"Tough." He reached for her hand across the table, had it in his when keys jangled outside the door.

Her eyes went wide as they met his. He squeezed her hand. "I guess this is it."

"I trust you," she said definitely, nodding just once.

Sheriff Stoke opened the door, a wicked grin curving in the depths of his beard.

Graf was glad that Jessa had so much faith in him. Because he had none.

Sixteen

Sheriff Stoke and three other men led Jessa and Graf to the school gym. Excited voices echoed down the hallway. All that was missing was the sound of squeaking shoes on the hardwood floor, and Jessa would have thought they were on their way to a basketball game.

Beside her, Graf stared straight ahead, his jaw tight, mouth drawn into a grimace. Jessa hoped he was pretending to be nervous, and secretly had a plan, because she certainly didn't.

They went down the stairs that led to the gym floor, through the narrow hall past the door to the boys' locker room, and out to face the population of Penance, which filled the bleachers, both "Home" and "Away," and lined the wall by the doors to the parking lot.

At the other end of the court, two huge piles of

firewood, pine branches, and fallen kindling surrounded railroad ties that had somehow been braced into a vertical position.

"What the fuck?" Graf muttered.

Sheriff Stoke slapped him on the back and cracked an unfriendly smile. "We did some of our own research on vampires. Fire works just as well for you as for a witch."

"I'm not a witch!" Jessa shouted. "If I were a witch, wouldn't I just cast a spell or something to escape?"

The sheriff didn't seem to have an answer for that question. He shoved her toward the center of the gym, to stand on the emblem of the school mascot at center court; the Penance Blue Devil, copied right off a pack of candy cigarettes, smiled up in evil profile. Beside her, Graf raised an eyebrow that echoed the expression on the Blue Devil's face.

"Today, you're all witnesses to justice here in Penance!" Stoke shouted to the roaring crowd, and the din grew louder. They didn't have the rally towels or the pep band, but if they had, the scene would have looked a lot like the one the year that they had beat the Madison Mohawks in the state semifinals.

"This is not good," Graf whispered to Jessa, apparently under the impression that she couldn't guess a room full of people cheering to see them burned at the stake was a bad sign.

Sheriff Stoke raised his hands and walked in a

circle around them, hushing the crowds on both sides. "We have witnesses who will testify to the evil nature of this woman, and her familiar, this vampire, and put to rest any doubts a body might have about the vile impact their presence has made on our town.

"We have evidence, studied by myself, and by an expert in the field of religious study. I will call him, first, to read his statement. Pastor Baird?"

Jessa's stomach dropped out at the mention of her old church pastor. He'd known her family since he'd come to Penance Baptist during her teenage years. He'd brought his family with him, four daughters that had been sent to school in dutifully modest outfits purchased from the Walmart in Richmond. Jessa and Becky had made it their personal mission to mock the Baird girls every chance they'd gotten, and Pastor Baird had made their behavior the barely veiled subjects of plenty of Sunday sermons.

The past five years had taken a visible toll on Pastor Baird. Two of his daughters had gone off to Bob Jones University before the town's borders became a prison, and he'd taken up the drinking that he'd so often decried in his sermons. He shuffled to the center of the floor like a man much older than his years, and began to speak softly, reciting lines from a crumpled notebook page. Several people called out helpfully that he should speak up, more shouted angrily that they could not hear, but Baird seemed not to notice until someone ran across the gym floor, a wireless mic in hand.

"...time as pastor here... Oh, thank you," Baird mumbled to the person who'd handed the mic to him, and then, not bothering to begin his speech again, continued. "Jessa was raised in as loving and Christian a home environment as any family could provide. Her father, James, struggled to keep his daughter in line, often calling me for advice as the family's spiritual leader about troubles with Jessa's boyfriends sneaking over in the night, Jessa's lying and staying out past curfew, and her insistence on wearing inappropriate attire.

"In these things, Mr. Gallagher could not have been more concerned, but her mother, a good and Christian woman until the last four years of her life, often opposed him. She began taking yoga classes on the weekend in Richmond, or driving to Columbus for 'women empowerment' seminars. She believed that Jessa's promiscuity and lying weren't hurting anyone. I tried to counsel Janis away from her dangerous addiction to New Age spirituality, but she was, unfortunately, still lost to the devil's lies when she passed on."

Jessa wanted to scream at Pastor Baird, or jump on his back and beat him until he couldn't stand, but that would only condemn her further. Graf watched her, and she met his gaze to reassure him that she wouldn't do anything stupid. She would just follow his lead, because he was the one who was supposed to have the plan.

Sheriff Stoke, who had been listening with his head bowed and his hands clasped behind his back as though listening to a particularly moving eulogy, stepped forward and shook Pastor Baird's hand. Then, taking the mic from him, asked, "Would you say that Jessa was exposed to her mother's interest in New Age practices?"

He leaned the mic toward Pastor Baird, like a television reporter interviewing an eyewitness. Baird nodded certainly. "My daughters once reported that Jessa wore a pendant of an I Ching coin, which is a fortune-telling device."

A fortune-telling device, or a cheap souvenir from my seventh-grade pen pal, she thought angrily.

"And, Pastor, can you tell the good folks of Penance what it was you examined in the Gallagher barn this morning?" Stoke canted the microphone at Baird's face again.

"There were a number of mutilated animals, chickens specifically, arranged in a pattern inside a chalk circle. There were various satanic symbols around them, and ritual tools lying nearby." The pastor turned to stare Jessa down. "It was most certainly evidence of a witchcraft ritual."

"Thank you, Carl, you can sit down now," Stoke said, patting the man on the shoulder. The sheriff motioned to the bleachers, and his wife, Marjorie, got to her feet, her angry mouth scored with even deeper lines for the special occasion. She came forward with a stack of four books in her hands. No sign of the binder, though. She handed them over to her husband, who fumbled awkwardly to balance them and still hold the microphone, but he managed. "Here we have further evidence that Jessa, instructed, apparently, by her mother, engages in witchcraft." He lifted one book up with the hand that held the mic, and turned around so everyone could see the cover. When he lowered it, he read the title aloud. "*To Ride a Silver Broomstick,* by Silver RavenWolf." He proceeded to do the same with the next three books, *Goddesses in Everywoman* by Jean Shinoda Bolen, *The Path to Love* by Deepak Chopra, and *Many Lives, Many Masters* by Brian Weiss.

Jessa thought she saw Graf's mouth twitch, as though he held back a laugh. All well and good if he thought this was funny, but he didn't know how scary the predominately Baptist population of the town would find these books.

"You can't be serious." Graf snorted, and Stoke turned. Graf didn't look the least bit apologetic. "Okay, so Jessa's mom was having a menopausal midlife crisis and started meditating and trying to fulfill her potential or something. I think that's a far cry from witchcraft."

"Demon, speak no more!" Pastor Baird shouted

from his seat, his voice impressively commanding in spite of his withered physical appearance.

"Now, Carl, let's let him hang himself, if he wants. It'll save us some of the work," Stoke quipped, and the crowd chuckled in near-unison.

Jessa closed her eyes. It was difficult to trust Graf's plan, not knowing what it was, not knowing how it would work. When she opened her eyes, her gaze locked on a familiar face in the front row on the "Home" side. Derek.

A few more townspeople stood to give their testimony. Times that Jessa had lied to them, as though lying were a talent available solely to witches. People who had never gotten along with her mother, who'd acted "high and mighty" and hadn't helped with potlucks and church socials. Jack Singer took the floor to explain that he knew Jessa had murdered Chad, because the morning he went missing a new bird came to his bird feeder, and he interpreted it as a sign from God.

"You're going to allow that as evidence?" Graf argued. "You're hell-bent on killing us. We get it. Don't make us sit through this bullshit first. C'mon, I'll light the fire myself."

"Graf!" Jessa snapped, but she actually agreed with him. Burning alive probably wouldn't be as bad as listening to everyone trying to involve themselves in the hottest gossip in town since Derek and Becky's shotgun wedding.

"Don't worry, vampire. We're getting to you," Sheriff Stoke assured him. "June, you wanna come up here?"

Normally, June walked like she was sure of her place in town and on the earth. Now, she kept her head down and tried not to meet anyone's eyes.

Sheriff Stoke seemed to enjoy her humility a whole lot. He placed his hand on her back and gently led her to the center of the floor, like an invalid walking for the first time. "Ms. Dee, you were the one who brought it to my attention that our guest here is a vampire. Can you tell the people of Penance why you would have cause to think something like that?"

She didn't take the microphone, but spoke loud enough that it carried her words through the gym. "He's kind of still. He's just *too still*. You can tell that he's thinking about moving before he does it. That's because they move faster than humans, if they don't try not to. And he doesn't blink. Least, not that I noticed."

"How often do you notice whether people blink or not?" Graf asked, his lids closing and opening rapidly, like he had something in his eye.

Jessa hadn't realized it before, but now that she did, it seemed so bizarrely obvious. He didn't blink. He didn't tap his feet nervously or do anything clumsy. He was still; it was the only way to describe it. That was what the air of danger was around him when she'd first met him. She'd known he was a vampire, but not knowing about the existence of vampires, she hadn't been able to put a name to it. So, how had June?

"June, do you feel comfortable sharing with these people the reason that you're acquainted with the ways of vampires?" The concern in Stoke's voice wasn't a put-on, not now. June shrugged and unbuttoned her checked-plaid shirt, then drew it off her shoulders to stand before them in a ribbed-cotton undershirt. Her shoulders, arms and chest, every visible inch of skin, were marred by bumpy scars. Teeth marks. And when Jessa recognized them, she unconsciously raised her hand to her neck, touching the bite disguised by the curtain of her hair.

The sheriff strode to her side and gripped her wrist, prying it away from her neck, then pushed her hair aside and revealed the scabbed punctures and ugly bruise Graf had left behind.

"Guilty!" someone in the crowd shouted, and the chant was taken up like a mantra.

"What are you going to do when you kill us and the monster's still here?" Graf challenged the sheriff. "What are you going to tell people?"

"The people won't care," Stoke replied quietly, then he whistled, calling four men from the front row. Two of them were the other council members. The other two were friends of Chad's, and they looked as though they were disappointed to see Jessa and the vampire killed by fire, instead of by hand.

"What are you going to do?" she whispered to Graf, and instead of answer, he gripped her hand in his and squeezed it.

A cold sweat broke out on her brow. He didn't have a plan. He didn't have any idea how they were going to save themselves. When two men grabbed her and dragged her backward, toward the stakes, she thrashed and screamed.

"Wait!" Graf shouted as he was similarly carried off. He cursed and shoved his captors off himself, and a group of ten people rushed forward to help them. Jessa's executioners pulled her arms behind her back and secured them around the stake, but she was too engrossed in Graf's struggles to put up a fight. He landed punches, even bit a couple of the townspeople, but there were too many of them. The stands were nearly empty by the time they managed to get him to his stake, men and women both leaving their seats to help wrestle him into place. They used the same nylon rope to bind his hands as they had used on hers. No stretch to those. No way to get themselves free.

"Wait!" Graf shouted again. "If she's a witch, couldn't she just call It here, right now, to kill you all and get her free?"

They were too far gone to their bloodlust, Jessa thought with a panic. She looked to the stands, where Derek still sat, his eyes intense. She turned to the crowd assembled on the floor. "He's right! I'm going to do it! I'm going to call It here, right now!"

Someone produced a blowtorch and set it to the dried pine boughs in the pile. Pine burned fast; smoke began to rise immediately. The kindling stuffed into the cracks between the logs started to pop, and Jessa's eyes watered as she called out words that she hoped sounded like a witch's incantation. From the corner of her eye, she saw Derek rise from his seat, and she prayed he was going where she thought he was heading.

The flames began to rise around her, and she screamed, backing up against the stake to stand on her tiptoes. The log beneath her feet had thankfully not caught yet, but it would. How long did she have? Had she waited until it was too late?

"Jessa, hold your breath!" Graf shouted above the terrifying cheers of the people as his pile was lit. "Don't breathe it in!"

It was good advice, but sadly not any that she could follow. Fear drove her lungs to gasp at double speed, each breath full of stinging, punishing smoke. Her vision swam with the waves of heat, her eyes burned as though the fire originated in them. She caught a glimpse of Graf's face, twisted in a grimace of agony, and then the flames closed a wall between them.

The screams of the people faded behind the violence of the fire, then rose again. An unearthly roar rang in Jessa's ears, louder than the buzz of pain that originated in her wrists, where the nylon rope melted into her skin. The general sense of chaos outside of the flames came to her, and she wished she could see beyond them. She didn't feel the heat anymore, except in her chest, but even that was getting better as her breathing slowed.

She tilted her head back to look up at the white painted beams of the ceiling high above, had the vague memory of looking at them while lying on her back to stretch for volleyball, then closed her eyes.

Seventeen

It burst through the wall like the Kool-Aid Man, only way scarier.

Not a poetic image, Graf acknowledged as he struggled against the rope binding him. Softened by the heat, they pulled apart like warm taffy—another unpoetic image—but wouldn't break, not fast enough. Dragging the stake with him on his back, he rushed headfirst through the flames, into the crowd. He bent at the waist and spun in a wide circle to fend off anyone attempting to stop him, then ran backward, full speed, until the end of the stake hit the wall with a force that jarred his shoulders but did eject his crucifix from the loop around his wrists. He straightened, shook the rope from his wrists and charged at Jessa's pyre. There was no time to stop and admire the cruel efficiency with which It dispatched one yokel after another, filling the air with the sound of shredding cloth and flesh and the screams of myriad victims.

He plunged blindly into the inferno surrounding Jessa, groping blindly and quickly for flesh. His hands found her in a crumbled pile atop the wood, and his heart would have stopped beating if he'd still been human. He pulled her free easily; the rope had melted around her wrists, releasing her to fall onto the pile, but miraculously, she hadn't yet burned. Her clothes and hair were singed, and a red stripe branded her left cheek. She was still breathing, a slow, noisy death rattle, but good enough. If he had to, he'd…do what was needed.

The thought paralyzed him for a second, just long enough for someone to knock him down. He struggled to his feet, pulling Jessa against his chest like a sleeping baby, and turned to face the sheriff's wife, her thin mouth pinched and wreathed with angry lines. She brandished a Bible, and hit him with it again.

"Lady, get out of my way," he snarled, showing his teeth, but before he had time to make good on his implied threat, one of It's long, spiked arms shot toward her. The monster gripped her in his massive fist and squeezed until her screaming stopped and her lower body fell to the ground independently of her head and all the mess still contained in the beast's fist.

Although Graf felt a kind of kinship with the

creature at that moment, he wasn't about to stick around and see if it felt the same way. He ran for the doors, faster than the screaming townspeople fleeing all around him could see, though he doubted any others would try to stop him. It stomped after him, bellowing in confusion as it speared people in its claws and tossed them aside.

With so many hysterical victims running in circles, It was slowed down a bit, just enough for them to escape. He crushed Jessa tighter to him and increased his speed, his preternaturally strong muscles tiring under the strain. Penance flew by, and he hoped that he guessed the way back correctly. There was nothing worse than getting lost really fast.

When he made it back to her driveway, he saw that the monster no longer followed. Neither did the crazed mob, hopefully. He still had to take precautions against that. What had Jessa said? They should board up the windows? Fat lot of good that would do them, with the kitchen wall missing and their love of pyrotechnics. Instead, he took the precaution of taking the shotgun up the stairs with them as he hurried Jessa into the bathroom.

While he ran water in the tub, he examined the extent of the damage. Her face was burned; that would leave a brutal scar, but nothing that would endanger her life. The melted rope peeled away from her wrists, pulling skin with it. Her shoes were burned, and her feet worse than any other part of her, but still, not as bad as they could have been. Nasty blisters covered the bottoms of her feet, shining yellow with fluid pressure in some places, burned to leathery white patches in others.

He'd run the bath cooler than would be comfortable for her, but not cold enough to cause her shock and not warm enough to encourage the heat trapped in her skin. He plunged her fevered body, jeans and all, into the water.

Sputtering, she sat up, her wet hair throwing an arc of water behind her. She gasped noisily, still panicked.

"Whoa, whoa!" Graf shouted, gripping her by the shoulders so she couldn't harm herself any further than she already was. "I've got you. I've got you."

Her entire body trembled, water making clean tracks in the soot that covered her face. Her eyes were almost comically large, irritated and red from the smoke. "Graf?" she asked, her voice barely a whisper.

"Yeah, it's me." He'd barely finished his sentence when she flung her arms around his neck, crying out loud, sobs racking her pitiful, wet body. He hushed her with soft words, grateful to feel that some of the unnatural heat had left her flesh. Still, she shivered in his arms like a wounded animal, and it was a long time before he could pry her fingers loose from his shoulders.

He coaxed her back into the water and gently

washed her hair and face with the homemade soap, her neck, her arms, and then gently tended to her feet. She sat in silence and misery, shaking all the while, until he helped her from the water and wrapped her in what was probably too many towels. He pulled her jeans down and carefully worked her feet from them, took her soot-stained shirt and bra and carried her, bundled in towels, to her bedroom.

He didn't know when the mob would come for them. They would, eventually, and that trick probably wouldn't work again. Derek wouldn't just keep playing along. Graf would have to kill him, and hope that would end the beast's reign of terror.

Then again, if it didn't, they'd have even more problems. Maybe torture would work better. Torture him until he spilled all the details of his pact with the creature, how he controlled it, how it could be killed. Graf closed his eyes and took an almost spiritual pleasure in the thought of what he would do to the sniveling human. In those fantasies, Jessa was there, not pleading for mercy on behalf of her ex-boyfriend, but cheering him on, her skin pale and healed, her unblinking eyes gleaming in the moonlight.

Graf shook those thoughts away. Making someone into a vampire was a huge commitment. Not something you did when you knew someone for less than a week. Not even if being trapped with that person made you think crazy things about the way you felt about her. It was the disorienting turn the night's events had taken that was playing with his head. If stress could cause health problems in humans, why not in vampires? Not ulcers and heart attacks, maybe just mental illness. Because he was certainly not in his right mind.

"Anybody home?" a voice called, and he jumped from the bed beside Jessa. She reached for him, clawing at his arms, and mumbled, begging him not to go, but he put a finger to his lips and eased her to the bed, pulling the blankets over her.

At the top of the stairs he grabbed the gun and put the hammer down. "Who is it?"

"It's June," the voice replied, and Graf dropped all pretenses of humanity.

"I should shoot you right there," he said, raising the gun to point straight at her chest. "Get out and tell your friends down at the bar that if they show up here, I'll kill every goddamned one of them."

June didn't flinch, even with the sudden appearance of a vampire pointing a gun at her. "You'd never be able to hold them all off. They'll form a mob and be here before sunrise."

"Nice of you to warn us before you run back and join them," he snarled. "Don't make me tell you again to leave."

"I'm not going to join them. Put the gun down, and I'll tell you what I know," she said calmly.

"I've already heard what you have to say. I was in the gym, remember? I was the one tied to a stake?"

His finger ached to squeeze the trigger. "If you knew so much, you could have at least told them stakes work best on vampires if they're shoved through our hearts."

"I know that," she said. "I also know where Derek went after he summoned It to try to get rid of Jessa."

This made Graf lower the gun. He reset the hammer, but he didn't let the weapon leave his grip. "What?"

"Is Jessa here? She needs to hear this." June glanced toward the stairs, and Graf stepped protectively in front of them.

"I'll decide what Jessa needs to hear right now. She's in bad enough shape as it is." He gestured at the couch with the barrel of the gun. "Sit down, and start talking. Because I'm awful hungry, and you look like you must taste good."

This shook her, when the gun had not. Her face went pale, and she sat, as instructed, but when she spoke, her voice still held that unflappable calm. It was a ruse, Graf realized as he listened to her.

"About that," she said, looking down at her hands. "I'm not real proud of my past. I know you're not interested in the details, but the people I fell in with weren't good. I did some things that I probably shouldn't have done, and ran up a debt to some people I should have paid back. And they made sure I paid them back, in blood. When I saw you here, in my town, well, you can understand why I wouldn't want your kind here, after what they did to me."

"I understand." And he did. He knew what kind of sadistic SOBs there were out there, blowing everybody else's cover. "I don't particularly care. Get to what you know about Derek."

She blew out a long breath. "I guess I don't have any excuse for not telling you sooner. I found out myself the night everybody was out looking for Becky. Derek was drunk, and he started talking."

"Derek being drunk seems like a pretty regular occurrence," Graf said, sitting in the floral armchair.

June shook her head. "Not like this. He could barely walk. He stayed until closing, and I figured he was just passed out in the back booth. Figured he'd sleep it off and that would be it. But he woke up a little, and started confessing things to me. You have to understand what life used to be like for Derek and Becky and Jessa. Jessa was homecoming queen, Derek was homecoming king. He was our star football player. Back when I was running a restaurant and not just a booze joint, he would walk in the door and everyone would want to talk to him about the game, and what colleges were scouting him. Him and Jessa and Becky were like the Three Musketeers, you'd see them everywhere together. Sometimes in a big group of friends that would come and go, but they were always together, 'cept when it was just Jessa and Derek."

Graf nodded. "I've heard this story. Get to the part where this means anything to me and you walk out of this house alive."

"I don't have any illusions about leaving here alive," June said, just as unblinking and stone-faced as he was. "When Derek got drunk that night, he said it was all his fault Becky left, which was pretty much plain to everyone in town. But I told him things would work out, and Becky would come home. That's how it always happens. They have a big fight, Becky always comes home. He said no, that's not what he meant. He never meant for everyone to get stuck here, he said. He just wanted things to go back to normal."

Graf frowned. "Back to normal?"

"That's what he said. After that, it was mostly nonsense about the scholarships he'd missed out on and how he'd sacrificed everything for Jessa, so it was her turn to sacrifice. He talked a lot about Sarah Boniface, too. Some folks thought there was something going on between them, but he'd married Becky… I didn't think Derek was smart enough to juggle three women, when he was doing so badly with two."

Something cold gripped Graf's stomach. "What else did he say?"

"He made me swear never to tell anyone. Said no one would be mad at him once he got his reward." She sighed as though a great weight had been lifted off her. "Put yourself in my shoes. If you knew what vampires are capable of, and one came to your town, are you going to worry about getting rid of him, or getting rid of the drunk who thinks he's got control over something that for five years has seemed utterly uncontrollable?"

Graf wanted to stay mad at her, and desperately tried to call up the fury that had caused him to point a gun at her in the first place, but he couldn't. Whoever the vampires were that she'd run into, they'd obviously made an impression on her. The scars she'd revealed had been worse than any Graf had ever seen. He'd known vampires with dedicated feeders. Sophia had even had one for a time, though she hadn't treated him as badly as the unnamed vampires had treated June.

Unfortunately, that left him with the problem of knowing what to say to her. He wasn't going to apologize for whatever had happened to her, because he was still mad enough to be spiteful. He wasn't going to thank her for the information, because that was the type of thing she should have told him, oh, maybe sometime before he was standing on top of firewood, tied to a fucking stake. "Why didn't you tell us? At least Jessa? People need to know if a monster is chasing them down."

"I was going to tell you, but then Chad disappeared. I think you killed him." She was asking for confirmation, Graf realized.

Fine, she could have it. "I did. I killed him after he tried to murder Jessa."

"Why would he try to murder Jessa?" June's face screwed up in disbelief and disgust.

"Derek told him to. I guess his little conversation with you explains why that would be." Graf put the gun aside. "For the record, I'm not an asshole who abuses humans."

"You bit Jessa," June accused.

"Yeah, but she wanted me to." He rubbed his eyes, and actually blinked a few times, even though he didn't need to. It was soothing to get the smoke and dust out. "I put Chad out of his misery fast, and he deserved it. You small towns love self-defense, right?"

"What are you gonna do now?" June asked, jerking her head toward the stairs. "You guys can't get out of here. You said she was in bad shape. And they'll be coming for you."

"They can try." It was a stupid thing to say, but bravery had a component of stupidity, didn't it? "What would you do, if it were you?"

"Murder-suicide." June laughed, a sound that rattled low in her chest.

"I'm not going to let anyone hurt Jessa," he vowed, and felt the helplessness of that vow immediately. There was no way out of this. They couldn't leave town. They couldn't hide. "Now that you've told me this, are you going to deny it to everyone else? Set us up again?"

June didn't answer.

"Fine. Just remember, now they know about you. You were in with vampires. There's something that makes you different from them. Eventually, they'll use that against you," he warned.

"I know. I've always known that." June's eyes were catalogs of every sadness a person could experience. Weary of the game, she'd just cashed in her chips and left the table, and she knew it.

So, that was how it was. Don't misstep, don't fall out of line, or the people of Penance will safely remove you. Well, fine if they wanted to live like that, but Graf wasn't going to. And he wasn't going to die like that, either.

He stood and faced the kitchen, eyeing the missing wall. There wouldn't be any time to repair that, for sure. But they could put up some beams to make entry more difficult. "Where would I find some lumber?"

"We don't have much in the way of lumber, Graf. There's a sawmill, but it only runs if someone needs it, and they cut their own trees down." June came to stand next to him. "You thinking of a remodeling project?"

"I was thinking of sealing us up in here." How long would that safety last? Eventually, someone would find a stray brain cell and bring over an ax. Then, they'd be right back where they'd escaped from.

"You could use the wood from the barn," June suggested. When he didn't answer, she continued. "It's mostly still good, at least it looks good. She ain't got chickens no more, so it's not like you need to keep it up."

"True." He rubbed his chin. "We don't have to stay safe forever, just until we can get Derek to talk."

"Or until someone wounds It again," June said quietly. "You know that's an option."

"Not an option." The thought of the sun filling the sky, the burning, helpless... Not again. No way.

"What's the plan, then? Just stay here forever?" She snorted. "You sound like Jessa."

"Well, sometimes fear can paralyze a person." That was all he would say on that particular subject. Sure, he had some pretty intense feelings for Jessa, but he wasn't thrilled to be compared to her in the agoraphobia department. "Let's concentrate on getting Derek out of whatever he got himself, and everyone else, into."

"Is that something you can do?" June asked doubtfully.

Graf faced her, considering. She hadn't been so keen on helping them when they were locked up in the high school, or when they were about to be barbecued. The scars on her body stood testament to why she wouldn't trust him, but she was here, now, alone with him without trying to stick a stake through his heart. Maybe he had to trust her, on general principle. "I think so. I don't know. But I know that I can't let them kill Jessa. And I can't protect her on my own."

June nodded, her large, blue eyes shining with unshed tears. Of regret, maybe? Or fear? Graf didn't care. This woman had betrayed them once, and he wasn't going to let it happen again.

Eighteen

Jessa woke to darkness and sat up, rubbing her eyes. Graf lay beside her in her bed, looking like a dead man, he was so still. Her whole body ached, and her face felt like she had a terrible sunburn. Her feet just plain burned, and when she flexed her toes, something popped and ran down to her heels. She didn't want to think about that too much.

Graf had probably stayed up with her as long as he could, then passed out from exhaustion. Even vampires could get tired; she'd found out that much when they'd had sex in the teachers' lounge of her old high school, of all places.

Exhaustion or no, one of them needed to stay up. He had probably been right about fear of It keeping people indoors. So, she hadn't imagined that, just before she'd lost consciousness. It had come; Derek had called the demon up to keep from blowing his cover. To condemn her in one final attempt to get rid of her.

Why hadn't that betrayal crumbled her? After he'd tried to kill her, it probably shouldn't have surprised her that he'd tried again. Surprise was different from hurt, though. A leg you broke twice hurt just as much the second time as the first time.

It was because of Graf. She could try to deny it all day long, but it wouldn't do any good. There had been a time, not too long ago, that she would have gone on loving Derek even after he'd tried to have her killed, kill her himself, and frame her to get her killed. It stung to realize how stupid she had been. The fact that she could think back on it was a blessing, though. And her new self-awareness wouldn't have been possible without Graf.

If Mom had been alive, she would have chastised Jessa for that kind of thinking. "There's nothing a man can do for you that you can't do for yourself," she'd always said. She hadn't liked Derek, definitely hadn't been thrilled with her daughter's devotion to a high school jock. Mom had been right, of course. She'd always been right. When Derek had finally left her for Becky, left her grieving and alone, she'd thought she would have been better off dead with the rest of her family. She'd even considered trying it out. In the end, though, she hadn't needed Derek. She'd only needed herself.

She didn't need Graf, either, but he was good to have around. A good distraction.

Who was she kidding? She was as in love with him as she had been with Derek. Falling hard and fast was a curse, but there it was. She loved Graf, despite what he was, and despite the havoc he'd caused in her life.

She rolled over, every movement causing her limbs to tremble in pain and her chest to burn, to put her arm over Graf's solid chest. She pressed her lips to his cheek. He didn't stir. He didn't even breathe.

Okay, maybe she wasn't so in love with him that she was totally okay with lying beside his dead body. She stood gingerly, biting back cries of pain as the blisters on her feet tightened and popped under her weight. Even if he seemed dead to the world, she had no doubt that any noise of discomfort she made would wake Graf so he could rush to her rescue, and he needed his sleep. At least one of them needed to be strong enough to fight this out to the bitter end.

And it would be bitter, she realized, limping to her dresser. They were still stuck in this town, with a whole mess of people who wanted to kill them to solve their problems. She pulled a rolled-up pair of socks out of the top drawer and made her way to the bathroom for the potted aloe plant that sat on the high windowsill. She sat on the edge of the tub and carefully smoothed the plant's sap over her burned soles, then pulled on the clean socks, hoping that would prove enough of a barrier that her feet didn't become horribly infected. The sap felt good and cool, and she shuddered with the small relief from the pain racking her body.

The living-room light was on, and as she rounded the landing, she saw the hooded sweatshirt over the back of the couch.

"I hope you don't mind, I drank a little of your shine." June stood in the kitchen doorway, a half-empty glass still in her hand.

Jessa's fists clenched at her sides. "Get out of my house. You're not welcome here."

"I didn't figure I would be. I thought I might be needed, though." June sat on the couch, her long braid flipping over her shoulder.

"Well, you were wrong. We're doing just fine." Jessa stalked to the armchair. She didn't want to sit. She wanted to pace angrily back and forth, but her feet wouldn't cooperate.

"You're doing just fine with one of you nearly crippled and the other one starving to death?" She shook her head. "You're not going to be able to feed him on your own, and you're not going to be able to fight off intruders in the position you're in."

"You would know all about feeding vampires, wouldn't you?" Jessa snapped, knowing it was unfair, somehow, to bring up June's past. Either way, she wasn't getting near Graf.

A hard expression came over June's face, as

unfriendly a look as Jessa had ever seen on the woman's usually cheerful face. "You wouldn't be so high and mighty if you knew what kind of people you were getting yourself in with, messing around with vampires."

"Graf is not like that," Jessa said, certain of her words as she was certain that the sky was blue. "Not all vampires are the same, like all people aren't the same."

"You think the same rules apply to them as apply to us?" June shook her head. "He's playing nice now. That's how they do it. But you don't understand their world. If you got out of this town, and he didn't need your blood, or there was some other human who looked good to him, he'd take them in a second. And what do you think he would do to get rid of you?"

A shiver went up Jessa's arms, but not from doubting Graf. "I'm sorry about what happened to you."

"You'll be more sorry when it happens to you," June said, refusing to relent. "I'm telling you, Jessa, the best thing you can do right now is give him over to the mob, when they come."

"Why? So I'll be defenseless, and they can take me then?" She closed her eyes, and the image of the flames still licked behind her eyelids. "No way. I'm not going to be helpless."

June's face crumpled as if she was going to cry. "Look around, Jessa. You are helpless. Give them the

vampire, tell them you've repented, tell them anything. You're a good liar, you can get them to believe
you."

"No. I'm not going to hand him over. It isn't an
option." Her gaze flicked to the gun beside the couch.
June was between her and it.

She didn't think June would do anything crazy.
But she'd misjudged a lot of people lately.

"Derek knows what the monster is after. He told
me. We could get rid of both the monsters in this
town, Jessa. You just have to trust me on this."

Jessa hoped it was the moonshine talking, or just
fear, because she didn't like this side of June. She'd
always played the role of the neutral party, the tough,
fair judge. Never the backstabber.

"First shift is over." Graf came down the steps
from the landing, his feet making exaggerated noise
as he descended. He'd been waiting for a while, listening. Something tight in Jessa's chest loosened at
the sight of him, and some long-missing part of her
recognized that feeling as safety.

June knew he'd been listening, that much was clear
on her face. She stood, looking almost guilty, and
faced him, but said nothing.

"Get upstairs, get some rest," he said to June, and
the implied threat of "Or I'll make you" hung in the
air.

She nodded, not meeting his eyes, and went up
the stairs.

"You can't trust her not to try something," Jessa whispered. "Maybe you'd better not sleep until she does."

"We can't all stay up around the clock. If she tries to take a run at me, I'll just have to wake up first." He sat on the couch and patted the cushion beside him. "You want to curl up here and sleep. You know you do. I'm all room temperature over here."

She forced away the giddy smile that threatened to erupt into a volcano of giggly idiocy. "You should be sleeping. I got enough. Besides, I need to get a look at that binder, while there's still time. All I wanted to do before was hide it, but it was in Derek's house. He had it for a reason, and he was looking through it for a reason."

"Fair enough," Graf replied with a shrug. He stood and helped her to the couch, and Jessa was thankful for the hand even though she would never admit it. When she was settled, Graf knelt and rummaged under the couch, emerging with the black plastic binder. "I like the glitter."

On the cover, a large star in a circle in silvery, glittery puff-paint peeled off in flecks. Jessa pushed the rubbery paint with her fingernail and made a face before opening the cover. "'The grim…grim ore.' Is that how you say it?"

"I have no idea."

"'The Grimoire of Raven Nightshadow.' I'll assume

that's Sarah." Jessa read on, flipping through pages. "I guess grimoire is a fancy name for a spell book. She must have really thought she was a witch."

"Well, the rest of the town did," Graf pointed out. "But none of this stuff looks that serious. Red candles for a love spell, stuff about getting back at the idiots at school. How old was she?"

"She'd have been about a high school senior when they took her. I guess Derek likes them young." Jessa rolled her eyes.

"What's this back here?" Graf pointed to where the paper changed sizes at the back of the book.

She flipped quickly, past pages of notebook paper to the thicker cardstock in the back.

"Must be serious, if she used nicer paper," Graf snorted.

Jessa's fingers trembled as she flipped over the first page, heavy with pasted-on photos.

"Oh my God, Jessa, that's—"

"Shut up." She touched her fingers to her mother's face beaming up from the page, and her father's, and Jonathan's. What had Sarah been doing with these? How had she gotten them?

Her stomach clenched. She knew exactly how Sarah had gotten them. The thought that Derek would have given them to her for some sick little game made her want to vomit.

Graf didn't disobey her, so he sat next to her like

someone watching the numbers count down on a time bomb.

"I don't understand…" She flipped again, but all that filled the next pages were Sarah's handwriting. "She didn't know my family. She shouldn't have had these."

"I think we know how It got here," Graf said slowly, cautiously.

"No. No, that doesn't make sense! Derek controls It. You saw him. You saw him." She realized that she sounded almost pleading. "You saw him, Graf."

His expression was pained. "I did. But I've seen the way he acts with you and with Becky. I saw him stand by and let them tie you to a stake to burn you. He was going to let that happen. What's to say he didn't do the same thing before?"

"What, you think he let them kill Sarah so that he could get control of the monster?" Something about that didn't make sense. "And what does it have to do with my family? Why are they in here?"

Gently, Graf took the book from her hands. "I don't know. Give me just a minute."

Though she could read the writing just fine over his shoulder, she didn't. Whatever sick thing Sarah thought she was doing with pictures of her family was something Jessa could safely lock out of her mind.

"It looks like they were somehow a component of whatever it was that she did. It doesn't say anything about Derek." He frowned and thumped the page with his thumb. "But why aren't you in here? Why just them?"

Jessa waited, numb, while Graf continued to read.

"I know why." A cold chill raced down her spine. "Because they're dead. That's why Derek wants me dead. To finish whatever this spell is."

They stared at each other, both of them shocked. Jessa more so, she decided. Somehow, the words had escaped her mouth before she'd even managed to piece together that thought. Now, her brain had to race to catch up.

Derek wanted her dead. He'd proved that much. Derek controlled the monster, somehow, and he knew how to get rid of it. So, why hadn't he? And what would have made Chad willing to murder her? What would make anyone willing to murder another person, on someone else's say-so? Why had Sarah done a spell that trapped them all in the town? Why did she die without telling the truth?

All it would take was her death, and the whole thing would be complete. Whatever the point of it was.

"You don't know that," Graf said, swallowing so hard she could watch his Adam's apple move in his throat. "You don't know that."

"You do." Otherwise, it wouldn't have hit him so hard. "If it isn't true, then why does he want me dead? What does It want?"

Graf didn't have an answer, and that was her answer.

"Look," he said slowly, quietly, "you can't tell anyone about that."

"Why not?" Her voice pitched up hysterically, though she felt oddly calm and detached. "They want me dead, anyway."

"Because we're going to figure something else out. We're going to get out of here alive. Both of us." He swore and ran a hand through his blond hair. "You didn't tell June this, did you?"

"No, but she's smart. She'll figure it out, if she hasn't already." She paused. "If Derek hadn't already told her. Shit, that's why she wanted me to get rid of you—"

"Because I'm protecting you…" He jumped to his feet and was instantly gone. Jessa knew where to follow, though she hadn't seen him move up the stairs with that unnerving speed. She was halfway up when she heard him swear and pound his fists on the windowsill.

"She's gone!" he shouted, striding back down the stairs. Jessa ran to her room, where that damned tree that had helped her sneak in and out so many nights in her teen years stood placidly beside the open window.

"Graf, wait!" She raced down after him, but by the time she reached the door, he was gone.

He'd left her alone, the door standing wide-open.

Outside, rain fell in huge drops that splattered themselves across the front of the house. She stared out the door at the darkness, paralyzed. It seemed like any second a group of angry people would swarm up the lawn, and she would be too late to shut them out.

Or It would appear, and rush at the house with its terrible claws, and she would still be standing there, framed in the doorway, the light from the lamp a beacon.

And Graf had left her there, alone.

She stood for a long time, unable to move to close the door and shut herself inside the safety of the house. Because it wasn't safe if he wasn't there to protect her. Once upon a time, she would have hated that thought. After Derek had abandoned her, she'd learned that she couldn't rely on anyone. She needed to cling to that lesson now.

The creature wanted her dead. Well, it was going to have a hell of a fight. It had already taken everything else from her; it wasn't going to have her life. She picked up her gun and carried it with her upstairs. She took a pair of her father's boots out of the closet, since her shoes had been burned in the fire and her feet would be too swollen to wear any of her mom's pairs, which didn't fit great under the best of circumstances.

If Derek was responsible for trapping them all in Penance, then killing him would solve the problem just as easily as her death would.

* * *

The walk to Derek's house was difficult. The burns on Jessa's feet made themselves painfully known with every step, and every step was impeded in turn by her damaged ankles inside her father's too-large boots and also by the rain that made the grass slick and turned ditches into mini-rivers. By the time the lights of the house became visible, her tank top and shorts were soaked through, and she shivered despite the warm July air. Her boots had filled with water, and they squished and sloshed like buckets on her feet, but she kept walking, hugging the gun to her chest like a baby.

You can do this. You can do this, she repeated as a mantra in her head. She could do it, despite the flood of memories that the very thought of Derek's name brought back to her. Prom. Driving around in his car. Making out in the woods behind her house. Stupid, childish memories she had clung to for too long. That wasn't love. That had been hormones and teen rites of passage. It wasn't enough to let someone walk all over her for. It wasn't enough to die for.

She didn't knock on the door. It wouldn't be locked. She pushed her way in, the gun in front of her, cocked and ready to fire, her arms trembling from chill and exhaustion.

"You really think you can do it?"

At the sight of him, Jessa's resolve quaked. Derek sat in an armchair covered in torn tweed fabric that had been patched with duct tape. He held a jar of moonshine on his knee, his handsome face made harsh and ugly by shadows of sleeplessness and the yellow light from the floor lamp behind him.

She didn't lower the gun, but she didn't fire, either. "You could do it to me."

"I could. If you were dead, I could leave. I could go find Becky and the kids. I could go down to Richmond and get a job. All of this would be gone."

"How do you know that?" Her palms sweated, and she wanted to wipe them on her shorts. But she didn't want to lower the gun.

"How do you think?" he snorted, lifting the jar to his lips to drink.

"Derek, what did you do?"

"I didn't expect it to be like this," he said so quietly she almost missed it for the rain on the roof. Was he crying? It certainly appeared that way when he dipped his head and covered his eyes. Then, he spoke loudly and removed all doubt. "I didn't want it to be like this!"

Jessa had only seen Derek cry one time before. The day he'd gotten his final rejection letter, the one from Arizona State, the twelfth school to break it to him gently that, though he was a talented player, there wasn't a place for him in college football at their university. It unnerved her to see it then, and it unnerved her to see it now. She didn't want to put the gun down, but she did want to comfort him. A sick, pathetic part of her insisted that she should hurry to his side and make him feel better, make herself more important and understanding than Becky.

She shook her head to clear that thought away. "What do you mean? What did you do, Derek?"

He looked at her, like a child admitting to stealing candy from the drugstore. "I did a spell."

Her finger relaxed on the trigger. She wanted answers more than she wanted to blow his brains out. "What do you mean, you did a spell? That kind of stuff isn't real."

He nodded stubbornly, drunkenly. "Yes, yes, it is. I got Sarah Boniface to help me do it, too. She had all these books, and she got on the internet and looked stuff up for me."

"Why would she do something like that?" Jessa asked, but she already knew the answer. Derek had charmed her. Maybe he'd promised her popularity or a way to get even with all the kids who teased her at school. Derek always knew exactly what to promise to get what he wanted.

"I didn't mean for it to happen like this!" His face screwed up in anger. "She did it wrong! She did it wrong, and worded it wrong, and lied about it and then that bitch got what she deserved!"

"She was just a kid!" Jessa's grip tightened on the stock; her finger twitched but did not touch the trigger.

He snorted drunkenly. "She was a witch! She

helped me get this thing here! She just did a bad job, was all."

"Why? What was she supposed to accomplish? What was that monster going to do, be your pet?" How could he be so stupid? And how could he really believe that a girl like Sarah could competently summon monsters, just because she wore black nail polish and had a spell book?

"It was supposed to make everything better. It was supposed to make everything go back to how it was, before we graduated." He sniffed as more tears came to his bleary eyes. "I just wanted to go back to how things were. I wanted to play football again. I wanted to mean something."

"To mean something?" Realization hit her like a fist to the stomach. "You thought you'd go back to being the big football star in town, is that it?"

"I just wanted everything to go back to normal. It was even part of the spell. It was supposed to stop things from changing." His voice died to a pathetic whisper.

Well, it had succeeded, in some aspects. No one had been able to leave town for five years, for a new job or a new home or college. But life in Penance had definitely changed. The only thing that remained from their time in high school was that everyone still knew Derek's name, still talked about him. That probably wasn't what he'd been hoping to accomplish.

"And what, you think killing me is going to make

this whole mess go away? Killing Sarah didn't make it go away." The hairs along Jessa's neck rose, attuned to some electricity that preceded news of the worst kind. She almost feared hearing it.

"It will make it go away," he said certainly. Deadly calm, he stood and approached her. "It needs your blood. I promised It your blood."

She took a step back, knowing she should shoot him where he stood but still craving answers. "Why would It need my blood?"

"Because I promised It your family's blood for what I wanted. See, there's a price you have to pay, when you do a spell like that. A sacrifice. We used some chickens at first. That's how I got the idea to arrange them in your barn. Sarah showed me how to do it. But It demanded a bigger sacrifice. And we did it. You came back. It was like it was working."

"So, you promised It…me?" Her stomach turned sour. She was going to be sick. "But then why—"

"It was an accident! Sarah said the price had to be paid in blood. A blood sacrifice. I had Chad help me fuck up the brakes on your mom's car. So it would look like an accident." He looked ashamed. "I didn't think it would want you, too. I didn't think it would want so much! But she said she would give It the blood of your family, and I guess… I don't know. I didn't realize… I guess that included you… Maybe Sarah knew it included you, but anyway, It came to collect."

A doll with a dirty plastic face lay on the floor between them, no children to play with it. Her blood ran ice-cold in her veins. "Derek, what happened to Becky and the kids?"

He cried harder, covering his face. For a sickening moment, Jessa thought she knew the answer. Then, Derek raised his head and tossed the jar of moonshine aside. "She left. It was sick. Something hurt It real bad, and she knew."

"Knew what?" It seemed unlikely that Becky could have known something about the existence of It and hadn't shared it with the entire town. No matter how much she might have loved Derek, she didn't love being trapped any more than the rest of them.

"She knew that when It gets hurt, it doesn't have any real power. That vampire got It and Chad shot It and it made It too weak so she got out." He wiped at his eyes, his expression hard.

They could have left. They all could have left, and they'd missed their chance. Now, she really would be sick. She doubled over, clutching her stomach.

He rushed at her, and she was unprepared. She pulled the trigger, and the gun kicked back, smashing her in the chest. The bullet ejected and blew a hole in the floor just inches from Derek's feet. She vomited, shaking, and knew she was safe for minute. Derek had the queasiest stomach on the face of the earth.

"Jesus, Jessa!" Derek jumped back to avoid the

splash of puke. Choking, spitting out the vile remnants in her mouth, Jessa turned and ran.

Derek grabbed the butt of the gun and tried to pry it out of her grasp as she got to door, and she whirled, gripping the barrel. She didn't like having the gun pointed at her abdomen as they tugged it back and forth between them, but she wasn't letting go. She would get the gun away from him and, this time, she wouldn't hesitate.

"You killed my family!" she screamed, and that renewed her strength. She gave one huge, hard pull, and the gun slipped from Derek's hands, releasing too suddenly and sending her backward through the flimsy screen door. The cinder-block steps scraped across her spine, and the pain shoved all the air from her lungs.

"Jessa!"

It was Graf's voice, she knew that much through the starbursts of pain that obscured her vision and shot fuzzy static through her ears. What was he doing there?

Not that it mattered as he scooped her up to set her on her feet and took off into the house after Derek. He would kill him, she realized in a moment of panic. She wanted him dead, but it wasn't Graf's place. Too many people had been wronged by Derek, and they deserved to see justice served. Real justice, not vengeance born of fear and hatred and prejudice.

"Graf, don't!" she shouted, but her fears were

unfounded. Derek flew through the door and landed with a sickening crunch on the ground. He coughed, and blood burst from his lips.

"Broken ribs," Graf said, dusting his hands off as he stepped out the door. "He'll be fine."

"He won't be," Jessa said coldly, resisting the urge to kick him as he lay there. "They're gonna kill him."

"Yup," Graf agreed. He nodded toward the road, where shapes of something moved in the moonlight.

As the shapes drew closer, she realized what it was.

The town of Penance, angry and urgent, swarming toward Derek's house.

Nineteen

The good people of Penance, still hungry for an execution, converged on the tiny lot like it was the last lifeboat off the *Titanic*. Graf pulled Jessa behind him, completely on instinct, and she pushed his arm aside. So, she was just as hungry for blood as everyone else. Good girl.

She had every right to be. When he'd caught up with June, Graf had been angry enough to kill her. She'd known that, and so she'd readily agreed on a compromise. Jessa wouldn't die tonight, and neither would June.

"If Derek controls that thing, he's the one who deserves to die," he'd reasoned, and June, terrified and pinned to where she stood because of his grip on her braid, had agreed.

"What if we kill him and the demon doesn't go

away," she'd squeaked. "What if we need him to get rid of It?"

"Then we deal with that when the time comes." Graf had pushed her away then, so she could see his fangs, long and intimidating in the moonlight. "Or I could ensure Jessa's safety by killing you right now."

Graf hauled Derek up by the back of his shirt and set him roughly on his feet. "We're here to have a word with you about your monster."

"I don't know what you're talking about," Derek sputtered as Graf marched him down the lawn.

The clouds moved away from the full moon, lighting the yard up like a spotlight. Human eyes glittered blackly in darkness, looking more monstrous than any vampires Graf had ever seen, and for a second, he was afraid himself.

June pushed her way to the front of the crowd. "Derek, you wanna tell these people what you told me the other night?"

"No," Derek spat, as stubborn as a child.

"I think you should tell them, Derek," Graf encouraged him, and then he twisted his arm behind his back for a little more encouragement.

Jessa hung back on the lawn, as if she were afraid to get any closer to the throng. Graf didn't blame her. He wasn't too keen on facing the people who'd almost roasted them alive just a few hours ago.

"If he won't, I will," June said, and there was

nothing friendly or hometown about her expression now. "You say a lot of dumb shit when you're drunk, Derek."

He hung his head, but said nothing.

"Derek did something he shouldn't have," Graf prompted. "Tell them about it, Derek."

Derek whined in agony as Graf's grip on his arm tightened, then he sobbed, "Fine! Fine!" He took a deep, shaking breath. "I...I did it."

Graf leaned close to Derek's ear and said quietly, "They know you did. We told them all about it. We showed them the picture book you made with Sarah."

"Get your monster out here so we can kill it!" someone shouted in the crowd, and they erupted in cheers of violence.

"I can't just call it!" he tried to shout over the mass of voices.

"Liar!" Jessa marched toward him, fist raised as though she would hit him. When she got close enough, though, she restrained herself. "You called it pretty easy to my house to search for me. You called it to the gym when you wanted to trick everyone into believing I was a witch!"

A few loud agreements went up from the crowd, but the reaction wasn't as vehement as Graf would have liked. He didn't need them still thinking Jessa was some kind of sorceress. "Cool it on the witch talk," he murmured under his breath. He didn't want them to remember he was a vampire, either.

"He knows where Becky went!" Jessa's voice rose over the resultant cries of horror and outrage. "They're okay. They got out."

"What are you talking about?" someone shouted.

"She's crazy!" Derek got to his feet, holding his side, and Graf ached to beat him to the ground again.

The crowd seemed less likely to listen to Derek now that their bloodlust had turned away from Jessa and on to him. She kept it short and sweet enough that they didn't take their eyes from Derek. "He said Becky and the kids got out. If It gets hurt bad enough, we could all leave. He just never had the courage to tell anyone."

"Call It here, right now," June ordered over the outrage of the crowd. "We're all ready for it."

In the low light, Graf took stock of the weapons they'd brought. Guns, most of them, but some axes and baseball bats. At least one person had brought a compound hunting bow and arrows, which struck him as a little ridiculous, but they would have to take what they could get. He hoped this worked. Otherwise, they would have a lot of angry people gunning for them again.

"If you won't get it here, I will," Jessa said. She clenched her fists at her sides, opened her mouth, and screamed, loudly and shrilly. The scream went on and on, even after she closed her mouth, as it echoed off the trees and the side of the house.

"What's that supposed to do?" Graf asked quietly. "Other than make them think you're a witch again?"

"It will come for me, because Derek promised me as a sacrifice," she said, determination hardening her eyes. She called out to the crowd. "Derek is the reason the monster is here, and Derek killed my family."

"Now what do we do? To get It here?" June asked Derek.

"We wait," he said miserably.

They didn't have to wait for long. A loud roar went up from a stand of trees across the field on the other side of the road. The monster emerged, a distinct black dot charging across the silvery leaves of the cornfield.

"Graf," Jessa said, her voice high and tight.

"I'm not going to let It get you," he promised, but she backed away from him, as though she didn't believe it. He didn't have time to think about that now. He had a monster to help destroy.

"You won't be able to kill It," Derek warned. "It won't die. It will just keep coming back until it gets what it came for."

It met the opposition in the middle of the road, its terrible claws spread as if to scoop them in, its mouth open and dripping stinking, fetid saliva from its jagged teeth.

The first shots popped off, and the creature swatted at its attackers. Its long, knobby fingers, made longer by its claws, swung like a double-dutch jump rope from hell. Someone screamed. Someone else ran.

Graf turned, and Derek was gone. The coward couldn't even face the monster he'd made.

Blood pounded through Graf's veins—Jessa's blood, which made him slightly horny on top of the excitement from the impending fight. He turned to Jessa and gave her an imploring look.

"Go get 'em, honey," she said with a sarcastic punch to his shoulder.

Graf shook his head and made a mental note to tell her to watch her smart mouth. Faster than she could blink, he was gone, running into the heart of the battle and skidding to a stop just in front of the monster. To his left, a man in overalls dropped to one knee, bleeding from the head.

"Help him!" June ordered, reloading her shotgun.

Though he would like nothing more than to tear into the monster's hide, the guy did need his help. And, remembering what had happened last time they had gone mano a mano, Graf figured the biggest help he could possibly be was getting people out of harm's way. Grabbing the man by the yolk of his overalls— he couldn't trust himself to touch him any further, with blood flowing freely from his wound—he ran up to the lawn in a flash and deposited the injured man at Jessa's feet. "This is how you can help," he told her. "But if that thing comes anywhere near you, you run, got it? If Derek gets near you, you run."

"Don't worry, I'm not stupid," she mumbled.

"I know you're not. You're with me." He winked and raced back into the throng. No one seemed to need immediate rescue, so he took his own run at the creature, hoping the crack shots in the crowd didn't use the opportunity to pick him off. He head-butted the monster in the abdomen, managing to knock it back a step. Graf himself fell back, colliding with the hard ground with an "oof." He got to his feet before the beast's massive claws struck the ground where he had just lain.

"You're gonna get yourself shot or killed!" June shouted over the seemingly endless volley of gunfire. "Get out of there."

He grinned at her and shook his head. The monster brought its fist down on a young guy with a shotgun. The massive clawed hand ground the poor kid into paste, but his gun escaped injury. Graf scooped it up and blew two fingers off It before it could attack again. That left It with a pretty wicked thumb, but one claw was better than three.

It roared in fury and turned its beady little eyes to Graf. "You tired of killing these pathetic humans yet? Wanna fight a real monster?"

There had to be some intelligence in the thing, because It responded by swinging away and snatching up a handful of the good folk of Penance. It hurled the bodies at Graf with enough force that a few necks got broken as they carried Graf to the ground. Trapped under a pile of humans, some of them dead, some of them badly injured, was not how Graf had intended to spend this fight.

"Come on," June shouted, commanding her fellow soldiers with impotent rage. She knew they were losing—that much was evident from the desperation in her voice. Graf struggled to move the stunned and the dead off him, asking all the able-bodied to get themselves the hell out of harm's way. All the while, the creature swung at the bullets flying at it, sending a few heads spinning off like daisies caught by a weed wacker.

Graf seized one of the broken bodies he'd been pelted with and swung it with all his strength at It's midsection. It batted the corpse out of the air with its ruined hand, spraying gore over the rest of the fighting force.

"Graf, no!" June shrieked in horror. The fighting seemed to momentarily stop as citizen after citizen of Penance realized that he had just used one of them as a weapon.

"You stick to helping the wounded, you fucking moron," she spat at him, and Graf sheepishly scooped up a woman with a broken ankle. When he'd gotten her out of danger, two other men needed aid, the victims of friendly fire.

The beast must have taken fifty hits at that point, the way Graf figured it. But It was still standing, still fighting as hard as ever. He didn't flatter himself that he'd done more damage with his bare hands than a group of pissed-off avid hunters with firearms could do. Why wasn't the fucker falling, or at least retreating?

He scooped up an elderly woman who'd taken a small-caliber ball through her ankle and ran her to safety despite her protests that she was fine to fight.

A familiar voice screamed, loud and shrill from inside the fray, and Graf struggled to make his way to June's side. It had her pinned, a claw through her thigh, and leaned over her with dripping jaws wide.

"June!" Graf grabbed the nearest available object, a pitchfork—Jessa had mentioned those hurt like hell—and slid it across the bloodied grass. He reached It, just barely, and shoved the pitchfork hard through the creature's lower jaw, screaming and pushing until the tongs protruded through the top of its head. When It pulled its claw free from June's leg to swipe at the farming implement jammed through its soft palate, Graf used the opportunity to pull June to safety.

"Hold on," he warned, throwing her over his shoulder. In an instant he dumped her on the grass next to Jessa and the wounded she was tending to.

"I'll be all right," she argued, hissing as she bent her leg to examine it. There was blood, a lot of it, but it didn't gush or spray like it would have if her artery had been nicked. Her luck hadn't run out yet, even if it was still fairly shitty luck.

Jessa grabbed his arm before he could disappear into the fray once more. "Something's not right. It should have run off by now."

"You're right," he agreed. "But I don't know what's going on."

"It has to be Derek." She chewed her lip, her gaze far away as she looked toward the monster. "Maybe he's doing another spell, something to keep It from quitting."

When she looked up at him, she got a scared, frantic look on her face. Her pupils dilated, and her pulse stopped and started in her throat. Then, almost as fast as a vampire, she dove for Graf. Not for him. Past him.

He whirled and saw Derek, holding Jessa's shotgun leveled at Graf's head. Jessa screamed, "No!" and grabbed the barrel, covering the muzzle with her hand. In an explosion of blood and bone, the shot ripped through her hand and into her face. She fell like a doll, her knees folding, then her torso tipping, arms crumpling beneath her.

It roared.

A blast of heat and light blistered through the

air, muting the screams of horror from the people fighting against It.

And then the monster fell to one knee, then appeared to sink into the ground. Nothing but bubbling black remained, and then even that disappeared into the ground.

The people of Penance froze with shock, staring at the place where the monster had been.

Graf didn't look at them. He couldn't take his eyes off Derek, who stood, shaking like a man who'd just realized he was facing down a tiger but has run out of ammo. Graf didn't even give him a warning snarl before he lunged for him. He didn't bite him. He knocked him down, waited for him to stand, then knocked him down again. Derek scrambled backward on his hands, like a crab, and Graf pushed him back down.

The people of Penance staggered toward the house, their faces and clothes black with soot and smoke. Some of them dropped their weapons. Others held them tightly. They all advanced on Derek.

When the first strike came—a blow from the butt of a rifle that caused Derek to spit out blood and teeth—Graf was satisfied that Penance's own brand of justice would be served. He dragged himself, suddenly devoid of energy, back to Jessa.

She lay facedown in a heap, a pool of blood

forming beneath her head. The sticky crimson had oozed through her hair and now rolled around sparse blades of grass, picking up sand as it went. As he looked down at her, Graf took a completely involuntary breath, a hiccup that caught in his chest and intensified the pain that already bloomed there. He knelt at her side and lifted one limp arm, still warm, but rapidly cooling in death. He rolled her to her back and turned his face away.

Gore didn't usually bother him; it came with the vampire job description. Looking at Jessa, though, was impossible. He didn't want to see her face ruined and half-gone. He didn't want to see proof that her fragile mortal life had been snuffed out.

Her mortal life. His fangs ached and descended from his gums. There was no question that he wanted to save Jessa. There was no question that it would still work, and he'd seen vampires created from far messier deaths than this one, ones that had healed to perfection. But did she want to be saved? There was nothing for her in Penance. Her family was dead. Her house had been destroyed. She had been deeply unhappy when he'd arrived. Did she want an eternity of that unhappiness?

It was hard for Graf to imagine anyone not being happy as a vampire. It was harder to imagine waking up tomorrow night and Jessa not being there with him.

Could he make her happy? Happy enough to want to live forever?

While the good, salt-of-the-earth people of Penance beat Derek to death on his lawn, Graf scooped Jessa up in his arms and quietly walked away.

Twenty

The room was dark, and eerily quiet. Despite the lack of light, Jessa saw the shapes of her bedroom furniture clearly, and she relaxed, sinking back to the bed she'd sat bolt upright from. She pressed a hand to her chest. Nightmares like that always made her pulse race and her lungs ache from panting.

Her hand remained still where it lay. Her chest didn't move. She sucked in air in a violent jerk; her hand rose and fell with the motion, just once.

She reached to her hair and smoothed it back. It wasn't damp from sweat. And she was thirsty. So, so thirsty.

Beside her, Graf sat up. He smelled so good, so familiar, she wanted to bury her face in his neck and breathe him in.

Wait, Graf didn't have a smell.

"You feeling okay?" he asked, rubbing her arm,

the way people had done to her at her parents' funeral. Feeling okay? "How are you holding up?" It was an odd question from Graf. It lacked his typical humor…

"I'm fine," she said mechanically, then corrected herself. "No, I'm not fine. Something is wrong."

"Nothing is wrong." He pulled her into his arms, and she went to him because she had other things to worry about than where her body was. He kissed her cheek and smoothed her hair. "What's the last thing you remember?"

The last thing? She could barely remember the last night, as a whole. "I guess it was fighting It… I remember It's claws, and I remember a lot of people shooting…"

Shooting. That was something. "Derek had a gun?"

Graf made a noise of affirmation low in his throat. "He did. You're remembering, that's good."

"Wait." She remembered the gun, and Derek pointing it at Graf. She recalled putting her hand over the barrel and— "He shot me!"

"Don't panic!" Graf held out his hands, like he was trying to keep her from jumping off a ledge. "I can explain."

The gun had gone off, the shot had scattered, plowing through her hand, splattering over her face and chest. She smoothed her hands over her face, which by all rights should have been missing.

"You made me into you."

"I can explain," he repeated, but his expression said, "Oh, shit."

"What's to explain." She shrugged, thinking that she should be stiff and sore from sleep, but she wasn't. She felt amazing. Not just her body, but her spirit, if there was such a thing. "You saved my life."

"No, I kind of killed you." He cocked his head to the side. "You're taking this awfully well."

"I am, aren't I?" She shrugged again. "It's better than being dead."

"It is." He scratched his head. "I've got to be honest, I was expecting you to freak out."

"I still might." Maybe the full impact of what had happened to her hadn't sunk in yet. When it did, she reserved the right to freak. At that moment, there were far more important things on her mind. "It's gone?"

"Yeah. And Derek is…"

"Dead," she filled in for him. A lump of mingled sorrow and anger rose in her throat. "That I might freak out about."

"You'd better not." Was that jealousy she heard in his voice? It pleased her in the most disturbing and shameful way.

"Did you make anyone else a…a vampire?" She thought about those people lying all bloody on the grass.

Graf shook his head. "Only you, as far as I'm aware."

Hearing about your own death was definitely an experience Jessa had never expected to have. She laughed at the absurdity of it.

"I need to tell you something." Graf looked mildly annoyed with her mood. Maybe whatever it was he was going to tell her would have been more appropriate for a brand-new, freaking-out vampire, instead of a brand-new, calm one. "I don't want you to think that what I did was so that you would be obligated to me."

She nodded, indicating that she was listening.

He went on. "You don't have to come with me, so don't think I'm forcing you to. I'm going to get out of here. I have a life outside this place, and I need to get back to it."

Was he brushing her off? She carefully fixed her expression so he wouldn't see her disappointment and hurt. "I understand."

"No, you don't." He gripped the back of her neck and pulled her mouth to his, kissing her like it was a different language, one that he could easier communicate his meaning in. When he broke his mouth away, he leaned his forehead against hers. "I'm just saying that I'm not forcing you to come with me. I need you to come with me. I need you, period. And I'll drag you out of here, kicking and screaming if necessary."

It wouldn't be necessary. She looked around her room, the room with pictures of her and Derek and Becky at graduation, the room with wallpaper covering the spot where she'd colored a unicorn on the painted wall in permanent marker when she was five. The room in the house where she'd lived another life, when her parents had been alive, when things had been so, so much different than they were now. The house that was an empty shell now that all of that was gone.

In the distance, she heard a siren wailing, an ambulance screaming toward its destination. An ambulance. In Penance. She laughed, even as the alien sound conjured a picture in her vampire brain of the plump Midwestern EMTs who would be riding along in it, the bleeding accident victim strapped helplessly in the back. Her mouth watered. She smiled slowly at Graf.

"What is it?" he asked nervously, clearly anticipating rejection.

She arched an eyebrow and wetted her lips. "Have you ever stolen an ambulance before?"

* * * * *

If you leave now, you'll always wonder, a tiny voice nagged from the back of my mind. For a fraction of a second, it seemed the gnawing fear would win. I would just walk out of the morgue and forget the whole incident ever happened.

But my father's words and Dr. Fuller's hurtful evaluation of my abilities bounced around in my brain. I didn't want to be the failure I'd been in my father's eyes. The failure I'd become in Dr. Fuller's. It spurred me toward the table.

I was no coward.

Before I gave myself a chance to change my mind, I whipped the sheet completely off the cadaver.

Every second passed in slow motion, frame by frame. The very instant I pulled the covering off the body, I saw a brightly colored sole of an athletic shoe poking from under the sheet. There wasn't time for this to register as I ripped away the shroud, revealing hospital-issue scrubs and the face of the morgue attendant, his features frozen in terror.

I didn't scream right away, either from shock or the fact that the scene didn't make sense. John Doe was supposed to be here, not this young man. The sight transfixed me.

His neck had obviously been broken. The flesh of his throat had been torn the way it would look after a dog attack. Extreme blood loss left his dark skin ashen, though the table and most of his clothing were spotless. His eyes were open. One was missing.

I saw the telephone perched on the gleaming steel counter, but it seemed miles away as I ran to it. My hands shook so badly that I could barely punch the numbers to issue a code blue. But no reassuring calm came over me when I hung up. I was still stranded, still isolated in this weird nightmare. I picked up the phone again.

I was dialing the number for the night security office when something brushed my shoulder. The touch was so light I barely noticed it, but I wound up inexplicably on my back.

The force of my landing knocked the wind out of me. Confused and frightened, I scrambled to my knees, but that was as far as I got.

In the next instant, I was airborne again. Shattering glass crashed, the consequence of my impact against the cabinets. I had flown into the glass with enough momentum to break it and splinter the wooden doors. Pain ripped down my spine. The shelves collapsed and the plastic tubs within slipped to the floor, overturning and spilling their contents. I fell to my hands and knees in a mire of formaldehyde and human livers, unable to efficiently crawl through the slippery mess.

A hand grabbed my hair and dragged me upward. When I tried to regain my footing I slipped to my knees again and writhed painfully in the grasp of my attacker. I looked up.

John Doe looked down at me.

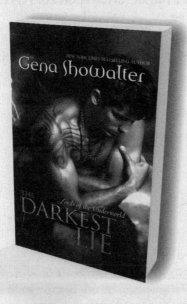

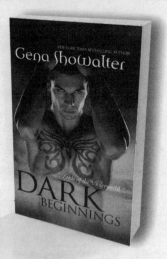

THE PSYCHOLOGICAL BASIS OF MORALITY

LIBRARY OF PHILOSOPHY AND RELIGION

General Editor: John Hick, H. G. Wood Professor of
Theology,
University of Birmingham

This new series of books will explore contemporary religious understandings of man and the universe. The books will be contributions to various aspects of the continuing dialogues between religion and philosophy, between scepticism and faith, and between the different religions and ideologies. The authors will represent a correspondingly wide range of viewpoints. Some of the books in the series will be written for the general educated public and others for a more specialised philosophical or theological readership.

THE PSYCHOLOGICAL BASIS OF MORALITY

An essay on value and desire

by

F. C. T. MOORE

First published 1978 by
THE MACMILLAN PRESS LTD
London and Basingstoke
Associated companies in Delhi
Dublin Hong Kong Johannesburg Lagos
Melbourne New York Singapore Tokyo

Printed in Hong Kong

British Library Cataloguing in Publication Data

Moore, Francis Charles Timothy
   The psychological basis of morality. — (Library of
   philosophy and religion).
   1. Ethics
   I. Title   II. Series
   170   BJ1012

ISBN 0–333–23664–5

'*If the will did not exist, neither would there be that centre of the world, which we call the I, and which is the bearer of ethics.*'

LUDWIG WITTGENSTEIN
Notebooks 1914–1916
p. 80

Contents

(i) Argument in one dimension

Books begin at the beginning and continue until the end (footnotes being the exception that proves this rule). This unfortunate one-dimensionality has led philosophers into various expedients of style, from Platonic dialogue to Cartesian autobiography, Spinozistic tabulation or Nietzschean declamation, expedients by which the complex internal relations of argument may be reduced to a tractable linearity.

This book has strayed from accepted linearities. It has a main argument presented in linear fashion. But there are in addition annexed sections which are intended to support parts of that argument, to lead into it, to explain it further, to defend it against various objections, and to show its bearing upon issues related to those arising in the main argument.

The main argument is printed in roman type with section numbers in arabic numerals, while the annexes are printed in italic type, and are separately numbered in roman style. The main argument has a degree of self-sufficiency, while the nature and intent of certain annexes imposed an allusive and sometimes fragmentary treatment.

(ii) The Metaphysic of Morals

In his book Individuals, Strawson made a distinction between 'descriptive metaphysics', which is 'content to describe the actual structure of our thought about the world', and 'revisionary metaphysics', which is 'concerned to produce a better structure'.

But is 'descriptive metaphysics', so defined, a task of philosophy at all? It may seem that this is an area of study belonging properly to various of the human sciences. To examine how men actually think, we may say, is in different ways the business of historians, sociologists, social anthropologists, psychologists, and so forth. Such studies have an empirical, rather than a philosophical, orientation.

What is true in this objection accounts, I believe, for some of the traditional hostilities and suspicions that arise between philosophers and others. But it is nevertheless a misleading objection. For philosophy too starts from, even if it does not always return to, how men actually think. Moreover, those very thinkers who might covet the title of 'descriptive metaphysician' customarily argue the existence of ordered relations between concepts, such that some are said to be logically more basic than others, or even such that some are claimed to be a necessary requirement for any thought or experience of any kind. We may put it by saying that such a philosopher wishes to disclose a necessary order within the natural order of thought.

Of course, this characterisation of a philosopher's task by appeal to a distinction between a necessary conceptual order and an empirical natural order raises major problems. We shall return to them in annex (xi) below.

For our present purpose, it is sufficient to observe that in philosophy and elsewhere the search for a 'necessary order' often manifests itself in an explanatory technique by which one set of propositions, concepts or terms is taken as fundamental, and some other set is explained in terms of the first. This is the procedure often given the label of 'reductionism'. Reflection on it will lead us to qualify the distinction between descriptive and revisionary metaphysics.

For the application of this procedure by the so-called 'descriptive metaphysician' to diplay what he claims to be the actual structure of our thought about the world will be the diagnosis of some necessary order within

2

the natural order of thought, and will always be open to challenge. In the case of such challenge, the philosopher who thought he was describing may well be charged with an unnecessary and implausible revision. Berkeley notoriously claims to be a champion of common sense, that is, to be describing the actual structure of our thought about the world. But what of Berkeley's critics? Are they to maintain that he has described wrongly, or that he has revised unacceptably? Or should we reject this dilemma, and claim that Berkeley is neither describing the natural order of thought, nor offering an alternative to it, but proposing a debatable account of a necessary order within the present and perhaps within any possible natural order?

Techniques of reduction, I suggest, whether in philosophy or elsewhere, cannot be justified on the basis of the natural order alone—by reference to brute facts. It is this that has led some to hold that not only are particular applications of such techniques open to criticism, but that they are of their nature vicious. 'Everything is what it is, and not another thing.' Such views constitute a radical and pervasive scepticism. How can dynamics, for example, be justified in treating idealised and not real trajectories? And what remains of the very profession of philosophy? This scepticism is not to be lightly dismissed; but if philosophy can be vindicated at all, it will be improper to object to a particular philosophical argument on the sole grounds that it employs a technique of reduction. In moral philosophy, for example, arguments against naturalism are generally question-begging in their bald assumption of the autonomy of moral concepts. There is no 'naturalistic fallacy' unless it be the fallacy of all philosophy.

I make no excuse, therefore, for arguing what is undoubtedly describable as a naturalistic position in moral philosophy, for offering a metaphysic of morals which is, I believe, truer than Kant's own position to his injunction that 'a metaphysic of morals has to investigate the Idea and principles of a possible pure Will'.

But it is the proper courtesy of an author to apologise to his reader for the imperfections which will certainly be found in his work, and to make it clear that those whom he wishes to thank are named for that purpose alone, and not with the impertinent intention of lending their authority, however subtly, to the finished book.

I am grateful to many colleagues, friends and students from Oxford, Paris, Birmingham and Khartoum, but particular thanks are due to Elizabeth Anscombe, Christopher Bryant, Jacques Derrida, Alec Fisher, Peter Geach, John Hick and Christopher Villars; to Bernard Mayo, Ingmar Pörn and Charles Whiteley, whose comments on the draft were invaluable; to Peter Lienhardt, whose pungent remarks on the dangers of the profession *of philosophy made a lasting impression on me; to the British Academy, the French Government, and the University of Birmingham, for important material assistance at various stages of my work on this book; to M. and Mme. Busnel, in whose congenial house the final draft was written; to Hilary Fancote, for her patient and efficient typing of the draft; to my wife, whose help and indulgence made this work possible; and to Alf Louvre, who said 'It's anarchy!'*

1 The Pure Will

Kant held that it was the will conforming itself to duty, not the will alone, which was to account for morality. I shall argue that the existence of the will by itself already implies the existence of value.

As a first step, we shall make abstraction of the specific human circumstances and contingencies of wills and values as we know them, and address ourselves to the relation between pure will and pure value.

The idea of a 'pure will' is, at its schematic minimum, the same as the idea of a source of change. Consider a universe containing just one such source of change. May changes take place in such a universe other than those produced by this source of change? Any such changes, clearly, would have to be such as not to originate from a source of change; for if they did, our universe would then contain more than one source of change, which is contrary to the hypothesis. Any such additional changes would therefore have to be of one of two kinds: they would be either changes produced by other changes which in turn were produced by other changes and so on (there being no first member in such a series, there would *a fortiori* be no source for any of the changes in it); or they would be changes occurring spontaneously (or produced by spontaneously occurring changes). These two cases—that of causal sequences of changes without a first member, and that of self-originating or unoriginated changes—may be problematic. Indeed we shall find it necessary to consider them further in section 13 below. But they are not obviously incoherent. And, what is important for the present purpose, nothing in the schematic initial condition of our hypothetical universe (that it contain only one source of change) permits us to *exclude* the possibility of changes occurring in it which are not attributable to that will.

We may now assert of this universe that any change that occurs in it must occur by the operation of the one source of change, or spontaneously, or as a member of a sequence of changes each producing the next. These latter kinds of change may not occur, but we cannot exclude them. But if they do occur, a further possibility is introduced—of changes occurring as a result of some combination of the three factors. This possibility must be open, since if it were not there would be no grounds for claiming that the three classes of events belong to the same universe. Moreover, a change which is due to more than one factor may be different from what it would have been if only one factor had been in operation.

We are now faced with a surprising result. It might have seemed that the idea of the pure will, abstraction made of the contingent forms of our actual experience of willing, was the idea of a source of change which would produce any change upon which it was directed without impediment, so that it would be absurd to suppose willing to occur without its corresponding change. But the construction of a model universe even with only one will has led us to require the *possibility* of the frustration of that will. For the model does not allow us to exclude changes attributable to other factors. If there are other factors, we cannot exclude their interaction. And if they interact with the will, we cannot exclude the occurrence of a change other than that towards which the will was directed.

Of course, just as the 'will' in this model universe is no more than the abstract form of agents as we know them, so too the 'value' distinctions which can now be seen emerging are no more than the abstract form of the real evaluations which we make and encounter in our lives. But these forms at least have emerged in our model universe, which is good so far as it conforms itself to the will, and bad so far as it does not, from the standpoint of the one will (*and there is no other standpoint*).

We take issue, then, with Kant's treatment of the *a priori* conditions of morality. An examination of the 'idea of a possible pure will' alone enables us to see in it the genesis of values, though the sketch here offered of a model universe calls for considerable elaboration (such as is adumbrated in annex (viii) and sections 8 and 13 below).

This condensed and abstract argument is a rehearsal for what follows. Our embodied existence, our varying and conflicting desires and pleasures, the intransigencies of the world, of others and of ourselves, all of these greatly complicate the various evaluative and psychological notions which are cast in the moulds respectively of what I have been calling the idea of pure value and the idea of pure will.

It will now be our task to relax the abstractions made, and to move back from the model universe just described to the very world of our joys and sufferings.

(iii) Objects of Desire

But as we turn to give an account of human desires, as a first concrete mode of the 'pure will', we encounter a philosophical reef. For we shall have to consider the objects of desires, and in so doing we shall naturally if not unavoidably speak of states of affairs, and of the propositions specifying them. These are problematic and controversial notions. I do not hope, in this annex, to offer a detailed solution to these problems, but to provide a chart by which my later use of the notions of states of affairs and propositions may be accepted without shipwreck.

We may start by observing the circumstances of our natural and perhaps unavoidable use of these notions. Men respond to states of affairs. They believe them to exist. They believe that they can be brought into existence. States of affairs provoke fear and pleasure. They are perceived and reported by the use of the appropriate propositions. They are striven for. But what account is to be given of these notions?

States of affairs may be envisaged either from the point of view of Wittgenstein's Tractatus *or from the point of view of Carnap. The two extremes (even if these labels for them are not entirely appropriate) are that in which we start from the universe as a whole, and consider a state of affairs as what corresponds to a complete state description of the universe, and that in which we start from the objects which exist in the universe, and consider a state of affairs as a specific combination of some of those objects. In the one, it is the universe as a whole which is supposed in some sense to be given; in the other, it is particular objects which are supposed to be given.*

But in fact neither of these is given. It is not an epistemological difficulty that I am raising here: not the difficulty of how we can know that a given state description of the universe is true, or of how we can know that we have securely identified a particular object, though both of these are difficulties. The problem is more radical. For if the universe is unbounded, then state descriptions of it of the kind envisaged cannot be given, and any partial description will fail in its logically primary task of providing an adequate criterion of identity for states of affairs. Equally, there could be no formally adequate identifying description of a particular object, enabling it to be

7

distinguished from other objects and then to form states of affairs by its combination with some of them. Thus the viability of the notion of states of affairs would depend on whether as a matter of fact the universe is finite.

The readiest solution to those difficulties is to weaken our identity requirements for states of affairs, incorporating into our account provision for the incompleteness of propositions specifying states of affairs, either in the sense of not being complete state descriptions of the universe, or in the sense of not deploying complete identifying descriptions (after the manner of Russell) of the objects composing the state of affairs: the two difficulties in certain respects coincide.

According to this solution we regard a state of affairs as an entity determined only in respect of those features included in the proposition specifying it. It remains undetermined of all other features whether the state of affairs has or lacks them.

An entity of this sort is pretty much a logical weakling: for instance, the law of excluded middle will be severely restricted in its case. Yet it is, I suggest, because of the tractability of a notion of states of affairs allowing this weak identity that human beings can readily deal with and appreciate the situations which they believe themselves to encounter. The provisionality and indeterminacy which is the logical weakness of the notion is at the same time its practical strength. At times, indeed, by variously motivated and effected restriction of our area of enquiry, we behave as though states of affairs were at least in principle fully determinable (in both the two senses formerly indicated), and for the purpose at hand this procedure may be legitimate. But it is a realist extrapolation from (or a creation of simplified model domains within) the prior—and not just epistemologically prior—case of states of affairs which are only partially determined; we should not be misled by it into attributing greater theoretical substance to the notion of states of affairs than it actually possesses.

For the notion is not only logically but also ontologically weak, since we have now made states of affairs relative to propositions held to specify them. The question now arises: what of propositions themselves?

It is a commonplace that here too we find ourselves in face of a form of the old realist/nominalist controversy. According to the realist position, a proposition is the thought of a sentence (at least in the case of declarative sentences)—a thought which a given sentence may succeed to a greater or less extent in conveying, and which may equally be expressed in other sentences, a thought whose existence is not dependent on the existence of any particular linguistic forms, nor on the existence of any particular thinker—a thought which is real—which is an abstract, non-spatiotemporal, non-linguistic, and *non-psychological entity. According to the nominalist position, a proposition—if we are to use the term at all—is a linguistic entity. The view is more or less flexible according to whether and how the phenomenon of 'saying in one's heart' is admitted (thereby providing suitably linguistic entities where they might not else have seemed to be found), and according to the ways in which syntactic or even semantic considerations are made to enter into the criteria for identification of sentences—of the linguistic entities which are the nominalists' candidates for propositionhood.*

On the simplest realist view the same proposition is expressed by the following two sentences: 'The morning star is bright', and 'The evening star is bright'. On this view, true sentences refer to or are made true by their correspondence with states of affairs. And in the present case, the two sentences say the same thing of the same object: they are both true in virtue of the same state of affairs. Consequently the thought they express is also the same. But on this view, as it stands, there is no uniform way of dealing with the non-equivalence of the two sentences in what are called 'intentional contexts'.

We may therefore adopt a modified and more subtle realist view—that of Frege. According to this view also, the two sentences have the same reference, which is not a state of affairs, but a truth value, in this case, truth. However, they do not have the same sense, since the sense of the expression 'the morning star' is different from the sense of the expression 'the evening star', though their reference happens to be the same. Thus though we admit realist propositions, as the sense or thought of sentences, we find them to be different in the case of these two sentences. Hence it is possible to deal with the difficult features of intentional contexts by maintaining that when a sentence appears in such contexts it then has as its reference what in non-intentional contexts would be its sense.

This modified realism provides a coherent solution to the problem at hand. Yet it has an ad hoc character, and introduces an intensional anomaly into the logic of intentional contexts which is plainly going to be awkward to cope with. Our problems are housed, but in a logical ghetto. If we turn to the nominalist solution, on the other hand, we find that the ghetto has been replaced by an unusually characterless suburb. For the essence of this solution is to claim that in these contexts what we are dealing with is not any kind of entity which transcends thought and language, but a particular linguistic form. The immediate reply to such solutions is to state baldly that when, for instance, we attribute a belief to someone, we do mean more than to attribute to him some actual, tacit or potential utterance of some form of words. Moreover, it is clear in the case of human behaviour (let alone the case of animals) that it is false to claim that whenever a man has a desire, a hope, a belief, there exists some form of words which in one way or another he must be taken to be manipulating, even in his heart. For belief in a proposition need not actually take a specific linguistic form at all.

The difficulty we are now presented with closely resembles that which we encountered in the case of states of affairs, and the solution I shall propose is also analogous to that solution. Propositions are characteristically, though not exclusively, expressed by sentences, and when we take a sentence to express a certain proposition, we are assuming in that context the agreement of a certain community, however wide or restricted, about what other sentences would rightly be taken to express the same proposition. It may seem that there is a fatal circularity in such an account of propositions—being of the form: a proposition is what is expressed by any set of sentences which are taken to express the same proposition! However, the agreement of the community is not happily described as an agreement that such and such sentences express the same proposition: it is rather that for some purpose and in respect of some state of affairs, a certain open set of sentences is such that any of them may be substituted for any other without such a substitution making any difference (for that purpose and in that context). Consider, for example, the case where I repeat what I have said in other words to avoid misunderstanding. It is true that when I do this, there is a way in which I am precisely not treating the two sentences as interchangeable. Indeed, I am envisaging the possibility that the first may not perform its desired function, whereas the second (or the first together with the second) may do so. Yet this is possible just because both are equally such as to perform that function (if successful—and of course it would be absurd to search for a guarantee that the hearer understands). Now, the consensus which expresses itself in such functional equivalence (whatever detailed account should be given of it) does not in general enable us to give a complete enumeration of the set of sentences so determined as expressing the same proposition; nor indeed is our assumption of consensus in particular cases always correct.

However, it is a matter of everyday experience that sets of sentences are granted as equivalent. Where this is so, it is appropriate to speak of propositions of such and such a form, since there is then no particular sentence with which we are concerned. Of course, no label of the form 'the proposition expressed by s' can of itself and independently of context identify a particular proposition: as is so for definite descriptions in general. Even where a list of sentences is given, it cannot be a complete list, and will not guarantee community of understanding, which is in general already in existence in the shared patterns of life and thought that are the informal basis for the philosopher's use of the notion of a proposition.

But the case of intentional contexts is precisely one where the community of understanding may be in question. For the subject matter of intentional statements is the beliefs, desires and attitudes of particular people, something of which for good reasons abstraction is made in other contexts of discourse. Yet this need not lead us to the extreme of claiming that in these contexts there can be no criteria for interchangeability of sentences, as the severe nominalist solution requires, at least in the admittedly unsophisticated version of it which I have indicated. Nor are we obliged to devise a special semantics such as that of Frege. For Frege's account takes as given what I argue to be in question in such contexts, namely the senses of those expressions which will now refer to their senses.

The fact is that in such contexts, sentences are taken as interchangeable with certain others, and thus as 'expressing a certain proposition'; but whereas elsewhere there is an assumed agreement about the range of sentences in question, the arbiter being communal practice, in these cases, on the other hand, it is precisely in question what proposition the person is entertaining, and it is he alone who is, exceptionally, the arbiter of what other sentences are taken as expressing the same proposition, no matter how unorthodox his understanding.

Of course, when I speak here of the individual being the arbiter, I do not mean that we are to refer the matter to him for adjudication. It is rather that the criteria of what is meant and understood lie now not in communal behaviour, but in his individual behaviour—the way in which his fashion of acting, speaking and thinking shows him to understand the sentence: of this he is not necessarily himself the best, and certainly not the only judge.

The account of intentional contexts that is now taking shape hinges on the claim that their peculiarities are not in fact logical: rather the problems concern the criteria for propositional identity appropriate in such cases, since the identity of propositions in intentional contexts, as has been argued, depends upon the person whose propositional attitude is in question. However, this account seems to encounter a serious difficulty in modal contexts, where the same difficulties (of referential opacity and so forth) arise as in the other intentional contexts already considered, but where there seems to be no possibility of generalising the solution proposed, since we cannot relativise the identity of propositions in modal contexts to some individual person. Thus it may be objected that the account proposed here is ad hoc, being able to cope with a certain problem in psychological contexts, but not with what is in the end the same problem in modal contexts.

*However, the approach suggested can be extended to cover modal contexts. Consider the interpretation of the modalities by the semantics of possible worlds. In this semantics, we read, for instance, 'Necessarily **F(a)**' as '**F(a)** in all possible worlds'. It will be in this way that we shall account for the* failure of the inference 'Necessarily **F(a)**, **a** = **b**, therefore necessarily **F(b)**'. But what does the adoption of such a semantics amount to? It amounts, I suggest, to the introduction of an uncertainty into the identification of the propositions with which we are dealing—not this time as a consequence of individual vagaries on this side of some agreed identification, but now of vagaries of possible worlds and contexts beyond the agreed identification. If **a** may recur in many possible worlds, and so **b** also, the identity of the proposition '**a** = **b**' is now in doubt. To which world is it to be relativised? (For trans-world identity of objects cannot be assumed, though it may be variously specified, connecting different worlds by structures of what have been dubbed 'trans-world heir-lines'.) If we relativise it to 'this' (agreed) world, then the inference will not stand. But if, for instance, it were true of any arbitrary world, then '**a** = **b**' so interpreted becomes equivalent to 'Necessarily **a** = **b**', and the inference will stand.

These are the lines of argument showing that in intentional contexts in general, and not only those where psychological notions are involved, the puzzles that have been so much discussed may be regarded as puzzles about the identity of propositions, and not about logical peculiarities of propositions of a certain type.

I am arguing that we should retain the notion of propositions for intentional and non-intentional contexts, and that there are no logical differences between such propositions arising specifically from the context difference, once the identity of the propositions concerned has been carefully ascertained. Now this position suggests that arguments like '**a** believes **p**; **p** implies **q**; therefore, **a** believes **q**', are after all valid, and that any appearance to the contrary is produced by introducing confusion about what proposition it is that recurs in the argument. For instance, it is rightly held that 'The morning star is a planet' implies 'The evening star is a planet' granted the truth of 'The morning star is the evening star'. But when it is further assumed that the man of whom we say (doing the best we can) that he believes that the morning star is a planet is necessarily entertaining the same proposition as was expressed in the above argument, then there is dangerous ground underfoot. Indeed, if this man does not believe that the evening star is a planet, this precisely raises questions about what proposition it is that he is being said to believe, when he is said to believe that the morning star is a planet. His ignorance of the fact that the morning star is the evening star must be taken to affect the meaning he attaches to sentences involving reference to the morning star, and sentences involving reference to the evening star. Referential opacity is not a property of a sentence or a proposition: it is in the eyes of the beholder.

Let us be clear about what is suggested here. In many ordinary *circumstances we assume with perfect felicity that we do for the purpose at hand understand each other perfectly. Information is commonly and often justifiably treated as a communal and communicable possession, and investigations are treated as methods of ascertaining the truth or falsehood of propositions quite transparent to the investigators. It is in this common world of the understanding that we act as though we had to do with Platonic propositions.*

But as soon as the possibility of misunderstanding arises (and the very existence of a common world of the understanding depends upon there being some means of coping with this), propositions—or their corresponding sets of sentences—become circumscribed. We have to rein ourselves in to that weaker form of identity of propositions according to which they are determined only in respect of a certain limited range of sentences taken as interchangeable. If **a** *does not believe* **q**, *though* **p** *implies* **q**, *then* **a** *does not believe* **p**, *even though he is rightly said to believe that* **s**, *and* **s** *is normally understood to express* **p**. *What it is that* **a** *does believe may be rather impenetrable. The root of the trouble may lie in anything from a minor piece of factual ignorance to an eccentric theory about the world, or even a radical confusion of thought.*

Thus propositions, like states of affairs, may be regarded as entities that are not fully determined, though in both cases and for many purposes we may properly act as though they were.

The idealised or Platonic picture which we are then using should not be attacked because it is idealised, any more than the idealisation involved in any scientific theory should render it open to suspicion. But idealisations need to be carefully handled. In this case, we should be taking the set of interchangeable sentences to which a proposition corresponds to be wholly determinate. The relation between sentence and proposition thus appears as analogous to the relation between token and type. Just as a class of tokens are tokens of the one type, so here a class of type sentences are expressions of the one proposition. And just as for many purposes it is appropriate to assume that it is determinate for any arbitrary token, whether or not it is a token of the one type, so it may be appropriate to assume that it is determinate for any arbitrary sentence whether or not it expresses a given proposition. But when the understanding of a sentence is in question, the class in which it is to be placed as expressing the same proposition is of course in question, so that it will be undetermined of certain sentences whether it is part of the way that a particular sentence is understood by someone that they should or should not be among the set of sentences taking which as interchangeable for the purpose at hand defines his understanding.

*Now in giving an outline of this position, we have apparently been led to reinstate as a valid inference 'a believes **p**; **p** implies **q**: therefore **a** believes **q**' (among the possibly unwelcome consequences of which would be not only that a person could not have an inconsistent belief, but that if he has a true belief, then he believes all logical truths, and that if he has a false belief, then he believes any proposition whatever). However, we have not committed ourselves to its reinstatement. What we have done is to show that the reasons sometimes advanced for holding the inference to be invalid, namely, the alleged logical peculiarities of so-called intentional contexts, should be dismissed. It is now open to us to consider any special features of notions such as wanting and believing without the burdensome assumption that intentional contexts are logically anomalous.*

It may indeed be found fruitful to formalise our findings, for instance by appropriate definition of modal operators, but we are not obliged to do so in order to escape intentional anomalies.

*We shall not here engage in any substantial discussion of formalisations of wants and beliefs, but some observations may appropriately be made. We may hold, for instance, that wants that are inconsistent with each other, and beliefs that are inconsistent with each other, can clearly coexist in the same person; on the other hand, we may wish to deny the possibility of holding a belief which is in itself inconsistent, or having a desire the specification of whose object would include inconsistent propositions. In this way, we are committing ourselves to the view that beliefs are to be distinguished from each other, and wants too. (We should not accept the view on which it would in the end be improper to treat different wants or beliefs as separable items rather than as more or less arbitrarily isolated segments of the totality of a man's wants or beliefs.) On the contrary, wants and beliefs are capable of individuation (this is primarily a psychological task). Individual wants or beliefs cannot be in themselves inconsistent (though the agent's attempted treatment of a set of sentences as not involving inconsistency may show confusion of thought on his part), but inconsistency may and does occur in the set of wants or beliefs of a particular person. If we wish to represent these views formally, we shall eliminate distribution in our rules for the modal operators. In other words, we shall disallow the inference from 'a wants (believes) **p**' & 'a wants (believes) **q**' to 'a wants (believes) **p** & **q**'; we shall also disallow the inference from 'a wants **p** & **q**' to '(a wants **p**) & (a wants **q**)' (though we may retain the inference from 'a wants **p** & **q**' to '(a wants **p**) **v** (a wants **q**)'. Such a position will be developed, though not formally, in section 2§4.*

But before we proceed to a more detailed consideration of wanting, a substantial objection to the whole procedure of this annex should be considered. It is conducted, we may hold, at the wrong level. Propositions and states of affairs are considered as entities, and—as if this were not bad enough—as unanalysed entities. On the contrary, it should be recognised that propositions only exist because of the terms which compose them, and states of affairs because of the objects which compose them. Thus any questions about the possibility or acceptability of treating propositions and states of affairs as entities must take second place to, or at the very least go along with, questions about the possibility or acceptability of treating terms and objects as entities.

This objection alone is decisive: it means that what has been said in this section cannot be treated as an adequate theory of propositions or of states of affairs. The crucial questions of their internal structure and of the possibility of reductivist accounts of them are left virtually untouched.

However, the purpose of this short section has not been to present such a theory, but rather, as was indicated at the outset, to say enough to make safe the use of the notions of propositions and states of affairs which it will be convenient to make in the account of wanting which is to follow.

And we have seen that it will be safe to use them so long as we bear in mind two provisos:

(1) we must fully recognise uncertainties in the identification of the propositions—and consequently the states of affairs—with which we are concerned (in particular, possible divergences between communally established understanding, and the—possibly confused—understanding of a particular person);

(2) we must consequently be ready to treat propositions and states of affairs as entities which are not fully determined.

These conditions may seem problematic, but they situate the problematic area where it is: neither in the perplexities of an outright Platonic transcendence, nor in the bleak theoretical landscape envisaged by the nominalist, but in the uncertainties of life, uncertainties which exist, both in the world, and in our response to it. To these responses we now return.

2 Wanting

§1. When a man has a desire, three conditions are satisfied. First, a description of some state of affairs in the form of a proposition or some conjunction of propositions will provide an answer to the question 'What does he want?'; secondly, this will be a description of a future state of affairs; and thirdly, the man will tend or intend to do something as tending to bring about that state of affairs. We may call these three criteria the *propositional*, the *prospective*, and the *conative*.

§2. It may seem that the propositional criterion does not always apply, since some desires are directed not upon states of affairs, but upon things. This is not so. Let Caroline want a rose. Upon what is her want directed? There need be no particular rose which she wants. In that case, what she wants is this: that the state of affairs in which she is in possession of some rose obtain, or that the proposition that for some rose she may be in possession of it be true. However, let us suppose that there is a particular rose—the one just out of reach on that bush—that she wants. Is it not then the case that what she wants is a thing, and not a state of affairs?

We ask here what would satisfy her desire. Would *that rose* satisfy it? In some way, certainly: but in what way? Would it satisfy her desire by remaining on the bush, by closing its petals, by being in her hand, by being in her dining-room, by being a gift offered to her, by changing colour? Caroline's desire cannot be satisfied by the rose as such (whatever that would be), but only by something being true of the rose.

A desire then is always directed upon some state of affairs; we can ascertain which one by asking what must happen to satisfy the desire. It is to be remarked that this question can in principle receive a definitive reply: that is, we can give a full specification of the state of affairs which would satisfy any desire by giving in full the propositions which the person who has the desire is (in respect of that desire) trying to make true. For instance, that I should pick the rose now and hand it to Caroline might be such a specification for her present desire. Notice that the state of affairs which is the object of desire is undetermined in all other respects, beyond those mentioned in the propositions given.

This may seem unsatisfactory: for I may make these propositions true while doing something that Caroline does *not* want. In picking the rose, I denude the bush; in handing it to Caroline, I thrust a thorn into her palm. She may want neither of these things. But then other conflicting desires have come into play.

It is important to notice here that there are two different cases of conflicting desires, the cases of extrinsic and of intrinsic conflict. As we have described our present example, the conflict between Caroline's desires might well be extrinsic in the one case, and intrinsic in the other.

An extrinsic conflict is one where no conflict emerges at the level of specifying the objects of desire: in other words, where the conflict occurs although we do not find incompatible propositions in those specifications. Here, we may say, the two desires just happen to come into conflict: indeed, it may be questioned whether conflict is an appropriate word at all. In our present example, Caroline had no reason to expect that receiving the rose would involve being hurt by the thorn. There is therefore (so far as we have stated the case) no reason to include not being pricked by the thorn in the specification of the original desire, and its conflict with the aversion to the pricking is extrinsic. (Note that aversions are treated as desires.)

An intrinsic conflict is one where conflict already emerges in the specification of the objects of desire, in that the specification of the one includes a proposition which is incompatible with a proposition included in the specification of the other. For example, Caroline may recognise that the picking of the rose in this case will denude the bush. And this may be unwelcome to her. Yet the description of the state of affairs which she wants in this case includes the proposition that the bush is denuded. We may wish to claim that since she does not want the bush denuded, this proposition cannot properly be included in the specification of any desire of hers. However, if she does take it that to have the rose handed to her is to have the bush denuded, then a description of the state of affairs which is her objective is incomplete if it excludes the denuding of the bush. Let her have other desires: for instance, that the description of whose object would include this—that the bush be left intact. These desires are in intrinsic conflict with the first precisely in that the specification of the one includes a proposition which is the negation of a proposition included in the specification of the other.

But now the claim that we can in principle give a full specification of the object of any desire looks much more problematic. Are we to include every proposition which the person whose desire is in question supposes will be true if his desire is fulfilled?

This question may best be answered as follows: when a person envisages and tries to bring about some state of affairs, he is concerning himself with a particular change in a relatively unchanging environment. A specification of the object of his desire will display that upon which his action is directed as distinguished from that which he will let be.

Of course, these limits to his field of action are notional: if he acts, there is no limit to the consequences, or alternatively, if he is to act, there will be no limit to the conditions to be fulfilled. This is the kind of dilemma often finding paradoxical expression in proverb and folklore (as, for instance, in the song 'There's a hole in my bucket'). Yet the same is true of the billiard ball in the classical model of causal action. It is only by an artificial and notional restriction that we consider the billiard table as a closed dynamic system. However, it is a fruitful simplification of a kind indispensable in the sciences, though the modes of simplification or idealisation call for careful scrutiny, as will be argued in section 13 below. Correspondingly, the boundaries that a person tacitly draws round his field of action, though they may be less clear cut, and much more changeable, are equally indispensable to his activity. In reality, he acts in the universe as a whole—and he knows it; but he can only know what he is doing, he can only act, by making the defeasible assumption that the field of possibilities within which his action will take place is effectively closed.

Thus the first boundary we find around a person's desire is a boundary determining the set of propositions whose truth-value is taken to be fixed by the accomplishment of that desire, and distinguishing them from those whose truth-value is taken not to be so fixed. Note that this distinction is determined by what the person whose desire is in question takes to be the case: he may of course be mistaken—the accomplishment of his desire may in fact fix the truth-value of propositions outside that boundary. It is also possible, as we shall see shortly, for it to fix the truth-value of propositions within the boundary in the 'wrong' direction.

But first let us consider the distinction in more detail. It is clear for some cases. If we return to Caroline, that the bush be denuded is a proposition which, she takes it, would be fixed as true by the accomplishment of her desire for the rose. But, for instance, the proposition that her brother will miss his breakfast the following morning is not so fixed.

However, the matter is less clear if we consider what may be called *background conditions*. A person will take it that there is a range of conditions (from general physical laws to more specific circumstances) without which his desire could not be accomplished. In that case, if the desire is accomplished, the truth of the propositions stating those conditions is fixed. On the other hand, we may object that the truth of such propositions is not fixed *by* the event in question. And the idea behind this objection is that the truth of the law of gravity, for instance, is not contingent upon the human will. The objection may be reinforced by appealing once more to the idea of the boundaries drawn—and unavoidably drawn—by a person around his 'field of action'. Surely, he will not draw them so as to include conditions of this kind.

But this objection is question-begging. And it seems to me that conditions of this kind are to be included, for the accomplishment of a person's desire would indeed be taken by him to fix as true such background conditions (without being taken to bring about their truth: what is brought about is the state of affairs designated by the whole set of propositions). Of course, for many purposes, these background conditions can be ignored. They will recur, in various combinations, for many different desires, for the same person or for others. They are therefore able to be cancelled out, or treated as a kind of fixed framework for action, as the Newtonian laws of motion, together with the various special forces, would provide a framework for the action of the billiard balls.

If we share a person's assumptions about background conditions, we shall be all the more inclined to set them on one side, and not to include them in the specification of any desire of his. But they cannot in general be set aside for the following reason. The sets of propositions which specify the objects of desire have it as their function to indicate what a person is trying to bring about. If his assumptions about the background conditions are different from ours, we shall not know what he is trying to bring about, if we have omitted them from the specifications. This may be especially obvious in the case of the desires of a 'mentally disordered' person, or of a person from a radically different culture.

Thus 'background' conditions are to be included in the specification of objects of desire. But this raises a further problem. Not only have these specifications now become extremely unwieldy:

they also seem to include propositions performing two quite different roles—those which, as we might say, really indicate what the person is after, and those which merely give the person's views of the accompanying conditions.

This is the distinction which we shall later consider in more detail between the essential and the non-essential occurrence of a pro-position in the specification of an object of desire. Putting it briefly, a proposition is said to occur non-essentially when the desire which it helps to specify would still be considered to be fulfilled even if, contrary to expectation, that proposition were not made true by the accomplishment of the desire. This is one way, as we said earlier, in which a person may be mistaken in the boundary he draws around his field of action.

Now the constant reference in what has been argued here to what a subject *takes* to be so, and the very terminology of propositions, may suggest an account of desire which would require in the wanter conscious and specific mental acts of entertaining propositions and considering their consequences. In fact, of course, the proposition which is the complete specification of an object of desire need not at any point be consciously entertained by an agent. It may be merely implicit in his thoughts or in his behaviour; and it may remain partially provisional or indeterminate until the moment of com-pletion. So the basic thrust of this interpretation of wanting—that it should be seen as the attempt to match the world to a blue-print—should not be crudely translated into the substantial (and bizarre) psychological thesis that whenever a man wants something his first step is to go through the intellectual process of framing certain propositions—of preparing and inspecting a blue-print.

§3. The second condition satisfied when a man has a desire is that the set of propositions specifying the object of his desire apply to a future state of affairs. It may seem that this condition does not always hold since a person may desire what is already the case. For instance, a man might want the company of a friend while already in his company. But what is in fact wanted here is that the meeting should continue, and the continuance of a present state of affairs is of course in the future. A person does not want what he already has. But I may be mistaken. I may be ignorant of the fact that the state of affairs which I am after already obtains. Let us say that my picking of the rose is intended to placate Caroline after my bad behaviour yesterday. But this placating, this attempt to make her once more well-disposed

towards me, is superfluous. She does not need placating. The desired
state of affairs already exists.

But of course we have not held that the set of propositions
specifying an object of desire will be true only in the future. Rather,
for a person to have that desire is for him to treat that set of
propositions as denoting a future state which he would try to bring
about.

§ 4. This leads us to the third criterion of wanting—that the man is
treating some proposition as something to be realised, that he tends or
intends to do something as tending to bring about the state of affairs
he has in mind.

Notice that this criterion implies the first two criteria. If, then, it
can be treated by itself as a necessary and sufficient condition for a case
of wanting, it seems to follow, if we grant that everything a person
does, *a fortiori* he tends or intends to do, that a person never does
anything that he doesn't want to do.

Is this conclusion tolerable? Suppose that Caroline and I are in a
public park. I do not want to pick flowers in such a place, but still I
pick the rose for Caroline when she makes it clear that she wants it.
Can I not say that though I did want to please her, I did not want to
pick the flower? Here we have once more the distinction between
propositions that occur essentially and propositions which do not
occur essentially in the specification of a desire. Let us take it that the
propositions that I am trying to make true here are at least the
following: that I should pick this rose in this public park, that I should
hand it to Caroline, and that I should thereby please her. Let us further
suppose that if Caroline were not pleased, my desire would not be
satisfied: in that case, the proposition that she should be pleased by the
gesture occurs essentially in the specification of the object of my
desire. If, on the other hand, the first proposition turns out to be false,
because the place is not a public park at all, and if in spite of this I
should still take my desire to have been accomplished, then the first
proposition does not occur essentially in the specification of the object
of my desire.

In general, if *a desires* (*p & q & r*), we cannot infer that (*a desires p*)
and (*a desires q*) and (*a desires r*); we can however infer that (*a desires p*)
or (*a desires q*) or (*a desires r*), for at least one of the propositions
specifying the object of his desire must occur essentially (in other
words, it could not be the case that someone had a certain desire, and
that it was satisfied, when *none* of the propositions in the set specifying
the object of desire was true).

Thus we should not claim that what a person does is always what he wants to do, but more carefully that the proposition(s) describing the state of affairs which he takes himself to be bringing about must be included in or must include the set of propositions which specify a state of affairs which he wants, even though the proposition(s) describing the state of affairs which he takes himself to be bringing about may not occur essentially in the specification of the object of that desire, and even though they may even be included in or include the specification of the object of some conflicting desire.

In this way, we can give a better account of the cases in which a person says of his own action that he did not want to do it; for we see now that though its description must overlap the specification of some want of his, it need not coincide; and where it does not coincide, such a description would not rightly be taken as the specification of a want at all: indeed, it may enter into the specification of a conflicting want.

Now in dealing with this first difficulty about the conative criterion, we were led to say that what a person does, *a fortiori* he tends or intends to do. And it may seem that two important questions are begged here: first, how do we distinguish actions from mere movements? (For there would arguably be no such *a fortiori* if 'unwilled movements' of a person's body were to be included in what he is said to do.) Secondly, it is clear (and here tacitly supposed) that a tendency or intention to act may exist without coming to fruition. Then what does such a tendency or intention consist in?

Tendencies exist as states of being actually and actively directed towards some future state of affairs. When accompanying the accomplishment of that goal, they constitute its being willed. In saying this, we bypass current controversies concerning the relation between intention and action, and whether it could be causal; we ignore traditional epistemological questions about how I can know what my intention is, or how another can know; and we offer no means of distinguishing the 'tendencies or intentions' to act with which we are concerned from activities of autonomous systems, for instance in the human body, which show the same formal pattern, but are not 'subject to the will'. Consider for example the homeostatic regulation of the blood sugar level. It would be correct to say that this mechanism is in a 'state of being actually and actively directed towards a future state of affairs'.

In ignoring all these questions, we are effectively treating the notions of a tendency or intention to act, and of the attribution of a change to such a tendency, as primitive. It may seem perverse, even though all explanation must start somewhere, to take as a starting-point what has traditionally been a major point of philosophical debate. But that appearance of perversity is perhaps attributable to philosophy's preoccupation with the special place of man, and hence of itself, in the order of things. Questions about the specific character of human willing are more properly attacked in biology, cybernetics, psychology, general systems theory, sociology, or even physics, than in philosophy. These are points to which we shall briefly return in section 13. For the present, we shall openly refuse an answer to these questions, and stipulate the notions in question as primitive.

But given that we have done this, a third difficulty arises for the conative criterion for wanting. It may seem that the strong connection established between wanting and acting would leave us unable to deal with the case of conflicting wants. For if one of the wants is not acted on (as must be the case), how on the present account can it be a want at all?

Consider a case. The park-keeper, in our interview after the plucking of the rose, begins to eye Caroline in an offensive manner. I hesitate for a moment, having two conflicting wants—one to placate him and avoid further fuss over the rose, and the other to rebuke his offence. Then I rebuke him. Note that throughout the interview and the moment of hesitation, I wanted to placate the keeper. That is, I did have a real tendency to placate the man at least until the moment of rebuke. Thus although two (practically or logically) incompatible actions cannot both be performed, nevertheless two *tendencies* which are tendencies to perform incompatible actions can coexist. Indeed, the existence of such tendencies to act independent of the actions in which they may (or may not) issue, is, as already remarked, an important part of the position being proposed.

But this case of conflicting desires raises the question of their strength or intensity. What account can we give of such variations between desires? An important dimension of the answer is closed to us here, for, as we shall admit and justify in annex (v) below, the present account of desires takes no account of their affective aspects—of their embodiment. As yet we have only partially relaxed the abstractions which enabled us to construct the model universe of section 1. In this case, it must be granted that the intensity of a desire may exist and be felt in the body: there is yearning in the bowels. But I would maintain that differences in the strength of desires do not consist in such sensations: they consist in different degrees of readiness to combat difficulties and obstacles to their fulfilment. And this readiness is itself an aspect of the tendencies to action of which we have spoken.

But what of cases where no action is open? Can a man not have a desire (even a strong desire), and yet be powerless, and believe himself to be powerless, to further it in any way? May I not long to fall in love, or want a fine day? This possibility constitutes a serious objection to the conative criterion for wanting, and will be considered in section 3.

(iv) Paronymy

But before we discuss the relation between wishing and wanting, it is necessary to consider a problem in the theory of meaning.

Sometimes the same term is applied to different things because they satisfy the same criteria; this is the case in which Aristotle used the term **synonymy**. Sometimes, however, the same term is applied to different things although the criteria of application of the term in the different cases are quite unrelated; this is the case in which Aristotle used the term **homonymy**. One intermediary case is discussed by Aristotle himself—the case in which the same term is applied to different things by an indirect appeal to the same criteria (as a food, a climate, a complexion, and a man may all be called 'healthy' in virtue of their different relations to the one notion of health in a man— πρὸς ἕν λεγόμενον). Another intermediary case is that in which the things are called by the same term because each of them satisfies a sufficient number of a set of criteria (though there may be little overlap between the criteria actually satisfied in any pair of cases); this is the case where Wittgenstein spoke of 'family resemblances'.

But there is a further kind of intermediary case—where things are called alike because they are deemed to satisfy the same criteria. This is the case in which I wish to use the term **paronymy** and of which I now offer some examples. (Note that this application of the term is different from that assigned to it by Aristotle at the beginning of the De Interpretatione.)

Consider the following regulation: 'A resident is any person who has resided continuously in the country for at least the six months immediately preceding the date of his application: except that persons who have left the country only for short periods during those six months may be deemed resident.' Here two classes of people are (rightly) called residents: those who satisfy a certain criterion, and those who do not satisfy it but are deemed to.

Again, when children play families, the one may call the other mother, though his 'mother' does not satisfy the criteria by which a person is properly so-called, when for the purposes of the game she is deemed to satisfy them.

These are merely examples, and the notion of 'deeming' which they illustrate is in need of explication. We have already in annex (iii) advanced reasons for holding in the case of sentence-meaning that outside a central *common domain where a Platonic extrapolation of propositions with strict identity is made, other domains such as those defined by beliefs, wants and modalities must be taken as disposing propositions with weak criteria of identity. As we have noted, this would emerge at the level of terms in the form of weakened (trans-world) identity criteria for the individuals in the worlds of belief, desire and so forth. We now have a corresponding thesis about predicates, for predicates in two 'worlds' may be analogous. Take the case of the children's game. Here the children create and people an imaginary world of a simplified kind based on some of their experiences of the real world. Now the girl who plays mother is not 'in fact' a mother: but she is a mother in the world of the game. Certain roles and attributes are assigned to her, and for the purpose of the game, so long as it is being played, she will be the mother. She is not improperly (homonymously) so-called, nor is she so-called for the same reasons as real mothers (synonymously): purposes at hand have established a recognisable and delimited context within which the predicate 'mother' is applied to her in virtue of criteria other than those in virtue of which it is regularly or primarily applied. One may say: 'because that is what it is to be a mother in a game.'*

Consider also the example of the regulation: the person affected by it may not in law be a resident, but the regulation itself (as administered by certain officials in the light of certain other practices and regulations, and as having a certain range of consequences when applied) itself establishes a delimited context within which a person who is not a resident may parony-mously—and properly—be called a resident.

Consider also Joule's experiment. In this experiment, a beaker of water is taken, and a paddle operable by a falling weight attached to it through a gearing and pulley system is immersed in the water. When the weight is raised, the system has a certain (potential) energy. The problem raised by Joule was this: if the weight is allowed to fall, that potential energy is lost from the system; hence the experiment constitutes a refutation of the principle of the conservation of energy. Joule's solution was to recognise heat as a form of energy. Then we find in his experiment that the movement of the paddle heats the water, and we are able to retain the principle of the conservation of energy.

Now before Joule, the term 'energy' was applied (in scientific contexts) in virtue of the mass and velocity of bodies: its primary application was therefore to moving bodies. An extension to stationary bodies becomes possible by allowing, for instance, a certain potential velocity to a suspended body in virtue of what will happen to it when released, or equivalently in virtue of the energy required in suspending it.

But on what grounds could heat be regarded as a form of energy? Joule's experiment provided an experimental and scientific context in which it was reasonable and fruitful to deem heat to be a form of energy even though at that time, and for a long time, scientists lacked that development of physical theory which would justify Joule's extension of 'energy' to include heat by showing how the term could be applied to both cases in virtue of the very same criteria. Pending that advance, there were on the one hand the cases of 'energy' which satisfied the conventional criterion, and on the other the cases of heat, which were thought not to, but were none the less deemed to. To make use of this insight, it was necessary to adopt, as Joule did, a quantified principle of equivalence between the two kinds of energy, which was arbitrary in so far as it had no theoretical backing, but justified in so far as it worked.

There is a further question: what made it reasonable to regard the new principle as a principle of the conservation of 'energy'? After all, heat simply was not energy in the received sense. Why not deem energy to be a form of heat? Or why not hold that both energy and heat are manifestations of some third phenomenon? The answer seems to lie in what may be called the theoretical geography of the principle of the conservation of energy (here, and throughout this section, there is an appeal to metaphor to give an account of a notion of metaphor: for a scientific principle and a watershed do not synonymously have a geographical position: there is a problem here which will be reverted to briefly at the end of this annex). The received principle played a certain role in the context of mechanical systems as conventionally envisaged. The new principle will play a closely analogous role with respect to systems in which heat too is involved. Such structural similarity or homology is what justifies regarding the new principle as a principle of the conservation of energy. For the time being, heat is properly, but only paronymously, called energy.

Thus, in general, predicates with a primary application in one domain may acquire secondary applications in other domains according to the purposes defining those domains. It is such secondary applications of a predicate that are sometimes marked by the idioms of deeming, and which we here characterise as 'paronymous'.

However, this account of paronymy raises major problems: first, it has inescapably itself been established by the use of some strategic paronymies, such as that of a 'domain', and such as that of being in an 'intermediate' position on a scale whose limits are homonymy and synonymy. Secondly, it has been an important feature of the notion of paronymy here advanced that terms used paronymously can nevertheless be properly so used. There is an appearance of paradox here, for we should commonly mark a non-paronymous use as proper. But the aim must be to make possible a distinction between those transfers of a term from one domain to another which are appropriate, justified, fruitful, correct, and those which are not.

The only way of establishing such a distinction that has been hinted at in our present discussion is a form of pragmatism. It was said, for instance, that Joule's principle of equivalence 'worked'. This can only mean that it was a device which enabled scientists to generate a wider variety of true non-paronymous statements. The paronymous form of the principle of the conservation of energy only became directly justifiable with the establishment of the molecular theory of heat. But at this point, precisely, the term 'energy' ceased to be paronymous in its application to heat. For in a wide range of cases heat was now literally a matter of the movement of particles—of mass and velocity. What were two domains linked by a strategic paronymy have now decisively merged into one.

However, this pragmatic or instrumentalist solution is really an evasion. Although it gives a justification for using a paronymous expression, it does not give an account of that in which the appropriateness of the paronymy consists.

We need, therefore, a solution such as that hinted at above in paronymous terms, namely that the paronymy is appropriate in proportion to the structural similarity between the position of the term in its own domain, and its position in the domain where it is to have its paronymous application—in proportion, that is, to an ascertainable homology between two predicates in two domains.

This is a line of solution which raises too many problems to be developed usefully here, but let us allow that it gives enough substance to the notion of paronymy to allow us to use it in what follows. The problems will recur in section 13. Meanwhile, let us consider the nature of wishing.

3 Wishing

Wanting has been defined by three criteria, the *conative* (there being a tendency to action), the *prospective* (the action being directed at bringing about what is believed to be a possible future state of affairs), and the *propositional* (the state of affairs being designated by a set of propositions).

Now human engagement in the world is not purely practical, that is, restricted to the consideration and implementation of what can in fact be done. Imagination, for example, is a faculty by which we can take pleasure or refuge in the contemplation of the unattainable, or in the pretence of its attainment. However, the distinction between the real world and the world of the imagination needs to be taken carefully. Certainly, the world of a novel, for instance, is imaginary: yet the world of, say, *Middlemarch* is by no means unrelated to the real world of nineteenth-century English society. Moreover, our attitudes towards what passes in that imaginary world are by no means unrelated to our attitudes towards what passes in the real world. Furthermore, imaginary worlds sometimes come into being. What begins in play may end in life. Or indeed, what begins in life may be transmuted into a relived dream.

We may return for a moment to what was said in section 2 above about an agent's delimitation of his field of action. This delimitation may be more or less realistic. The man may subtly or grossly modify his purchase on the world: he may, for all kinds of motives from experimental curiosity to pathological fear, modify his map of what is and of what is possible—and this is also to modify the kinds of actions open to him, even to the extreme point at which nothing resembling an 'ordinary action' is open at all, so that all that is left to the agent is to go through a kind of magical charade, a ritual which may be experienced as the natural expression of the 'desire' in mild cases, or may be pursued with passion in extreme cases as though it were an attempt actually to bring about the desired goal.

It should not be thought that the first step outside a severe pragmatic view of one's field of action is a step into pathology. For there is in any case no single or clear criterion to determine a particular boundary delimiting a field of action as discussed in section 2 above as normal, pragmatic or rational. Anomalies may enter from the moment at which any boundary at all is drawn. But as we have seen, action is impossible without such boundaries. This is man's predicament: at the same time his will is not master of the entire universe, and on the other hand there are no closed and predetermined limits to its exercise: so our boundaries may be ambitious or cautious, closed or permeable, fixed or shifting, and so forth.

It is on these complex boundaries that the notions of wishing and wanting range. A stern distinction between the two worlds would lead to a sharp distinction between the cases where, it is held, we can and do try to get something, and the other cases in which we have set ourselves unrealistic goals, but English idiom, unlike that of some other languages, such as French, is less strict. For we do sometimes regard ourselves as *wanting* what we cannot get, and do not believe ourselves able to get.

This idiomatic point is rather instructive: where in English the homology between a 'realistic' and an 'unrealistic' desire is marked by using the same term in both cases, in French we use the same verb but in 'unrealistic' cases it appears in the conditional tense. Thus in French we assume the practicability of a distinction between the central cases where there is a real tendency to action (and where we may use the verb *vouloir* in tenses other than the conditional), and the other cases where there is what *would be* such a tendency if it were possible (and here we use *vouloir* in the conditional tense). The distinction between the English *wanting* and *wishing* is analogous, save that wanting is allowed greater scope. In what follows, it will be convenient to mark the distinction between cases where there is a real tendency to action and cases where there is not as a distinction between wishing and wanting, and it is in this sense that we shall henceforth use these terms.

Now what is the relation between wishing and wanting? A first attempt at an answer might have been to claim that whereas cases of wanting satisfy the three criteria already suggested, cases of wishing satisfy only the first two of these criteria. This, however, would be insufficient: for wishing is more than merely envisaging a state of affairs and taking it to be in the future. It is, after all, what has pallidly been called a 'pro-attitude'. What then in the case of wishes constitutes their directedness towards the desired goal?

Let us take a clue from the French conditional idiom noticed above.

We may start by attempting the following account. A person wishes
p if and only if he would want p. But 'would want' under what
conditions? Presumably that some action were open to him in the
matter. We now say that if an action is open and the man has a
tendency to perform it, then he wants p; while if no action is open, but
if there were a suitable action the man would have a tendency to
perform it, then he wishes p.

But this account is unsatisfactory for many reasons. Consider a
person of sternly pragmatic temperament—one who does not harbour
many wishes. Now consider any situation such that from our
knowledge of the man, we can be sure that if any action were open to
him, he would tend to take it, to achieve a certain goal. For instance,
he sees some artichokes in the shop, but has no money in his pocket.
We can be sure from our knowledge of his tastes and habits that if he
had some money he would have a tendency to buy some. In that case,
on the suggested account of wishing it would be a matter of definition
that he now wishes for some artichokes. This is clearly unsatisfactory.
It may be the case that a person would want p and that he does not
wish p.

Let us then follow the clue of conditionality in another way: a
person wishes p if and only if he does what would be wanting p if the
conditions allowed it. In this case, we suppose in the wisher some
substitute for or analogue of the tendency to action which occurs in
wanting: we suppose that some predicate homologous to 'ξ wants p'
is true of him. Consider the boy who repeatedly telephones the girl
who will have no more of him. The actions that he performs (and the
tendencies to perform them) are of course perfectly real, considered in
themselves. But they are notionally aimed at a re-establishment of the
boy's relations with the girl, which, in the case we are imagining, he
sees no way of achieving, though he yearns for it—he wishes it. The
telephone calls are not genuine attempts to achieve a goal, but they are
expressions of his yearning, since they are at least notionally, at least in
an imaginary world, directed towards that goal. The daydream that
the right words spoken into the mouthpiece will heal the breach is
real, but not realistic.

Of course, there is a certain oversimplification involved in our
account of this case, even given the way in which we have set it up.
For who can say that the right words would not have the desired
effect, even though the boy may be sure in his heart that he will not
find them? In other words, in an actual case like the one described, it
would not be as unequivocal a case of 'wishing' as we have tended to

suggest. Suppose one of his 'phone calls is successful, and the girl relents. It is not clear how he will react, and this may be left indeterminate in his present wish/want. If he is frightened and paralysed by this success, not knowing what to do in a situation which was quite unexpected, we shall be inclined to treat him as having a mere wish, belonging to a well-insulated imaginary world. If on the other hand he immediately takes advantage of her relenting, enthusiastically but practically, surprised but not disturbed by it, then we shall be inclined to think of him as having entertained a want—long shot though it may have been and seemed. A continuous range of cases may lie between these two extremes.

But so far we have considered only a case of wishing in which the actions and tendencies to action, though unrealistic in their goal, are nevertheless real actions with only a tinge of ritual. There are cases, however, where the ritual gesture is the only available expression of the wish, like the man at the railway station whose gesture of outstretched arms at the departing train may be paronymously pulling the train back to prevent his separation from a lover.

We have now made explicit what was implicit earlier in this section: namely, the importance of the notion of paronymy discussed in annex (iv) above. By it we are enabled to express our account of wishing as follows: whereas in the case of wanting, the propositional, the prospective and the conative criteria are all satisfied; in the case of wishing, the first two criteria are satisfied, but the third only paronymously.

But there seems to be a further artificiality here. For the requirement of the prospective criterion excludes wishes directed upon the past or the present, although idiomatically there are such wishes. Indeed, the English idiom 'wish that' never takes a straight future tense; this is reserved for the case of 'making a wish'. This is indeed precisely the purest example of the class of cases for which it will be convenient to reserve the term *wishing*. The other cases fall under a different category to be considered in section 4.

(v) Abstraction

But first let it be noted that the analysis so far offered is achieved by a sort of phenomenological abstraction of the body. Thus while we have indeed moved some way back to this world from the model universe of section 1, the account is still proceeding at a certain level of abstraction. In fact, though any desire does satisfy our three conditions, and though these conditions are necessary and sufficient, yet because we are embodied (and it is not to our present purpose to discuss the possibility of a disembodied existence), our desires are characteristically lived through and in the body, and the yearnings in the bowels which may supervene have been excluded from our account.

It is important to bear this in mind, since the abstraction is much more noticeable in the case of the third variation which we are going on to discuss, where an account will be offered of pleasures. For bodily sensations are often the most notable aspect of pleasures. Nevertheless we shall maintain the abstraction of the affective in order to draw attention to the links between wanting and wishing on the one hand, and pleasures on the other, since the nature of these links is central to our argument, and easily obscured by urgent sensation.

4 Pleasure

We have so far considered two modalities of the pure will of section I in the case of human agents—*wanting* and *wishing*. But there is a third modality. Whereas the second satisfies the three criteria for wanting save that in the passage to 'imaginary worlds' the conative criterion is only paronymously satisfied, in the case of the third modality, the prospective criterion also is only paronymously satisfied.

The conative attitudes with which we started (wanting) were at home in the world of the attainable. When we turned to what is beyond the attainable, however, we found a set of cognate attitudes (wishing). What will happen when we turn to what is on this side of the attainable—to what is already attained? What when what is *to be attained* is neither attainable (something we want), nor beyond the attainable (something we wish for), but something which is attained already? Here, I argue, we have a further set of cognate attitudes, of which the characteristic example is taking pleasure in a thing. Taking pleasure is what would be wanting, but that what is wanted is already present.

We have here an explanation of that supervenience of pleasure to which Aristotle drew attention in another way. For the appetite produced by the pleasurable situation (and which constitutes its being pleasurable) has no function, since that which it is the tendency to strive for is already present. So a desire may be awakened by the advent of the very situation for which it should be the desire. This superfluous desire, this purely paronymous striving for a present situation which is through that striving only paronymously treated as being in prospect, naturally overflows into the smiles, the deep breaths, the expansive gestures which form a happy charade of striving for that which has been vouchsafed from the first. Such is pleasure.

34

(vi) Perfect Peace

We have now the outlines of a map of human appetite: a monochromatic map, since we have left out of account the fact that man has a body. But there are two main features of man which are held constant in this map. First, that feature of man which is captured by calling him a rational being: it is a feature which emerges in our map in the production of propositions to which the world may be matched, or against which it may be measured; secondly, man appears in our map as an essentially active being.

We may instructively ask what lies beyond our map at these points. In other words, what lies beyond the boundary of propositions, and what lies beyond the boundary of activity?

It seems that beyond the boundary of propositions lies the animal world. For at best we can only paronymously attribute the entertainment of propositions to animals; yet we cannot avoid thinking of them and treating them as having at least some desires. We descry at once a whole further area linked to the original ground which we have surveyed in sections 2–4 above by another strategic paronymy, that according to which animals are properly but paronymously said to be trying to make certain propositions true. However, it will not be part of our present task to explore this area.

Up to this point we have considered a number of modes of the will, each new mode linked to the central case by a strategic paronymy. And the central thread throughout is the presence of some form of activity. Yet do not some pleasures call into question the primacy of the will? Man may be an active being: in that case, he does not know 'what to do' when confronted with the unlooked for and unworked for fulfilment of desires that he has not even had the time to formulate: hence we have claimed that his pleasure is his treating that situation, as best he can, as an object of desire.

Yet why should he be held in a trap of ceaseless activity, especially when activity is superfluous? This question should lead us to acknowledge what is obvious: that the present account of pleasure cannot be regarded as more than a foothold on very difficult terrain. It is not a primary purpose of the main argument to develop a theory of pleasure, and it would be absurd to think that a few words would suffice for this. Thus, though the few words of section 4 may strictly suffice for the main argument, we shall not here leave them entirely without support or development.

35

It is in the first place rather easy to discern a development which would enable us to deal with displeasure and similar phenomena. For just as avoidance may be assimilated to wanting (by treating it as wanting not-**p**), so displeasures can be interpreted within the framework of the existing account of pleasures as the presence of a tendency to bring it about that not-**p**, which is idle just to the extent that it is too late to bring it about that now not-**p** when **p** already now obtains. Such a move becomes problematic, however, in the case of pain, since it omits an essential: pain as a sensation. Moreover, the same difficulty already confronts us in the case of pleasurable sensations. We have, it is true, already adverted to, and given some justification of, our abstraction of the body, but it may still be held that there are cases, such as sexual pleasure, in which the account given cannot stand, since embodiment is an essential feature of such pleasures, which are at least in part irreducibly a matter of sensation, rather than of an attitude towards some sensation.

This objection seems to me sound, in that it shows that not everything that can reasonably be considered to be a pleasure can be directly accounted for by our account of 'pleasure'; and parallel considerations apply to pain. There is, however, a strategy for dealing with these cases which takes rise from the general structure of the argument presented. For we have already referred to a world of animal desire generated by the paronymous application of the propositional criterion to animals. Now man too is an animal. And in the animal world we find the physiological correlates of desire, hitherto defined in non-physiological terms. Thus physiological phenomena, say of the organism 'striving towards' ejaculation, or showing aversion from a painful stimulus, are formally homologous (in terms of the applicability of our three criteria) to the non-paronymous causes of wanting, of which the subject is a person, and not a purely organic entity.

Yet it is not clear how this observation can help us. We may grant animals wants, and allow even physiological processes to be paronymously so classified. But how can this help us with animal pleasures? If the paronymous shift is consistently made, a pleasure in this animal world would be an excess animal appetite, a superfluous physiological striving for an already existing condition. That this abstract possibility is not merely speculative will be indicated in section 13 below. However, even ignoring the problem of the gap between a physiological event and a sensation, it seems clear that such an account would be at best insufficient to deal, for instance, with the case cited of sexual pleasure. For this case, quite apart from the essential involvement of sensation, has two important features not captured in our account: first, that of pleasurable activity, and second the pleasure of satisfied desire.

Now activity becomes problematic for us to the extent that it may be its own end, that in doing it, the agent has no end beyond doing it. In our account not only of pleasure, but also of wanting and wishing, we have in fact taken as our examples of objects of desire only states (such as being in possession of a rose), and not activities (such as digging the flower bed). It is true that nothing in our appeal to the notion of states of affairs excludes activities; but the problem arises from this—that whereas in the cases hitherto cited there is a ready distinction between the actions or activities which manifest a desire and the state of affairs which is its accomplishment, we now have cases where that distinction does not exist. Consider the desire to be playing squash. Certainly, this desire can be manifested in just the same way as others which we have considered: for before the game, the player will find another person to play with, collect his equipment, see to it that there is an available squash court, and so forth. But is not his desire to play also, and indeed pre-eminently, manifested in his actually playing? That which above all brings it about that he is playing is that he is playing. Here is an activity which may be considered an accomplishment of its own end. Such an example differs from cases of wanting, under our definition, in that the prospective criterion does not apply (not even paronymously); but it differs from pleasures, under our definition, in that the conative criterion does apply non-paronymously. That is, the activity which is the object of the person's present desire is not taken to be in the future (so that we do not seem to have a case of wanting, as here defined); while on the other hand the tendency or intention to act in the matter is really and not just paronymously present.

Thus whereas our account is generated on the basis of the primary case of wanting in which there is a gap between desire and possible fulfilment (the prospective criterion applies), now we see a further dimension of variation produced by dropping the prospective criterion—cases of 'wanting' in which striving collapses into achievement. What would pleasures be along this dimension? The following strategy may be suggested: we shall appeal to an awareness in the agent not only of the coincidence of his activity considered as an object of desire with his activity considered as producing that object; but in addition of their coincidence with that which would be a striving for that state of affairs or activity, were it not present. In short, just as there is a variety of wanting in which the goal and the action directed towards it collapse into each other, so there is a variety of pleasure in which the 'extra' paronymous striving which characterises more central cases of pleasure collapses into the activity itself. This then would be a strategy for exploring what may lie behind Aristotle's metaphor for pleasure in an activity, that it is like 'the bloom of youth'.

But at the opposite limit to that of pleasurable activity, there seems to be the pleasure of satisfied desire, where no additional paronymous desire is excited. In other words, though not all satisfaction of desires need be *pleasurable, yet in some cases we do find an essentially tranquil pleasure which again does not conform to our main account of pleasures. We now envisage the granting or attaining of a state of complete tranquillity, a state in which desire (including that mode of it which we have called pleasure) would have been quite transcended—the state of perfect peace.*

That there must be an end of all striving, and that it must be a state of tranquillity (in which there is no striving for goals) has been a persistent theme in moral speculation from Aristotle's somewhat sophistical arguments that the state or activity of intellectual contemplation—of θεωρία—is the aim of all aims, to the arcana of religious mysticism.

We shall have occasion to revert to this topic in section 13. Meanwhile, with these brief observations on strategies for developing the theory so far advanced (particularly in respect of its application to pleasure), we shall review our conclusions up to this point.

5 Appetitives

What we have so far observed is a common structure in a wide variety of different psychological situations. The whole class of cases considered may be called *appetitives*, since they all involve some form of (real or paronymous) striving for some state of affairs.

The primary sort of appetitive is the *conative* in which all three conditions of section 2 hold. This is the case of which wanting is the paradigmatic example. But, of course, wanting in the sense defined is a feature of many different psychological states. The analysis adumbrated will enable us to display what may be called the appetitive skeleton of all such cases. We may instance looking for (wanting to find), being curious about (wanting to know about), loving (wanting to benefit, to be with, etc.), competing (wanting to defeat), hating (wanting to destroy), attacking (wanting to render innocuous), being ambitious (wanting to advance oneself).

Alongside conatives are the two cognate branches of the family of appetitives: *optatives* (cases in which the conative criterion is satisfied only paronymously and of which wishes are paradigmatic), and *fruitives* (cases in which both the conative and the prospective criteria are satisfied only paronymously and of which pleasures are paradigmatic). Optatives would include, for instance, cases of despair, anxiety, anticipation; fruitives—pride, regret, admiration. Alongside this family are the families of *animal appetitives* (where the propositional criterion is satisfied only paronymously), and *energetic appetitives* (where the prospective criterion is not satisfied), both adumbrated in annex (vi) above.

However, it must be remarked that a particular psychological state need not necessarily fall under only one of these categories. A particular case of admiration, for example, might include a conative component (wanting to imitate), an optative component (wishing to be the other person), and a fruitive component (taking a particular pleasure in the fact that such a person exists). Animal appetitives too might be in play. Moreover, there is no once for all appetitive analysis of all cases to which we apply a term such as 'admiration'.

In fact, the analysis would enable us to disengage certain complexities in any particular situation according to rather simple general principles. Thus the 'appetitive skeleton' which it enables us to display is not the skeleton of, for instance, ambition or admiration in general, but of any particular case of these or other psychological postures. The application of this analysis would be a matter of psychological practice.

My purpose here is not to carry out such an applied investigation, but to base a theory of value on the possibility of carrying it out.

(vii) Ends and Means

But there is a difficulty to be confronted before we turn to values. For are not the specifications of the objects of appetitives which we have discussed at length specifications of ends? What of the means? Nothing has been said, it may be held, about the adoption of means to those ends, about the ways in which those ends can provide reasons for acting, or act as motives. In short, the operation of what since Aristotle has been called 'practical reason' has been left out of account. This omission is serious enough in the area of theoretical psychology to which the main argument has up to now been confined. It will become unacceptable if it is carried over to the theory of value.

The brief answer to this difficulty is that the propositions specifying the objects of appetitives are precisely not Aristotelian major premises in a practical syllogism. We are not dealing here with relatively independent psychological forces or entities postulated in such a way that they open up as the main topic of enquiry the links between them and any actions which may issue. On the contrary, a want as we have defined it is a tendency to act in certain ways with a certain end in view. Consequently, the connections which are the concern of practical reason belong within the structure of the objects of appetitives. The reason for an action, or its motive, the end and the means, these things must appear in a full statement of what it is that a person wants in acting in such and such a way. In effect, then, these questions are just some of the many different kinds of question that can be asked about the way in which a particular proposition occurs in the specification of the object of an appetitive.

A first important distinction is one already noticed, that between the essential and non-essential occurrence of a proposition in such specifications. Starting from this distinction, we find approximate outlines of the account to be given of traditional topics of practical reason. For instance, essentially occurring propositions may be said to denote an end, and if a means to that end has been adopted, the proposition(s) specifying that means will occur, but not essentially, in the specification of the appetitive.

But questions about the internal structure of appetitives arise because they and the actions arising from them may be criticised and called into question in

41

various ways. This impetus to the analysis of appetitives is at its most powerful where an appetitive is itself subject to another appetitive—where there are wants about wants. This case acquires a special importance for value theory, and we shall revert to it in section 7.

However, the relegation of the means/end chain to the interior of an object of desire leaves another traditional problem unsolved, or rather raises it even more acutely: the problem of ἀκρασία, of the weakness of the will. For the position advanced here, even more sharply than a number of other positions similar in this respect, would make the means/end chain unbreakable: more precisely, our position seems to entail that if a person has a desire, and the circumstances are propitious to his action, and there are no conflicting desires, then he must act on it. Or if he does not, he cannot properly be said to have the desire.

In fact, exploration of the variety of cases to which the term 'weakness of the will' may be applied should show that this position is not paradoxical. The term is commonly applied, for instance, to cases of conflicting desires, especially when the prevailing desire is 'less worthy' or concerned with short-term goals. It may also be applied where a professed desire turns out not to be really serious: it is not a want but a wish, in our terminology. And thirdly, what is to prevent what might be called the spontaneous degeneration of a desire: what is to prevent a tendency to action simply ceasing to be? A weak-willed person in this sense would be one in whom tendencies to action did not sustain themselves very long in the absence of occasions for acting, and tended as it were to peter out even when the occasion presented itself.

It is not our present task, as we have already declared, to engage in psychological case studies. The topics of the present section, though interesting and important, belong to a more substantial treatment of psychological topics than is possible here. For it is time to make the move from what we desire to what we value.

6 Values

But how can this be done? How do we move from what is wanted to what is good? From the concrete modalities of what we called the idea of pure will, to the concrete modalities of what we called the idea of pure value?

Recall once more the model universe which was sketched in section 1. Values were said to emerge in that universe at the point where we were obliged to recognise that the one and only will which *ex hypothesi* existed in it might be frustrated. The universe, we said, was 'good' so far as it conformed itself to that will, and 'bad' so far as it did not. More precisely, we suppose that the will is tending to bring about a certain state of affairs. This state of affairs could be described in some set of propositions forming a kind of blue-print for a possible future. When the universe comes to match this blue-print, that is good; when it fails to, that is bad.

Now all appetitives satisfy the propositional criterion. In their case, that is, some set of propositions (some blue-print) is always to be found which denotes the object of the appetitive. For this object we may introduce the technical term *appetitum*. The transition to values is then simple to the point of banality. For we simply state that any appetitum is a value, against which the world is to be measured, and in accordance with which it is to be transformed.

It is in this sense that I am claiming that everything that a person wants, wishes for or takes pleasure in is thereby and to that extent good. The consequences of this claim, and objections to it, will be considered in the sections that follow.

43

(viii) Sciences of Value

Ferdinand de Saussure wrote: 'In linguistics as in political economy we are confronted with the notion of value; *both sciences are concerned with a system for equating things of different orders—labour and wages in one, and a signified and a signifier in the other' (1959, I.iii.1, p. 79). These are words which should draw our attention to the extreme narrowness of philosophies of value which ignore economics and linguistics. Indeed, de Saussure found it natural to discuss value ('valeur') without referring to what we call moral values at all:*

> *'Even outside language all values are apparently governed by the same paradoxical principle: they are always composed:*
> > *(1) of a dissimilar thing that can be exchanged for the thing of which the value is to be determined; and*
> > *(2) of similar things that can be compared with the thing of which the value is to be determined.*
>
> *Both factors are necessary for the existence of a value. To determine what a five-franc piece is worth one must therefore know: (1) that it can be exchanged for a fixed quantity of a different thing, e.g. bread; and (2) that it can be compared with a similar value of the same system, e.g. a one-franc piece, or with coins of another system (a dollar etc.). In the same way a word can be exchanged for something dissimilar, an idea; besides, it can be compared with something of the same nature, another word. Its value is therefore not fixed so long as one simply states that it can be 'exchanged' for a given concept, i.e. that it has this or that signification: one must also compare it with similar values, with other words that stand in opposition to it. Its content is really fixed only by the concurrence of everything that exists outside it. Being part of a system, it is endowed not only with a signification, but also and especially with a value, and this is quite different' (ib. II.iv. 2 pp. 114—5).*

De Saussure's reference to exchange in his first criterion for values suggests the possibility of passing in both directions: that is, it seems that either of the two items may be taken as the value, and the other as the valued.

44

For instance, if the value is an amount of money (a value possessed by a coin), it may be treated as the measure of a certain quantity of labour; alternatively, that amount of labour may be treated as a value to measure that amount of money. In the case of language too, if the value is a Fregean sense (a value possessed by a word) it may be treated as the measure of a given object (as understanding the sense of the word on the shopping list enables us to judge that the object in the shopping bag is wrong), or vice versa (as recognition of the object in the bag enables us to judge whether or not a certain word is the correct word for it).

But are we not inclined to give one of the two orders priority in each system? For labour can exist without money, and objects without words. Money and language are like rulers brought in from outside to be laid against a preexisting reality. Yet this is a naive and misleading picture. Consider the case of the ruler. It may seem that things in reality are already related in terms of lengths and distances, and that a ruler brought in to measure these quantities will change nothing. Then we shall say that the value is or is possessed by this yardstick (that by whose means we measure) and that the reality which it will measure is prior to it. Yet, short of a transcendent yardstick, we must recognise that the yardstick itself is just another object. If reality already contains relations of length and so forth, then reality already contains rulers (as many as you like!). Alternatively, if reality contains no rulers, the making of something into a ruler brings into being both orders—that is, the measure and the measured. In this sense, it would be misleading to ask whether money precedes labour, or labour money, whether language precedes reality, or reality language: neither order can be understood except as forming part of a (linguistic or economic) system.

Yet is it not absurd to suggest—as we seem to have done—that things did not exist before words? Certainly; but what is not absurd is the view that things considered as having their place, and at certain points their essential place, in a certain system of multiple and possibly constitutive relations between things—things considered in some such specific way must be considered as one order in a system of which the other order is furnished by a particular language and culture. Of course, questions about the genesis, change and decay of linguistic or economic systems are in order: they are important questions. But they should not be perverted into unanswerable perplexities about the alleged priority of one order over another within the system. That way lie sterile disputes such as those between forms of materialism and idealism (do words create things, or vice versa?), or between monetarists and the apostles of productivity (is what counts in an economy the amount of work done or the amount of money in circulation—gold or productivity?).

Thus we must distinguish (which is not to say dissociate) questions about the origins of systems from questions about the operation of systems: in de Saussure's terms, we must distinguish their diachronic and synchronic aspects.

In the case of appetitive value systems in particular, we must distinguish synchronic from diachronic considerations. It will be argued in section 11 below that failure to do so is partly responsible for misconceptions about the autonomy of moral values.

There are further lessons which we may draw from de Saussure's remarks about values. The world of appetitive values must be envisaged as comprising two structured orders: first, the system of values of an individual or group which has its own internal structure or 'syntax' (and we must avoid the atomistic error of considering such systems as mere agglomerations—see section 9); and secondly, the order of the sets of states of affairs taken as able to be affected by the action of that individual or group, or as constituting its field of action; the matching of these two orders may take place in both directions within the system as a whole: we may measure the world by our values, or try to transform it in accordance with them. A further lesson is that appetitive values may be regarded as forming a segment of the totality of human value systems in the Saussurean sense—of the diverse forms of exchange and equivalence practised in and constitutive of human societies, from their language to their kinship systems and their economy: areas now the object of various sciences of value. Moral philosophy should take its place in this configuration, as a branch of the study of appetitive values.

But what is the relation between appetitive value systems and others? For instance, appetitive values clearly enter into economic, kinship and linguistic relations: it is vital to all these that we want to buy or earn something or to produce it, that men want to acquire or give a wife, that they want to say or learn something. All these wants use and bring into play and are made possible by the other value systems. They do not, however, constitute them. Relative to these desires, the other value systems become an objective framework for what is attempted.

However, this is perhaps only so at the individual level. At the communal level, these other value systems may be seen as themselves special varieties of appetitive, as expressions of the 'will' of the community, which is other than the summation of the individual wills of its members. If this were the correct view, the value systems with which we are primarily concerned would be generated by just one kind of appetitive—that involving individual desire (being the main preoccupation of the main traditions of Western moral philosophy). It is not as evident as Dummett has recently suggested (1973, p. xv) that 'moral philosophy' is prior to 'political philosophy'—though we entirely accept his claim that philosophical psychology is prior to ethics. The question here is whether individual 'psychology' is prior to group 'psychology'.

It may be held that the notion of the will which we have been using cannot admit the will of collectivities in other than an aggregative or metaphorical sense. But mere aggregation of individual wills does not allow us to deal with economic or linguistic systems, which are essentially communal. And the priority of individual willing which would be implied by taking collective willing as only paronymously so-called seems to leave no room for the essential role of society in man's emergence from an animal state, or indeed its likely role at some much earlier evolutionary stage. There is a dilemma here: we admit a collective will, and then Hegel is with us; or we give priority to the individual will, and then we have the intellectual phenomenon known in some circles as 'bourgeois individualism' in its various political and philosophical manifestations.

Let us then try to clarify the notion of the will by returning to the will of the model universe of section 1. On what grounds can that will—the source of change—hypothesised as being in that universe be said really to be in it, as opposed to acting upon it from the outside? We may try to answer this question by adding a further requirement to the model: that if the will is to be considered as forming part of the model universe (rather than being a transcendent source of change), then it must be able not only to act on the universe, but also itself to be acted on. Now if it is acted on, some change must be produced in it. But a change in it will also ex hypothesi be a change in the universe. Thus we now have a further classification of the changes which may occur in our model universe: changes which occur 'in the will' and changes which occur 'elsewhere'. We must then postulate a 'zone' in the universe which will be the zone of the will (let the quotation marks indicate that this is not necessarily a spatial zone). Now this zone will be one from which changes occurring elsewhere may originate, and which is itself liable to undergo changes originating from elsewhere. If we consider changes said to originate from it, in what does their originating from it consist? An arbitrary assignation is insufficient. At least the following two elements seem to be required: a prefiguring of the change to be produced, this prefiguring being itself a change in the zone of the will (we may call it the appetitum), and a feedback by which the change can be monitored, and if necessary correcting action taken either to adjust the change or to adjust the appetitum according to which the change is being produced. We now have the following scheme: the occurrence of an unattributable change in the zone of the will (the appetitum); the occurrence of a change outside that zone and attributable to the first; and the occurrence of further changes in the zone of the will attributable to the change produced outside, together with possible adaptations consequent upon this feedback. Of course, there are still many dark areas in this model, when we have it in mind to understand agency as we experience it and to assess philosophical views about agency as we know them. For instance, in a sense the model still fails to capture agency. It is merely stipulated that one change may produce another. Moreover, it may seem that the transcendence of the will which it was part of the purpose of this extension of the model to dispel has persisted. For why is this zone called the 'zone of the will'? Is the will still to be regarded as being outside the universe, but, as it were, attached to this special zone through some pineal gland? Or could we simply identify that zone with the will?

It is striking that the development of our model is leading us on the one hand to questions of transcendent metaphysics, and on the other to the abstract description of self-regulating organisms—to that branch of general systems theory which deals with open systems, for example. These topics will recur in section 13.

But for the present let us turn from these questions and ask what the extension of our model universe offers with respect to the question of the 'will' of collectivities. The essential step in filling out the will of the model has been to give it an 'appetitum', something which governs, and may itself be adapted by external changes. If we have good reason to attribute the existence of some such appetitum to a collectivity, then we shall have good reason to speak of the will of collectivities. There is some reason to think that languages and economic systems (for example) are entities of this kind. They belong essentially to collectivities; they cannot be explained as the aggregation of individual desires (the dependence being rather the reverse), they regulate—and are subject to adaptation as a result of the consequences of such regulation. To make the point as modestly as possible, we may say that nothing in the model yet excludes a communal will. We shall return to the form which such a will may take in section 8 below.

7 The Differentiation of Values

Moral philosophies which give pride of place to psychology by taking benevolence, pleasure, the will to power or some other psychological notion as cardinal have usually suffered from the crudeness of their psychology. Thus the simple occurrence of a certain psychological state has not in the end seemed sufficient to account for the intricacy, subtlety and variety of evaluation as we live and experience it, still less for specifically moral evaluation, whose particular qualities have led many philosophers to regard it as completely *sui generis*. And those who have held the contrary have often been forced into a kind of positivistic iconoclasm. It is important to observe that a more carefully laid basis in theoretical psychology will eliminate this weakness in such positions.

In this section, we shall outline six chief distinctions between kinds of values which flow from the analysis of appetitives so far offered and which will establish the flexibility and power of the proposed account of values.

§ 1. First, we may distinguish *primary, secondary* and *tertiary values*, according to whether the corresponding appetitive is conative, optative or fruïtive. In addition, primary and tertiary values may also occur in the *animal* and *energetic* dimensions indicated in annex (vi).

This gives an initial framework for the place of efforts, dreams and pleasures in evaluation. What a person values is given in all these modes. Primarily, however, his values are displayed and exercised in his active engagement in the world. Only subordinately do they find expression in his wishes and pleasures.

Thus if a person is a pacifist and has a tendency to act in the matter, for instance by refusing to bear arms, that there be peace is a primary value of his. But if he merely wishes for it, believing there to be no action open to him, or merely takes pleasure in it once achieved, it

49

remains a value of his but only what I call a secondary or tertiary value.

It is important to notice here that the position argued in this book is not hedonistic, either in psychology or in value theory. For it is not true in fact (still less analytically true) that human actions are always aimed at a pleasure. They are aimed simply at the fulfilment of their corresponding appetitum. Correspondingly, pleasure is not the one touchstone of value. For pleasure is not to be defined simply in terms of the satisfaction of a preexisting desire. One case of what we call disappointment is sufficient to undermine this view. Rather, as has been explained, pleasure is itself at least in many central cases a new 'desire' awakened by the very situation for which it would be a desire. Pleasure in this sense does play an important but secondary role in evaluation—just because of its appetitive structure.

§2. Secondly, there is a distinction between *quasi-values* and *real values*. A value is a quasi-value when someone acts as though it were a value of his when it is not. For instance, consider the man whose hatred of war is entirely confined to the fact that war involves injury and death for men. He does not dislike fighting as such: indeed, he may favour all forms of conflict and competition from boxing to economic struggle, but have a 'humanitarian' distaste for overt and physical suffering. This man's view will be different from that of the man who really wants peace. The state of affairs aimed at by the one is that men should not fight each other; but by the other, that men should not fight each other *and* thereby cause injury and death, where the first of these propositions does not occur essentially. Now in many situations, these men may act alike; indeed, their appetita overlap. These are the situations in which it is appropriate to say of the second man that he acts *as though* he simply wants men not to fight each other. This second appetitum—the value of peace—is a quasi-value of his.

Other cases of quasi-values occur in hypocrisy. A man acts as though he wants to give a donation to a charity, when in fact his appetitum is that he should give an offering *and* be seen to do so. Again, an apologising child acts as though he is sorry for hurting his sister by hitting her, when in fact he wants not to excuse himself, but to avoid punishment by being seen to excuse himself.

Now quasi-values are a degenerate species logically as well as evaluatively. For there is no limit to the number of quasi-values generable from any one real value by addition or subtraction of propositions. In other words the criteria of identity for quasi-values seem even more problematic than those for values themselves.

The potentially disorderly quality of quasi-values, however, is kept in check by the purposes of referring to them. If one has in mind some real value that a person could have, and that some other people do have or have had, it may be important to notice that the person already has it as a quasi-value, or to create circumstances in which he is likely to acquire such a quasi-value. One central case, for instance, is educational. In moral education, transformation of a quasi-value into a real value is a characteristic process. The parent (let us say) is concerned that his child should value truthfulness. He begins by concentrating upon it as a quasi-value, that is, by applying punishment and reward. The child at first comes to aim at the cultivation of truthfulness with a view to avoiding punishment and pleasing his parents. In due course, he may come to aim at truthfulness without qualification.

Again, when we pay attention to values which are shared in a community, the notion of quasi-values enables us to take full account of the realities of moral consensus, that it is not universally whole-hearted and single-minded. Many individuals in a community, apart from children, may tend to adhere to a given common value for extraneous reasons—may hold it as a quasi-value. This does not prevent the consensus from being real, since the appetita of the members of the community do in fact overlap at the relevant point. Nor is this a weakness in the values of the community, except from the point of view of the more stern or fanatical moral conservative. It is rather a mark of adaptability. A classical case is Mosaic law, and the challenge of Jesus to attitudes towards that law. There was, no doubt, a moral consensus in Judaic society at that time—that the law should be obeyed. No doubt some wanted to obey it and thereby avoid social disapproval, some—to obey it and avoid punishment, some—to obey it and thereby obey God, some—simply to follow the law. All these appetita overlap, so that following the law is at least a quasi-value for all the kinds of people mentioned. Thus the original Christian value—to love God and your neighbour, and therefore among other things follow the law (in which arguably following the law does not occur essentially), though revolutionary from many points of view, nevertheless had important continuities with the past, retaining following the law as a quasi-value.

Thus, quasi-values, too easily despised in the individual for hypocrisy, provide in the community a great means of conserving the moral experience of the past, and a fertile ground for moral evolution or even revolution.

§3. A third distinction to be drawn is that between *open* and *closed* values. A closed value is a value such that there could be a time by which the corresponding desire could have been fulfilled—for instance, that John should not quarrel with Roland over their inheritance. An open value is a value such that there could not be a time by which the desire could have been fulfilled—for instance, that mankind should live in peace. For even if universal peace were established in the year 2000 (which would conform to the value), war might break out again in 2001; thus that there should be peace is an open value, never to be definitively fulfilled. John and Roland, however, cannot quarrel over their inheritance after one of them dies, so that if they have not quarrelled over it before this time, the desire that they should not do so (whoever may have had it) will have been definitively fulfilled, and thus the value corresponding to it is a closed value.

(ix) Eschatologies

It may seem that this distinction between open and closed values breaks down in face of any eschatological moral position. For the last day is precisely the time at which so-called open values are found to be fulfilled or not.

Yet the last day is a very special sort of 'time'—a final or limiting time. In religious eschatologies, paradise is outside or beyond time as we know it. In Marxist eschatology, the final utopia is equally beyond time as we know it (that is, time as determined by the strictly historical process of class struggle, warring and resolved contradiction, etc.).

Thus we may either deny that the last day is a time, or say that it is that limiting time at which even open values become closed. For closed values are already closed within the temporal sphere; but open values are closed only sub specie aeternitatis.

7 The Differentiation of Values

§ 4. A fourth distinction to be made is between *negative* and *positive* values. A negative value occurs where the proposition(s) occurring essentially in the corresponding appetitum is (are) negative. A value that is not negative is positive.

This is a logically trivial distinction, since we could always pass from a negative proposition (say, one in the semantics of which must occur an expression of the form $\sim F(a)$) to a positive (in which $G(a)$ takes the place of $\sim F(a)$), merely by defining G as the contradictory of F (so that $(x)\ (Fx \equiv \sim Gx)$).

Moreover, equivalences of this kind certainly occur in natural languages. Are we to say, for instance, that my desire that you should be present is positive, while my desire that you should *not* be absent is negative?

The answer is that while there are appetitives which may indifferently have either positive or negative form, such as the one just mentioned, nevertheless, such conversions are not generally possible. Let us consider moralities characterised by prohibitions: if these prohibitions could indifferently be transformed into exhortations, our description of these moralities as concerned above all to forbid or stop certain actions would be a purely formal or artificial one. We do not feel it to be so: 'Do not kill' seems unequivocally to be a prohibition (even if transformed into a superficially unnegated form such as: 'Leave alive'); likewise, 'Do not commit adultery' (even if transformed into 'Be sexually faithful to your spouse'). It is not our present purpose to discuss what could justify our persuasion of the priority of the negative form in these cases (the issue is related to that raised by Nelson Goodman's 'grue' emeralds, and Hempel's 'non-black non-ravens', as Quine's discussion of the natural or animal priority of certain predicates in his essay 'Natural Kinds' clearly shows): it is enough to notice that it is such a persuasion which ensures that the statement of any corresponding appetita will be in negative form, so that the criterion mentioned above may be applied in distinguishing negative from positive values. The pattern for this distinction in the model universe of section I and annex (viii) will be that between cases in which the will has to bring about a change in order to fulfil its appetitum and cases in which it has to abstain from bringing about, or resist a change.

§ 5. Fifthly, there is a distinction between first order values, and values of higher orders. A first order value is a value in the specification of which no other values occur essentially; a second order value is one in whose specification one or more first-order values occur essentially; a third order value, one in whose specification one or more second order values occur essentially, and so on. Put simply, this means that higher order values occur when there are wants about wants; when, in describing the state of affairs which is a man's appetitum in some case, we have to include reference to other appetita or wants, whether of the man himself, or of others. Take the case of a man wanting peace; we may find that what he really wants is that people should not *want* to harm each other, while another man might merely be concerned that any such harm be prevented.

But what of the non-essential occurrence of a value in the specification of another? A man wants to marry a certain girl. The marriage is unlikely to take place unless the girl also wants to marry him. Knowing this, the man will have the following appetitum (to give it in some more detail): that the girl should want to marry him, and that the marriage should take place. But there are two possible cases here: one in which he really does want the girl to want to marry him, because the kind of relationship with her which he envisages would be impossible without that desire on her part, and another, let us say, in which he wants the marriage for purely economic reasons, so that, though he wants the girl's consent, it is—as we say—only as a means, and if the marriage were to take place without such a desire on her part, his desire would be satisfied. The reference to the girl's desire, therefore, does not occur essentially in the specification of his desire (in the second case), since his desire could be satisfied by a state of affairs in which she did not have the desire to marry him.

To take another example, suppose that a man makes a private sacrifice to help someone in need. He doesn't do it from a Kantian sense of duty—he merely wants to help. In his case, we are dealing with a first order value. If we praise his action, we introduce a new value—our own: for we want people to have such desires, including ourselves.

We may illustrate the point further with yet another and more complicated example. A boy is progressing well at school, but unsatisfied. He is bored, inarticulate and withdrawn. He seems to want a change, without knowing what. The boy's parents, noting what they take to be his desire for revolt, send him to another school where they hope that this desire will be suitably satisfied. Here is a second order value. Now the promoters of this school want to satisfy the desires of parents to satisfy their children's desires for revolt. This is a third order value. In a letter to a newspaper, a traditionally minded correspondent expresses his hostility to such schools, saying essentially that he does not want the state of affairs in which the promoters of schools want the state of affairs in which the parents want the state of affairs in which the teachers want the state of affairs in which the child who wants revolt should have his desire satisfied. This is a fifth order value (though style, as well as other considerations, may well have obscured this hierarchical appetitive structure).

Is there any limit to this ladder of values? There is, I think, no limit of principle, save that there are desires the specification of which essentially includes reference to other desires *regardless of their order*. For instance, I may want the good of others to take precedence over all my other desires. Now this desire, though it may conflict both logically and practically with other desires which I have or may have, as well as with other desires of other persons, yet includes all my other desires within its scope, and subordinates them explicitly to one goal, whatever their order may be. A value of this kind may be called an *architectonic value*, after Aristotle. There could not be a value of higher order, though there could of course be other architectonic values (even in the same person) in conflict with it.

Here, then, is a central complication that we meet in moving from the model universe of section 1 to the world of our experience, that wants come into conflict, not only with practical intransigencies, but also with each other, even in one person; it is this fact which introduces higher order values into our world, for it is so that our desires come to be directed not only upon certain states of the universe, but also upon bringing about or eliminating desires for those states. And it is in this region that much moral activity takes place, that we are urged to love each other, to cultivate inner virtues, that we are praised, blamed, punished and rewarded. To this extent, Kant was right in fastening on the motive of duty as a locus of morality. This is so, however, only because of the specific imperfection of our world which is the disharmony, including the inner disharmony of human desires. If this disharmony did not exist, most higher order values, and with them duty, would be superfluous and would disappear. So too, we might argue, specifically moral values would disappear, being that refraction in values which is produced by their intersection with the impurities of the world we experience.

§6. There is a further, and particularly notable distinction between what I shall call *relative* and *absolute* values. A value is relative if reference to the person whose value it is occurs essentially in the specification of the value; and a value is absolute if it is not relative. This is a distinction related to the notions of selfishness and altruism. It may be clarified by an example. Suppose that there is a man in danger of drowning in a lake. A bystander notices his predicament, and wants him to be saved. So he prepares to dive in, but as he is about to do so, a boat comes into view, and the man is rescued by someone in the boat. Now suppose that the bystander's original desire was this—that he should swim to the drowing man and save him. Did mention of the bystander (as the rescuer) occur essentially in the description of the object of his desire? If his desire would be satisfied by a rescue from the boat, then mention of him does not occur essentially: what he really wanted was that someone should rescue the man, believing at first that he would himself have to be that person. In the other case, his desire would be frustrated by the boat coming to the rescue. His desire might essentially have included this—that *he* should be the rescuer. Then reference to him will have occurred essentially in the specification of the value. It would then be a case of a relative value; whereas the other situation, where he simply wants the man to be rescued (no matter by whom), would be an absolute value.

Thus on our basis in theoretical psychology, we are able to create an array of independently varying distinctions in values. Every value must be situable for each of the six distinctions, but no position on any one distinction requires any position on any other. Our account may be reviewed schematically as shown in the diagram on the next page.

This diagram illustrates succinctly the flexibility of the proposed account of values. It is a flexibility that is dramatically increased when we recognize that we have largely restricted ourselves to single values. In fact, as has been briefly noticed, some evaluative attitudes, even in a single person, may be appetitively complex. A particular

Appetitivity	Sincerity	Scope	Positivity	Relativity	Order
primary	real	open	positive	absolute	first
					second
secondary					third
	quasi	closed	negative	relative	. . . . .
tertiary					architectonic

case of admiration, for example, might involve first—wanting the admired person to be imitated in respect of his desires (a primary, real, open, positive, absolute, second-order value), acting as though one wished to be the other person (a secondary, quasi, closed, positive, relative, first-order value), as well as taking pleasure in his existence (a tertiary, real, closed, positive, absolute, first-order value).

But what of specifically moral values? Before we consider them, we must progress from the analysis of particular wills and particular values to some account of multiplicities of wills and multiplicities of values.

8 Wills in Harmony and Wills in Concert

Until now we have been primarily concerned with an account of value and desire based on the model universe with one will of section 1. But the world we know has a multitude of wills. Thus for any given value we have three possibilities: first, it may be a value of only one person (an appetitum of only one will); secondly, it may be a value shared by a number of persons (where several wills are directed at the same appetitum—wills in harmony); third, it may be a group value (where the appetitum is such as to be possessed only by a group of wills—wills in concert).

The difference between the second and the third cases becomes manifest in the distinction between actions that may be performed by individuals severally, and actions that may be performed only by collectivities. For instance, rioting, discussing, making war, electing, going on strike are all actions properly or primarily performed by a group. Correspondingly, the desire or tendency to perform them exists in the group, and the corresponding value is essentially collective. These group values are different from values shared by a group, where the members of the group severally desire the same object, like the punters, trainers, jockey and owner all wanting the same horse to win.

It will be convenient to speak of those whose appetita constitute a given value as the 'reference group'. We may now elaborate the earlier point. A reference group always has at least one member. In the case of some values it may necessarily have more than one member. Moreover, a reference group having more than one member or may not be identifiable independently of the corresponding appetitum; that is, the persons concerned may or may not have something which brings them together beyond the sharing of this value. For instance, the desire that Pegasus should win the three-thirty is likely to be the only thing that marks off its reference group; whereas war can be made only by a nation, so that the group that makes war must also be identifiable as the nation that it is (the term 'nation' here should be allowed to cover various marginal cases). In such a case, of course, the fact that war is the somehow determined will of the nation does not imply that it is the will of every member of that group.

However, the distinction between wills in harmony and wills in concert, though it may seem clear when we refer to some chosen examples, gives rise to perplexity. For the case of wills 'in concert' has in fact been explained by reference to *a concerted will*: the question then arises—what in these cases is the relation between the wills that are in concert and the concerted will? What is the will of the collectivity in rioting, and what is its relation to the wills of the individual rioters? What is the concerted will in discussing, and what its relation to the wills of the parties to the discussion? and so forth.

Let us start by considering the case of a discussion. Could we not understand this activity by reference to the wills of the (say two) parties to the discussion without in addition appealing to a concerted will? We may grant that discussing can be regarded as an action performed by a collectivity, but deny that it is anything over and above the contributive actions of those who take part in the discussion. In other words, a discussion is nothing other than a sequence of speeches in the question/answer relation, or some other such relation, and the successive utterance of such speeches with the appropriate intentions constitutes a discussion. We have no need of a collective will.

Consider the following minimal discussion:

'What is the number of the house?'

'Seventeen.'

This, it seems, can be simply accounted for as follows. John is concerned with some house, but he does not know its number. Consequently, he asks Richard, whom he thinks possibly to know the number, and in asking the question he is trying to get Richard to tell him it. Richard, on the other hand, in replying (we assume that he is not lying or answering at random), is trying to inform John of the number of that house. Schematically, John's aim is that John should know the number, and he tries to bring it about that Richard should try to bring it about that John should know the number.

It may seem very clear that two wills are enough here, that we do not need a third will—that of the John–Richard collectivity. In other words, if 'John knows p' be represented by '$K_j p$', and 'Richard brings it about that p' by '$D_r p$', then the conversation above can be sufficiently represented by the formula $D_j D_r K_j p$.

But there is a weakness here. It is true that if we take the conversation as given, the above representation is adequate. We take it that $D_a p$ implies p. Then from $D_j D_r K_j p$ we can infer $D_r K_j p$, which is true of the conversation, and from that in turn $K_j p$, which is also true at the end of the conversation. But by starting from the conversation as a whole, we are begging the question, which is whether that whole can be treated by summing the wills of John and Richard. For what is John's action, considered as *one of the two* constituent actions of this discussion? It is that he asks a question—and asking a question is not bringing it about that an interlocutor causes you to know the answer; it is trying to bring that about. Equally, Richard's reply is not of itself a bringing it about that John knows the number, it is an attempt to bring that about. Then what brings it about that the first attempt (the question) can achieve its goal (and consequently the second also)? It seems to be a tacit agreement of Richard and John that they should engage in a question–answer exchange such that if successful it would conform to the pattern schematically given above. This specific agreement is of course itself made possible by more general conventions of language and society. What is suggested, then, is that to understand a discussion as an interaction of two wills, we have to appeal to a joint will that the discussion should proceed according to a certain pattern. Of course, this joint will need not be exercised in any other way than in the several actions which constitute the discussion. It is that which plays the same role with respect to the components of the discussion as rules of inference play with respect to the steps of an argument. Thus, though we need to refer to the collective will, we must not treat it as another coordinate component of the discussion. Attempting to do this would produce something of the form $D_{j-r} D_j D_r K_j p$, and would be subject to the analogue of Lewis Carroll's Achilles and the Tortoise paradox.

Let us consider an example of the conditions which must be jointly secured in order that the discussions proceed. John and Richard must assure that they are speaking about the same house. But then why should this assurance be regarded as something achieved by the collectivity of John and Richard? Let us allow p to be the proposition ' "The house" in the discussion is the one and only house such that . . .;' then the condition to be secured is that both John and Richard know this—$K_j p \& K_r p$. But can this not be brought about by, say, John? We should then have an expression of the form $D_j (K_j p \& K_r p)$. But there is a flaw here. John may know that he will use the term 'the house' in the required way in the discussion (he may intend to do so), but he cannot know that it will be so used in the discussion unless he also knows that Richard will so use it. But the only reason he could have for supposing that Richard will so use it, *ex hypothesi*, is that Richard will follow his stipulation. But this is viciously circular, since $D_j(K_j p \, \& \, K_r p)$ was introduced precisely as giving the form of that stipulation. Here then is a specific example of the need to refer to a superordinate (joint) will, and of the importance of not treating it as coordinate with the individual wills.

It is indeed an example of the role of conventions in language and understanding, of that 'common world of the understanding' which we had occasion to discuss in annex (iii). In outline, just as language and understanding in general require reference to communal arrangements and their maintenance, to some kind of communal will: so too in a particular linguistic situation, the participants must as a collectivity be taken to see to it that the specific conditions obtain which are necessary for the success of their particular project.

But suppose that both John and Richard as a matter of fact do make the required assumptions: why do we need additional reference to the pair as a collectivity? It is because the assumptions required can only be specified as those which are to govern *their* discussion: but the discussion only exists if the assumptions are made. Just as we have seen a connection on the one hand between the problem we are discussing and the Lewis Carroll paradox, so on the other we see a connection with traditional social contract paradoxes, by which there could not be a first contract since any contract implies a prior contract in terms of which it may be established.

On this side, we may profitably recall Russell Grice's position in his *The Grounds of Moral Judgement*, or that of Rawls in *A Theory of Justice*. The contract becomes in a special way hypothetical: we draw attention to situations in which it would be in the interest of the parties to them to have contracted or to contract to act in a certain way. The analogy in our case will be that the parties to the discussion should act as though they had agreed that they should jointly ensure its conformity to certain conditions. This requirement of conformity is sometimes realised in the person of a chairman, who is supposed to be not a party to the discussion coordinate with the others, but a superordinate representative and guardian of what makes the discussion possible.

An account now takes shape of certain actions of collectivities. Beyond the several constituent actions of the members of the collectivity, appeal is made *in addition* to the will of the collectivity as such, since the conventions or contract underlying the collective action can be explained only by such an appeal. But we must beware of an unbalanced diet of examples. This account of the *concerted will* is being constructed on the basis of a solitary example, that of the highly sophisticated collective action of discussing. Moreover, discussing is a dubious candidate for a collective action. And though it is instructive to have discovered a need in this marginal case to appeal to the collectivity as well as to its members, we cannot be confident that the account emerging will apply to more central cases.

For instance, we have mentioned rioting as a case of collective action. We shall not debate the *centrality* of this example. It is in any case clear that the rioters are not bound together by any convention or contract, even implicit or hypothetical. There could not be a chairman of a riot, whose task it would be to see that the parties to the riot broadly observed some agreed procedure.

But it might be maintained that a riot could be 'stage-managed': it is a mere turn of idiom that this stage-manager would not be called a chairman. But no: there is at least an implicit chairman in every discussion; for the chairman's role is part of the structure of discussion as such—the chairman stands for the collectivity, and the collectivity stands by certain conventions, and the discussion stands on those conventions. But the stage-manager of a riot would not be structurally part of it. It is not only that a riot could take place without being stage-managed: but the stage-manager of a riot that was stage-managed would be outside it, calculating the effect of various interventions on the mob which was under his observation. The chairman is on the platform with the speakers; the chairman may be up-stage: but the stage-manager is off-stage.

In the one collectivity, then, there is a strongly articulated internal structure assigning various roles to its individual members in various circumstances: indeed, the collectivity has its existence in and by maintaining this structure. In the other, however, we find a virtual absence of such structure: the individual who riots in a way ceases to be an individual—he 'loses himself', he is 'swept along', he becomes 'just one of the mob', he is 'carried away'. The rioter does not of course cease to be an individual organism: he breathes and moves; but he is more likely to run than walk; much more likely to shout than talk; and he tends to stop thinking as an individual: such instrumental intelligence as is displayed in a riot is displayed at the collective level by actions like changing route to avoid an obstacle. But it is 'intelligence' of a very low order, and rather easily outwitted. The rioting mob is superhuman—for it is composed of individual human beings and is an entity of a higher order than they (in some sense): but it is subhuman—for the rioting individuals tend to lose human characteristics, and the resulting collective being is more bestial than human. This is perhaps why the parties to a riot as well as its victims may be frightened by it—and frightened in more than a merely prudential way.

Differences between our two examples may be further illustrated by considering ways in which collective actions of the two kinds may be balked. How might one set about sabotaging a discussion? One range of methods depends upon a crude physical interference with what makes the discussion possible: we bodily separate the parties to the discussion—we cut a telephone line—we turn on a radio so loud that the participants can no longer hear each other. But there is another range of procedures aimed with greater or less subtlety at disturbing the tacit conventions of the discussion. An unsubtle example: use of a word considered *obscene* in a *polite* discussion is likely to stop it, since there will rarely be any way of regarding it as a move in that discussion; or again, the introduction of an irrelevance into a directed or purposive discussion may have the same effect. The latter case is of some interest, since 'changing the subject' is in fact allowed for in many, if not all kinds of discussion (it is even called for: the bore, too, is a conversation stopper). In what is loosely characterised as 'casual conversation' the governing conventions are rather weak and there are few *thematic* restraints on changing the subject; there are, however, restraints on frequency (it would not do for *each* speech of a party to a two-person conversation to be a change of subject). In other cases, though there may be much stronger restraints on changing the subject, they are nevertheless not absolute: in other words, breaching these restraints does not necessarily end the discussion. For it may be treated as a tacit proposal for a change in the governing convention, and a reply may establish and further delimit that change.

Of course, it is rather rare for the establishment, observation or alteration of such conventions to be a matter for conscious attention. On the other hand, consciousness of them at a theoretical level emerged rather early in Western thought. And it emerged interestingly in two rival models of the direction of discussion and speech in awareness of such conventions, and of the possibilities of exploiting, developing or codifying them. For the proponents of the rival versions of this new insight, their dispute was of the first importance.

Nothing could be further from Plato's Academy than the school of Isocrates. But the rivalry between philosophy and rhetoric was as nothing to the layman, for whom, as Aristophanes had already made clear in his parody of Socrates, the *Clouds*, these men, whatever their rival doctrines, indifferently exploited their indecent study of conventions of speech to 'make the better argument appear worse, and the worse better'. For the Platonists, truth was independent of forms of speech, though attainable by privileged forms of argument: the rest was trickery or ornament. Here were the impulses to formal logic (and the first important step here would be taken in Aristotle's *Topics* with the codification and classification of certain underlying conventions of discussion), and to the philosophers' notion of timeless and context-free propositions. For the rhetoricians, on the other hand, the proposition is an abstract monstrosity, and the logical schemata of inference a mischievous extrapolation from the realities of human communication through language. Since this seminal dispute philosophy and literature have been increasingly at odds in Western thought. And if the rhetorician is devoted to speech, philosophy, at times, has seemed to be devoted to its annihilation: Socratic irony is the supreme conversation stopper: the mother and father of red herrings and indecent interjections.

But it is not necessary to substantiate these brief observations on the genesis of rhetoric and philosophy in order to show the possibility of disturbing or breaking off a discussion by interfering with or playing on its underlying conventions. The question that now concerns us is whether there is any parallel to such interventions in the case of another form of collective behaviour, rioting, in which we have agreed that no such conventions are present. Certainly, the analogues of cutting the telephone line, or drowning the conversation with loud noise and so on, are to be found in the armoury of a riot squad, though its weapons are more sinister. But, as we have seen, a conversation can be stopped by tampering directly with its mechanisms: can this be done for a riot? The following case was once reported to me. A rioting crowd paused at a police barrier, in a moment of tension; the man in charge of the police stepped forward, and all eyes were on him: would his action unlock the next stage of the riot? He did not harangue the crowd, raise his arms, or issue a threat—he gave no orders to the squad of police. Instead, he took a bunch of keys from his pocket and juggled with them: the riot ended.

Now the creation of a mob from a group of individuals seems to require, as we have seen, a certain loss of or merging of their individual identity. The mob once constituted has a limited number of rather simple responses to a few broadly defined categories of situation, such as situations which present obvious obstacles to its objective, and situations which offer an obvious approach to that objective. In the case quoted, the whole attention of the mob came to be directed upon an unassimilable action: the juggling resisted interpretation as a threat or as an encouragement. Thus, in attending to this event, the mob ceased to exist, dissolving into an aggregate of individual people in the same place all observing a particular inconsequential act.

Now if we may disrupt a discussion by tampering with its *conventions*, what would we be tampering with in such methods of disrupting a riot? Here we seem to need a theory of sympathy, a theory by which it would be possible to explain forms of solidarity between men not based even on implicit conventions.

A serious study of sympathy belongs to various sciences, and we cannot embark upon it here. But the general form of the questions to be asked about collective action in collectivities based on sympathy, as in collectivities based on convention, is: how are such superordinate persons constructed? This is no more or less than the question how human society, organisationally or affectively, is constituted. As I have said, it is not part of our task here even to sketch the emergence of organisations, of possibilities of mass action, of corporate personalities, or to outline the diversity of types of communal will from that exercised by a highly organised and hierarchical bureaucracy, to that evident in a casual street-corner conversation, or manifest in the pure violence of an undifferentiated rioting mob.

But when we consider these phenomena, our individualistic predilections may make us revert obstinately to the question which has recurred in various forms throughout this section: are not individual wills prior to collective wills? Do not the latter exist only upon the condition that individuals freely and for as long or as brief a period as they wish enter into their creation? A rioter may at any moment walk away; an interlocutor may at any moment leave or sabotage the discussion, and so on. These observations, no doubt, are true. But they display a distracting anxiety for individual freedom.

It is an anxiety provoked by the idea that a collective will might be a mysterious force able to subject individual wills to its determination. We should dismiss it; and remark that collectivities make individuals possible just as much as individuals make collectivities possible. It is a mistake to think of either form of the will either as prior or indeed as firmly delimited. This is what gives importance to the notion of wills in concert: for it is only in special cases that the will of a collectivity (the concerted will) can be thought of as having an existence of its own (through legal fictions, and so on); and equally only for special purposes that individual wills can be thought of as having an existence independent of collectivities (in the sphere of morality, for instance).

In our model universe, we have only one will, and we have supposed the delimitation of its 'zone' to be unproblematic. If additional wills are introduced into the model, we shall not be able to exclude the case of an overlapping of zones: at this point, an atomistic/additive account of their interaction ceases to be suitable, for we are quickly faced with analogues in theoretical psychology of the three-body problem. This is a point to which we shall return in section 13. Meanwhile it will be enough to note that we give priority neither to the individual will (in the manner of Mill) nor to the collective will (in the manner of Hegel).

9 Values in Harmony and Values in Concert

In addition to the harmony or concert of wills in respect of their values, we must consider the harmony or concert of values themselves.

In the first place, values can be regarded as forming systems by what we may call *compresence*, that is, their presence together in the same person (or independently identifiable group of persons). However, mere compresence will not sufficiently account for the unity which value systems may be experienced as having. In fact, it is a matter of experience that the value systems of individuals and groups do not spring from arbitrary collocations of appetita. What further principles then concur in defining value systems?

We may appeal to a second and a third criterion: to *compatibility* and *compracticability*. Now it is clear that it is not a condition of there being a value system that its component values should be perfectly compatible and compracticable. Indeed, the modification or collapse of value systems in the face of emergent contradictions (whether logical or practical) is a leading feature of the history of mankind, as well as a frequent dilemma for the individual man. But the very fact that these modifications and collapses occur shows that compatibility and compracticability act as a constraint upon value systems. The more blatant the incompatibilities or incompracticabilities, the less likely is a system of values to survive or even to exist. For the group or the individual will in the end be obliged to alter at least some of its values. There is a limit to good luck, and to the possibilities of self-deceit.

However, the compresence of a number of values in a person or group as constrained by their compatibility and compracticability is still, it seems, insufficient to account for that other unifying feature of value-systems which we may provisionally call their style. What constitutes such a style has been a recurrent problem for historians and social scientists, who, from Marx and Durkheim to Weber and Mannheim, have given very different answers to the question. How in general such an investigation of style is possible will be the topic of annex (x).

(x) Thematics

We return to part of the argument of annex (iii), where a justification was offered for the use of a notion of a proposition. Now at that point, a proposition was defined as what is expressed by a set of sentences where the set is granted to be the set of sentences which are for a certain purpose interchangeable. If we ask a similar question about the identity of a sentence, similar problems arise. A sentence too is to be defined with respect to a set of what have come to be called 'token sentences'. But yet again similar questions can arise about the phonetic identity of a token sentence.

There seems to be here a scheme of argument capable of repeated application, and generating a hierarchy of formal entities whose properties and relations may be investigated at each level by the appropriate enquiry: phonology, morphology, syntax, semantics.

But is there any reason for supposing that propositions are the highest entities in this ladder? That is, just as interchangeability for a set of sentences is the genesis of propositions, could there be a higher order interchangeability between a set of propositions which would be the genesis of a yet higher order entity?

Our first answer might be: certainly not. For it is necessary to language that while we may use a number of different sentences indifferently to express the same proposition, we may not propound a number of propositions indifferently; for to propound a different proposition is to say something different; and it is never indifferent that we say something different. But this, of course is to beg the question. The question is precisely whether sometimes in saying something different, we are at another level saying the same thing.

It seems that there are such cases. Consider for instance a socialist saying of someone: 'He disapproves of death duties', or 'He is unwilling to put his child in the State educational system', or 'He opposes nationalisation'. It is clear that we are dealing here with three different propositions (each of which evidently could be expressed in many different sentences). But it is also true that there could be circumstances in which the propounding of any of these propositions would amount to the same. Indeed, it is in general possible to ask what a person is trying to say, although it is quite clear what propositions he is propounding.

Thus the postulation of higher order entities bearing a similar relation to propositions to that which they bear to sentences turns out to be far from idle. I introduce the term 'thema' for a higher order entity of this kind. And now, corresponding to the study of the relation between sentences and propositions (namely, semantics), we have a study of the relation between propositions and themata, which we might call 'thematics', or 'hermeneutics'.

Of course, many objections to this picture of language, with or without its corollary of themata, can be made. In particular, it might be held that it, like much other progeny of Aristotle's De Interpretatione, *supposes erroneously that the assertoric uses of language are primary. Is the point that I have made, for instance, by speaking of the relation between propositions and themata, simply a confused version of Austin's distinction between the illocutionary and the perlocutionary act? This is a question which I shall not pursue here. I shall allow myself merely to indicate a line of answer by the assertion that the ability to propound propositions is central to all uses of language from assertion to exclamation, and that themata enter as a corollary, once the door has been opened to propositions.*

Let us look more closely at themata, and begin by considering the relation between syntactic, semantic and what we may call hermeneutic rules. An important initial point to observe is that each set of rules may be seen as constructing higher order units out of lower order elements. These units are then subject to further rules, become themselves elements out of which entities of a higher order again are constituted.

But how are all these rules related? We might at first think them to be logically independent. That is, in the case of syntax and semantics, we might think that a particular syntax imposes no particular semantics, and a particular semantics no particular syntax. But this view is subject to important qualifications. First, if a language is to be sufficiently powerful, it is essential that semantic rules should cover open classes of syntactic units, these classes, plainly, being defined and related syntactically: in this way, a given syntax will impose semantic restrictions (apparent counter-examples from codes and ciphers are properly dismissed as parasitic). Equally, though it would be possible, given a particular set of semantic rules, to substitute different syntactic units for the ones on which they presently operate, there are again restrictions on how this could be done if inconsistency in the application of semantic rules as applied to the new units is to be avoided. In general, to give a string of words a meaning is thereby to give it a syntax, to make it into a sentence. In a favourite example, giving one meaning rather than another to the string 'I like cooking apples', is also giving it one syntax rather than another, making it one sentence rather than another.

Now, like syntactic and semantic rules, semantic and hermeneutic rules are restrictedly independent. Nothing about the proposition that a man disapproves of death duties compels it to be taken as conveying the thema which it did in the context hinted at above. Yet, plainly, the proposition delimits a range of themata. Equally, nothing about the thema compels it to be conveyed by that particular proposition. But, to pursue the analogy, in taking a syntactic unit (a sentence) as conveying a certain thema, we are thereby taking it as expressing a certain proposition. For instance, in taking the syntactic unit 'He disapproves of death duties' to convey the same thema as may be taken to be conveyed by 'He opposes nationalisation', we are thereby taking that syntactic unit as expressing the proposition which is also expressed by 'He believes inheritance taxes to be wrong', rather than that which is also expressed by 'He thinks that supposed duties arising in the event of a death should be disregarded'.

Thus, the notion of higher order meanings given or perhaps hidden in lower order ones—the notion of themata—is acquiring some substance. But there are some serious challenges to it. First, does it represent an unnecessary multiplication of entities? Secondly, is it a notion which would have application only in what are broadly called the cultural sciences? Thirdly, is this corollary of a traditional view of language which we have been trying to establish actually no more than a reductio ad absurdum of that view?

First, then, ought we to use Occam's razor and deny the existence of themata altogether? It might be argued that these themata can only be set up by tacitly adopting the false view that the same sentences always or generally express the same propositions. In a certain context, let us admit, the sentences 'He disapproves of death duties', 'He is unwilling to put his child in the State educational system', and 'He opposes nationalisation' might be interchangeable. But so far from showing that we are dealing here with different propositions conveying the same thema, the case should simply be regarded as one in which the three sentences are used or understood to express the same proposition. Let us not multiply entities beyond what is needful: the work to be done by themata can in fact be done by propositions alone.

This objection is, I think, easily disposed of. It is perhaps enough merely to repeat the observation made earlier, that it is perfectly possible to wonder what a man is getting at even when it is clear what propositions he is propounding. For instance, let someone admit an error. He does so by expressing a certain proposition. And he is understood to do so by being understood to express that proposition. But in admitting his error he may further be expressing a desire for reconciliation with the person addressed. In this case, he is conveying the thema of a desire for reconciliation by expressing the proposition that he was in error; and although certainly this is not the only means by which such a desire might be conveyed, if it is so conveyed, it is indeed by the use of that proposition that the man conveys it. Again, 'He disapproves of death duties' may be true or false. But even granted that the propositional ambiguity of this sentence is resolved, and that we know the proposition to be true—a thematic ambiguity will remain.

Thus the first objection is not enough to make thematics collapse into semantics. Let us turn to the second difficulty. Does thematics exist only in the human sciences? The following argument may be put forward. Any plausible examples that may be given of themata are in the field of human behaviour and expression. It is certainly the case that human behaviour calls for interpretation multiply and at many different levels. It always makes sense to ask, given any description of a man's linguistic or non-linguistic behaviour, what he's getting at. This is a fact that raises many vexed philosophical problems concerning motives, intentions, reasons for action, and so forth, as well as many empirical questions in the same area. The human sciences try to deal with such questions, and such endeavours themselves raise conceptual problems. But such problems, which belong essentially to theoretical psychology, are simply obscured by wrapping them up in the terminology of 'themata', by suggesting that they arise as problems in the theory of meaning. It is, after all, clear that a proposition like ' The sun is about 93 million miles from the Earth', or ' The photon has no charge', does not convey any thema. What has been called a thema is really nothing more than a motive or intention with which someone acts or speaks.

This is a more substantial and difficult objection. It will be suggested in reply that the view in the theory of meaning put forward is in fact quite general, and the argument will proceed by showing how themata are after all conveyed by propositions in the natural sciences.

Let us start by considering the shop-window presentation of scientific conclusions. In such presentation, the scientist may lay out what he knows as a deductive system, with general laws at the top, and particular observation statements at the bottom. The system may be presented by the most hard-nosed as a closed system such that the topmost laws are to be understood as doing nothing more than stating more concisely what is already stated by all the bottom-most observation statements.

But given a hierarchically ordered system of the kind described, can we see there any place for themata? The answer stands out. Thematic relations between propositions will be those which are given by the grouping of those propositions under some higher proposition (or law). Thus the proposition that the photon has no charge will, together with many others, be taken to convey as a thema the corpuscular theory of light.

There is an objection to be met here. Are we not dealing with a single ordered system? Has it not been claimed that the higher order propositions *which it contains state no more than is already stated by lower-order propositions? Must it not then be that there is only one set of semantic rules, and that between various propositions in the system, nothing more recondite is needed than relations of implication? Consider the analogy of a game of chess. Here the rules of the game specify how the pieces are to be moved. It is a consequence of these rules that there are other higher order rules governing sequences of positions of the whole board. In turn, from these positions, we can construct sequences of moves (including those called gambits), and there will be yet higher order rules governing these yet higher order entities. The introduction of themata in language is like the introduction of higher order entities (and rules) at chess: it is a superfluous elaboration upon the set of semantic rules, just as the other is a superfluous elaboration upon the one set of rules of chess.*

This objection does not cut as deep as might seem. For though themata are indeed a superfluous construct in the case of the shop-window positivist formulation of scientific results, they are precisely not so in the case of the practice of scientific enquiry. For in that practice, the 'thematic' relations between scientific propositions are precisely a crucial problem, and moreover the thematic ambiguity of scientific propositions is a crucial means of advance in its capacity to suggest future lines of enquiry. Consider the thematic ambiguity of propositions suggesting that the atom was like a small solar system. The investigable uncertainty of how far such propositions concerning atoms could be correlated with established propositions concerning planetry systems properly so-called was a heuristic advantage.

A similar point may be made for a case already considered in annex (iv) above, that of Joule's treatment of heat as a form of energy. And we at once remark that themata have brought us to the borders of paronymy. For it is often the thematic principles characterising different domains which also suggest ways of relating or amalgamating those different domains.

Thus the case of the natural sciences, while it seemed at first to provide a strong counter-example to the claim that the notion of a thema is required in a general theory of meaning, in fact turns out to provide further exemplification of the claim.

But the claim still has to meet a third objection: that it should be taken seriously only as a reductio ad absurdum of the theory of language of which it is allegedly a corollary. On this objection we shall say that things have already gone wrong at the point at which we begin speaking even of semantic rules, as though they not only existed, but were analogous to syntactic rules. There is, it will be urged, no branch of enquiry called semantics at all—there is nothing left over for it from all the special sciences and disciplines. Still less, if semantics be banished, shall we find any home for 'thematics'. The chess analogy might have been taken more seriously: for clearly there are no higher order rules beyond what corresponds to syntax—namely, the rules of chess.

In reply to this objection let it be said that in fact the argument of the present section in no way requires the autonomy of semantics and thematics. Further, the elaboration of the chess analogy was a bad move by the objector: that a certain move will constitute 'putting the opponent into check' is indeed part of the semantics of chess; that another move is an 'attacking move', or that **B** *to* **K3** *made by Fischer in a match against Byrne played when he was 13 was 'one of the best in the history of chess' (Gerald Abrahams,* The Chess Mind*)—these are hermeneutic judgements, bringing us into the area of themata.*

Certainly, interpretation in general is not a specifically philosophical task (the above interpretations need chess players, not philosophers, to make and assess them), though the rivals among the more holistic interpretative systems (such as Marxism and psychoanalysis) certainly pose philosophical problems.

Yet there remains the task of discerning general features of interpretation, both formally (as in work done in formal semantics), and through discussion of the leading notion of a thema (a discussion which the present annex is intended to display rather than conclude).

10 Styles of Life

We have now the abstract apparatus to account for that feature of sets of values which we called their style. For sets of values may be unified by their thematic structure, the simplest case being that in which all the appetita convey the same thema.

But this formal anwer is exceedingly bare. What kinds of thematic structure are there? What determines them? What limits are set upon them? How can we set about that work of interpretation which would elicit the thematic structure of a particular set of values?

(xi) Human Nature

There is one strategy here which has been widespread in moral philosophy: we set out to discover an anchor for human values independent of what men happen to desire. This anchor is often found in 'human nature'.

It may be argued, for instance, that men's needs or interests are objectively determinable, independently of what they may desire. Such needs or interests will then be held to have a determining role at least for some parts of human value systems, and to set limits upon them. This position is all the more in need of consideration since we have not yet made any mention of needs or interests.

From the point of view of our argument, the leading question is whether needs or interests could indeed be established independently of desires. We should distinguish four theses at this point:

(1) that it is possible to establish what a particular man's interests are independently of what his desires are;
(2) that it is possible to establish what human interests are independently of human desires;
(3) that it is possible to establish what human interests are on the basis of some general facts about human nature;
(4) that it is possible to establish what ought and ought not to be done mediately or immediately on the basis of human interests.

We shall consider these theses in turn. It will be convenient to allow the term 'desire' to cover the whole class of what I have called appetitives, and to consider only interests, on the supposition that closely analogous considerations will apply to appetitives other than wanting, and to needs as well as interests.

There are several versions of the first thesis:

(a) that it is possible to establish what a particular man's interests are independently of any particular desire of his (i.e. a desire for **x** is never sufficient ground for saying **x** is in his interest);

*(b) that it is possible to establish what a particular man's interests are independently of the totality of his desires at any particular time (i.e. his total aversion to **x** now is never sufficient ground for saying that **x** is not in his interest);*

(c) that it is possible to establish what a particular man's interests are independently of all his desires.

The first two versions of the first thesis (together with corresponding versions of the second) are entirely plausible. It is the third version which we shall question. Could we reasonably say that something was in a person's interest even though it neither matched nor helped the attainment of any of his desires, then or later? It may be said that saving the life of a would-be suicide is doing something in his interest, whatever his desires may be, now or in the future. But what if for the rest of his life he regrets and resents his survival?

'You say that I am at least alive: yet life holds nothing for me. You say that securing my survival is securing an interest of mine: but in that case my interest has become a technical and biological condition to which I am indifferent. My life is not my survival. . . .'

Yet this is only one example, and we may find in Mill's satisfied pig and in his dissatisfied Socrates a plausible example suggesting the independence of a particular man's interests from the totality of his desires. For a vegetable life which answered grosso modo to the totality of a man's actual desires would yet not be in his interest if he had latent and unexplored talents, even if the exploitation of those talents might produce suffering and discontent. It seems to me that this sort of case—and indeed that of the suicide—is precisely a matter of dispute: of moral dispute. In other words, if we are inclined to accept Mill's view, it is in the light of our own values. It is not, therefore, an example that can settle the issue: for a person holding, as I would, that interests are not independent of desires may simply observe that the term 'interest' in this example may have one of two functions: either it is camouflage (in saying what is in this man's interest, I really mean that I want men in general and this man in particular to develop their talents), or it involves tacit reference to hypothetical desires of that man (I say that it is in his interest to develop his talents not only because so will he better serve his desires, but because if now per impossible he could make an informed choice, he would desire the development of his talents and not their atrophy, and correspondingly would, if they were not developed—and if per impossible he were able to appreciate what he had not experienced—regret it).

The corresponding third version of the second thesis, that it is possible to establish what human interests are independently of the totality of human desires, is even harder to accept. If then we must reject the first and second theses, at least in this strong form, we shall be in a position to reject the view that interests are primary, and to argue that they are on the contrary secondary to desires. The topic of interests would then be a subordinate theme within the appetitive framework already proposed (and our strategy would in outline be this—to analyse consulting the interests of **a** as desiring the state of affairs in which **p**, and in which—because **p**—certain desires of **a** are more readily fulfilled).

However, the attempt to subordinate an account of interests to the general account of value and desire offered here may be countered by the third thesis, that interests are established not on the basis of human desires, but on the basis of human nature. But now we are confronted by a range of Thomistic problems. Will it not be the nature of all things to seek the good? How, then, could we distinguish basing interests on desires from basing them on human nature? Some have envisaged facts about the nature of the human organism such that certain things are necessary to its survival, so that anything which procures or safeguards those things could be said to be to that extent in man's interest. But why should the survival of individual men have a determining role for human interests, especially since men are in any case mortal? With what justice can one say (appealing to such considerations) that it would be in the interest of the peoples of the Indian sub-continent if the sacred cow were desacrified? One would mean, of course, that a more 'rational' livestock policy would contribute to the elimination of famine, which brings suffering and death to many people. But those people themselves may hold that survival at that cost cannot be in their interest. . . . There is a genuine conflict of values here: it cannot be resolved by a straightforward appeal to supposedly objective interests.

Thus theses (1) to (3) seem to me to be misleading or false, though thesis (4), which would give a role to interests (or needs) in the grounding of moral notions, seems to me to be unexceptionable. It is, however, a thesis which can be accommodated within the general structure of our present argument, so long as it is not held that interests be ascertained independently of desires.

In any case, it should by now be rather clear that even if accounts relying on the independence of needs or interests could be established, they would not provide a means of accounting for what we have called 'style' in value systems. Rather they would tend to show a basic core within different styles of value. They would separate two kinds of value: the first an indispensable minimum, a critical or social morality thought of as providing a necessary framework for human life, within which the second kind of value—total value systems with their differing ideals and styles—would appear as it were as 'options': a matter for man's free choice. And here we confront a certain philosophical obsession; or a certain obsession of philosophy: the obsession with man.

Lévi-Strauss detects this obsession in existentialism, which he describes as 'an exercise in self-admiration in which contemporary man is duped, shut up in colloquy with himself, prostrate in extasy before himself. It is cut off from scientific knowledge which is despised, and genuine humanity whose historical depth and ethnographical dimensions are not recognised, in order to set up a closed and private world: an ideological Café du Commerce where the habitués, safely inside the four walls of a human condition made to the measure of a specific society, all day long go over problems of local interest, beyond which the smoky atmosphere of their dialectical fug prevents them from seeing' (1971, p. 572). Again, more generally, Michel Foucault has outlined the historical appearance of that configuration of knowledge which constitutes man as a central but problematic object: that which is studied by several sciences, but never fully—a being in the end impermeable to science. Foucault forecasts the erasure from our universe of this enigmatic outline which is man, like the face in the sand which is obliterated by an incoming tide.

The point of these observations seems to be as follows. Western philosophy, since the moment of Socrates's rejection of the sciences of nature, has never ceased to construct defences against science, by attempting to appropriate or exploit its findings, by attempting to discredit it on philosophical grounds, or—as a last resort—by attempting to secure an area as the proper preserve of philosophy, the enclosure taking a different form according to each advance of knowledge which philosophy, in her reactionary guise, takes to be a new encroachment. Thus we find philosophers—nomads whose title to land for grazing always yields to advancing sedentary communities which cultivate the land—occupying temporary camps in various corners of the intellectual universe. The boundary of one such camp is staked out by the 'problem of the freedom of the will': in this camp, a central part of the study of man is reserved for philosophy. Another camp is delimited by the currently widespread view of philosophy as concerned with 'conceptual problems'. On this view, the distinction between conceptual and empirical truths is held to be axiomatic, and conceptual problems are supposed to be susceptible only to a specific kind of non-empirical investigation, that of the philosopher.

So do we set man outside nature, detecting that peculiar position in his consciousness, his freedom, his concepts or his language: in his ability to apprehend, through philosophy, a realm of necessity distinct from the natural order. And so our first question to the present schematic account of value and *desire is: how does man come out of it? Is he absolutely unconditioned, free to will what he will? What determines values, and what limits them? These are questions with the wrong spin, when they are thought of as philosophical questions. In fact, they are scientific questions, and what is said in this book is a schematic part of an ethnology, a sociology, a psychology, an ethology, a biology, a cybernetics, as much as part of a 'philosophy'; it should be read as advocating the destruction of the boundary fences between these fields, or rather as urging a recognition that the boundaries which they are intended to mark are in a number of important respects illusory.*

10 Styles of Life

Returning to the style of value systems—to forms of life—we are chastened: the substantial claims about what constitutes them are to be found in the various sciences, and such claims are beyond our present scope. That section of our main argument which would show its point turns out to be empty. However, the formal account offered of styles in value systems in terms of a common thematic structure enables us to see how particular claims of this kind would take their place in our general account of values.

One thing is very clear, that we are placed at some distance from conventional moral philosophy. For certainly what is comprised in a style of life or of values goes much beyond what has come to be thought of as a matter of morality. For the Greeks, by contrast, it was quite natural that the aristocratic style of life marked by magnificence should be a topic in moral treatises. On our terms too, the inclusion of such a topic would be entirely appropriate.

But we are faced again with the strong tradition of the autonomy of moral concepts: is it wholly erroneous? What are the special features of 'moral values'? Indeed, more generally, what species of value are there?

11 Species of Value

It may seem that since the present account purports to deal with all values by referring them to corresponding desires, no justice can be done to the insights of those who have insisted on the autonomy of moral values, or the special character, for instance, of aesthetic values. To take a more specific objection of the same kind, it may seem that no justice can be done to cases described and experienced as cases of conflict between a moral principle and a desire.

The specific objection is rather easily countered. For if having a moral principle is itself having a desire of a particular kind, there will be no more difficulty in accounting for conflicts of the kind in question than for any other cases of conflicting desires. But even if this be granted, we may still ask what kind of desire constitutes having a moral principle.

It is in the end a historical and sociological question why and how some distinctions between kinds of value receive greater emphasis and attention in a particular society or period than in another. The existence of a wide range of discriminations between kinds of value has been discussed at some length in section 7. It remains to show how a sufficient characterisation of what may broadly be called a contemporary Western notion of moral as opposed to other values may be given in terms of these distinctions, though it must be remembered that this characterisation is not only subject to correction by the historian or social scientist, but is also a characterisation of something which is itself subject to change, so that views according to which moral values are autonomous are displayed as in that respect mere rationalisations of local prejudice.

Moral values, then, may be characterised as follows, using the distinctions of section 7: they are *primary* (involving a commitment to action); they are *real* (for the hypocrite, for instance, is precisely one who does not believe in the moral value in question); they are *open* (for closed values lack the universality taken to be an important feature of moral values); they may be either *positive* or *negative* (we are perhaps witnessing a historical change of emphasis from negative to positive values); they are *architectonic* or *higher order* values (for lower order values, especially first-order ones, do not have the intrinsic feature of regulating other values, a regulation which introduces all kinds of disciplines from rule-following to spiritual exercises, and which is important in morality); they are *absolute* (for morality is thought of as independent of the at least partly selfish concerns represented by relative desires).

This characterisation of 'moral values' should not be thought of as a theory of morality. Nor would there be any purpose served by testing and challenging each of the offered criteria in turn. For if, for instance, one said, 'But it is not *necessary* to morality that every value be "primary" in your sense', the reply is that there is no necessity here. There is a cultural and historical evolution in values, a particular configuration of which in modern Western society is in fact relatively distinct from other values, is thought of as such, and is moreover called by this special name: 'morality'.

But the description of that configuration given above, is a description of one of many possible different kinds of configuration, which is to say possible species of value; of these possible species many have also existed, which is to say, acquired currency as lived distinctions. We have known law-style moralities, and corresponding theories of morality, which give a special place to negative values; utilitarian moralities and theories of morality, which give a special place to tertiary values (those maximised satisfactions taken to be the final measure); moral theories and moralities giving a special place to universality (such as Christian or Islamic as opposed to say, Judaic moralities), and which in our terms emphasise absolute and open values; deontological theories of morality and moralities in which duties take first place, which lay emphasis on architectonic values; teleological and technical value systems (not only moralities) which draw attention to the internal 'instrumental' structure of appetitives discussed in annex (vii) above; aesthetic values, which are tertiary values primarily concerned with human artefacts, or what can paronymously be treated as such.

All these and many other configurations of human values call us insistently away from the abstractions governing the present argument. To suspend them completely is to let our theory rejoin our practice. Indeed, the abstraction which permits theory to emerge can be vindicated nowhere else.

(xii) Neutrality in Moral Philosophy

A. J. Ayer writes that any theory of morality

'is entirely on the level of analysis; it is an attempt to show what people are doing when they make moral judgements; it is not a set of suggestions as to what moral judgements they are to make. And this is true of all moral philosophy as I understand it. All moral theories . . . in so far as they are philosophical theories, are neutral as regards actual conduct.' (1959, pp. 245–6)

The remarks just offered should make it clear that this is a misleading view. For it supposes that in morality we are dealing with a given phenomenon in human behaviour which we could thus attempt to observe, describe and analyse impartially. But rival views about what is essential to morality do not offer, whatever the appearances, different accounts of the same configuration of phenomena: they draw attention to, or even create different configurations. Groups differ, not only in their moral beliefs, but also in their conceptions of what constitutes morality, if indeed they have any distinction between moral and other values.

Moral philosophy can only hope for a degree of neutrality by taking its place as a difficult branch of general value theory: such is the argument of this book. But if it is correct, and if this degree of neutrality is possible, the important reproach levelled at neutralist moral philosophies comes into play, that they admit, or even licence and encourage, any abhorrent and aberrant position, on the sole condition that some formal requirements be met.

12 The Evaluation of Values

How then will our theory rejoin our practice? Will it not be assimilable into *any* practice? Will it not sanction *any* wilful action? Does it not at least imply that there could be no rational basis for condemning any action? If by *rational basis* is meant some set of principles from which it could be deduced or cogently argued that such and such an action is wrong, independently of any desires of the person making the judgement or of some other person involved, then indeed there can be no rational basis for such condemnation. Condemnation can only be based upon a value.

Of course, there is the possibility of the evaluation or assessment of values not with a view to praise or blame, acceptance or rejection, but *technically*: we may discuss their practicability, their scope, their compatibility and compracticability with other values, their internal structure, and so on. It is in this way that much moral discourse, practical and theoretical, turns out to be technical. But we can and do also assess values morally—we evaluate them. In so doing we are adopting or expressing another value. But when a conflict arises, how can it be settled? Since what we are dealing with is in the end a conflict of desires, that conflict can only be settled by one or both of the parties abandoning or modifying his desire, or having it overriden. Indeed, moral debate is essentially the attempt of one or both parties to it to bring the other to recognise that he does not really want what he thought he wanted, or if he does, to change this desire. And it proceeds by such techniques as drawing out the consequences of a desire, appealing to some commonly held value, and showing that it applies to the case in spite of appearances. The latter technique is merely a special case of showing that something does fall under a certain concept. There is nothing to be said for giving it a special name (such as 'universalisability') and claiming it to be a distinguishing feature of moral discourse; nor is there anything to be said for a revision of this position by which universalisability is held to mark all descriptive terms, but to have a particular importance in the case of moral terms, since they also have 'prescriptive meaning' enabling us to infer imperatives.

Indeed, concentration upon the meaning of moral judgements is a poor starting point in moral philosophy. For too many important questions have to be begged in assuming in advance a clear and agreed distinction between moral judgements and others. On our account, value judgements in general will be any judgements to the effect that some value is or is not satisfied (that is, that the propositions in the corresponding appetitum are or are not true). Around this central case will be a variety of peripheral cases in which a more indirect appeal to a value must be made in understanding a judgement, where something, for instance, is judged conducive to or symptomatic of the satisfaction of some value. If the value entering into a judgement is that of the person making the judgement, he does have some commitment to action, because of the nature of values, but not because of the meaning of the judgement. For instance, a value may come into play not only in transforming the world, but also in measuring it. When the world is measured and comes up to scratch, no action is called for; but the meaning of some judgement which was once a guide to action, and is now the sign of its successful completion, does not change. Values may find expression in prescriptions, but value judgements do not have a special kind of meaning called prescriptive meaning.

The ways in which values enter into the meaning of terms is a complex topic which has been well opened up by Julius Kovesi (1967). But considerations of meaning do not enter into the evaluation of values. If I say that I think that the exploitation of the weak, the defenceless and the poor is wrong, this can only mean that I do not want them to be exploited, can only mean a fight against the desires which contribute to that exploitation, even if they are found in myself.

This view may be a threat to the morality which is aloofly consciousness of the truth of its pronouncements, but it leaves in clear view the morality which is a practical commitment to a different world, which is the work of men of good will.

13 The End

Throughout this book, we have argued good to be the end of all human striving—we have composed an extended footnote to the ancient definition of the good as 'that for which all things strive'. But in so doing, we have consistently taken the existence of desires to be the fundamental datum. That certain desires exist has been the brute fact; we have neither asked for nor allowed explanations of their existence. Such questions lay beyond the metaphysical limits of our position. Putting it more brutally, 'I just want it' has been made the final word in all questions of value. Is this not an infantile and anarchic position? Why should desires exist at all, and why should those desires exist which do? Why should we ever expect ourselves to be able to persuade others of the desirability of certain states of affairs?

Let us return to our model universe with one will. Why should that will produce some one change rather than another? In a revised version of the model (pp. 47–8), we were led to say that the 'intention' or 'appetitum' which appears in that zone of the universe which is the will's is not attributable, or that it can be attributed to no agency other than that of the will. It is this arbitrariness present in the original model which has persisted throughout our account and which is now being challenged.

Let us note that further consideration of our model universe may itself impose that challenge. For if we allow it to be arbitrary what the will in that universe directs itself towards, what distinction will remain between a change produced by the will, and a change occurring spontaneously? Indeed, etymologically, 'spontaneous' means 'willed'. On the other hand, if we try to escape arbitrariness by allowing determinations of the will from outside, then the will ceases to be a source of change, and the distinction between a change produced by it and a change produced by previous changes will also collapse.

This is a dilemma apparent in the confrontation between executive/mechanistic and voluntarist views of choice, between an Aristotelian view of choice as the putting into effect of pre-existing policies, and an existentialist view of choice as the sovereign creation of policy. Ricœur's attempt at a compromise between these positions (1950) seems to me to be unsuccessful. The dilemma, which seems to require us to take one of two positions, each of which is unacceptable, arises from certain underlying assumptions about the will. These assumptions are made plain in our model universe, and it is there that we shall most fruitfully consider how the will could remain distinguishable from what we called spontaneous events on the one hand, and from deterministic series of events on the other.

There seem to be two lines of solution to this problem. The first is to abjure completely the transcendental residue in our revised model universe. We have already noticed in annex (viii) above that on the interpretation of the 'zone of the will' in our model, the will must be other than and outside all the items in that zone: it will transcend the universe: it will be that 'centre of the world' of which Wittgenstein speaks in the passage which forms an epigraph to this book. We shall now simply identify the will with its zone. The description of that zone will tend towards and should merge into the theory of self-regulating organisms, and the way forward will be with the sciences dealing with such organisms.

But is this solution merely an adoption of the mechanistic horn of the dilemma? To suggest that this may not be so, we must look rather far afield.

For long the understanding of the universe, and the solution of particular problems about it, depended upon the drawing of boundaries in experience which would clearly delimit and abstract the entities concerned and the area of study, within a universe conceived as a single, globally determined whole. These boundaries were of such a kind as to delimit closed systems: that is, they were not permeable boundaries. Thus Newtonian mechanics deals essentially with closed dynamic systems. In a particular problem concerning such and such bodies, the influence of other bodies on the system cannot be taken into account at all, except indirectly, by being transmuted into so many special forces considered as acting within the system in question. The success of Newtonian mechanics is all the more remarkable when we consider that it is unable to deal with systems of more than two bodies, except by *ad hoc* methods of approximation, and that it was obliged to multiply special forces again in a very *ad hoc* fashion.

Thus the other face of the tremendous and fruitful simplification of problems achieved by this approach is a tremendous complexity of solutions of actual problems, or indeed the unavailability of solutions except by *ad hoc* procedures in all but the simplest cases.

One method of dealing with complexities of this kind is to treat the phenomena within the closed system under consideration statistically. In a sense, then, it becomes unimportant that there are questions that cannot, in principle or in practice, be answered about the behaviour of particular particles in the system or about their interaction. We now confront that triumph of closed system thinking: classical thermodynamics. But it is a triumph gained in the teeth of life. For the phenomena of life, at the level of the particular organism, or at the level of the evolutionary process, present remarkable and consistent examples of the maintenance of highly improbable states, and of their regular evolution in the direction of even greater complexity and improbability.

Now the Newtonian model exemplifies a pattern of enquiry and thought which is in no way restricted to physics, and it may be useful to summarise its leading features:

(1) items are considered only as belonging to *closed systems*, though the closure need not restrict us to a finite number of items, nor need it necessarily be considered to represent a closure in the nature of things, rather than being one convenient application of a methodological necessity—to restrict our field of enquiry (this pattern can be widely detected, from literary criticism and chemistry to formal semantics);

(2) the items of a systems are *atoms* of it—within that system they cannot be decomposed or explained, and if they behave differently from each other, this has to be treated as a brute fact (in classical chemistry, the elements have to be atomistically conceived in this way, but again we are dealing with a widespread pattern of thought, from economics to folk-lore);

(3) the interactions of items within a system are governed by laws, forces or constants which can be ascertained but not explained from within (such as gravity in classical dynamics, or Grimm's Law in philology);

(4) the overlapping of systems may occur and occur systematically, but this is only where a new system can be envisaged comprising both earlier systems (such would be the case for an envisaged collapse of chemistry into physics); otherwise overlaps have to be treated as arbitrary or merely coincidental.

Indisputably, all these features of classical science, indeed of classical thought, have been very fruitful. But they are all open to question. We may begin with the fourth feature—with overlap problems. Jacques Monod has written:

> In roulette, uncertainty is operational and not essential. . . . But in other situations the notion of chance takes on an essential and not purely operational significance. This is so, for instance, of what may be called 'absolute coincidences', that is, those which result from the intersection of two *totally independent* causal chains. Suppose that Dr. Smith has an emergency call to visit a patient, while Jones the plumber is carrying out an emergency repair to the roof of a nearby building. When Dr. Smith passes at the foot of the building, the plumber inadvertently drops his hammer the (deterministic) trajectory of which intersects that of the doctor who dies of a fractured skull. We say that it was bad luck. What other word could we use for such an event, unforeseeable *by its very nature*? It is clear that chance here must be considered as playing an essential role, inherent in the *total independence* of the two series of events whose interaction produces the accident (1970, p. 128: my italics).

Now the notion of absolute coincidence is an inevitable corollary of the closed system approach; for if two systems of events intersect but are quite distinct, then *ex hypothesi* there is no system within which that intersection could be explained.

We may remember Evans-Pritchard's well-known description of Zande beliefs:

> In Zandeland sometimes an old granary collapses. There is nothing remarkable in this. Every Zande knows that termites eat the supports in course of time, and that even the hardest woods decay after years of service. Now a granary is the summerhouse of a Zande homestead, and people sit beneath it in the heat of the day and chat or play the African hole-game or work at some craft. Consequently it may happen that there are people sitting beneath the granary when it collapses and they are injured, for it is a heavy structure made of beams and clay and may be stored with eleusine as well. Now why should these particular people have been sitting under this particular granary at the particular moment when it collapsed? That it should collapse is easily intelligible, but why should it have collapsed at the particular moment when these particular people were sitting beneath it? Through years it might

have collapsed, so why should it fall just when certain people sought its kindly shelter? We say that the granary collapsed because its supports were eaten away by termites. That is the cause that explains the collapse of the granary. We also say that people were sitting under it at the time because it was in the heat of the day and they thought that it would be a comfortable place to talk and work. This is the cause of people being under the granary at the time it collapsed. To our minds the only relationship between these two *independently caused* facts is their coincidence in time and space. We have no explanation of why the *two chains of causation* intersected at a certain time and in a certain place, for there is no interdependence between them. Zande philosophy can supply the missing link. The Zande knows that the supports were undermined by termites and that people were sitting beneath the granary in order to escape the heat and glare of the sun. But he knows besides why these two events occurred at a precisely similar moment in time and space. It was due to the action of witchcraft. If there had been no witchcraft people would have been sitting under the granary and it would not have fallen on them, or it would have collapsed but the people would not have been sheltering under it at the time. Witchcraft explains the coincidence of these two happenings. (1937, pp. 69–70, my italics)

It is not my purpose here to construct any argument intended to suggest that the Azande may be right in their beliefs about witchcraft. The point rather is that Monod finds it natural in presenting and justifying an important methodological assumption—which results in a belief in absolute coincidence—to appeal to what seems plain common sense. But the Zande example shows what Descartes was neither the first nor the last to point out, that though common sense may be regarded as a common possession human opinions may nevertheless differ, and differ on the most fundamental assumptions.

The appeal to common sense here, as everywhere, is therefore unsatisfactory. It is open to us—indeed, incumbent upon us—to challenge any belief in 'totally independent causal chains', and therefore in 'absolute coincidence'. That the creator of relativity theory—a decisive break from classical science—should have been reluctant to accept the uncertainty principle (to believe that 'God plays at dice') is itself not a coincidence: for the belief in *absolute coincidence* is as ineluctable a feature of classical thought as the belief in absolute space and time. What positive form such a challenge might take we shall consider shortly. Meanwhile, it is enough to observe that the appeal to coincidence which is a corollary of the closed system approach when different systems overlap is a reason for discomfort.

If we now turn to the forces, constants and laws which are appealed to to explain events occurring within the system, there too we find cause for unease: for such principles, lying at the metaphysical limits of such a system, are incapable of explanation from within it. Valency for example is an essential concept of classical chemistry. The attribution of valencies to the elements is a necessary condition for the description and explanation of chemical reaction. Yet there can be no chemical explanation of differences of valency. Again, in biology, the old dispute between mechanistic and vitalist views of life was metaphysical shadow boxing, since the disputants commonly shared a closed system approach: consequently, the principles appealed to in accounting for biological systems were not open to biological explanation.

What has happened in such cases has commonly been the establishment or envisaging of a wider system; or at least the appeal to another system. Valency receives an explanation in physics; and phenomena of life may be held to receive their explanation in chemistry. We begin to glimpse a hierarchical and possibly re-ductionist view of the structure of science. But the urge to reductionism is itself a kind of challenge to the classical approach; here also, then, we should be ready to question that approach.

We may now turn to the next feature of the approach, its atomism. It is not only the dark areas of Wittgenstein's *Tractatus* that should give us pause here: in many sciences the view of systems as composed of independently identifiable items which interact is proving un-satisfactory. Phonetics is powerless if it attempts to give an inde-pendent acoustic definition of each sound in a language, and then tries to ascertain how such items may be combined. Studies of folk-lore are sterile if they stay with Stith Thompson's or even Propp's lists of folk-tale components. Physics has long ceased to be a straightforward study of corpuscular interactions.

Finally, if we turn to the leading notion of the approach from which its other features stem—that we should always regard ourselves as treating closed systems—there is every reason to hesitate once more. For the most obvious examples around us—biological systems—are obviously and essentially *not* closed: they depend upon and are characterised by the exchange of matter and of energy with their environment.

If we detect a challenge to classical thought on all these fronts, what positive form may this challenge take? We shall approach this question by adverting briefly to contemporary movements in mathematics, biology, social anthropology and linguistics.

There is a recent movement in mathematics arising from the work of the Bourbaki and calling itself category theory. According to this view, the segmentation of mathematics into a number of sub-disciplines each dealing with its own kind of system is harmful and intellectually malfounded. We start with the existence of structural homologies between different (including widely different) math-ematical sub-disciplines, and treat them by a kind of general theory of homology reminiscent of the technical homology theory of top-ology, but perfectly general in scope. Mathematics is one: and not in the traditional sense whereby we attempt to show that all the (admittedly different) branches can be variously traced to the one set-theoretic root, but by appealing to structure rather than foundations, and showing that these 'branches' are varyingly homologous systems of transformation themselves transformed in accordance with a general theory of such transformations.

This movement offers the perspective of a radical challenge to the disciplinarity which is a feature of the traditional approach in the sciences (and elsewhere): and not a challenge which would proceed by praising attempts at 'interdisciplinary' cooperation. If we accept the traditional notion of disciplines *at all*, crossing of the boundaries in any systematic way is impossible: there is no intellectual space for such commuting. Each kind of closed system is a separate object of study: at the overlaps we find brute coincidence, and any apparent analogies between different systems are themselves haphazard; to give them serious attention would be intellectually disreputable: at best they may provide flashes of insight like electrical discharges occurring at random, and flashes of insight whose only justification can lie in their proper incorporation in the receiving discipline.

Thus category theory enables us to conceive the possibility that where traditionally two 'disciplines' were separated by an imperme-able boundary, they now emerge as linked by one or more specific articulations or hinges on the one hand, and perhaps display some perfect continuities or abrupt discontinuities on the other. If this is so in a particular case, the emergence of analogous structures in what we used to think of as the two domains will no longer be a coincidence, a 'mere metaphor'. In particular 'absolute coincidence' will disappear, since there will no longer be 'absolutely independent causal chains';

rather the independence of causal patterns will be strictly relative to the structural relations between the domains in which they are displayed.

In addition to such challenges to disciplinarity, there are more direct challenges to the appeal to closed systems, in particular those associated with the name of von Bertalanffy in biology. Bertalanffy has argued that we cannot deal with biological phenomena adequately unless we recognise that we are dealing with open systems, namely, those in which there may be exchange of matter and energy with the environment. Such systems are capable of rigorous treatment, and there are flourishing programmes of research in the area for instance of non-equilibrium thermodynamics (such as the work of the Brussels school under Prigogine). They show a number of special characteristics. In the first place, they may maintain themselves in a state of high statistical improbability, a steady state different from the classical thermodynamic equilibrium. Secondly, they may display what Bertalanffy calls 'equifinality', a property by which the steady state, if reached, is effectively independent of the initial conditions of the system, being determined by its parameters. The notion of open systems (of which cybernetic systems, or 'Ashby machines' displaying negative feedback, and open only to information and not energy exchange, are special cases) is fruitful not only in biology, in studies of growth and metabolism, genetics and evolution (where it allows us to envisage a new turn to the acrid disputes over nature/nurture distinctions), but also in the suggestive power of a 'general systems theory' in a variety of other areas.

Finally, we may consider direct challenges to classical atomism. These are perhaps most clearly displayed in social anthropology and linguistics, where 'structuralist' movements are precisely characterised by their refusal to take the elements in the field under study as given items of which it may independently be ascertained that they occur in such and such combinations and not others. On the contrary, it is held that the identity of an element is determined only by its place in the system. In phonetics, for instance, a vowel is the vowel it is not because of the physically measurable nature of the sound emitted, but because of the constitutive systems of relations between sounds which are the phonetics of a given language. In the case of studies of folklore, we find Vladimir Propp writing (although he is supposed to be a forerunner of structuralism): 'The total number of elements, the constituent parts of fairy tales, is about one hundred and fifty. . . . While in biology, a change in one part or characteristic entails the changing of another characteristic, in the tale, any part can change independently of the others. . . . We may conclude, then, the constituent parts can be studied out of context of the story which they compose.' Propp's resolute atomism in this area seems inherently unconvincing: at all events, its inadequacy is sufficiently demonstrated by Lévi-Strauss's *Mythologiques*.

We glimpse here emerging severally in different branches of knowledge what may in due course be recognised as a new organon. The formal theory of this organon may be emerging most dramatically in the work of René Thom, whose qualitative dynamics would have two important consequences from the point of view of the arguments of this book: first, the reinstatement of certain analogues of teleological explanation for local processes, and secondly, the rejection of a Laplacian belief in global determinism in favour of a characterisation of science—including the human sciences—as concerned to discover and analyse local determinisms within a generally rather labile and chaotic universe. Among such local determinisms there would indeed be found those which we have called 'wills': but a rigorous description of them through an appropriate science need no longer commit us to a traditional mechanistic view. Moreover we may well have no special reason to adopt that conventional philosophical position known as reductionism, by which the apparent autonomy of the human will would be reduced to some other globally deterministic level of explanation.

In short, there may be emerging new configurations of knowledge in which, on the one hand, classically severe disciplinary distinctions will disappear, and, on the other, the study of 'wills'—that is, of active self-regulating organisms, of autonomous but not closed systems—will have strategic importance. It is beyond my present purpose and competence to give a serious review of these developments; yet they are connected with that model universe which was constructed in section 1, and has guided the whole argument of this book. They are developments, moreover, which have other specific bearings upon our arguments.

Paronymy, for instance, was a notion indispensable in our treatment of wishing and of pleasure. And it emerged as an intractable notion. But the possibility of general theories of homology at a formal level (such as in category theory), and of specific treatments of specific homologies made possible by the replacement of disciplinary boundaries by disciplinary articulations, opens up the prospect of challenging the basis of that definition of paronymy which gave it a questionable and mysterious status: namely, the assumption (particularly dubious in the psychological case which was our first concern) that there really are *different* domains, where *difference* would connote incommensurability, and paronymy would be the transfer of a term from one to the other, a paradoxical transfer supposed to take place in the absence of any space in which it could be effected.

Pleasure, for instance, was argued to be homologous to wanting for a domain in which (unlike that of wanting) the desired state of affairs is taken to be already present. Now the existence of this homology (already recognised in a formal notion such as that of the 'pro-attitude', since the presence of a pro-attitude could be manifested indifferently in any of our three modes) is able to be set in the context of a general possibility of detecting such homologies, where different domains are accessible to each other through regular transformations of their defining conditions.

Moreover, our divagations in this section give us a glimpse of a biological homology of the psychological want/pleasure relation already alluded to in annex (iv). An open system of Bertalanffy may have parameters tending to keep it in a steady state distinct from classical thermodynamic equilibrium. This has two consequences; one, that the system is 'naturally' active (it displays autonomous activity), and secondly, that if a case occurs in which that activity is anticipated in its goal by other forces, then that activity, directed at producing a state which already exists, is superfluous and forms an 'overshoot' (see Bertalanffy, 1968, p. 143). The existence of such a biological analogue of what pleasure would be on the account offered in section 4 above is an important consideration, and should not be dismissed as a *mere* analogy: for man *is* a biological organism: we have envisaged an organon in which psychology and biology would emerge as structurally linked domains.

Thus, to return from this rather dizzying detour, the rejection of the transcendental interpretation of the 'zone of the will' in our model universe, and the corresponding identification of the will with that zone, will not necessarily commit us to a classical mechanistic view of what we should in that case scarcely be entitled any longer to call 'will': the mechanistic/voluntaristic dilemma which we outlined has now taken a different form. Our problem was whether the three classifications of changes in our model universe of section 1 could be kept distinct. In particular, could the 'will' be distinguished from changes attributable to causal chains, and changes attributable to nothing (or to chance)? The tendency of our observations has been that the classical distinction between chance and necessity (from Democritus to Jacques Monod) is simply a feature of an obsolescent ideology of science. Under a rival approach, the admission of mechanism and chance to our model universe will be seen as misleading: the autonomous action of a system (call it 'the will') is a starting point: it is the extrapolations (if they are such) to pure mechanistic causal chains, or to pure chance, which now become problematic. On this rival approach, man remains a natural phenomenon, but his ends belong to a teleology susceptible of treatment in a configuration of the sciences made possible by their escape from the old dilemma—chance or necessity, a dilemma which received schematic form in our model.

But there is another view, in which man appears also in a supernatural world. Teilhard de Chardin wrote:

> I have observed that for the best of unbelievers morality comes down to the precept 'do not do to others what you would not wish them to do to you'. This morality, in my opinion, is anodyne and static. It oils the wheels, but it is not enough. The human machine must do more than not squeak. It needs energy or fuel. This energy, this essence (that is, being obliged to act, or having the taste for action)—it is the whole problem of morality to provide. Now I see no other possible source than submission to a universal ideal object (*believed in* and *hoped for*, but not tangible; for it is universal and in the future, while we are individuals and in the present). (1965, pp. 53–4).

On this view, recognition of teleology places human striving in necessary relation to a transcendental goal—the forms of Plato, the non-natural goodness of G. E. Moore, the Divinity as the end of all ends, though like the case of immanent causality discussed above, transcendent causality too will take on a quite different form in a structuralist/open system perspective. Indeed, will the two coincide?

We may start once more from the necessary presence to the will in our model universe of a projection of a possible change. It is this *being directed towards* a possible future state of affairs that is characteristic of the will. Can we account for such directedness merely by reference to a tendency to produce the end? Why *should* the will tend to produce it? One reply might be that ends are not made so by being aimed at: they are aimed at because they already present themselves as ends—as an imperfect reflection of the one End.

But is there any longer a distinction between that End as a perfection beyond our striving and as contained within it? Such speculation is the beginning of many books (most of which have not been written): of this one, it is—the end.

Summary of the Main Argument

Defining the will as a source of change does not entitle us to exclude the possibility of the frustration of the will. The source of values schematically lies in the possible failure of the world to match the project of a will.

There are three chief modes of the will in man: first, wanting (determined by three criteria—the conative, there being a tendency to action; the prospective, this action being aimed at bringing about some state of affairs in the future; and the propositional, there being some set of propositions which the wanter is trying to make true); secondly, wishing (in which the same criteria are satisfied, save that the conative criterion is only paronymously satisfied); and thirdly, taking pleasure in something (in which the same criteria are satisfied, save that the conative and prospective criteria are only paronymously satisfied).

Any psychological state falling under this general account may be called an appetitive, and the object upon which an appetitive is directed may be called an appetitum. Any appetitum is a value, in accordance with which the world is to be changed, or by which it may be measured.

Values may be classified according to the corresponding appetitive structure. They may be primary, secondary or tertiary (according to the three broad classes of appetitives); they may be real or quasi-values (according to whether the value in question is a value of the person in question, or the person merely acts as though it were a value of his); they may be open or closed (according to whether or not they could be finally satisfied); they may be positive or negative; they may be first order, higher order or architectonic (according to whether other values figure essentially in the appetitum); they may be relative or absolute (according to whether or not reference to the person whose value it is occurs essentially in the appetitum).

In addition, values may be classified according to the reference group, that is the group of people whose values they are. Here there are three cases: values which are possessed by only one individual, values which are shared, and values which belong primarily to a collectivity.

Further, values may form systems, by compresence (being held together by the same person or group of persons), by compatibility or compracticability (being logically or practically able to be achieved together), and by style (forming together what is, by some criterion, a coherent picture of a possible future world).

Within this general framework, different species of value can be discerned. The number of possible combinations of the distinctions given is very large, but only certain configurations acquire or are given importance (such as the configuration called 'morality' or 'aesthetics'). Which they are and why they are is finally a historical and sociological question.

Values can be assessed technically (having in view their practicability, their scope, their compatibility and compracticability with other values, their internal structure, and so on). We may also assess a value evaluatively, but only by accepting some value which will act as a basis of that evaluation.

If we ask why do those values exist which do, there are two possible answers, one that it is the life sciences (and only they) which can give and are in fact giving the answer; and secondly, a transcendental view according to which certain ends of themselves attract our desire.

Bibliography

There follows a selective list of books which I have referred to or made use of.

Aristotle, *De Interpretatione*
―――― *Nicomachean Ethics*
Ayer, A. J., *Philosophical Essays* (London, 1959)
Bertalanffy, Ludwig von, *General System Theory* (New York, 1968)
Bourbaki, Nicolas, 'L'Architecture des mathématiques' in *Les Grands Courants de la pensée mathématique*, ed. F. Le Lionnais (Paris, 1948)
Carroll, Lewis, 'What the Tortoise said to Achilles', in *Mind*, IV (1895), pp. 278–80.
Derrida, Jacques, 'La Mythologie Blanche (la métaphore dans le texte philosophique)' in *Poétique*, Seuil, Paris, no. 5 (1971): translated by F. C. T. Moore in *New Literary History*, vol. VI, Winter 1975, no. 2
Descartes, René, *Discours de la Méthode*
Dummett, Michael, *Frege: Philosophy of Language* (London, 1973)
Evans-Pritchard, E. E., *Witchcraft, Oracles and Magic among the Azande* (Oxford, 1937)
Foucault, Michel, *Les Mots et les choses* (Paris, 1966)
Frankfurt, Harry G., 'Freedom of the Will and the concept of a person', in *The Journal of Philosophy*, vol. LXVIII (1971)
Frege, Gottlob, *Translations from the Philosophical Writings of Gottlob Frege*, ed. P. Geach and M. Black (Oxford/New York, 1960)
Grice, Russell, *The Grounds of Moral Judgement* (Cambridge, 1967)
Hare, R. M., *The Language of Morals* (Oxford, 1961)
Hart, H. L. A., *The Concept of Law* (Oxford, 1961)
Kant, Immanuel, *Groundwork of the Metaphysic of Morals*, tr. H. J. Paton as *The Moral Law* (London, 1948)
Kenny, Anthony, *Action, Emotion and Will* (London, 1963)
Kovesi, Julius, *Moral Notions* (London, 1967)
Kreisel, G., 'Category Theory and the foundations of mathematics' in Lecture Notes in Mathematics, no. 106, Springer-Verlag, 1969, *Reports of the Mid-West Category Seminar: III*, pp. 233–47
Lévi-Strauss, Claude, *Mythologiques*, 4 vols. (Paris, 1964–71)
MacIntyre, Alasdair, *A Short History of Ethics* (London, 1966)
MacLane, Saunders, 'Foundations for Categories and Sets' in Lecture Notes in Mathematics, no. 92, Springer-Verlag, 1969, *Category Theory, Homology Theory and their Applications: II*, pp. 146–64

Mayo, Bernard, 'The Moral Agent', in *The Human Agent*, R. I. P. Lectures 1966–7 (London, 1968)

Mill, John Stuart, *On Liberty*

—— *Utilitarianism*

Monod, Jacques, *Le Hasard et la nécessité: essai sur la philosophie de la biologie moderne* (Paris, 1970); tr. A. Wainhouse as *Chance and Necessity* (New York, 1971/London, 1972)

Moore, F. C. T., *The Psychology of Maine de Biran* (Oxford, 1970)

Moore, G. E., *Principia Ethica* (Cambridge, 1903)

Piaget, Jean, *Le Structuralisme* (Paris, 1968); translated by C. Maschler (London, 1971)

Plato, *Phaedo*

Pörn, Ingmar, *The Logic of Power* (Oxford, 1970)

Propp, Vladimir, 'Transformations in Fairy Tales' in *Mythology: selected readings*, ed. P. Maranda (Harmondsworth, 1972)

Quine, W. V. O., 'Natural Kinds', in *Ontological Relativity and other Essays* (New York/London, 1969)

Rawls, John, *A Theory of Justice* (Oxford, 1972)

Ricœur, Paul, *Le Volontaire et l'involontaire* (Paris, 1963)

Saussure, Ferdinand de, *Course in General Linguistics*, ed. C. Bally & S. Sechehaye, tr. W. Baskin (New York, 1959)

Strawson, P. F., *Individuals* (London, 1959)

Teilhard de Chardin, Pierre, *Lettres à Leontine Zanta*, (Paris, 1965)

Thom, René, 'Structuralism and Biology', in *Towards a Theoretical Biology*, ed. C. H. Waddington (Edinburgh, 1972)

—— *Structural Stability and Morphogenesis*, tr. D. M. Fowler (Reading, Mass., 1975)

Warnock, G., *Contemporary Moral Philosophy* (London, 1967)

Wittgenstein, Ludwig, *Tractatus Logico-Philosophicus*, tr. D. F. Pears and B. F. McGuinness (London, 1961)

Index